The Baptism of Billy Bean

The Baptism

of Billy Bean

a novel

ROGER ALAN SKIPPER

COUNTERPOINT

BERKELEY

Library of Congress Cataloging-in-Publication Data
Skipper, Roger Alan.
   The baptism of Billy Bean : a novel / Roger Alan Skipper.
   ISBN-13: 978-1-58243-460-5
   ISBN-10: 1-58243-460-3
      p. cm.
      1. Witnesses—Fiction. 2. Drug traffic—Fiction. 3. Appalachian Region—Fiction.
I.Title.
   PS3619.K568B37 2008
   813'.6—dc22

                                                                    2008034648

Cover design by Natalya Balnova
Interior design by Beth Kessler, Neuwirth & Associates, Inc.

COUNTERPOINT
2117 Fourth Street
Suite D
Berkeley, CA 94710
www.counterpointpress.com

Distributed by Publishers Group West

10   9   8   7   6   5   4   3   2   1

Printed in the United States of America

as all
as ever
for Connie

.1

THE CONVERTIBLE SPEARED OUT OF THE BLIND
*turn with its engine screaming for more. But there was no surplus
to be had and if the coaltruck hadnt appropriated its trajectory
the little red car would have struck about the first fork of a light-
ning-tormented chestnut oak that stood a half-dozen rods down
the mountainside. The truck was there, though, squatted under
twenty tons of coalvein that rode its back black and sullen as the
late-August West Virginia sky that hugged Cheat Mountain. When
the car wedged in under the dropaxle the truck hunched up in the
back and down in the front like it had been kicked between the
legs as the tandems found purchase and climbed up onto the lighter
frame. The Jakebrake hammered and the retreads that still rested
on ground slid in the gravel along the pavement's edge. Coal spilled
from under the tarp on the far side. A pale orb that the man in the
vehicle behind the coaltruck momentarily took for a pumpkin shot
through the cascade of coal and bounced once off the gravel and
careened down and away through the trees.*

*The man braked his not-quite-babyblue Ford pickup to a stop
on the berm behind the coaltruck and the flashers came on and he*

stepped out thin and tall if he didnt stoop. A rough-sawn face soft-ened by the novelty of the situation. He zipped his too-big Carhartt jacket and scratched his thinning hair and ambled to the truckdriver's door and stepped up on the gastank and examined the driver who was still staring ahead all ox-eyed and clutching the wheel with both chubby hands. Like maybe if he didnt look in the mirrors the past would wither away unacknowledged.

The tall man reached in the open window and touched the driver on the shoulder.

There wasnt a thing you could have done, he said. A voice steady and kind.

The driver's head came around in slow motion. The lower lip with a bad case of the yips. I been driving seventeen years without an accident.

You still havent had one that's any fault of yours. No more than if a meteorite fell down and kliped you in the head. Unless you're the type to convince yourself that you shouldnt have been standing in that particular place.

He must of been going seventy.

Every bit of it. If he intended to make that turn he went about it all wrong. Come on. Slide down from there and see if you can throw a half-hitch on your breathing. Air's a good thing but it's like everything else. Too much of it will stunt your growth.

The driver sat with his head back and eyes closed for a bit before he released air pressure to lock the brakes and switched off the big Cummins diesel and when it had spooled down they stepped to the ground and squatted to look beneath the truck. The truckdriver in a wifebeater and cut-off jeans and sockless brogans and the tall man in a heavy coat, as though seasons and not vehicles had collided. The tall man duckwalked in alongside what had been a convertible and eased his head up among the truck's crossmembers where he could look inside the wreckage and when he waddled out again he had blood on his chin.

I need to get on the radio and get some help out here, the truckdriver said.

There's no hurry on that fellow's account.

Aw no. He aint dead is he? His voice heavy with the desperate hope that the steel and flesh wadded under his tires had suffered only cosmetic damage.

I'm pretty certain his head flew down the hill. Unless he didnt have one to start with.

When he'd digested that information, the truckdriver walked to the front of the truck and placed his forehead against the fender and his shoulders hunched a couple of times and he spat between his feet after each spasm. In the back of his bare leg a tendon trembled like his lip had. The bellow of another truck coming up the grade seemed to steel him and he wiped his mouth on the back of a hairy arm and stood waiting for a bright-waxed new '89 Mack to clatter to a stop.

You all right, Harry? the new driver hollered out his open window.

There wasnt nothing I could of done, Harry said. *This fellow said so himself.*

I can see that. Let me get out some flares so we dont get run over.

He opened the door and fumbled behind the seat and emerged with two red cylinders and a pack of reflective triangles and the tall man said, *Give me half of those and I'll set them up the hill a piece.* When he'd erected triangles around the bend and at the end of a straight stretch he sparked the flare to start the phosphorous sizzling whitehot and foaming and propped it on its wires and returned to the accident site.

Tugboat's callin it in, Harry said. His voice steadier. *You're gonna stick around aint you?*

Sure. Yeah. I saw the whole thing. He squatted and looked under the truck again. At the fluids finding separate pathways down the hill. *You ever see anything that red?* he asked.

Harry's lip shivered again and he glanced at the thin man and said, *You got some of it right under your mouth. You ought to wipe it off before it dries.*

The tall man touched fingers to his throat and examined them and took out a blue paisley hanky and scrubbed at his chin. *The car's what I was meaning,* he said. *That's the color God intended red to be.*

A faded green Impala crept down the mountain followed by a beat-up Datsun pickup and up the hill came a Strohman Bread van and before long there was a long string of four-way flashers and knots of people talking and then the blue-and-red lights of the Union County sheriff's cruiser and a Ralph's Towing truck with a rollback bed with a yellow light and the red-and-white ones of the rescue squad.

He's around here somewhere, Harry said to Sheriff Dick Trappel. *That's his pickup right there. He seen the whole thing. Said there wasnt a thing I could of done.*

That . . . blue F-150? the sheriff said. *That's Lane Hollar's truck. There's not another one that color in the world. Lane Hollar, where you at?* he yelled at the bystanders.

He went down in the woods, someone hollered back.

What color do you call that truck, anyhow? Dick said. *In case I have to write it down?*

Shit-muckle-turquoise? one of the bystanders said.

Robin-egg blue, Tugboat said. *With the robin stirred in.*

Here he comes now, said a man with bright green two-inch-wide suspenders with Weyerhaeuser printed down the fronts who'd been sizing up the stand of red oak and poplar below the road. Then another said, *Oh my god.* There was a scramble to see and a collective groan and the tall man's head appeared over the cutbank and he grappled with a sassafras bush but nobody offered a hand and he hauled up into view with a streaked and bloody mass like a frozen dirty limbless newborn baby dangling from his other hand.

The tall man stomped his sneakers to rid them of dirt from the fillbank and looked at the bottom of both feet. *I thought I saw the head go flying, he said. It rolled clear to the creek. He stooped and placed it on the ground and extricated his thumb from two-knuckles deep in the misshapen mouth and the tips of two fingers from the noseholes. Like one would disengage from a too-small bowling ball. He wiped his fingers in a flurry of coltsfoot growing from the gravel and then on his handkerchief.*

The circle of people tightened, nobody wanting to see but not desiring to be the only one who hadnt seen, either.

I smell alcohol, Dick Trappel said. You been drinking, Lane?

A beer or two. But this head cant say that. He nudged the bald head with his boot. Stinks like a brewery.

That the only way you know to carry a man's head?

It's been so long since I graduated highschool I dont even recall who taught head carrying. Or even what department it was under. There's no hair to get hold of. And I tried the ears. That's like picking up a thirty-pound oyster with rubber gloves. What do you think's in there to make it that heavy? Blood dripped beside his shoe and he looked at the headspring on the back of his thumb and wrapped it in his handkerchief. If he was carrying anything a shot of penicillin wont fix you probably dont want to kiss me. I considered knapping his front teeth out but by then he had my thumb half gnawed off. He evaluated their expressions and laughed. It was a joke.

You come up to the cruiser, the sheriff said. When they'd gone there he said, Close your eyes and touch your finger to your nose nice and slow.

No. If someone needs a sobriety test that bad take one yourself. You get your little booze sniffer out here and I'll blow in it if that's what you want. But I had two beers like I told you. Not enough to perform for all these folks.

The end of a gnarled root black with fresh dirt protruded above Lane's shirt pocket and the sheriff took it by the end and pulled it up where he could see it. Where'd you dig ginseng?

It wasnt up here on the hard road.

Dont dare tell me you dug that while you were . . .

One week a year, Dick. That's all the vacation I ever take. I take my birthday week to hunt sang, and that's what I'm gonna do with it. Whether some baldheaded flatlander picks that day to try to knock a coaltruck over the hill or not.

The sheriff looked away with an expression akin to Harry's when he'd leaned against the truck fender. How old are you?

Lane looked at his watch. Till you get done with me I'll be forty-one.

I dont know, Lane Hollar. The sheriff shook his head. You're one I just cant decipher.

You dont need to. Not unless I break some law. And I dont. Go worry yourself with them that do. He put his coat back on and walked to his truck and shook the ginseng root down into an empty breadsack and started the engine and rolled down the side window. No way Harry could have avoided what happened. No way at all. The window ascended and the pickup nosed away through the people and vehicles.

When the brakelights had disappeared Dick Trappel walked back to the group of men standing looking at the coaltruck. Or what was under it. You able to do anything here, Ralph? he asked the towtruck driver.

Not with the rollback. I done called for a big rig.

Thank you for doing that.

You ever see anything to beat the likes? Ralph nodded to the dark stain where the head had rested in the gravel.

Not that I've chose to remember.

Carrying that thing the way he did. Ralph shook his head and spat like the thought had brushed his tongue.

It aint no mystery why he wears a coat all summer, the driver they called Tugboat said. That Lane Hollar's one cold sonofabitch.

. 2

eyes touched and ratcheted back and the shorter man said, Hey. I
know you. You're Lane Hollar.

Not until the lower lip quivered did Lane see past the gray hair
and bifocals and the extra weight. Harry? he said. Harry the coaltruck driver.

How you been? The hand was cold and firm like half-hard clay.
Not like his voice.

Better but I'm getting over it.

Me and the woman used to come dance when your bluegrass
band played at the Legion. We miss that. He glanced over his shoulder. She's got too fat to dance anyhow so it's likely for the best.

If Lane had ever seen Harry's face in the Legion's dim-light swirl
of cigarette smoke he'd not attached it to an owner. Yeah, he said.
Meaning nothing.

We were at the Mid-Atlantic Banjo Championship one time too.
Up at Cumberland. Watched you win it. You still pick some?

Havent played a note for years.

That's a shame. There's nothing but country music nowadays. If you could call it that. Bunch of noise.

Yeah. Impatient to get his groceries and be gone but snagged on a splinter of shared experience. The way Mary's underpants used to catch on his calluses. You still driving coaltruck?

No, hell no. I kept on another couple weeks after that baldheaded feller run under me but I couldnt sleep for thinkin about it. At every turn I just knowed another little red car was going to dive under my truck. Another noggin would ricochet down the mountain.

It sticks with you. Even after . . . what . . . ten years?

Harry laughed. 1989 it was. Same year I took up weldin. Down at Union Container. Best move I ever made. Even if it is ruinin my eyes.

Seventeen years, Lane said. Seems like five.

Or a hunderd sometimes. Others like it happened yesterday. But I'm shed of it finally. My head knowed all along I wasnt at fault but my heart finally figured it out too. It bother you any?

More now than then, Lane said. At a loss to why he'd tell a stranger what he wouldnt share with his best friend. Even if he had one.

You still at the lumber company?

No, Lane said. My wife passed on in '97. That's when I quit the band. My ticker got lazy then and I had bypass surgery and after that I went back to selling plywood for a while but one morning I just couldnt figure out a reason to do it anymore. I bought a baitshop out on Ford Road. Tinker around there.

That's your place? No kiddin. I go past all the time.

Stop in, Lane said. Wondering if Harry wouldnt find another route so he wouldnt drive past. Now that they'd prodded at a past neither wanted to wake.

Harry stood tall and peered around like a few inches could circumvent shelves two feet taller than he was. I got to find Susie, he said. If she gets loose in the tater chips I'll have to take out a second mortgage to spring us loose from here.

They shook hands and Lane watched him go but what he saw was a bald head wedged between a whiteoak and a lichen-covered rock, just before it would have rolled into the creek.

Lane had yet to witness anyone peel a dead cat from the highway and clutch it to his breast, and he'd never seen a cat dead with the same certainty as an unattached head. When he'd seen it was hairless he'd perceived the difficulties of carrying it and had a notion to leave it for another to fool with. But that hadnt been his propensity then or now.

The Carhartt coat he'd been wearing that day was a birthday present from Mary. Brand new, sixty dollars. The lubricious nature of those ears came back with a rush, and the incredible weight of the orb. Only one practical way to carry it. But he wished he wouldnt have.

Vaporlocked in the WalMart aisle, he wondered if he was done with death. Not the everyday passing-on kind yet to be endured, but the violent endings like he'd seen in Nam. The Nashville boy's death, when he stumbled across a bouncing Betty. Or the Nevada lieutenant standing drinking from a canteen listening to mortar fire, then the mortar arrived and the lieutenant was no longer. The black boy from Bangor dancing just before he fell down full of holes. The Brown Banger, they'd called him. Till then. Lane hadnt mentioned him again, nor did he talk about the ones our side had killed, the boys in the other army.

Death hadnt even been the worst that could happen. Being dead couldnt have been any more terrifying than the rash of bloodsuckers that werent leeches or bugs either but a tormenting agent straight from hell. Like John the Revelator described. He'd seen nothing like them before or since. They'd worked half the night burning them off with cigarettes, the whole gnawing deeper as the individual suckers fried and withered. The following morning the fat little private from Arizona was dead. He still walked and blinked and farted but the components that lent definition to life were sucked dry. Shortly after that he was sent home but Lane couldnt imagine he ever arrived. Or what he'd have done if he had.

Lane couldnt recall their names. Just where they were from. The interesting part. He'd been to West Virginia and a little bit around it and Parris Island and Southeast Asia, and the last two were so far back he couldnt recall them enough to complete an entire picture. Just a brushstroke here and there. Even if he wanted to remember.

Please God dont let there be a Nam for Toby to go to when he's of age, he thought and wondered if he was praying and to whom. Thought it without his usual amusement at such notions. Let this Iraq thing be done with and nothing else take its place. Though he wasnt sure school wasnt just as bad. Toby didnt say much about school—considerate of an old man's sensibilities—but Lane couldnt miss it on the TV: guns in the bookbags and dope in the lockers and sex in the bathroom. And then there was highschool yet to face if they made it through that.

Lane looked around him and pushed his cart ahead and scanned the shelves as though somewhere in the neat rows of bottles and boxes and cans he'd find what he'd left behind over there. The missing element that allowed him to lay down a man's head and dig a ginseng and take it up again as though it were a lunchbag.

But that had changed. He'd held Mary's hand and felt the life slither away and just when he should have broke entirely inhuman whatever left her found a place inside Lane. The moment she died he realized how special life is. Mary was dead and Frank might as well be, the worthless piece-of-trash excuse for a son, but Lane still had Toby and Darlene. Right there with the canned salmon and tuna and Spam and deviled ham and Vienna sausages as witnesses, Lane vowed that as long as he was alive, nothing was going to foul up their lives. Not if he had anything to say about it.

. 3

NICKEL BALLEW ANTICIPATED THE REEK OF FEAR
but what he got instead was tobacco smoke and yesterday's beer
and antifreeze and garden chemicals and gun-cleaning solvents. The
young man they'd come to see took the fishing pole he'd been rig-
ging and propped it against the garage workbench, then lit a Camel
and leaned back against the dented steel top. Billy Bean's hands were
as battered and rough as an old man's, his arms leathery and lean.
Like his extremities had been birthed before the balance. Two inches
shorter than Ballew but still tall.

You aint learned a thing yet, have you, Billy Bean said to the short
heavy bruise-faced man behind Ballew. He considered his two visitors
as though they were mouse turds deposited there in the center of his
garage floor. Something to be swept down the floor drain between
Ballew's feet. His eyes lingered on Ballew's ostrich-skin boots and his
mouth turned down on one corner.

Talk to *me*, son, Ballew said. Harold's just along for the ride. He
stood tall and loose and easy, jingling change in the pocket of his
black jeans, but tension radiated from him nonetheless.

Billy Bean's eyes coursed one last time over Harold's ponytail and greasy denim jacket and runover boots and refocused on Ballew. A tremor in his voice that might have been adrenalin. Dont get me wrong, Mr. Henry. I know you're an important man up Cumberland way. But when you start running dope down here you lost all respectability in my book.

Mr. Henry?

It aint because you got nigger blood in you neither. Until I seen you I didnt even know that. It dont mean nothing to me. Mesicans either.

Ballew turned and looked askance at Harold and got nothing but a sullen shrug in return.

How'd he come up with that name?

It aint like I'm too stupid to figure it out on my own, Billy Bean said.

All I told him was he didnt know who he was fooling with, Harold said.

You didnt give him my name?

Nickel, I swear . . .

Ballew shook his head. Just shut up.

I thought you was Larson Henry, Billy Bean said. It was on the dealer tag. Larson Henry Motors.

Well, Ballew said and turned to him again. What I had planned for you was a mini-seminar in circumspection. But I just hate that *n* word plumb to death.

N word?

Things need gnawed down before they'll fit in your little bitty brain pan, dont they. No bigger than a possum's. You suppose maybe you were created on the *morning* of the sixth day? Couple hours ahead of the rest of us?

Billy Bean's face went flat and the line of his lips drew thin. Dont call me stupid.

Ballew turned to the open garage door that had given them

unexpected easy access to the kid. As though he'd been waiting for them. Individual trees were coalescing in the fading blackness, the birds tuning for the morning symphony. Occasional headlights flickered beyond the trees that lined the long driveway. He caught his own reflection in a side window and adjusted his chambray collar.

Free of Ballew's gaze, Billy Bean gained confidence. No matter who you are, you two need to get back down over the hill where you belong. Before I open another can of whupass.

Now, though, there's the matter of my pride. A hard thing to heal once it's injured.

Dope dealers dont have call to have any. And your punk there dont deserve none a-tall.

Hatred twisted further Harold's bruised misshapen face. That and fear.

Who invested you with such authority? Ballew said in his preaching voice. The Bible had never caught fast in his heart but he relished its words and rhythms and inflections, and its violence. Did God lift you on high? That I might tremble and obey? Or have you ordained yourself? An earthly priest with a foolish calling. Ballew watched Billy Bean's reflection in the side window, confusion and doubt working under the skin. Ballew turned back and withdrew a folded piece of literature from his pocket and handed it to the young man. Do you read, my son?

Billy Bean looked at the tract without comprehension. What's it say?

You hold in your hand the salvation message. Have you time to clasp it to your soul?

All I'm saying is that I got a fiancée went to that school where you're sellin dope. Where our kids will go.

That's all we need. Illiterates wedding retards. Spawning mental amputees.

Watch out, Harold warned Ballew, but Ballew had already seen what was coming and delivered a vicious blow with the edge of his hand, just over the ear, and the ballpien hammer Billy Bean had taken up clattered on the concrete floor. His eyes went from confident to empty without intervening doubt as he rolled sideways against the workbench, then slid to the floor.

I'll kick your guts out, Harold said and moved forward and drew back his foot.

Huh uh, Ballew said.

We need to teach him a lesson he wont forget.

How about one he wont remember. Ballew picked up the tract that had fluttered to the floor and blew the dust off the words: THE WAGES OF SIN IS DEATH.

The skin on Harold's face juddered like his brain had hit a pothole. Let's get out of here then, he said. If we aint going to rough him up. It's getting light out.

Billy Bean was going fishing this morning, Ballew said. I will make you fishers *of men*, he shouted, his eyes yellow-tinged and crazy. Will you be a *fisher of men*, Mr. Bean? Or will you drown in the gene pool? I want every eye closed, every head bowed. God is *speaking to hearts*, folks.

Let's go, Harold said. Please.

Ballew glanced outside. Saw all there was to see. Trees. Beginning to stand out against the sky. He considered the canoe in the back of Billy Bean's rusted pickup. We pass a lake just out the road?

It aint really a lake. Just a water dam.

As opposed to?

Harold stared blankly. Dont be fooling around.

Have you been baptized, Harold? Is your soul secure?

If any comprehension had entered Harold's overtaxed brain, it hadnt yet worked around to his eyes.

Give me a hand, Harold.

What are you going to do?

We're going to put this new convert in that canoe and we're going out to the lake to baptize him. When they bent to pick up Billy Bean, Ballew caught the stink of fear on Harold that he'd expected to smell on the kid. Ballew grunted as he shouldered the lax body over the side and into the canoe. He polished the toes of his cowboy boots on the back of his jeans and then wrapped a shop rag around the handle of a tacklebox and set it in the canoe and added a fishing pole. Let's go out to that lake. Water dam, I mean. He opened the pickup's door and when he saw the empty beer cans and sardine tins and cigarette packs and Slim Jim wrappers he said, Tell you what, Harold my man. You drive this one, and I'll follow along in mine.

What if someone stops me?

Tell them you're on the way to the emergency room. It doesnt have to be a lie, if that's what concerns you.

Emotions worked at Harold's lips but never produced sound and when his eyes left Ballew's they touched here and there on the landscape and then like an old bear entering a cage he slid into Billy Bean's pickup.

One more thing, Harold.

Harold ground the starter and when the valves had steadied into a hard clatter he said out the open window, Yes sir? Staring straight ahead.

Was the package where I told you it would be? Am I not a man of my word?

Yes sir. You seem to be.

I made a mistake in getting anywhere near the little bag of goodies I gave you. Now it's not even a week later and already you've gotten yourself in a jam and threatening to drag me into it too.

I'm sorry.

We're going to take care of this and you are going to do the job you owe me and after that you wont even *think* my name again.

You never even said what it was I had to do.

When it's time you'll know. Until then, stay away from me.

But you came to . . .

Do not mention my name. Or you will join our young friend here. Is that clear?

Harold gripped the wheel and blinked through the early morning fog and the cloud of oilsmoke. His white knuckles and blackened face unlikely on the same body. I understand, he said.

.4

LANE GRIPPED HIS GRANDSON'S SHOULDER AND eased a step further into the cattails. Careful, he said. Because I'm using you for a cane, he thought but didnt say. The water was tepid in the shallows but already sucked at what little warmth reached his legs via blood that only seemed to go around once every two weeks. Roots snarled his feet and bottom muck clasped his sneakers. The cane's finetoothed edges slashed at his arms when he stumbled. Should have worn a wool shirt instead of a flannel. A mass hard but alive bumped his leg. A little snapper. When the water lapped at his groin he sucked at the damp air and closed his eyes.

Smells like shit, Toby said.

Lane cracked a knuckle against the sunbleached head. You watch your language or I'll take some of it and scrub out your dirty mouth.

Some what?

What you said.

What was it? He grinned.

I wont dignify it by repeating it. Keep that reel out of the water. I dont intend to grease reels all night just because you're too dilitary to take care of them.

You just keep from falling down and spilling the minnows and I'll worry about the reel.

Lane parted the final stalks and gazed out into early summer fog. The water still and clear but opaque over the dark bottom. Be quiet now. Dont spook him off.

Is this where he took the duck? Toby already stripping braided line from the big Ambassadeur knucklebuster reel, checking it against a thumbnail for abrasions, feeling of the Palomar knot at the junction with the steel leader.

It's why we're here. Not fishing off the dock.

Maybe we ought to catch a duck, use it for bait.

You dont do that. Cause pain to a warmblooded creature. Not ever.

Was it a fullgrown duck he ate?

I told you ten times already.

Tell me eleven.

It was a little one swimming in line with the others. The last one in line.

The boy clipped a fist-sized red-and-white float to the line three feet above the forged stainless hook. His eyes full of muskellunge big enough to take a duck, even a baby one.

Dont be last in line, Lane said. Remember that.

I thought we were going fishing. Not to school. The boy grinned and thrust his hand into the minnow bucket that floated between them.

How old are you again?

You know how many.

Twelve years is a short time to get so smartmouthed. Keep it up and you wont be a teenager. I'll see to it. Get the biggest one.

The boy removed his hand from the bucket and looked inside. There's only three.

If he wont bite on three he wont bite on thirty.

The boy reached in again and withdrew a white sucker nearly a foot long.

Hook him behind the dorsal fin so you can steer him up and away. Not in the lip. The boy had already done that, slicker than Lane could have. Dont lam him down onto the water, kill him before he gets a chance for something to eat him. Lob him out underhand.

The line swished through the guides, and the bait and float landed with soft plops just a few yards away. Far enough?

That's perfect. Now keep the line tight so he pulls away. Dont let him head in or we'll be tramping on him. The float was already nodding as the sucker tried to escape whatever had it by the tail. What do you suppose a fish thinks when the minnow jerks it out of the water? the boy said.

Fish arent long on philosophy, I dont reckon. They just figure it for what it is. That getting yanked out of the water is a common occurrence they just havent experienced yet.

How big you think that old muskie is?

Keep your voice down. Makes vibrations the fish can feel. He's almost exactly the same size he was the last time you asked me.

How big is twenty pounds? the boy whispered.

He might be bigger than that. Thirty maybe.

My science teacher said there's no muskies in here.

That'd be difficult to determine from here to the school. And I never saw him out here.

It's a her. Miss Davis.

Well. I didnt see a her for certain.

Behind them, up on Ford Road, an unrestricted exhaust bellowed past and behind it Lane heard for one moment the more subdued voice of a heavier engine well muffled. There comes Billy Bean, the boy said.

The cacophony of mechanical neglect proceeded around the lake and gravel crunched at the access road and at the launchramp, two hundred yards across the water. The engine raced and backfired and died and the door rattled shut. The sounds of the canoe sliding free of the rusted bed and the engine roared again from the launchramp to die again at the parking lot.

He's losing a clutch. Either that or he's too drunk to let it all the way out. Lane glanced at his watch.

What's a clutch do?

Ties the engine to the wheels. Or turns it loose when you dont want it to go.

If there're muskies in here why doesnt anyone ever catch one?

Good jeeminy, boy. You ask more questions than a woman.

Tell me why.

I guess it's just the way you are. Probably because you grew up without a man around.

No, tell me why nobody ever catches one.

Nobody fishes for them. Once in a while someone hooks one but their tackle doesnt last long enough for them to know what they had ahold of. Most think they hooked into a big snapper turtle.

Dont they ever catch a little one?

There's not any little ones anymore. They're tiger muskies. Hybrids. Half muskie and half northern pike. They cant reproduce.

Then how'd they get in here?

The game commission put them in one time about fifteen years ago. I helped carry the milkcan they were in down to the edge of the water. They've all died out but just a few. Maybe just this one. Whispering irritated his throat. Now shut up or I'm gonna have you fixed so you cant reproduce.

How do you do that?

Lane thumped him on the head again, and the boy grinned.

The fog was thinning fast as the June sun eased upward, clear of the trees. Crouched in the cattail cane, Lane felt as though he were hunkered in a high cold meadow. A hard clunk against Billy

Bean's canoe. A voice, lowpitched and unhappy. A splash, loud and careless.

Billy Bean has someone with him, the boy whispered.

No he dont. He never fishes with anybody. Sounds to me like he fell down. He must be drunk. Early as it is.

A pair of voices, argument in the tone.

I told you, the boy said.

Lane shifted in the clammy water, tried to move some blood into his legs.

Across the lake an engine started and rumbled and two doors opened and closed and gravel rattled as another vehicle pulled away. Where'd that one come from? Lane said.

They must have already been there.

We'd have heard them. They must have come when Billy Bean did. You couldnt hear an Army tank over his junker. The engine noise faded and then grew as the vehicle left the access road to the launch-ramp and accelerated toward them on Ford Road. Watch your float.

There's Billy Bean's boat. He's not in it.

Lane peered into the mist, saw nothing.

Behind them the hiss of brakes pumped hard, the clunk of a trans-mission into reverse, the uneven throttle of someone backing up. To where Lane had backed his pickup off the road and into the brush.

When Lane looked back to the water the boat was there, not emergent but all of a piece, driven by the softest of breezes that had sprung up in their faces. Monochromatic but for a crimson smear across the gunwale and down the side. High in the water, empty.

Lane leaned forward to improve his perspective. Doors opened and closed behind them, on the road, and suddenly the mud around them smelled of water buffalo and human waste. The cane exotic and strange.

Lane touched a finger to the boy's lip as though they were on a deer stand. He held the boy's eyes till he knew he'd been understood, then pushed him forward out of the cane and into the open waistdeep water and stepped out himself and took the pole from the boy and squatted and pushed the boy down with him. The chill claimed his breath without argument or preamble.

Like an orange beacon the minnow bucket floated in the cattails and he reached in and retrieved it and pushed it down between his legs. The two sucker minnows banged against the insides and he tripped open the lid and felt them swirl away.

The boy looked as though he were going to ask a question. Lane shook his head and mouthed the word No.

Just on the other side of the cattails someone coughed and Lane caught a flash of blue. He eased lower into the water until only his nose was clear, tugged at the boy's jeans until he followed.

There aint nobody here. A voice full of smoke. Let's get the hell out of here.

Behind them, the float went under with a splash.

In one continuous motion Lane found the line and put it in the proper place between his teeth and bit it off and felt it zip through his fingers and gripped the boy's neck to keep him from turning.

What was that? A softer voice. Hello?

The morning was so still that the ripples from Lane's shivering made tiny lapping noises where they encountered the cane.

Ten yards beyond the cane the water boiled and churned and after a moment the slap of a heavy bullet into the water and a split-second behind that the flat bark of a bigbore pistol. The unmistakable clack of an automatic.

Aw, man, dont be shooting. Not after . . .

What was that?

It must of been a fish. Please dont shoot no more. Call attention to us.

It would take a world-class fish to make a stir like that.

Probly a carp. I dont know. But it aint nothing to shoot at. The voices moved away toward a point that thrust into the lake and Lane already had a handful of the boy's shirt and was cramming him back up into the cattail cane. The fishing rod snapped beneath his sneaker and the minnow bucket popped to the surface and Lane snagged it and dragged it behind and crowded the boy into the stalks and crouched over him and mashed the bucket down and into the mud. Dont even wiggle, he whispered, and smeared a handful of bottom muck across his own face and dropped his eyes and held his hand over the boy's face and squeezed the protest out of him. Not until the doors closed again and the engine accelerated away did he release the boy and stand shivering in the cane.

Why did you bite him off? Toby's voice shook with what Lane first thought was cold, but it was pure anger. He was *on* there. We *had* him.

The mist was already patchy and Lane could see the rear end of Billy Bean's truck. Parked in the wrong place and pulled in, not backed. Where you couldnt get the jumpercables to it if it wouldnt start. Do you not comprehend that you've just been shot at? he said.

He took it. And you bit him off.

Come on boy, move. Lane gathered the broken rod and the minnow bucket and crowded the boy toward the bank.

Where we going? He's right *there*, Pap.

Go, go, go. Lane hustled them toward his pickup.

The boy looked back toward the water. Damn niggers, he said.

Dont you ever say that word again in my presence. Dont say anything, dammit. Just *move*.

You said it. You just said it yourself.

Not that word. The other one.

. 5

of bottom muck that squished in their shoes. Lane threw the broken
rod and the minnow bucket into the pickup's bed and started it and
leaned forward as it spun up the soft ruts toward Ford Road, nudg-
ing it along. The boy up on his knees looking out the back window
as though with the proper attention the bit-off line could be retied.
When they'd clawed their way up onto the hardtop, Lane accelerated
back toward the launchramp, the steering wheel biting into his ribs
when they dropped onto the access road, the boy's fingernails mark-
ing the dashboard.

They slid to a stop at the launchramp and Lane jammed the stick
into reverse and killed the engine and clattered out to the end of the
dock, running splay-legged to keep his balance on the shifting boards.
Billy Bean, he yelled.

He's not here, the boy said. The dock rocked and clunked as he
joined Lane.

Hush. Just listen a minute.

They heard geese and the splash of a fish working up in the reeds
and the gravel voice of a raven. Billy Bean, he yelled again.

Down there he is, the boy said, and after a while Lane could make out a man's head and shoulders along the shore past the wood-duck boxes. Is that you, Billy Bean? His voice echoed from the woods beyond, and with it came another.

You're fixing to get your butt kicked, callin me Billy Bean.

Who is that? Who's there?

Shut up the hollering, you wasted old fart.

The man's silhouette moved toward them and when the squat dark form and the dense black hair that bushed from under the ball-cap came into range a shaft of irritated recognition shot through Lane. NoBob Thrasher, he said.

What's left of him.

Lane crawled the perimeter of the dock, looking down in the water. Help me look, he told the boy. He's in the water somewhere.

NoBob's heavy canvas pants swished when he walked and when they'd stopped he said, What you looking for? You lose your false teeth? He leaned his fishing pole against the dock's walkway and dug a cigarette from somewhere inside his dark work shirt and lit it, all in one practiced motion.

Billy Bean's in there somewhere.

I believe the old man must of took too much medicine, NoBob said to Toby.

I had on a great big muskie and Pap bit him off.

Lane looked up and said, Time is of the essence here. Help me look, daggone it.

NoBob appraised the mud Lane had smeared across his face and his wet clothing and laughed. He's done lost it, son. Thinks he's back in Nam.

It was big enough to eat ducks, the boy said.

Insanity aint contagious, is it? NoBob said. If it is I need to get back a piece.

Somebody else was here, but they're gone now. Lane pointed at the canoe, drifted across the lane and nosed into the rushes on the far bank. His canoe's blooded up and he's not in it. Billy Bean, he hollered again, and started along the bank, wading out into the water as far as he could and still walk.

There wasnt anybody else that I seen, NoBob said. If there was Billy Bean most likely went with them. Either that or he's passed out up in the woods somewhere.

Last time I checked the bullfrogs werent packing sidearms. So who did the shooting?

I was here before you came and I didnt hear no shooting.

The boy heard it.

I didnt hear nothing, Toby said.

Lane stopped and looked at him. You heard the shot. Heard them talking about it.

My ears were under the water. But I'd have still heard a shot.

Well, you didnt hear it, so you obviously wouldnt have. Didnt you hear what they said?

You likely heard a beaver smack, NoBob said. I seen one swimmin the shoreline.

Lane stepped out on the bank and stomped the vegetation and mud from his shoes and turned his anger NoBob's way. What if it was you in the water? Would you want Billy Bean to stand here and smoke while you drowned?

If that piece of white trash was all there was between me and the promised land I'd just as leave drown. Rather than face the idea I owed my life to him every morning. NoBob's little black eyes glistened like greasy ball bearings.

The old hardness hove up in Lane. White trash comes in a variety of sizes and colors, he said. Most of it would pitch in to help a dying man, though.

NoBob's face was burned dark as the mud on Lane's pantslegs but it turned darker still. If he's in the water like you say, it's too late for him. Any idiot could figure that out.

Lane's adrenaline sprung a leak and left him tired and old and cold and muddy. I shouldnt have said that. Felt the apology bounce back like spit off a griddle.

NoBob nodded across the lake. Did you look in the boat?

It's too high in the water for anybody to be in it. But it wont hurt to look. Toby, you keep searching, he said. Like the boy had commenced at some point. Lane and NoBob got in the pickup and slithered along the muddy tracks that followed the lake's perimeter partway around.

How old is this thing? NoBob said.

It's an '84. Surprised someone would think it so old. Bought it new.

When Lane guessed they were closest to the canoe he stopped and they fought their way through the vegetation and stood with their feet in the water's edge and stared into the empty boat. The blood on the gunwale had begun to dry and blacken and a patch of thin blond hair swirled outward from a rivet like hackle on a dryfly. Hellykerdam, NoBob said. You might be right. He pulled his hat down close over his eyes and looked back toward the launchramp where Toby stood on the dock looking out over the water. You'd think he'd float.

Like an anvil, he would. If Billy Bean had an ounce of fat he'd trim it off and fry with it.

This might be one black day for the Pabst Blue Ribbon Beer Brewing Company, NoBob said.

Let's heist this thing out before the wind shifts and blows it away. They grasped thwarts on opposite sides and dragged the boat through the grass to the pickup and hipped it up and into the bed and Lane hooked a long black rubber tarpstrap to a seatbracket and the other end into a rusty hole in the fender. The tension dragged the canoe crossways, but it stuck out on the passenger side where it wouldnt hit an oncoming vehicle. Lane twanged the strap and they climbed in and he backed and filled on the narrow muddy track until they were headed back the way he'd come. We probably ought not have moved the boat, Lane said. Should have left it there for the police to look at.

NoBob made a noise that could have meant anything. How much of a ass you're making of yourself aint sunk in yet, has it?

His truck's one place I havent looked. Just in case, we better. The parking lot deserted but for the battered and rusted Ford Ranger pickup. He pulled in beside it and switched off the ignition and they got out. You ever park like that? he said. Nosed up into the corner where you cant get at it with jumpercables if it should happen not to start?

No. But then again I aint burned up my brain quite as bad as Billy Bean did.

Lane looked in the window. His emergency brake's pulled and it's out of gear. The keys gone. The windows rolled up. He straightened and hawked and spat into the weeds. I doubt Billy Bean did one of those things in his whole life. Nobody that lives around here would.

Like I said. NoBob made a drinking motion and crossed his eyes.

Where you parked? Lane said. You got a cellphone?

I'd as soon be caught wearin pantyhose. My truck's parked down at the gate on the old Garner farm.

I'm going to run out and call 911 and get the boy back. Lane looked at his watch. Darlene'll be throwing a fit. He yelled for Toby and started the pickup. You're going to hang around, arent you?

Since you've totally screwed up the first day off I've took all summer, probly so.

•   •   •

NoBob lit another cigarette and when Lane's exhaust had faded he gave his surroundings a careful evaluation and then peered through the sideglass of Billy Bean's truck. With his handkerchief over his hand he opened the door and worked the stick into reverse and released the emergency brake but could tell by the way the pull let go all at once that the never-used cable was frozen in the guides. He crawled underneath, cursing the winter road salt that destroyed everything remotely mechanical. With a rock he tapped the brakedrums while he wiggled the cables until he felt the shoes release. Then with the heel of a hand as hard as the rock he scuffed at the dings on the drums until they faded into the surrounding rust.

He slid out and brushed off his clothing and gathered his fishing pole and walked along the shore to fetch his truck. Before all the foofaraw got started. Pleased with himself beyond what the situation warranted.

.6

the access road and got out and dug in his pockets and said, You
have a dime, Toby?

The boy didnt answer or look away from the corner of the passenger window where he sulked.

Muskies arent the most important things in the world. We'll
have another go at him. Lane discovered a quarter in the ashtray but
when he opened the booth's door he found it contained nothing but
a crooked walking stick and a gnarl of desiccated crap and toiletpaper. You knew there was no phone there anymore, didnt you? he said
but the boy ignored him. Lane glimpsed his own still-muddy face in
the rearview mirror and scrubbed away the worst with his shirttail.
Wondered about the kind of person who would defecate in a phone-
booth. In a glass outhouse.

A black cloud of depression blindsided him as he accelerated
back toward the baitshop, and with it came memories he'd thought
were gone but were merely sequestered where he hadnt visited.
Flying home on a cargo plane, a long line of gaunt soldiers har-
nessed to the wall, puking into their laps. A single broken tooth

lying on the bumper of his truck the morning after a bar fight; NoBob's claiming it for a trophy though he hadnt participated in its extraction. Staring at the calendar at the lumberyard, dumb-founded at the missing years. For a moment time skittered from its groove and the boy beside him was Frank, quiet and unreadable and fathomless as a minutely crafted but specialized tool with no discernible purpose.

The Mexican boy and the whistledick waited at the baitshop, the boy sitting patiently against the wall and the whistledick's lowslung broken-springed faded K-car oozing squirming dirty kids and listing to the right from the fat woman in the passenger seat. Lane sat for a moment before getting out to regain his bearings, to make himself acceptable to public scrutiny. Such as it was.

It's about time, the whistledick turkey-mouthed and tossed a cigarette butt into the lot.

Lane unlocked the door and said, Come on. Lane had never asked his name, nor did he care to. Sorry I was late. Too tired to go through the endless explanation that would ensue if he explained why. Two dozen each? A procession of whistledick kids poured in behind the thin man, fingering here and there and, Lane knew, sliding half of what they touched into worn pockets. Why the state didnt spray insecticide wherever the whistledick lived was beyond Lane.

Them last minnies wasnt worth ten cents. Died fore you could get em on the hook.

Well, you're lucky I didnt charge you ten cents for them then.

Not when you charged four dollars I aint. I remember when minnies was fifty cents.

I remember when people had jobs instead of living off the taxpayer, Lane thought but didnt say. He netted shiners from the big stainless tank into the dented whistledick bucket without counting, likely giving twice good measure but not caring, then grabbed two Styrofoam cups of crawlers from the refrigerator. Just take them, he said. Not wanting to get the moneybox from its hiding place with whistledicks watching.

The whistledick dug in a wallet with no particular shape and licked his thumb.

They're on the house today, Lane said. Since you got some bad ones.

Where they bitin at today? No thanks for free bait.

I'm not trying to be rude but I dont have time to talk right now. A problem's come up that I have to take care of. He hustled the sullen bunch out the door and shut it and then opened it long enough for Toby and the Mexican boy to come in and locked it behind them. He dialed 911 and stuck his finger in his off ear to cut out the minnow tank's bubbling. This is Lane Hollar, he said. From out on . . . yessir, that's the address I'm calling from. 94 Ford Road.

Wondering how they already knew that.

But dont send anybody here. To the baitshop. The problem is out at the reservoy. We got a man missing and I think he's in the drink.

The reservoy, he said. Where your drinking water comes from. At the launchramp.

He shrugged. Yessir. Some people say it that way.

He looked at his watch. I'll get there quick as I can.

He pressed the button on the phone and dialed Darlene's number and when it rang unanswered he fumbled for his reading glasses under the sales counter. As he searched through the phone book for the diner's number he said, How many you got for me today, Chico? The Mexican boy's name was Juan, but after he'd been corrected twice—Whhhhhhaun, not Wan—he'd resorted to Chico.

The hard-muscled brown boy set his jagged-topped tin can on the counter's edge. Only ten. The ground is too dry.

That's ten more than anybody else has brought me. Lane's night-crawlers and minnows came once a week from a commercial supplier but he was always ready to reward industry in the local boys, though Chico was the only one who demonstrated any. Lane found the number and dialed it and asked to talk to Darlene. While he waited he searched his pocket for change and finding none took a dollar bill from his wallet and placed it beside the tin can. Bring me all you find, now.

Darlene came on and he listened and said, I know, I know. I never do call you there and you know it. The reason . . .

He shook his head. Shut up and let me talk and then you *will* know. A fellow drowned out at the reservoy this morning. We've been looking for him.

No, he's fine. I just didnt get him back in time and I'm sorry.

He started to speak and wet his lips instead. Well, the youth group's already gone by now so he's not going swimming with them anymore.

I'll keep him here. You know that's no problem. I'll be gone for a little bit but not for long.

He ran the fingers of his free hand through his hair and rubbed his eyes. If I dont leave him here I'll have to take him back to where a man's drowned. I *have* to go back out there.

All right, he said. I think that's best. Lane placed the phone back in the cradle and watched two more vehicles pull into the gravel lot. Toby, he said, how'd you like to tend the store for a bit?

The boy made eye contact with Lane for the first time since they'd left the reservoir. By myself? He looked at Chico and back to Lane.

You gave me too much money, the Mexican boy said. Ten worms are only fifty cents.

Chico, your crawlers are the best ones I get. Not pulled in two. Took good care of. So I'm going to give you extra for yours this time. Dont tell it around, now, or everybody will be wanting that much.

That's $1.20 a dozen. More than you sell them for.

Worms of your caliber make people come back. I can stand to lose a little bit for that.

No, the boy said. I cant do that. He placed the dollar bill back onto the counter.

Lane considered and with Chico watching retrieved the money-box from the refrigerator's produce drawer and set it beneath the sales counter and gave the boy two cold quarters from it. Now you know the combination to the safe, he said.

Thank you, the boy said and unlocked the door and let himself out and as he exited the other customers crowded in.

Think you can handle it if I let you here? Lane said to Toby. It's Thursday, so we shouldnt be too busy.

Except if somebody wants a license. I'm not sure . . .

No. Dont try that. They'll have to wait for that till I get back. But you can sell worms and minnows, cant you? Plugs?

Sure.

A tremor in the boy's voice that Lane felt within himself as pride.

Lane ducked into the bathroom and changed into wrinkled but dry clothing from a garbagebag atop the water heater and put his wet discards in another. I forgot about sales tax, he said when he emerged. That'll be too hard.

It's just percents. We learned them a long time ago. I watch you do it all the time.

All right, he said. If you have a problem just write it down. We'll fix it up later. You need to get into some other clothes.

These are dry, Toby said, plucking at his light cotton shirt. Can I tell about the fish that got away?

If you dont make me look too awful bad doing it.

Toby grinned and Lane knew it would be all right between them.

Can I tell Mom that I took care of the store all by myself?

Let's see how you do at it. See what happens out yonder. Then we'll figure out what to tell Darlene. When you dont have customers you can sweep the floor and dust off the shelves. Get the plugs all on the right hooks. Make sure there's no sick minnows in the tank. All things the boy could do.

Good deal, Toby said, his sense of vast responsibility leaking from the whites that showed all around his eyes.

.7

than he'd intended, and parked behind a five-year-old patrol car pulled up tight behind the pickup NoBob had retrieved in Lane's absence. NoBob sat on the flat wooden bed, smoking a cigarette and talking to a muscled young man Lane thought both too short and too young for law enforcement. When Lane stepped out the deputy adjusted his hat and patted at the implements on his belt. Like a civilian would check his zipper. His pistol toward the front like an erection. MARTIN, his nametag said. If he hadnt stolen it from an adult.

You're not the one I talked to on the phone, Lane said. Some woman.

That was the dispatcher.

You got someone just to answer the phone?

That's what a dispatcher does.

Isnt Dick coming out? The sheriff, he felt obliged to add. In case this punk hadnt yet met his boss. Or not long enough to learn his first name. Maybe it was his very first day on the job. Deputies supposed to be lean and lanky, casual and friendly. Not like this one.

Annoyance with no effort to hide it flickered across the deputy's face. Tell me what *you* think we got here.

Lane spoke to the uniform, ignored the man. What we got is a canoe with blood and hair on it and no man. The three men stood and stared into the canoe. The man's in the water.

Says you, NoBob said. I aint seen no evidence of it.

His head hit on the boat. I heard it. Or someone hit it there for him. Then they came around and shot in where I was.

What's the boat doing in your truck? Close-up Martin smelled of shoe polish, an odor that always made Lane feel like he ought to either stand up straighter or take cover. Where was it when you found it?

It came drifting across the lake to where I was fishing. It was foggy. Lane pointed to where he'd crouched in the cane. Belongs to William Bean. Strange on Lane's tongue, the name said that way, two words. His pickup's in the parking lot, too. But he's not.

Ol Billy Bean. If Martin made any effort to hide his delight it was too short in duration to notice. Maybe drowned.

Or not, NoBob said.

A blast of static came from the cruiser and Martin looked at his watch and walked over and sat with his feet out in the gravel and talked into the mic.

You could help me a little bit here, NoBob. Instead of making me out to be an idiot.

Just because you went wormy in the head dont mean I got to follow along too. I didnt see and hear all this stuff you're claiming.

Other cars were coming in the lane now. An old blue four-door sedan with a red light suction-cupped to the roof above the driver. Right behind that the sheriff's new Crown Vic and then a Subaru Justy that Lane didnt think there were any of anymore. Back toward town the distinctive *whoop whoop* of the rescue squad's siren.

Where do these people come from? Lane said.

Everybody with a scanner is a cowboy. There'll be a hunderd of em here before you can bat your eyes.

The sheriff said something to Martin and came over and looked into the canoe and said, You called this in, Hollar?

Yessir, Dick. I was fishing across the lake and I heard a real loud clunk. The kind a head makes in a boat. It was foggy and when I saw the boat floating empty I knew something was wrong.

You're sure there's somebody in the water? Once this show gets started there's no calling it off. And it's not cheap.

Looking in the water shouldnt be that costly, I wouldnt think.

Anymore we dont do that ourselves. Once a call goes in to search and rescue, we're out of the picture.

He's in there. There's no doubt in my mind.

There is in mine, NoBob said.

The sheriff walked out onto the dock and Lane and NoBob followed and it sunk further than was comfortable and when Martin started out the walkway Dick Trappel said to NoBob, Thrasher, how about you standing back a piece. When Martin took his place the dock assumed both an incline and a sideways tilt. Like Martin was made of rocks.

NoBob stood sullen on the launchramp with his hands stuffed into his pockets. Ask him why he had mud smeared all over his face, he said.

We'll get to you, Dick said.

I'd go ahead and put that call in, sheriff. To the search and rescue.

Ask him where he was hiding at. What he was doing.

Thrasher, you pipe down. I dont want to tell you again. The call's already in, Dick said to Lane. There's no stopping it now. He stared into the water with no apparent curiosity. Somehow I figured Billy Bean would die of something other than drowning. In water, at least.

He didnt drown on his own, I dont think. Whoever was with him came around where I was and took a shot at me.

Shot at you? With a gun?

No. With a spitwad. Of course with a gun.

Why are you just now telling me this?

I been trying since I got here but nobody will listen.

NoBob says different, Martin said.

They didnt shoot *at* me, per se. I was hiding in the weeds and they shot into the water just behind me.

Who was it?

They got gone without my seeing them. I was hunkered down in the weeds. In the water.

Mud smeared all over his face, NoBob said from where he'd been listening. Rambo Hollar.

Trappel turned his attention to NoBob. Where were you, Thrasher?

Down past the woodduck boxes. Come in over the Garner farm. But I didnt hear no shot. Or another vehicle like he says.

Exactly where?

Probly fifteen yards past the duck box. Twenty, maybe. I could show you.

You had to hear them, Lane said. You were closer than I was.

NoBob shook his head and spit in the water.

Where were you when you got shot at? the sheriff said.

Lane held the sheriff by the arm and looked over his shoulder and aimed his finger where they could both sight down it. Smelled coffee on his breath. Right where that cattail cane comes out into the lake.

Was there anybody else here? You see anyone?

Just his grandson, NoBob said. He heard what I heard. Nothing.

Well where's he at? The sheriff looked around like maybe they'd stepped on him or something.

He's back at the baitshop. I called from there. His mom dont want him out here. Dont want him exposed to dead people.

They paused to watch an arriving procession of vehicles led by a little white Neon with a magnetic THE WEEKLY HERALD sign on its door. Dick muttered something under his breath when a skinny red-headed girl stood out and looked around. Martin, go head her off. I dont have the time to fool with this right now. And get some tape strung around or everybody and his halfsister will be down here. He returned his attention to Lane. If there's been a crime scene here it dont matter what his mother wants.

You tell her that, cause I stutter. When I talk to her, I do.

The sheriff hitched at his belt and rested his forearm on the butt of his revolver and looked out over the water. Dammit any-how, he said.

Right now he'd be easy to find. But if he drifts off into that milfoil.

The professionals are on the way. The sheriff looked at his watch.

Or if the turtles drag him off. There's a million of them in here. I'm just saying.

Those S&R boys dont like it if the body dont get hid good so they can play with their million-dollar toys.

There was a time I'd have peeled down to my skivvies and went in there looking for him. You would have too.

Take me over and show me where you got shot at.

A little bit of a current comes past here. When you load a boat you notice it. If it takes him out in that . . .

Dammit Lane, that's not our job.

Would you want the turtles to get you if you were in there?

If he's in there like you say he's beyond caring. Now come on. Martin, he yelled. Keep this area clear till I get back. Except for emer-gency personnel.

Yessir. Smug like nothing would suit him better than to be in charge.

Come on, the sheriff said.

Lane climbed into the cruiser but before they cleared the parked cars he said, Wait. Stop here at Billy Bean's truck. I want to show you something with his vehicle.

What? Not stopping.

It's pulled in instead of backed in, for one thing. And it wont start half the time. Twice I've jumped him myself. And it's out of gear and the emergency brake's pulled.

Trappel looked hard at him and veered into the lot and they dismounted behind the rusted Ranger. The sheriff looked in the window and opened the door and jimmied the stick. It's in gear. He depressed the clutch and the pickup drifted back a few inches. The brake's off.

Lane leaned in over him and had one of those moments when he wasnt sure where he was or why. It was. I swear it was.

Well, it's not now. Trappel pushed him back and said, Let's go before S&R gets here.

It's been monkeyed with.

By who?

I know what I saw. It was out of gear and the brake pulled. Somebody's fooled with it.

It dont mean anything if it was. Billy Bean didnt know whether he was punched or bored most of the time.

They drove around as far as the cruiser would go in the muddy tracks and when they got out Trappel looked back at the launchramp the same way a boy looks back at home when he leaves. How much further out here is it? We should of gone around by the road.

Lane didnt answer but set out through the rushes and hadnt gone fifty feet when his foot found a mudhole shoemouth deep. Trappel heard the suck when it came loose and made a noise not much different. You wanted to see, Lane said. So come on. Till they'd reached the point where Lane and Toby had crouched in the cane both men's pantslegs were smeared and their shoes were unrecognizable as such. Trappel breathing hard.

Right here's where they'd have been standing when they shot.

And you were where?

We were just outside the cane there. Lane pointed.

How'd they keep from seeing you?

We were under water except for our noses.

The sheriff looked at Lane for longer than Lane was comfortable being looked at. Why did they shoot? If they couldnt see you?

Lane looked out into the water and tried to see it as it had been. The boy had a muskie on. A big one. And it rolled out there and in the fog I reckon it spooked them and they popped one at it.

What happened to it?

I bit it off.

You bit it off.

There ought to be a shell casing around here. It sounded like an automatic. Lane started kicking at the grass.

They shot more than once?

No. The action sounded like an automatic. That clack sound.

What kind of tip did it sound like? Hollow point? Wadcutter, maybe? How about the caliber?

There's no call to get smart with me, Dick. But if you got to know, it sounded like a big bore auto. Like a .45 ACP. I heard enough of them to know. Flat and barky. Like a shotgun.

Do you hear that? That right there?

Lane listened and looked back toward the launchramp where more cars had shown up. I hear some stuff. Not any one thing in particular. What you want me to hear?

The sheriff looked at his shoes and said, Shit. Let's get back over there.

Then Lane heard the whup whup of helicopter blades, coming fast.

There's just certain tones I cant hear, sheriff.

Maybe if you got out there with water up over your ears you could hear it. The sheriff started back the way he'd come. He paused and looked back. If we dont find a body I swear I'll run you in for something. If I have to make it up.

Lane wasnt that far behind the sheriff when they got back to the cruiser, but it left without him. Walking around, he slipped in the rut and enlarged the mud's coverage to include his knees and his hands and his mood. I know what I heard, he said, and wondered if someone didnt have a telephoto lens, taking video of him talking to himself.

•   •   •

Grass flattened under the helicopter's downthrust when it took off again, lighter by four men and an entire pallet of gear. Two of the men were already in wetsuits and within a minute of landing had sprouted tanks and flippers and entered the water towing floats. After a slow pass across the lake, staying high, the chopper swooped closer and followed the shoreline.

He wont be up that way, Lane said.

He might be. NoBob shook out a smoke and offered one and for some reason Lane couldnt fathom his hand went out and took it and then it was in his lips and lit and he drew it in and just like that he was smoking again. Like he'd never quit.

Not unless he floated upstream he wont be.

NoBob snorted. Billy Bean would do just that. He was contrary enough to.

Lane looked at the cigarette. Sonoma? What for kind of smoke is that?

NoBob shrugged. I buy whatever's cheap.

It tastes all right. I just never seen one before.

Got em up at Deep Creek.

The helicopter eased lower and sediment streamed from the tangles of milfoil and clouded the water behind it, where the divers were headed. The whole affair as official and impersonal and ignorant as a training exercise. I remember when we used to drink out of that, Lane said.

They still do.

I mean without treating it. Course we pissed in it too. It's all that vegetation that makes it look dirty. They wont be able to see a thing after they whip all the mud up.

They got infer red, someone said. NoBob watched Lane flick ashes from his cigarette. When'd you start smoking again?

Now. Though I dont have any idea why.

Just once I'd like to enjoy one the way you look like you are. I dont have anything left but the habit. Maybe I ought to quit something so I could take it up again when I wanted to show how much I was bothered. Like you're doing.

Nearly an inch of cigarette remained beyond the filter but Lane dropped it into the gravel and ground it under his muddy shoe. Stick it in your ear, you little rat.

The words could have gone either way—rough banter or serious insult. NoBob spat between his boots and scooted up onto the flatbed of his pickup. I'm startin to remember why I liked you.

Lane didnt bite into an argument but stood wishing he hadnt snuffed out the smoke. He watched the chopper.

After a while NoBob said, You know, maybe I will quit smokin before it gets ahold of me like it does some.

Fifty-some years is most likely pushing it. You might have waited too long. Probably just over the line.

It'd be close.

What are you up to, anyway? I know daggone well you heard the same things I did this morning. And since when do you fish at all, much less on a weekday?

You gonna Mirandize me before you get out the rubber hose? I worked the last seventeen days straight finishing a job up at Deep

Creek. If that dont earn you a morning off, I dont know what does. But now that's screwed up till I should of went ahead and worked.

Inconsiderate of old Billy Bean, wasnt it.

Not the way I meant it. And you know it. White trash breeds and births and eats and fights and dies without any special kind of assistance from us. If they dont knock each other in the head they'll die from bad livers or of the syph. Get drunk and dont fix the fire and freeze their feet off. Pass out in the road and get run over.

From out in the water came a shout and a diver held up a dirty camouflage ballcap. I told you he was in there.

Or fall in the water and drown. I didnt say he didnt drown. Just that somebody didnt drowned him like you got conjured up in your imagination.

An orange buoy splashed into the floating vegetation beneath the chopper. Further down the lake than Lane had expected.

NoBob slid down off the bed and opened the pickup's door and eyed the combobulation of parked vehicles. This place aint going to be fit to fish in today. I'm gonna go cut a load of firewood. The engine fired with a roar and dust blew from underneath.

Lane held onto the rear-view mirror for a minute. As though he could restrain it long enough to defuse the tension between them. To restore some small measure of their old friendship. Though Lane didnt care but felt that he *should* care. If there was a difference. You ever count on getting old? he said.

Thinking on it wont change a thing. NoBob pulled the stick back into reverse.

I have, though. Maybe too much.

That could get tiresome. Wear a feller down. If God had wanted me to think He'd a made me a horse. Or a hog, or a dog. One a them smart animals that's got the time for it. While we fetch water and food and scratch behind their ears.

Lane released the truck. You really think I was just imagining things this morning?

One of us was experiencing an alternate reality. NoBob grinned and backed away at a steady throttle, sliding the wide bed through parked cars with inches to spare.

• • •

Lane edged close to the sheriff when they brought Billy Bean in, white and puckered and as dead as Methuselah's tallywhacker. The rescue cowboys whipped him into the ambulance and away before Lane could study him further. Like they owned him. Like they could bring him back to life if they were official enough. The canoe's gunwale was impressed across his temple like his head had been molded around the canoe, but Lane couldnt see any sign of what he'd feared. No missing chunks. I'm glad they beat the turtles to him, he said.

They're good at what they do.

Billy Bean's canoe's in my truck. What you want me to do with it?

Could you slide it off at your place? Till we see what's happening?

Dont you want to test it for fingerprints?

The sheriff turned and leaned close and confidential, like he was telling a randy joke at a Sunday school picnic. Lane, we'll do an autopsy. We have to in unattended deaths like this. But I can almost tell you what Doc Crawford will find: that he fell and knocked himself out and drowned.

Arent you going to talk to the boy? At least that much?

Thrasher said the boy didnt seem too enthusiastic about your version of what happened.

Toby was ticked off about the fish.

Imagine that. The sheriff stepped back a pace. You dont drink anymore. Did someone tell me that?

Not since Mary died. Nine years.

Not at all? Even at parties and stuff?

I havent been to a party since then.

Dick Trappel watched the flashing lights of the ambulance out of sight. I could talk to the boy. I could do that much.

Billy Bean would appreciate it.

Billy Bean's beyond caring. Way past.

Some folks are lucky like that, Lane said. After a while he kicked a stone into the water and turned and walked back to his pickup.

. 8

LANE STOOD JUST INSIDE THE BAITSHOP DOOR
and evaluated an assortment of lead sinkers and tried to keep his
heart from showing through the back of his coat while he listened
to Toby give fishing advice to Sid Lore. The bass are in the post-
spawn, the boy said. Maybe in a couple of weeks they'll bite again,
but I wouldnt waste my time on them just now. Bump your minnow
along the bottom out past the weeds. Around twenty feet. The wall-
eye and pike are both out there deep. Big perch, too.

Sid winked at Lane.

The boy knows, Lane said. Knowing that Sid would tie the nose
of his boat to the same stump he always did. Stare at a bobber and
listen to the radio till the Orioles' game was over and then he'd go
home and go in his house and nobody knew what he did there. The
same, Lane suspected.

Toby made change and Sid put it in his pocket without counting
it and picked up his battered old minnow bucket and paused where
Lane stood. His face as rusted and dented as the bucket. The boy's
growing up, Hollar, he said. As though the boy wasnt there.

Like a dadblamed weed. Trying not to sound like other grandfathers but hearing himself he knew he'd failed.

Things settled down out there so I can get the boat in yet?

The people are gone. They got the water stirred up hateful though.

The fish are all chased down to my hole. That's what I figure. Be laying in there so thick my minnie wont be able to get down to the big ones without getting ate.

Some remote part of Lane suggested offense at such indifference to death but it was a detachment he knew in himself. You might be right, he said.

There aint but one way to find out.

Sid shuffled out the door and when he was gone Toby said, Did they find him?

Lane nodded and went over to check what the boy had been doing. Yeah. I'm glad they got to him before the turtles did. Trying to soften the blow of a death to the boy and realizing he'd introduced an idea infinitely worse. Everything all right here?

One man wanted me to give him a discount. He laughed when I told him he'd have to ask you.

My price is my price. Folks know that.

Dick Trappel's cruiser was easing into the lot. Toby, Lane said, the sheriff wants to talk to you. Just tell him the truth.

The sheriff? Toby seemed to shrink a few millimeters. About what?

Lane patted him on the shoulder. There's nothing to be worried about. Just tell him what happened out there this morning.

I didnt do anything.

Nobody thinks you did. Lane recalled his own ungrounded fear of the law when he'd been Toby's age and the memory was an icicle that speared him hard and deep but somehow sweet.

How you doing, Mr. Hollar, Dick said when he came in.

He's talking to you, Toby, Lane said. He dont ever put a mister on mine.

Good. Sir.

Lane turned the sign around so that the CLOSED face was out. Knowing customers would beat on the door anyway, as long as his vehicle was in the lot.

Do you care if I sit down? Dick asked the boy. He eased into Lane's old rocker and Lane sat up on the counter and boosted Toby up beside him.

You play baseball?

Toby shook his head. Not on a team or anything.

It's hard for his mom to get him back and forth. With the hours she works, Lane said. He about has to ride the bus.

Your daddy sure played, Dick said. Old Frank had him an absolute rifle. Still does, I wouldnt doubt. I was leaning on the left-field fence one time where I could watch one of his throws to the plate, and I swear that ball never got ten feet off the ground. One bounce, right in the catcher's mitt.

He did?

We dont talk too much about Frank, Lane said.

He could knock a ball egg-shaped, too.

I throw pretty good.

How about your batting?

There's nobody to throw to me very much.

You ought to get this old coot to throw some. Dick swatted Lane on the knee and Lane felt like swatting him back with a closed fist. For the first time he realized how good Dick Trappel was at his job. Lane looked at his watch. Maybe you ought to go ahead and ask him what happened. Saw that the boy's affinity had passed from him to the sheriff.

We could do that. You had a big fish on this morning, I understand.

Pap bit the line off. Let it go.

Why do you think he did that, Toby?

When I saw Billy Bean's boat he crowded me out in the water and pushed my head down. Till just my nose stuck up.

He do that just because he's old and mean?

I guess not. Toby told about how the muskie had eaten a duck and of the size of the sucker minnow he'd put on the hook. Where he'd hooked it. How the fog had made his hair wet.

If it was that foggy you probably couldnt see over to the launch-ramp. What did you hear?

Billy Bean came and the thing that hooks the engine to the wheels wasnt working right.

The driveshaft?

No, Lane said.

Let the boy tell it. Was it the driveshaft? That's what hooks the engine to the wheels.

Toby looked at Lane with doubt in his eyes, not of his own memory but of Lane's account. I think so. Maybe.

All right. The driveshaft wasnt working right. What else did you hear?

It was the clutch, Lane said.

What else did you hear, son?

Somebody talking. And something hit in the boat. And I heard a truck leave.

Was it in that order?

I think so.

How do you know it was a truck?

It was loud like one. That kind of a sound.

Could it of been Mr. Bean moving his truck to the parking place that you heard?

It might have been. Yeah.

You're sure you heard something hit in the boat before you heard an engine again?

No. I dont know. Toby looked at Lane with the same trepidation in his eyes he'd had when the sheriff came in. I was paying attention to the bobber.

Big fish like that around, that's what I'd do too. Could you tell whether the truck you heard was down at the launchramp or up at the parking lot?

No.

What else did you hear?

Nothing.

Yes you did, Toby, Lane said. Tell what you heard after the truck went past.

That's all I heard.

You heard people talking.

Kind of.

Could you tell what they said? Dick acting like someone's grandpa, warm and interested.

Huh uh. My ears were under the water.

What else did you hear?

Something slapped on the water. I think it was a beaver. Smacking its tail down.

It was a pistol shot, Lane said. Not as sure as he was earlier.

Could it have been a shot, Toby? Do you think?

The boy looked at Lane as though a licking would be forthcoming if he said the wrong thing.

It's all right, Dick said. Just tell what you heard.

I didnt hear any gun.

Lane released air he hadnt realized he was holding.

Seems you're the only one heard anything, Lane. Dick turned again to the boy. Did you see anybody?

The boy looked away and out the window. No.

The sheriff leaned back in the chair and linked his fingers behind his head. His belly not pulling up into his chest like it once did. What do you think, Hollar?

I'm thinking maybe I ought to give that particular exercise up for a lost cause.

Are *you* sure of what you heard? And saw? About the sequence? After what the boy had to say?

Not as much as I was.

Tell you what. There'll be an autopsy. And I'll check out Billy Bean's house and his truck and anything else I can think of. Talk to NoBob Thrasher again. But unless something new comes up, I dont know where else to go with this.

Neither do I. Lane drummed his fingers on the counter. Billy Bean's canoe's still in my truck. What do you want me to do with it?

Slide it off here if you got room. Or run it out to his place. Whatever works for you. Or I could send someone out to get it.

I'll run it over directly. Billy Bean got any kin around that might need to be notified?

Knowing how Cricket was, Billy Bean's likely got three-four hundred halfbrothers and sisters strung around. But nobody legal I know of. Maybe that gene pool's finally dried up.

Lane extended his hand and found the sheriff's as firm and dry as it ever had been. I thank you for following up. Sorry to waste your time.

That's my job. But not for much longer.

You'll be missed. Whoever the next sheriff is.

That'll be Martin, most likely.

Martin? Somehow Frank's face had gotten installed atop the young deputy's uniform. He's a *kid.*

He's older than I was when I took over this job.

Still. It's not the same.

Looking back always is different than looking ahead.

But Lane's mind had wandered back to the reservoir. Hoping he was just crazy. That thinking about Nam again had twisted his screws, maybe had made him see and hear things that hadnt really happened. That Billy Bean really had fallen and hit his head, and as soon as they got him in the ground, life would ratchet back to normal.

. 9

LATE IN THE AFTERNOON THEY CLOSED THE baitshop and drove out past the buffalo farm to the edge of town to Toby's mother's home and entered without knocking.

Hey, Pap. Darlene's fine blonde hair was frowzy and smelled of grease when Lane hugged her. Under her faded sweatpants and baggy shirt a softness that didn't contribute to womanhood was accumulating, but it was mostly in all the right places.

DeeDee, I'm sorry I didnt get him back in time to go swimming.

People ought to have more consideration about when they drown. I dont like Toby swimming where there's no lifeguard anyway so it's just as good he didnt go.

If he was mine, I wouldnt let him run with that church bunch anyhow.

They're good people. And he needs to be with kids his age.

I'd worry more about him drowning in their doctrine than in the water. You ought to just let me watch him every day.

He let me run the store all by myself, Toby said. I made change and everything.

Oh, for heaven's sake, Lane. He's not big enough to be doing that. If I'd known you were going to do that I'd have taken off work and come to get him.

It didnt hurt him any. Sure as hell better than hanging out at the diner all day. For some reason Lane couldnt discern, his language coarsened around Darlene.

He's just a *boy*.

Lane grasped Toby by the shoulders and turned him in a circle for inspection. No bullet holes or needle tracks or sucker bites or anything, Lane said. When he let go Toby shot them both a look and disappeared toward his bedroom.

Dont even talk about needle tracks, Darlene said. That scares me to death.

But bullets and sucker bites are okay?

Bullets dont come around with any regularity and I could do with a sucker bite myself once in awhile. But the damn drugs are everywhere nowadays.

Lane considered that and judged it a stretch. The product of too much television, maybe. You got any of that coffee left? he said. Darlene's house was about the only place Lane ever felt warm. He tossed his jacket onto a Sears treadmill and picked it up and brushed the dust off it and placed it on the back of a kitchen chair instead.

Throw it around some more places while you're at it. The whole place needs dusted. She plunked Lane's big mug at his regular place and sat heavily across from him. You want a burger or something? The dishes are still out.

I got things to do. But I'd take a smoke if you got an extra one.

How the mighty have fallen. When she leaned far back to retrieve her purse from the countertop her sweatshirt pulled up above a creamy belly and bright red panties that Lane couldnt not look at. Her Salems were on top but she had to dig for the lighter and when she did a Keno ticket and a birth control pill box were among the rubble. Give me hell, she said when she stuffed them back inside.

Lane lit the cigarette and tried to ignore the menthol and get to the tobacco while he wondered which item she was talking about. Or if there were more he hadnt seen. Kind of proud that she didnt seem to care. What you do is your business. I didnt say a thing.

You dont have to. It sticks out all over you.

Whatever you're seeing sticking out it's not that. Lane added to the already full ashtray. Dick Trappel told Toby some stuff about Frank today.

What was the sheriff talking to Toby for?

Women always fixed on the wrong part of any sentence, it seemed to Lane. Just asking him about what happened out at the reservoy.

Why?

Lane examined the end of his smoke and considered a self-imposed ban on all communication with the opposite sex. Making Frank out to be some superhero, he said.

What happened at the reservoir? Other than someone drowning.

Nothing that I know of, Lane said and wondered how it was women downright forced you to say the opposite of what you thought. Billy Bean fell and hit his head in his boat and drowned.

That's what he gets for leaving quarter tips all the time.

That's hard, Darlene.

Life's a bitch and it's the good part. Hows come you started smoking again?

I guess I dont know why I stopped in the first place.

Let me see. Lung cancer. Emphysema. Public ostracism. Bad breath. Stinky clothes.

If I die with any parts not wore out or ruined I'm going to feel like I cheated myself.

She smiled and looked ten years younger. Raised cheeks framed the eyes differently and somehow changed the blue from sky to stream. The trick is for everything to crap out at the same time. Like my Ford does.

There's that, he said and stubbed out the butt and couldnt help but smell his fingers or laugh along with her when he did. Dont be surprised if Toby has questions about Frank. After Dick brought him up.

Frank is his daddy after all. It would kind of be expected.

Daddies stick around and take care of their family. Assholes dont. It was an old argument. I dont know why you dont find you a good man.

Good men are all married. And like I told you before, I had a good man and I let him go. Good men are boor-ring. I like em with nose rings and nasty tattoos. Motorsickles.

Aw, Darlene. Knowing she was jerking his chain but not as hard as he wanted to believe.

She laughed. I thought you had stuff to do. Even if you dont, I do. He rose and hugged her and she fastened a button on Lane's flannel shirt and brushed something from his shoulder. You need to quit worrying about me. Us. We're doing good.

You'd be better with a man. That's all I'm saying.

Well let me say it a different way, then. Butt out. Men are like that treadmill over there. They seem to have a whole lot more purpose in the store than you can bring to mind once you get them home.

DeeDee . . . you know I wasnt being critical of you. If everyone was like you . . . When he couldnt find the words to finish his thought he turned and opened the door and walked away.

I'm off tomorrow and Saturday, so dont be picking up Toby in the morning, she said from the stoop. There's enough work around here for ten of him. And Sunday there's a church picnic.

You ought to sleep in and get some rest on your days off. Let me watch the boy.

It's time he learns to work some around the house.

Funny that had to happen just now, he thought but didnt say. Just when I could use some company. Just when the boy could use a man around. All right, he said, you're the chief, and turned back down the walk.

You got a hole in the seat of your pants. Bring them over and I'll mend them. Unless you're showing off your butt on purpose. Either that or get you a pair of denim underwear.

He felt of his jeans. How'd that get there? I wasnt showing off.

You ought to.

He stopped and looked back at his daughter-in-law and pondered anew how he could have spawned a son idiot enough to leave her.

Better yet, she said, why dont you buy you a new pair. Get some of those hiphuggers like people wear nowadays.

I've been wearing these kind for a half a century or so. I reckon they'll work yet for a spell.

•　•　•

Lane checked Billy Bean's garage door and was surprised when it came open in his hand and even more surprised to see that the pickup had either been driven or towed home. He examined the garage door's lock and realized that it had none and wondered why that seemed peculiar to him. Since his own lock was seldom engaged.

He backed his pickup around to the door and slid the canoe onto the concrete floor and the chore felt incomplete so he hung the life preserver on a nail on the wall and stood and looked into the boat and then into the bed of his own pickup. Then into Billy Bean's. Where's the paddle? he said, and his eyes went to where it leaned against the workbench close to where he'd hung the cushion. You must have really been drunk, he said. His voice lonely and old. Knee-walking drunk. To forget your paddle.

After he'd removed the rod and tacklebox and placed them on the workbench he turned the canoe over on its top and took a last look around and lowered the door and felt something close off from his life. Not knowing for certain if that was a good thing or bad.

He drove into Hardly to the Lewis Funeral Home and found all the doors locked and sat in his pickup for a while and then drove down the street to the Get-n-Go and waited empty-handed in line with people he didnt know carrying bags of potato chips and twelve-packs of beer and cups of coffee. Let me have a pack of Sonomas, he said when he reached the register and laid two dollars on the counter.

You want to give me a hint as to what they might be?

Sonomas. Cigarettes.

Never heard of em.

Marlboros, then. Soft pack.

They're $3.99, the girl said.

I just want one pack.

Maybe wherever country you been living in where they make Sonomas you can get a pack of smokes for two dollars. Alphabeckistan, maybe. She repeated the price and not until he reached for his wallet again did she claim a pack from the overhead rack. $4.23, she said. Tax. She fingernailed the counter while she waited for Lane to extract yet another dollar.

You got any matches?

Why me, someone in line behind Lane said. Every stinking time.

I can sell you a lighter.

Lane left the store six dollars poorer than he entered and he paused outside and lit up and looked at his cigarette and said to it, Thirty cents apiece. That's about twelve cents an inch. You can bet you're going right to the filter. He drove back to the funeral home and when he found it still deserted he returned to the baitshop and turned on the lights and flipped the OPEN sign around just in case, though hardly anyone bought bait or tackle in the evening. He found a pair of battered WalMart reading glasses and with some difficulty found Lewis's number and when he called there was a series of switching noises and a quiet little voice said, Hello?

I was trying to get the funeral home, Lane said.

Oh, yes. This is Cliffton Lewis. How may I help you?

A fellow died this morning and I was wondering if there were any arrangements for him yet? I dont imagine there are but I thought I'd better check. This is Lane Hollar, by the way.

Would this have been Mr. Bean by any chance?

Yessir. William Bean. Again finding the two-word name strange.

The arrangements are complete, but there wont be any funeral. He's to be cremated after he's released from the coroner's office.

Lane was temporarily at a loss for words.

Was there anything else?

Well who made those arrangements? I didnt know that he had anyone.

Mr. Bean prearranged it a couple of years ago. At the time of Mr. Bean the elder's . . . at his time.

Lane vaguely recalled a story someone told about Billy Bean getting hung up and using Cricket's ashes under the tires for traction. The old man finally of some use to someone. Billy Bean did all that himself?

Mr. Bean. Yessir.

Are you sure we're talking about the same person? Billy Bean. Skinny, and tough looking. About as sharp as a watermelon.

I havent seen him in a couple of years. But yes, I suppose his physical condition could have been described that way. I dont feel qualified to comment on the other.

When's all this going to take place?

I expect the body to be released yet this evening. In fact, I thought this would be the call.

Well.

Pre-arrangement is something you should consider as well, Mr. Hollar. There's a considerable savings, and there's so much less stress on your loved ones. It's becoming a very popular option. For those concerned with their families.

I'm not planning on going anywhere for a spell yet. I got to be honest with you, I'm still having a hard time swallowing this.

Is there anything else I can help you with?

No, I guess not. A fellow gets down to where he needs your help, there's not much help for him. Is there?

It's all a matter of perspective, sir. A certain amount of ceremony is of tremendous benefit in the healing process.

Well, I cant see it from here, Lane said and hung up and felt empty and misdirected. After he'd smoked two more cigarettes he turned off the inside lights and stood looking out into the dusk toward Billy Bean's house, two miles away. He locked the shop and drove back to Billy Bean's garage and lifted the door and stood in the semi-darkness and listened and felt and smelled his surroundings.

Billy Bean's pickup was small and smelled of hot grease and stale beer and garbage and the seat collapsed under one cheek so that Lane felt like he was sitting in a child's toy car he'd scavenged from a dumpster. After a bit he pulled the emergency brake and released it slowly and pulled it again and released it quickly and both times could tell it didnt release at all. Like any old vehicle that had been driven in road salt all these years did.

He turned on the ceiling lights but could see nothing underneath so he fetched a flashlight from his own truck and crawled under the frame and stared at the fresh dings in the brake drum. Where someone had tried to scrub them out. A chill unrelated to the evening air found the back of his neck.

His back cracked when he crawled out and he groaned and stood crooked until he worked the kink out and then he walked to the workbench and opened the tacklebox he'd placed there earlier. Stared at a live bait box full of sinkers and floats and hooks and snapswivels, then at the flyrod he'd put there. That's some trick. Throwing sinkers with a flyrod. Without any bait.

Maybe he heard a noise or maybe he felt eyes. But he was not alone. Lane gripped the flashlight hard and turned as casually as he knew how under the circumstances and his eyes found the darker shape under the trees at the yard's edge and he let them slide on past and looked at his watch like he was late for something and walked to the door and switched off the lights and immediately stepped back into the darkness behind Billy Bean's truck.

From the dark garage he knew he couldnt be seen so he waited and watched and after a while the man under the trees stepped forward and Lane recognized both the short muscled shape and the voice. What in the sam hill you doing in there, Hollar?

Waiting to see who's lurking in the weeds. Like a common criminal.

Lane stepped forth from the garage and met Deputy Martin in the unshaded driveway and this time smelled sweat and heat instead of shoe polish and realized the man was wearing shorts and a tank top. I was jogging past and saw lights, Martin said. Where there shouldnt be any.

I was bringing back the boat, Lane said. Putting Billy Bean's stuff away where it belongs. Wondering how long he'd been watched. Lane switched on his flashlight and shone it on Martin's sweat-streamed face and the deputy stumbled back with his hand grappling where his pistol usually hung and Lane realized the younger man was afraid of him. Easy, hoss, he said. Fairly certain that the deputy had watched him for a while.

Martin's laugh had an adrenaline jitter. Caught me by surprise.

I didnt know you lived close to here.

I dont. I'm out past the old tannery.

Lane looked behind him. Where's your car?

I jogged over.

On foot? Knowing how stupid that sounded but unable not to say it. That must be five, six miles.

Probably just over seven to here. Thursday I do twenty miles.

You ought to do it in some other direction. Where folks dont care on Thursday if you skulk around in the shadows. Out that way. The second Thursday of the week is the day people this way dont care.

Look, Martin said. I got to get going before I tighten up. Shut this place up and let's get out of here.

Lane pulled down the door and listened to Martin's footsteps recede down the driveway. The sound too insubstantial for a man running hard. He got in his pickup and where the lane struck the highway, the empty lonesome baitshop came to mind and he paused to light a cigarette and the smell took him back in time and as though the past sat navigating beside him on the seat he turned right instead of left, toward Rooster's Bar and Grill. Just for a bit, he said aloud. Just to talk for a spell.

.10

THE OLD BLUE FORD PICKUP EASED INTO LANE'S regular parking spot like a milk cow into its stall. Like it hadnt been gone for nine years. He stood in the parking lot under the buzzing pole light and finished his smoke and recognized none of the half-dozen vehicles but the doorknob felt familiar and when he shouldered the sticking door open he felt like he was entering his own dark bedroom. Like he could close his eyes and walk directly and with confidence to the bar or the pool table or the bathroom. He took a stool at the end of the bar and swiveled around to look the place over. If anything had changed he couldnt tell what it was.

Hey Larry, he said when the bartender came over.

Lane. I didnt know you were due to get out yet.

Lane evaluated his self-imposed exile and found it not unlike what he imagined prison to be and carried on with the jest. Another week or two I was up for parole, he said. But I sawed my way out anyhow. Got too bored.

Larry drew a Coors Light draft for Lane without asking, his head tilted sideways so his cigarette ashes wouldnt fall in the mug. He'd gotten skinnier than ever, his eyes gone flat.

How you been? Lane said. You're looking good. When Larry answered with a twist of the corner of his mouth, Lane sipped and then swallowed and the cold shaft of beer was intimate. Like riding a bicycle would be. That's not as bitter as I remember it, he said.

Surely you've had some since you were here last. That's been what . . . four years?

Nine years. 1998. Last beer I had. Lane looked up and down the bar. I dont know anybody.

Larry shrugged. It's the same bunch. Who dont you know?

Lane squinted into the cigarette smoke. Everyone. Where's Tuesday Price?

Tuesday straightened up and got married. Got a couple of kids. Swallow the rest of that so I dont have to come right back.

Lane emptied the mug and passed it back for a refill. I dont see Neutral either.

Larry grinned. No. He got it in gear finally. Some quit or die, but someone else always starts or comes of age. They have different names but it's the same bunch.

There's a depressing thought. Trying to picture the one he'd displaced, feeling a certain rightness and comfort at the thought.

You want to run a tab?

I'll cash out as I go. Lane placed some folded bills on the countertop and Larry took a dollar and stuffed it in his shirtpocket. Drafts used to be a quarter, Lane said.

That was four raises ago. I give you the first one on the house.

A dollar. I'm not sure a draft beer's worth a dollar.

You dont have to drink it.

I'd forgot how depressing this place is. I should have gone to church. Got as down in the dumps without spending a dollar for a draft beer.

Larry laughed. Lane Hollar. How'd we ever get by without your charm and grace.

Aw. I'm just in a mood. It's good to see you.

You too, Lane. Real good. I'd about give up on you. You got your banjo with you?

I havent picked since the band broke up.

Get it out some day. Bring it down and play us a tune.

By yourself it's not much fun.

Get NoBob. He still likes it.

Shit, Lane said, as though he'd discovered a bit of it between his teeth.

Eddie and Paul're still around. I bet they'd take it up again.

You heard about Billy Bean, I reckon.

Who didnt? I'll likely have to take out a second mortgage without him settin there to keep the light bill paid. Pabst stock went down thirty-seven cents this afternoon.

I wondered if he still came here.

Sometimes I wondered if he ever left. Larry moved away to replenish drinks down the bar and while he did Lane walked to the jukebox and deciphered its workings and examined it for a coin slot and found instead a place to insert bills and found nothing smaller than a five in his wallet and glanced toward Larry and muttered a curse and let the bill get sucked away through the slot. Lane finally found some bluegrass over on one end next to German marching songs and big bands. There were only two bluegrass albums and he went down the line and punched in the numbers till he ran out of credits. Way sooner than he'd anticipated.

See, Larry said when he returned. You still like bluegrass. If you're gonna be coming back in I'll get some more of it on there. This bunch comes in here now mostly dont listen to it.

Lane missed his five-dollar-bill and said, Dont bother. He lit a smoke and realized Larry never even knew he'd quit. Who'd Billy Bean hang out with?

Anybody that would listen to him. There aint many. He evaluated the customers one by one. Sandy, maybe. She'd put up with him if he wasnt too far in the can.

Lane looked again and finally detected the dark-haired girl half hidden behind a video game sitting on the far end of the bar.

That looks like Jodie. At least in this light it does.

Sandy's Jodie's girl. Jodie's got something wrong with her. Dont get out much.

Last time I saw Sandy she was just a little bit of a thing. Came up to here.

I hear you're the one called 911 on Billy Bean.

Yeah. Me and the grandson were fishing and I heard a clunk on a boat and then after a while here came his boat out of the fog with blood on it.

Drownding was what I had figured for him, but I'd of thought it would have been in a bottle. Larry set two shotglasses on the bar and poured them brimful of clear liquid from an unlabeled bottle and pushed one toward Lane.

Now what might that be? Already tasting the hard clean burn of the moonshine Larry sold to tourists for twice the price of blended whiskey.

Mineral water, Larry said. Here's to old Billy Bean.

They clinked the glasses together and the liquor went down Lane's throat like an icicle covered with cayenne pepper. Felt the cold glow spread from his core like a mushroom cloud.

Billy Bean went to sleep on the bar last night, Larry said. I woke him up and said, I dont piss in your bed so dont you sleep in my bar. Those were the last words I said to him. That maybe anybody did.

That doesnt make sense. Makes it sound like the express purpose of a bar is for pissing.

Talking to Billy Bean dont require sense.

Was he in some kind of trouble? That you know of?

When wasnt he? Nothing special that I know of.

Just thought maybe he'd said something.

You ought to stand back here for a week. Hear what all I hear. It all runs together.

Listen to that song. "Muddy Waters." The Seldom Scene recorded that. Half of them's dead now. Duffey. Charlie Waller.

Waller wasnt in the Scene. Never was.

Yeah, but it's hard to think of Duffey without Waller. All those years together. They're both dead, anyhow. All the old good ones are. Jimmy and Carter and Lester.

Auldridge aint. Listen to him stroke that Dobro. The whole of Larry's musical ability would fit inside a shotglass and still allow space for an ounce of liquor but he knew the words to every song Lane had ever heard and what brand instruments the musicians played and the thickness of their picks and the names of their grandchildren.

Resophonic guitars you have to call them now, Lane said. Dobro dont care for their name being bandied about.

That's how the world stays cosmopolitan. Change the names of everything and if you dont know the new one you're backward and stupid. Even though the thing's the same and they cant recall the old one.

Not much changes, he said. Just the way we see it. Which things we choose to look at.

Larry made a pass down the bar and when he returned said, So what have you been doing besides not drinking?

Not one solitary thing. Selling worms.

You have any idea how boring you are?

Lane laughed. Maybe you'd rather I was like my grandpap Hollar. He wasnt boring. He and his six brothers used to go to town just to fight.

What do you think *my* granddaddy was doing while they were doing that? Larry wiped at the bar with a stained rag.

You're kidding me.

Tending bar runs in the family.

No wonder you treat me like dirt.

Larry shrugged. They paid for what they broke, and they werent boring.

Lane looked around the bar. What you want broke? So I can come up to snuff?

Larry laughed. Rubin Tichnell was the sheriff then. His deputy went tearing into his office and said, Them damn Hollar boys is back again. Rubin rocked back in his chair and said, Smokey, I can *hear* when the sonsabitches arrive. Your job duty is to advise me when they *leave*. Lane had heard the story, a little different, but he let it pass uncorrected.

Larry refilled their shotglasses behind the bar and they turned them up and shuddered. What you think Dick Trappel would do if he had the Hollar boys to deal with? Lane said.

Same as Rubin. Dick's a good old-type sheriff. Has sense to know the difference between the illegal and the inevitable. Between crackheads and kids working their way through growing up.

How bad are the drugs around here, Larry? Lane asked straight out. Surely it's not got as bad as in the city.

Sometimes I think it's worse. Like gypsy moths. There's more good out here to hurt.

Lane let that assimilate as much as it was going to at one shot. How's an old-time sheriff deal with that? he said. Drugs are more than busted chairs and hangovers.

He dont. He retires and turns it over to a new generation that can get their minds around it. Like Dick's fixing to do.

Martin.

Good as any I know. If there was anything bad to know I'd of heard it. There's some comes in here that's well acquainted with the sheriff's department.

Now I'm really worried. If he was doing his job these folks would hate his guts.

They do. But they hate him fair and square.

I reckon that's something.

You know who Martin reminds me of? Your boy Frank. Has that same kind of intensity to him. Like a possum eyein a chokecherry he cant quite reach.

Maybe that's what I dont care for about him.

Larry gave him a look and returned to his other customers and Lane returned to his beer and felt the moonshine working soft and warm and tried to imagine what it would be like to be a deputy. The sheriff makes a decent salary but you're not the sheriff. You're living in a trailer and driving a ten-year-old pickup with three hundred big ones on an odometer that's been broke for four years. If you ever accumulated enough money to get married, now your kid needs braces bad and you have dental insurance but cant make the copay. You got through highschool but didnt get overloaded with vocabulary on the passage. Suddenly you have a .41 Mag that you play with in the dark like it was your peder and a big cruiser with lights and siren enough to make a dead man pay attention. The power of the law where there's never been anything but a hillbilly's sense of predestination and lack of choices.

Till now. Out around the lake and the ski slopes are the party mansions. Sixteen bedrooms and three kitchens one of them has. Inside there's drugs and whores and money. Choice one is to wade through those Porsches and Lexuses that spill out and block the county road and knock on a door that cost more than your trailer did. Knowing that the high-brass dandy that opens the door is on first names with the governor. Maybe it will be the governor himself. Or, you can go cruise the back roads and watch the bars and look for someone like Delbin who just got locked up DWI on his riding mower. His lawyer will get three thousand dollars and the court will get three thousand dollars and you'll get an attaboy. And if you get enough attaboys without an aw shit that cancels them all out, you'll make deputy of the month. Get your name in the paper for making fifty-seven traffic stops and settling eleven domestic disturbances and serving papers on forty-three civil complaints. God forbid you'd get tied up in court on a long case that would get settled over dinner at the country club anyhow.

One day the idea finally bores through your thick skull that the lawyers are rich and the judges are rich and all the people around the lake are rich and your kid still needs braces. So your next DWI arrest is someone you half know and never particularly disliked, someone who'd just cashed his check before he stopped at the bar and he's drunk enough to make you an offer and you're in the right mood and that particular case gets settled right on the spot and you're better off and the guy you caught is better off. Good deal all around.

You do that a few times and suddenly you're not so proud of yourself. Your soul's been sold for the price of an orthodontist and you cant get it back. All you can do is get more for it. So one night you stop a Corvette with two kids with more money and more cocaine and more to lose than they have sense and upbringing and it's second verse same as the first, a little bit louder and a little bit worse. Just like that you're a criminal. And you're not the only one who knows it. So you find that the selling of your soul doesnt take place in a single transaction. The word gets around. Your boss—the sheriff—is no fool. But he's got his eyes on the finish line and that blinds him to the truck that's barreling down the sidestreet. What he wants is one more quiet year without a scandal, without anyone getting killed by a drunk driver, without any senator's son spending a night in the drunk tank. Without a murder. So he can ease into retirement with his reputation intact. So folks will sit with him at the diner when he's old. All around, he knows, every kind of violence and perversion and vice has spread like kudzu. But not here. One more year and folks will say, It was never like this when Dick was sheriff.

For one moment Lane could see it end-to-end. Dick Trappel was retirement-blind. Martin was likely corrupt in some smallbore manner short of murder. NoBob was a weasel but Lane didnt figure him for a criminal. And if he had to quit believing in Toby, Lane didnt much care to proceed with life.

But somebody had tampered with Billy Bean's pickup. He knew that for certain. But what if Billy Bean had got drunk and pulled his own emergency brake and done the dinging himself?

Lane wondered if other crazy people were aware of it when the last of their sanity slithered down the drain. Or whether they walked around thinking they were gifted to hear and see things nobody else did. Without warning Lane perceived himself as his grandson must have. Mud-faced and Nam-eyed and crazy as a pocketful of hornets.

Larry returned and waved his hand in front of Lane's face and said, Hello. Anybody in there?

I was just thinking, Lane said.

Thought I smelled rubber burning. While Larry refilled Lane's mug he said, Yesterday you could of asked ol Billy Bean about drugs. Said he kicked a dope dealer's ass.

The world was rotating under Lane's feet in an unusual way so that he wasnt sure if he was crazy or drunk, but he hadnt had but a couple of drinks so he wasnt drunk. Maybe he was just rearranging reality to accommodate truth or a facsimile of it. A dope dealer? Lane said. Billy Bean? What all did he say?

Well, let me think. He talked about how he can find ginseng where nobody else cant and that George Bush is really Jesus Christ and that when you're playing Keno you pick four numbers but dont bet them till none of the four comes up five games in a row and that the reason Budweiser dont taste good is because it's made out of rice that Chinamen's growed in shit . . .

I mean about drug dealers.

Hell, I dont know. I dont pay attention to his crap. I was just saying. About drugs. Beanhead was likely just trying to impress the girls. Larry waved his rag toward the other end of the bar. But he couldnt imagine a drug dealer unless there was one. Man dont have the capability to imagine something that aint.

Now you're starting to sound like a philosopher.

The education you pick up behind a bar aint but a inch deep, but it's wide as Mildred Gooding's left ham.

Lane worked on his beer until Larry moved away and then he walked down to the end of the bar and stood behind Sandy and watched her play a video game that he couldnt comprehend the object of. From behind she was Jodie, not Sandy, and Lane caught the smell of perfume over the cigarette smoke and beer and something stirred inside him that had been dormant for a long time.

When her game was over and before she could start another he said, Sandy?

She turned like she hadnt known he was there and smiled and said, Hi, her voice just like Jodie's. Same dark eyes. Same thick hair and quick grin. Same little frame. As soon as she'd appraised him she turned back to her game. But Lane could feel that her attention hadnt left him.

I'm Lane Hollar. I've known your mama a long time. Can I buy you a beer?

Sure Lane. I know who you are. Mom talks about you. Says you were crazy in love with her but was too shy to ever come out with it.

Aw. Jodie said that?

Is it the truth?

Lane felt his ears glowing. I dont know. That was a while back. When we were just kids.

Sandy laughed the way Jodie used to and Lane had to look away to get his thoughts rowed up again.

I didnt know she ever suspected.

You cant fool a girl about things like that.

Lane looked around the bar and found it more amenable from this direction, larger with bar lights reflected back from the windows. Larry said Jodie's not been feeling well. Anything serious?

Sandy shrugged. They wanted to run some tests on her but she doesnt have insurance and she said she wont pay big money she dont have to learn what she already knows.

What the taxman doesnt get the doctors do. I need to stop over to see her.

She'd like that.

Larry brought the beers and said, Two bucks, horndog, and Lane felt heat in his face while he dug the bills from his pocket.

Shame about Billy Bean, isnt it, he said when Larry was gone. I heard you hung out with him some.

Naw. I just didnt run away when he set beside me like some did. Billy Bean talked big and carried one fist cocked but he was a big old softie. If he'd of took a bath more often he could of gotten a woman.

He in any trouble you know of?

Said he beat the tar out of a dope dealer. Those werent his words quite. But you know how he was.

When was this?

Yesterday or the day before. I cant keep days straight.

I've just about got surrounded the fact that drugs are everywhere but the idea of dope dealers is giving me the slip.

She turned and gave him a look full of pity. There aint often one without the other.

Lane tried to imagine Toby handing over lunch money for drugs and couldnt and understood that the inability lay within himself and not in the boy. Billy Bean say any more about it? Where it happened, or who it was?

I'm trying to remember. It was on the back part of his property, I think. Where you can see the school from. Said he caught someone parked in a van there and he smelled marijuana and he slipped up and looked in and there was a big bag of it on the seat. She drank from her mug and punched at the buttons before her as though the story were finished.

Well what happened?

He told the guy to haul butt and he give Billy Bean some backtalk and you know how he takes to that.

They fought, I reckon.

To hear Billy Bean tell it there wasnt much fight to it. He must have given him a pretty good thumping. And then the guy told Billy Bean that he didnt understand who he was fooling with. That when whoever it was got through with him he'd wished he'd stayed back at the barn with the cows and minded his own business. So Billy Bean said he gave him another thumping to take home to whoever that was. But you know how he is. His imagination gets overheated once in a while.

He mention any names? Who it might of been?

Yeah, but I dont remember it. Henry somebody.

Lane catalogued the Henrys he knew: Henry Paugh? Henry Gnegy? Henry Moats?

No. It wasnt nobody from around here. Nobody I know.

You sure you dont remember?

Sandy laughed. Yeah, I'm right certain of that.

I wish you could. I got a grandson in that school. I'd sure hate to see drugs get in there.

Shoot, there's more drugs in there than you could shake a cat at.

It's a daggone *grammar* school. Part of it is.

And part of it aint. But the dope dont pay no attention to that.

Hard to get my mind around. Lane finished his beer and considered and dismissed another. Anybody else? That might have heard and remember who he said?

You're a persistent old fart, aint you. But she smiled and rubbed her knuckles against his belly like they were old intimate friends. She dug in her purse for a cellphone and pushed a button without looking at it. Hey, she said. Whose hind end did Billy Bean kick? No, not the whole list. Just a day or two ago . . . Good deal. She punched off and put the phone back in her purse. Larson Henry. Whoever that is.

Larson Henry. The name rang a soft fuzzy bell somewhere in Lane's memory. An important name but one he couldnt get a grip on. Who was that you were talking to?

Lisbeth. Taylor. She's another one that treated Billy Bean nice like I did. He asked her to marry him and she said she'd just as soon eat broken glass out of a spittoon. But after that he told everybody they were engaged. Just because he got up nerve to ask.

Lane laughed and set his mug on the bar. That sounds like the Billy Bean I know. Well Sandy, thank you for talking to me. Tell Jodie I said hi.

You ought to tell her yourself.

I'm going to. I really am. You take care, now.

Hey, horndog, Larry yelled as he was headed out the door. You dont fall off the wagon and drink just a couple and jump back on.

Some do, Lane said. He closed the door behind him and drove back to the baitshop.

.11

baitshop and smoked cigarettes and drank stale cold coffee and listened to the airpump in the minnow tank. He tried to think about
Billy Bean but Jodie was on his mind, a childhood crush unsullied
by reality. It was both invigorating and shameful. He could think of
nothing else.

He felt under the counter for the moneybox where it had set
unconcealed all afternoon and shook it and said, If you had a brain
you'd be dangerous. He put the box in the refrigerator's produce
drawer and the light killed his night vision and made him feel comfortable and warm. Like he was in the womb. Instead of in a falling-
down business that barely paid the electric bill. He opened a Coke
and drank half of it and held the cold can against the side of his head
and cherished its cold.

When his head began to droop he finished his drink and leaned
back in his chair for a moment. When he woke his bladder was burst-
ing and his back and neck were stiff and aflame and the windows
were pale with morning's first light. After a while he realized that
he wasnt at home, that he'd slept in the shop again, and he washed

his face in the bathroom sink and wet his hair and combed it back with his fingers. An early flurry of customers livened but cluttered the morning, and then the shop sat dank and dismal and lonesome. Lane made a new pot of coffee and swept the floor and said, Hell, and threw the broom into a corner without gathering the sweepings into a dustpan.

Depression didnt often settle on Lane but when it did it sat down heavy and hard. He looked around the baitshop and perceived a lonely dirty boar's nest populated with refrigerated worms and aerated minnows and an old man lacking life support of any kind.

Lane extracted with some difficulty a garbagebag of dirty clothing from behind the bathroom's water heater and closed and locked the shop and tossed the bag into the bed of his pickup. A customer entering the lot blew the horn but Lane waved without looking to see who it was and drove the two miles to his home with the window down and noticed the smell of cut hay and wondered if he hadnt been able to smell for a while or if he just hadnt bothered to. The moments in the cane had perked up his senses but suckerpunched his spirit till he wasnt certain the trade was a good one. When he reached his house he stopped in the driveway and contemplated the lawn and shook his head and said, White trash. He parked in the carport and went inside.

The house was musty but he didnt open the windows. He assembled a cheese sandwich with frozen bread that he thawed in the toaster and smelled the milk and drank some from the jug and poured the rest down the sink. He considered the doilies and ornaments that made him feel clumsy and claustrophobic and considered packing some away in the attic and decided that he couldnt do that.

When he had a big load of laundry going he went outside. The lawnmower was hard-starting and cantankerous and he was sweating hard before he cut the first blade of grass. He hogged down the front lawn and drank water from the hose and made a face at the vinyl flavor and finished the sides and back and considered raking and said, Not hardly. Understanding the work would last longer than he did.

While the dryer thumped and rattled Lane eased the worn case from under the bed in the little bedroom and opened it and admired the old Gibson banjo inside and brushed his thumb across strings gone dull with corrosion. I've heard yellow squash with better tone, he said, and hefted it from the case and was surprised anew at its weight. One at a time he removed the old strings and wound on a fresh set and brought them up to what he guessed was pitch and strummed a chord or two and moved the bridge slightly so the frets noted true and turned the banjo over and rubbed his thumb over the curly maple back, felt the briarpatch of beltbuckle scratches.

The metal picks had grown small now so he bent them until he could tolerate them on his fingers and picked a couple of rolls and a verse and a chorus of "Cripple Creek" and the first part of a melodic tune he didnt remember the name of. Appalachian something or other. The fingers of his right hand were clumsy at finding the depth and spacing of the strings but his left remembered things that he'd forgotten. Already tiring of the song. Like he'd been before. Too lazy to learn new tunes himself and too bored and ineffective to urge others to. The others happy playing in a rut, tickled to incessantly repeat the songs they already knew.

Well, he said, and adjusted the stops on his Keith tuners and dropped down into D tuning and hooked the fifth string under a spike and noodled at "Home Sweet Home" and "Reuben's Train." As he played, a remnant of his old drive rebirthed and he punched the low notes hard and choked the second string up the neck and heard the train and his foot did too and he grinned and swung into "Randy Lynn Rag" without pause and after the first pass his fingers located the tuners at the proper time and dropped the strings and hauled them back again the way he remembered.

Lane played until he heard the dryer kick off and like another switch had been thrown elsewhere the house was again as lonely and empty as a cavern. He put the banjo away and stuffed his laundry into two pillowcases and went out and threw them into the front seat and left without looking back.

Now where do you think you're going? he asked the pickup when it turned right instead of left at the end of the driveway. Like it had caught him by surprise.

• • •

The house had begun to follow the contour of the hillside, and for a moment Lane wasnt sure he was at the right place. If the driveway had ever sported gravel the dirt didnt recall it. An explosion of myrtle consumed what lawn might once have been but not so thoroughly that dandelions didnt flourish in the midst.

The foundation sills were rotted and the pilasters sunk into the clay, the aluminum siding dented and faded and a strip at the bottom torn away to reveal roughsawn timber underneath. The roof soft-edged and rounded with countless layers of tarpaper. A board broken in the stoop and the porch cluttered with garbage bags and a three-wheeled wagon and a charcoal grill that showed daylight through its rusted bottom. Lane knocked on the wooden screen door and found the wood so pumpkinlike it made no more noise than if he'd knocked on his arm. He opened the screen and rapped against the glass beyond.

From inside came a voice or he imagined it did so he opened the door and stuck his head into the gloom and said, Jodie?

Is that you bangin on the door, Lane Hollar?

Some's accused me of being him, he said.

Get on in here if you can. The maid aint showed up yet today.

Lane picked his way through a kitchen as cluttered as the porch and infinitely darker. He ducked through a curtain and stood squinting into a room that smelled of cats and tobacco and of old age and of sickness. Where are you? he said.

A light on an end table came on and a bony arm withdrew and Lane tracked it back to the woman. Or part of a woman. Not enough bumps under her blanket for a whole one. How you doing, Jodie?

No use to complain. Nobody will listen to you anyway. The same thing she'd said every time since Lane had known her. Grab you a seat.

Lane eased into a crooked-looking chair across the room from Jodie and found it comfortable and turned it to face her.

You dont look a bit different, she said. Still just a pup.

She looked even worse as Lane's eyes adjusted to the gloom and began to separate her from her surroundings. Hair still black but flat and lifeless as the eyes. A face somehow both pale and rashed. So skinny. I ran into Sandy, he said. She said you hadnt been feeling up to snuff.

That girl always did let out more than was good for her.

She's hardly a girl anymore. Clear growed up.

In some ways anyhow.

So what's troubling you?

Heart dropsy. I've dropped down and aint got the heart to get back up.

Serious, now.

Just because I look like a syphilitic witch with rickets dont mean I'm not fit as a fiddle. You ought to see me on a bad day.

You look good. You really do. But I can tell you aint feeling proper. He was talking like she did, the way he always had around her for some reason he couldnt fathom.

She sat up and let the blanket fall to her hips and gravity did something with her features that didnt hurt them any and he could see that she was still Jodie. Still pretty underneath the rind of ill health. Her boobs under the thin material of her nightgown still lumps instead of smears. Smoked too many of these things, I figure, she said. Out of a pack she shook a cigarette longer than Lane remembered seeing before and when the lighter flared he saw how long her eyelashes were. How thick and dark. She coughed for a while and sucked again and placed the cigarette in an ashtray and lay back down and pulled the cover under her chin.

After he'd seen her sitting up she didnt look as bad lying down. Gravity not as disconcerting after you saw how it worked. Lane had wanted a smoke but watching Jodie had thrown a wet sack over his desire.

You want something to drink? I could make some coffee.

Lane thought about the kitchen he'd navigated on his way in and said No thanks.

Hear you had some excitement yesterday, she said.

Yeah. Billy Bean's number come up. Lane looked down at his feet and there was a cat there black and glossy and he started and his foot jumped out at it without hitting it. The way you'd kick at a rattlesnake barefooted. Faster back than out.

He's as evil as he looks, she said. Eviler. Aint you, Booger.

The cat didnt purr or rub against his leg but regarded him with yellow eyes slit vertically with fire showing through the crack. Lane looked away but still felt them on him. Now that he'd seen one, he imagined scores of cats but he couldnt spot another. It's a shame, he said. Billy Bean was just a boy.

She laughed. That's the same thing Bo Heller said when Arthur died at the age of seventy-two. Course Bo was a hundred and three at the time.

It's all relative.

Yeah. A minute ago you was talking about how growed up Sandy is and Billy Bean was older than she is. Jodie smoked and stared off through the wall as though they'd opened a truth that required contemplation before it trickled away.

Lane got his cigarettes out and lit one and already they'd lost their taste and had become merely a habit. He looked for another ashtray and didnt see any but Jodie's so he rolled his jeans and flicked ash into the cuff. If Jodie noticed she didnt let on, but the cat disapproved and faded away into the junk and gloom.

Tell me what happened, she said, and Lane heard himself doing just that, all of it, of hiding in the rushes and of his suspicions and his discovery that someone had monkeyed with Billy Bean's truck while he was off calling for help and of his fear that he was losing his mind and of falling asleep again in the shop and of being lonely and desolate. He'd forgotten what a good listener Jodie was or maybe he'd remembered without knowing and that's why he'd come here and when he realized what was happening he said, You dont want to hear all that silliness.

You really think somebody might have done Billy Bean in? That'd be like backing over a willy worm after you'd squished it going forward. Overkill, like.

I know. It sounds idiotic. But Sandy said Billy Bean was fighting with a dope dealer just the day before. Somebody by the name of Larson Henry.

Jodie laughed.

That wouldnt be much of a fight. *I* could whip Larson Henry.

Who is he? The name rings a bell but I cant hang it onto a face.

Dont you read the paper?

Not if I can help it.

He sells cars and mobile homes and dented cans of peaches and used clothing, anything you can think of. Up Cumberland way. I've bought cars and rags both off of him. There wasn't a lot of difference in the two, now that I think of it.

Lane recalled the ads, bold and brazen and outlandish, more superlatives than there was room for on the page.

He's no dope dealer. I can hair near promise you that.

Well. Somebody's up to no good.

Who could have fooled with Billy Bean's pickup?

NoBob was there. A Deputy Martin. Now, there's one I dont trust.

Boob's a cocky little butthole, but I cant picture him messing with evidence. If it's like you say.

Boob?

Boob Martin. Deputy Martin. My ex's nephew.

I didnt know that.

Boob's all right. He's the only one checks in on me other than Sandy. He's smart as a coal bucket but he wants to be sheriff so bad it flavors his buckwheat cakes. He wouldnt do anything to jeopardize that. Sheriff's the summit of his imagination and it's there for the taking next year. He's never had anything in his life but he's going to have that.

Lane pondered how Billy Bean's demise could help Martin be sheriff and when he gave up he said, It's beyond me then why NoBob would mess with the truck.

No. That dont seem likely either. Jodie stubbed out her smoke and lay back and closed her eyes. A valve job's what I need, she said. Her eyes came open again and she smiled, maybe at his expression. One of mine is leaky. That's what I think from what they say on the TV.

You havent been to a doctor?

She snorted. Not for twenty years. I guess you have been to one.

When my heart was blinky I did. You should get it fixed. Heart valves are purely routine operations nowadays, Jodie. Not near as much trouble as a valve job on a pickup.

It's not the money. I'm poor enough someone would take care of the bills. But I feel good except that I'm tired all the time.

Couple of weeks you'd be out jogging. Working in the garden.

Right there's the two best reasons I know for not lettin them carve me up.

Fishing then. You always did like that, near as I can recall.

Pain scares the poop out of me. That's why I'm a old woman living alone. When I had Sandy I determined that wasnt ever going to happen again. There aint a marriage on God's green earth can withstand that resolution. I'd rather just lay here and be tired and feel good than to have my breastbone wedged open like they was splittin firewood.

Somewhere there had to be someone who'd had heart surgery without a lot of pain but Lane couldnt think who it might be.

My arteries got to be gunked up too. They'd take some out of my legs to fix them up. Lynn Sweitzer had it done and she looked like they'd stitched her together with hog rings. A slim but shapely bare leg emerged from under the blanket, a flash of dark blue panties at its root, and they both examined it, Lane deliberately examining the lower end instead of the upper where it hooked on. My legs are too pretty to be sliced up.

Lane wondered what kind of a sick woman wore blue panties to bed and his groin moaned from where it had been quiet for too long and he swallowed and didnt trust himself to speak till the leg went in again and the blue faded to black.

My legs always was the best end of me.

You're a young woman yet, Jodie. Maybe if you had your heart fixed you'd hurt for a little spell. But think how much better life would be. Sandy'd sure be tickled to have a mom she didnt have to visit at the graveyard.

It aint gonna happen.

Get up and get dressed and we'll go get a bite to eat. Do you good.

I havent been out of the house for a year or more. Dont reckon I ever will be again till they tote me out on a board.

When you let your world get little it's hard to make it big again. You end up shrinking the smallness if you try. Quit watching the TV instead of reading more. You eat less instead of better.

I didnt know you'd took up philosophy.

Had to, to keep from going crazy.

There's times some craziness would of done you good. Always so logical and rational you was cold-blooded.

That's what a madman is. He's so rational he cant get beyond his own logic. Cant let any question go unanswered even if he has to answer it wrong.

You saying you got beyond that?

I not only dont know anything, I dont even suspect much anymore. But come on. Roust up out of there and let's go eat.

If you'd asked twenty years ago things might be different.

Till I got up the nerve you already had a man. And then I got Mary before you got shed of him.

That's what made you so attractive. That shyness. Hid behind your hard old heart. Her smile further lifted her features and not until the black cat reappeared beside Lane's leg, watching Jodie now, did he realize that she'd gone to sleep. How long he watched her, he didnt know. Eaten up with sorrow for the loss of a love that had never been. A line from an Osborne tune—*they've never seen a mule but they're nostalgic too*—came to mind and he let himself out and drifted the truck down to the bottom of the hill before he started the engine so as not to wake her.

He drove away in a depression formed not by experience but by some experience he'd feared and never had. Even enough to attach a name to it.

● ● ●

Short of the baitshop, as he was passing the reservoir, Lane braked hard and backed with the mirrors and parked at the end of the slippery road where he'd parked the morning before. He drummed his fingers on the steering wheel for a bit before he stepped out and walked down to stand at the cattail cane and stare out over the water. A flight of resident geese flew honking and squawking the length of the water, their droppings splashing behind on the still surface like a foul corrupted rain.

Lane observed the broken cane where he and Toby had entered and left the water and the crushed grass where their feet had passed but if there was anything to be learned from tracks it was beyond his ability to comprehend it. He walked down to where the two men had stood when they'd shot at him and while he smoked the last cigarette in his pack he looked around to make sure he wasnt being watched.

He tossed the butt into the water and crouched down and combed the weeds, like someone looking in hair for lice nits. A faded 16-gauge low-brass shotshell and a broken turtle egg and an eroded heap of coon crap and a Slim Jim wrapper and a green flipflop with a broken toestrap. Closer to the water a desiccated bluegill—colorless skin dried over a bone frame—and a snarl of monofilament line waiting to snare a waterbird but nowhere the brassy flash of a pistol's shell casing. Then on the edge of the cane a flash of white. A cigarette butt resting in the grass, not yet sullied by dew or dust or rain.

He held it at arms length and read the name Sonoma above the butt and as though he'd found it still afire, tossed it into the water.

When he stood too quickly the blood drained away and the world tilted and he staggered for a moment before he found his bearings again. Such as they were.

.12

NICKEL BALLEW DROVE WEST ON ROUTE 50 OUT of Union County. The steady carving of the damp air by Backbone Mountain's interminable line of windmills vested him with purpose. Mindless or not. Pollen frosted his black pickup and he powered down the window and reached up to grip the rollbar and breathed deep of the summer air. Where the highway plunged steep and crooked down Allegany Front he pushed the big pickup to the limit, spraying gravel over the guardrails when a tire edged onto the berm. He passed three nose-to-tail coaltrucks on a blind turn without tensing. Knowing today was not his day to depart this life. Finding that information in the harsh hot brakes, in the sunlight that strobed across his windshield.

Short of Clarksburg, where the city bumped against the country and the satellite dishes and outbuildings faded from the lawns, he stopped at a filling station to use the bathroom. Feeling crazy and godlike. Like a god would. Should. Deserved.

The bathroom was large but barren with a single urinal and an unwalled toilet and a tiny sink. Ballew loosened his belt and pants and stood far back from the urinal and before he was finished a tall slim man with graying hair and a face full of good cheer and honest industry and small success stuck his head inside the door and said Oops and Ballew hated him and said Come on, brother. It's a two-holer.

The man hesitated and entered and glanced at Ballew and assembled his mouth into something resembling a frown. But not. That look that allowed Ballew to be crazy.

You have a problem? Ballew said.

The man edged around to shield himself and stared into the toilet and said nothing.

I'm talking your way brother. I asked if there is a problem.

I didnt say anything or do anything. So I dont know how there could be a problem. Still looking down and away.

Ballew rearranged himself and zipped and buckled. The problem is you come in here spouting opinions and then you act as innocent as a newborn lamb. He moved to stand just behind the man.

I didnt say a word. And I have no problem with you.

Your face said all I needed to hear.

Whatever. The man flushed and moved quickly but not as quickly as Ballew who stood between him and the exit door.

Dont you even wash your hands?

Do you? Defiant and scared, a vein jumping in his forehead.

Not till I'm finished the job. Especially if it's a dirty one.

The man backed away and felt behind him for the sink and leaned against it and crossed his arms. I have no problem with you, buddy. And I dont want any.

Anyone who *wants* problems is a freak. That's not our nature. His voice climbing as he worked into it. Yet it's our *nature* that brings problems down upon our heads. It's inevitable. This war with our *nature*.

The man looked at the door. I'd like to leave now.

You havent repented yet, my son. Dont walk out that door with *sin* in your heart.

The man glanced at himself in the mirror and when he did red flushed above his shirtcollar. Repent for what? Just what is it that I've done to you?

You entered my life with sin in your heart. Sin that *showed on your face.*

The man shrugged. Well, I'm sorry. I didnt mean anything by it.

Sorry. You think *sorry* is *repent?* Sorry dont mean *nothing.* Sorry's not worth the letters it uses up.

The man measured Ballew's size and clothing and tone of voice and then his eyes and a conclusion firmed up in his own eyes. I didnt make the language.

Ballew straightened a rolled sleeve on his western shirt. Maybe if you said it on your knees. Perhaps some body language would lift that sorry word sorry *out of the miry clay* and give it some *sincerity.* Even if it was artificial.

A stiffness came over the man. Into his face and into his voice. By god, I wont get on my knees. I apologized, and that's all I'll do.

Pride goeth before destruction and an haughty spirit before a fall. Folks always get that wrong. Say pride goeth before a fall. But since you cuss God you likely dont even know it the wrong way. That next verse is a dandy too, but nobody knows it. Better it is to be of an humble spirit with the lowly, than to divide the spoil with the proud.

If it's money you're after, I'll give you what I have. It's less than twenty dollars. The man made no move toward his wallet.

Those words were from Proverbs 16. Verses 18 and 19. It's a shame you wont get a chance to look them up yourself. Ballew opened the door and looked out and closed and locked it and when he turned to the man again his face reflected the flames of hell and he held an automatic pistol with a large hole in the barrel. Those that wont humble themselves will *be* humbled.

A groan eased from the man and he placed one hand on the sink's edge and looked at the floor and made the same face he'd made when he entered the bathroom and then he eased down to his knees. I'm sorry. I'm truly sorry. I repent.

Hell's full of people repenting right this very moment. But their time is passed and I cant help them. Yours has too. For *every* goddam—forgive me, Father—thing there is a season. A time to break down and a time to build up. A time to die. A time to kill.

The man moaned and put his hands over his eyes and lowered his head onto his knees. As though he were praying to Allah for new eyes. The smells of pine detergent and of urinal deodorant biscuits and of undershot piss were thick near the floor and made his eyes water. He shivered there for a long time but could find no words for repentance and when he looked up to die the man with the gun was gone though he'd not heard the door open or close. He put his head back down for a few seconds and then looked around the ceiling as though for spiders and stood and brushed his knees with trembling hands and locked the door and then washed his hands and arms to his elbows and dried them under the hot air blower. He leaned on the sink and looked into his own eyes from six inches away and said, You sickening son of a bitch.

He combed his hair and saw that he'd dribbled on his khakis so he sprinkled water on his shirt like he'd spilled something down his front and then he lowered his pants and sat on the toilet with the heels of his palms mashed into his eyes and his fingers in his ears.

•　　•　　•

Just outside the bathroom door a Subaru wagon with a crumpled front fender and rust over the rear wheel wells was nosed up to the curb. Ballew stopped beside it and considered the small black mixed-breed dog that yapped behind a two-inch gap in the side window. Hey boy, he said. The backseat was littered with packs of vinyl fencing brochures held together with rubber bands. Six-inch chunks of fencing. A sports jacket and two shirts hanging behind the driver's seat.

A road map stuffed between the console and the passenger seat. An open pack of cigarettes on the dashboard. Emblems of purpose and desire and necessity and pleasure.

Ballew glanced at a teenage girl talking on a cellphone while she pumped gas into a Ford Taurus and then he inserted his thumb and forefinger through the gap between the window and the doorframe. The dog licked his fingers and whined. Little sawed-off tail making frantic circles, waving for approval. Ballew waited for an opportunity to grip the nose and when it came he placed his thumb between the eyes and gradually increased pressure until one of the dog's hind legs drummed the seat and the front paws slipped from the window ledge. He squeezed harder until a small bone collapsed under his thumb and the dog went limp as its life slunk away. Ballew turned and entered the women's bathroom and washed and dried his hands and returned to his pickup without looking at the Subaru and headed south on I-79 toward Charleston, toward home.

.13

LANE REOPENED THE BAITSHOP AND BUMBLED

and mumbled through the day and when suppertime came he felt he should be hungry but wasnt so he drank a Coke from the refrigerator and got through the Friday evening rush, all five customers, and at dark closed the shop and put the money away and sat in the soft glow from the Trilene clock and rocked and savored and hated the solitude.

When a vehicle pulled into the lot and the headlights went off and the door rattled under a fist Lane slid down in the chair where he couldnt be seen and said nothing.

Come on you baggy pantsed old fool, came NoBob's voice. Open the door.

Lane switched on a light and unlocked the door. What do you want? I'm closed here.

NoBob pushed past and went directly to the refrigerator and removed a flat of nightcrawlers to make space for his thirtypack of Keystone Light.

Why dont you just make yourself at home, Lane said. Not be

bashful like you always were. Not much jest in the tone. He caught with one hand the can NoBob tossed his way. Expecting it.

You started smoking again. Now drinking, I hear.

Good to know my conscience is still working. That it shows up uninvited like conscience does. But never around when you need it.

Next you'll be at the women again.

The beer was cold and refreshing in his palm and when he drank the clean familiar bite switched off one thing and on another. Not much danger of that, he said. Doubt I could recall what to do with one. Something to do with high-heeled shoes, I think. Once I started I could likely suss it out.

Dont ask me.

You ought to know. You're still married, arent you?

They still call me NoBob, dont they?

I reckon.

Dont you ever go home? I hope you aint left the mower out in that yard. You wont never find it.

Shows what you know. It's fresh mowed, ready for a magazine cover. When were you out?

Last evening. Couldnt find you nowhere. Never thought to look at the bar.

Lane drank more of the beer and let it fill more of the place it had found that needed filling. I've been meaning to find some kid to keep it mowed. Half the time I sleep here in the chair. Too lazy to drive a couple of miles to a good bed.

Get your grandkid to mow it. Toby.

Then I wouldnt have anybody to fish with.

There's that, NoBob said. Against a pale pinstripe shirt with shiny snaps he was the color of plug tobacco. You were down at Rooster's, I hear. Playing Dick Tracy. He relocated a box of meaningless papers and ancient magazines from an old metal spring chair onto the floor and sat back in it and hooked a leg over its arm and Lane sat in his wooden rocking chair and settled his heels into the worn place beneath the sales counter.

You get your firewood cut yesterday? Lane said.

No. A lazy front blew through before I got the chainsaw sharpened.

Probably started counting your money and it took all day.

Shoot. I can count all my money without taking it out of my pocket. Except for the pennies and dimes. They're hard to tell apart.

Where you working next?

Out on Sugarcamp unless someone else calls and raises more hell than that woman is. That Deep Creek job got me behind.

Lane discovered that his beer was gone and retrieved another pair from the refrigerator. You remind me to put those worms back in when there's room. He sat and rubbed his arms. You think it's cold in here? I hate to build a fire in the middle of the summer but I've been freezing all day.

NoBob crinkled his empty can and grinned. We was out in the cabin last deer season, he said. Bobby and Mutt and me. Mutt let the fire go out and when we got up in the morning there was these brown fuzzy things rollin around on the floor. None of us could figger out what they was at all. After breakfast, after the fire got goin good, I swept them up and throwed them in the stove and they got to goin *phhht phhht* and blowin the door open. And I said what the hell is that and Bobby got to laughin and said them's frozen farts. That's what it's got to be. From them beans we ate for supper.

Lane laughed. I knew that was a lie when you got to the part about you sweeping up. That stretches the imagination more than mine will cover without rupturing.

That's what you are. An old frozen fart.

Lane lit a cigarette with his new lighter and turned down the flame so it wouldnt run out so quick. Birds of a feather fart together. He held out his can and NoBob leaned forward and touched his to it and they drank and belched and laughed.

They sat and stared at their feet until Lane said, What is it you want, NoBob? You didnt come out here to tell jokes.

NoBob bobbed in the chair for a while before he spoke. This thing with Billy Bean. I'd just as leave you let it go.

That's been kind of clear.

I told it like I seen it. Or heard it. There wasnt a thing to see. No gunshot. Nor any of that other stuff you said you did. Other trucks and stuff.

I always could tell when you're lying. Your lips do this funny thing. Move.

NoBob's lips did something funny just then but he didnt make any sound.

Lane considered all that he'd said at the reservoir. Who said anything about other trucks?

It wasnt me. And the boy didnt hear a thing. So it must of been you.

What are you trying to hide, my friend?

I dont know what you mean.

Billy Bean's truck was one way when I left, and another when I came back.

You say.

And I know you're dumb, but you're not deaf too. You heard a shot. You even went out and picked up the shell casing. I found your cigarette butt. A Sonoma.

NoBob's eyes, dark and feral, found Lane's. I was out there. Just to see if there was something to find, but there wasnt. Sometimes you dont understand everything, you know.

You made me to look like a fool and turned yourself into a criminal.

NoBob lit a smoke and dropped the ash in his empty can. You always was a fool and I aint no more a criminal than I ever was.

You've got me to convince of that yet.

NoBob smoked in silence for a while. You know what I do for a living.

Last I heard you were a stonemason.

That's just part of it. I got two schoolbus routes and a HCR mail route that I sub out.

I did see your name on a schoolbus. Struck me as ironic.

Right there. That's why you're loved by everyone that knows you. Never miss the slightest chance for a put-down.

Being loved isnt what I set out to do when I started this life.

You done good, then. NoBob's cigarette ash was long and firm, the tobacco not having time to burn properly. Rental houses. I got some of them, too.

The one out by the Dairy Queen I know of.

I got seven of them.

I didnt know anybody hardly rented anymore. Loan payments are cheaper than rent.

Not everybody can get a loan.

Lane thought about that for a while. Those kind wouldnt be staying in my houses, I dont think. If they're too worthless to get a loan.

Lots of good hardworking people cant borrow. For reasons that have no bearing on whether they're worthless or not. They got to stay somewhere.

I dont know any.

That's cause their names are Juan and Alfredo and Emilio and Marcos. Like that.

Mexicans? You're renting to Mexicans?

Mexicans. Cubans. El Salvadorons, or whatever you'd call em. I dont ask.

Chico's still brown face flickered across Lane's thoughts. There's some around, I heard. Not seven families, though. Not enough to fill up your houses.

NoBob snorted. Seven families wouldnt quite fill up three houses. Aw, get out. Where do they work?

For the logging companies. Farmers. Restaurants. The women clean houses. The car dealers use em to wash and detail. Two of them work for me. Mixing mud and tending. Anybody that's got grunt work uses them.

The Trilene clock ticked loud in the silence.

I had no idea there was more than a few around.

You dont get the best grip on the whole world sittin here watchin minnies.

What's this got to do with Billy Bean, anyhow? With you tampering with evidence.

It was just something I done on impulse. Like I do. If I'd of done what you say, that would of been why. Not that I'm saying I did it.

Lane knew impulsiveness to be one of NoBob's defining characteristics and didnt contest it or dignify it with a response.

Part of it is that the one day, the only one solitary day I've took to go fishing all year, this happens.

Billy Bean likely didnt pick the day special just to spite you.

If Billy Bean really got popped, I can guarandamntee you it had to do with drugs. Sandy told me the same thing she told you.

Are your renters running drugs? Is that what you're saying?

If they are, I dont know about it. But they're the first people will get looked at.

Lane raised his eyebrows in question. There's something here I'm missing.

Look. My house rentals cant stand close scrutiny. But you were sure as hell going to get them scrutinated. Then they'll move on to my other businesses. I dont run crooked businesses. But I do a lot of cash transactions. The less money I give the IRS the better American I've been. Dont look at me that way. You turn in every nickel you get selling bait, I'm sure.

Lane looked at the flat of crawlers. I hope those worms dont go bad. They dont last long out.

That's what I thought.

You figured wrong. Maybe some year I'll make enough to pay taxes but not this one. My books will be the same one way or the other. Why tell the truth with your mouth and lie with your pencil? Someday the twain will collide and leave you with a hard choice.

You got one now. Raise a stink about some white trash without a nickel's chance at a tent revival of surviving till he was thirty. Nobody would ever do time if he *did* get killed. Which he didnt anyhow.

Lane admired his feet for a while and then got up and cupped his hands to the window and allowed his anger to bubble back down into the pot. Nothing like white trash to point out the same qualities in others, he said.

Your other choice is stir up muck that will splash on folks that was minding their own business. That wont make you any friends. Dick Trappel included. He wants stuff quiet.

Look at the lightning bugs, Lane said. They've never been that heavy. He turned off the interior light so they could sit and observe the moving constellation.

Yes they have, NoBob said. Lots of times.

With nothing but fireflies for illumination Lane felt easier. Like the barrier between the two men was visual. Billy Bean was somebody I never cared for, he said. A load on the taxpayer.

You got that right.

When I realized he was a goner, though, it twisted a place in me I didnt know still turned.

I seen that it did. NoBob lit a cigarette. In the flame his face was the color and texture of a weathered cliff. Watchin you done something to me. Made me wish I still had a place that could hurt without hittin it with a hammer.

All the same. Billy Bean was a person. With feelings and wants and sorrows.

Dogs have them things. Spring lizards.

You're fifty-eight, same as I am, right?

Fifty-nine. I got held back in the second grade.

It wasnt my intent to get that old. Or I'd have taken better care of myself.

Have another beer, NoBob said.

I dont care for more.

Cigarette ashes hissed in NoBob's can, tenor to the airpump's soft lead. You're thinking in the right direction. Dont put your pecker in a rattrap by blowing up the morning into a big problem that aint never going to get solved anyway. Just leave it be for a spell.

The boy never had a chance. Cricket dragged Billy Bean to the bar and paid him money to cuss when he could hardly say mama. Not that he had one. What kind of raising is that?

I aint concerned with how white trashhood comes about. It's like oily rags. Spontaneous combustion.

They were quiet for a while and Lane thought he had vented but more words crowded out. At least the turtles didnt get to him.

NoBob tossed his empty into the trashcan and groaned when he rose from the chair. I got to find something easier to do. I aint a puppy anymore.

What's easier than stonemason? Pick up little rocks and set them on the wall. Pack some cement in the cracks.

NoBob snorted and went to the bathroom and urinated without closing the door.

When NoBob had returned to his chair Lane said, What you reckon will become of Billy Bean's property?

Let's get done with Billy Bean. I didnt come over here to hold a wake.

Worth good money, I bet. Out there on the highway. Close by the school.

You cant leave hold of it, can you. All right. Talk it the hell out and get done with it. When Lane said nothing, NoBob said, How'd it feel to start smoking again? How'd that first beer taste? I was envious. Just once I'd like to experience that again. But I'd have to quit first.

Lane was silent, brooding. Hearing again Billy Bean's head clunk against the canoe. Without suspecting he was going to he turned and kicked the trashcan and caved in its side and he clattered through the cans and papers and switched on the lights and leaned on the counter with his head in his hands. Dammit, he said.

NoBob bobbed a little harder. Dont break stupid on me, old buddy.

I will have another one. Lane retrieved two beers from the refrigerator and set his on the counter and started picking up trash and replacing it into the dented can. Nam screw you up?

Nothin that stuck. Second grade's what done me in. But I didnt see the action you did.

How you know what action I saw?

Cause you never bragged about it like we did. Trying to make more of it than there was.

You called me an old frozen fart. Thirty-three years ago I left that hellhole. For almost three days there I hid in the water and I got old and cold and havent ever been young or warm since. But not till today did I realize how bad it changed me. In my head.

You was contrary when you went. Come back the same way. Maybe a mite more dilitary. So it must be something other'n that.

Lane sat in his rocker and leaned back and closed his eyes. Pap told about how his granddad did good duty in the Civil War till Shiloh. Then he laid down his gun and walked home and hid out till it was over. Never farmed another lick or shot even so much as a polecat again. Just sat on the porch and drank moonshine and remarked now and again that after what he'd seen the south end of a mule wasnt all that spectacular. Made the boys do all the work.

They was some like that. Hated fightin but it got in their blood. Made everthing else too tame to keep down.

That never made sense till today. Squatting there in those rushes I was back at An Loc and I *wanted* to be there. Not one solitary breath I've drawn since I left there ever had that much life in it. Bad as I hated it.

When I first started smokin and drinkin it made me dizzy, NoBob said. But not as goofy as you're actin. You best ease off sinnin till your head clears.

Back when we had the band you worked up Cumberland way for a spell.

The route this conversation's taking is one I aint. You're going to ask if I worked for Larson Henry and the answer to your next question is there's no way in God's green earth that cheap old bastard is running drugs. It dont matter what Sandy said Billy Bean said. Passing facts through them two is like eatin the same food twice. It aint the same second time around.

Tell me about Larson Henry.

I'll tell you what you need to know. The man is too cheap to lay out the money it would take to run drugs. And he aint the type. Please leave this thing alone. Please.

Sit behind the mule again?

You think you're the only one ever observed the wrong end of a mule? Mule's asses come in a variety of shapes and textures. Like rocks. Go get a tattoo. A motorsickle. Mess with Buster Doolan's woman. Get your blood stirring without messin up everybody else's life.

Some folks would be better off with their lives shook up a little bit.

What the hell is that supposed to mean?

It means what it means.

You are one ignorant stupid dumbass retard asswipe baldheaded sonofabitch if you dont throw this thing down and leave it be.

I'm not baldheaded. Lane ran his fingers through hair that wasnt as thick as he'd have liked it to be. But it was there.

Stupidity aint a particularly distinguishin characteristic in these parts, but if you do this thing you're going to stand out some.

Lane drank from his beer and said nothing.

What about the boy? You consider what kind of doodoo you're dipping him into? If Billy Bean really was into some nasty people, you think they're going to drink hot chocolate while you bring the law down? Ask Billy Bean about that.

Lane thought about Toby and then tried not to and couldnt.

Dont you never go to the bathroom? NoBob said on his way there.

Shut the door this time. You sound like a cow watering a flat rock.

You're jealous.

I go when I need to, Lane said from inside the bathroom after they'd traded places. Not every two minutes like old men do. Lane washed his hands and stared out into the darkness beyond the window but with the lights on he could see nothing. NoBob's reflection, studying him from both sides.

Make me a deal, NoBob said. Think on this over the weekend. If you still got to roll the applecart over the hill give me a day or two to get my turds all in one toilet. Just that much. For old time's sake.

I'm sorry you got to be caught in the middle of this.

Right there's a first: Lane Hollar sayin he was sorry. NoBob grinned. Preston Ringer had just the one arm. Claimed he woke up one mornin in bed with a woman and she was layin on his arm and after he got a good look he gnawed it off instead of wakin her up to get it loose. Said he was forever sorry he'd got drunk the night before but he never once regretted not wakin her up.

I'd just as soon all this had never happened. You know that.

Yeah. I'd just as soon be young and rich and hung like a donkey.

But two of them things is out of the question and I'm about to give up on the third one. It's hair near quit growin.

Lane laughed and laughed again at being surprised by a laugh. He thought about Toby, and about mules. About how pleasing life could be till something evil reached in and gave it a stir and after that it was never quite the same. No matter how good it got.

We got a deal? You leave it be unless you talk to me first?

Yeah. I reckon. For now anyhow.

.14

again in the baitshop rocker with a stiff back and a headache and a
tongue that felt like he'd pulled a dirty sock over it. His brains scrambled
and muddled till he didnt know dreams from thoughts. Like he'd never
quit drinking. Like all the bad times he'd lived had been distilled into
that thirtypack of beer, and he'd swallowed them down again. Before
he stood he smoked one of his last three cigarettes and found it harsh
and bereft of any satisfying property and wondered what he'd found
so unappetizing about a mule. He thought of the previous two day's
events and found them surreal and fantastic and in an intuition that
passed over him like a chill he understood that he'd do nothing. That
the time for doing so had passed without his notice or participation.

He brushed his teeth and scrubbed his face in the bathroom and then
gathered beer cans from the sales counter and carried them out back to
the big garbage can. The worms were still sitting out on the counter and
he smelled each Styrofoam cup before he replaced the lid and returned
them to the refrigerator. Hoped it would be a Saturday when nobody
needed worms. A day when nobody in hell hankered for icewater.

He turned on the overhead lights and flipped the sign around and when customers came he was as nice as he could be but could hear the surliness wanting out. No, I just got some kind of a bug, he said to the ones that asked if he were sick. The Keystone flu, but he didnt say that. Figured they knew anyway. Never hard to spot.

When the early customers were gone he went outside and stood in the damp mountain air to clear his head and recalled his moments in the rushes when he could smell and hear and see like he hadnt for years and compared that to the morning's smoke-choked sinuses and alcohol-fuzzed senses. Suspected that life would accelerate in that wrong direction, the moments of youthful sensations briefer and more scattered till maybe he wouldnt recall having them. But suspected too that he wouldnt be that lucky. Finding no refreshment in inactivity, between a trickle of customers he gathered poptops and cigarette butts from the gravel and swept the walk and ran the trimmer around the shop to cut back the goldenrod and burdock that was steadily taking over. With the weeds cut away the ragged bottom edge of the Insulbrick siding showed rotting boards beneath and he wished he could uncut the vegetation. The light exercise started his blood pumping again and he went inside and scooped dead minnows from the tank—way too many—and he'd just decided to drain the tank and clean it when Lester Kelso's battered old three-color Malibu wheeled into the lot, Lester hollering Whoo wee out the open window.

A hidden function of Lane's brain beyond reason or perhaps bereft of it grasped what the exuberance was about and he said Dammit and watched Lester lift a fish as long as his leg from the trunk. It was only ten o'clock in the morning but the fish was stiff as a board and pale with the stripes nearly soaked off.

Where'd you find it? Lane said when Lester shouldered his way through the door.

Find it? I caught it. He heaved the fish up onto the sales counter without preamble. The stink of mud and decay washed over Lane and brought back the taste of the last night's beer.

That thing's been dead a while.

Since real early. Just after daylight. You ever see one like that? My gawd, aint it a monster.

Lane calculated the value and the cost of calling Lester the flat-out liar he was, and came up short. Not that there was any physical risk, little bit of a thing that Lester was, or that Lane would suffer any monetary damages since Lester hadnt bought so much as a split shot in the eight years Lane had operated the baitshop. Lester did stop in to tell stories, though, and if he suspected everybody knew he was a liar he might quit, and he was as imaginative and entertaining a liar as any Lane had ever heard.

Like the time Lester couldnt recollect the name of the shotgun he'd inherited from his granddaddy and Butch suggested if it was worth as much as Lester claimed it was likely a Stradivarius and Lester said, That's it. It's a Stradivarius shotgun. And no, nobody could see it because he never took it out of the vault. Not even to look at it himself. If the inert gas escaped the vault and the air got in, the gun's value would drop to 4 percent of what it was.

How you know there's anything in the vault, Lester? one of the fellows who heard the tale said. Maybe your granddaddy just made it up that there was a gun in there. Lester said, My granddaddy was a Fox and before you lay accusation of a lie onto a Fox you'd best contemplate what you was undertakin.

The fish was dead. Nothing Lane said or didnt say would change that.

If you're going to eat it you best do it quick, he said.

Aw, I wouldnt eat it. Gonna get it mounted.

That'd be the best option of the two, Lane said. I didnt even know you fished.

I aint for years. But I always was good at it.

Lane examined where Toby's steel leader had fed back through the gills, where the dragging line had abraded the gill filaments that absorbed oxygen. A hard way to go. By suffocating. At least the turtles hadnt been at it. Something about the way turtles chewed yanked a drawstring in Lane's guts. A meateater ought to exhibit more enthusiasm. Less relish and more gusto. How'd you catch it? Lane said.

Lester manufactured a tale of how he'd seen it cruising along the weedline and tried everything in his tacklebox but nothing worked till he was ready to give in.

What all did it turn down?

Lester didnt know the names anymore. Most of them had been his daddy's plugs. He described a big red-and-white one that had to be a Heddon Pikie and some that Lane couldnt make head nor tails of because they existed only in Lester's imagination.

Bring those plugs in here and let me look at them, Lane said. Antique lures are worth their weight in available virgins.

That's why I already took em home and locked em up. It aint important anyway what that big ol boy didnt bite on. I need to tell you what he *did* eat.

Go ahead. You've told me everything else.

Lester had been about to give up when a ringnecked snake—the blue ones with the orange bellies and a ring around their necks— crawled past and he hooked it through the lips and cast it ahead of the fish and the snake swam so fast that it was clear of the water but for its tail and the fish pushed a wake ahead of it like Jaws did and when it caught up, the snake was gone. It took Lester two and a half hours to land the fish.

It must have died sometime in the process then, Lane said, because the good Lord called the poor thing home some time ago. Unless it was about midnight when you hooked him. Lester squinted hard and Lane realized he'd tiptoed too close to outright insult. Now I'll have to stock snakes, I reckon, he said. Everybody will be wanting some. Minnows wont be worth five cents a dozen from now on.

Lester lifted the fish's head every minute or so to admire it. The skin parting from the countertop made a noise like tape peeling off the roll. How much you figger this thing weighs?

I'd put it between twenty-five and thirty pounds. We'll hang it on the scales and find out for certain. First, though, I need to call the Department of Natural Resources.

What would you want to do that for? Lester said. As though Lane had suggested summonsing the devil.

A state record has to be certified. Line weight. The reel and rod you were using. The bait. I hope there's no problem with that kind of a snake being a protected species. Exactly where you caught it. They'll want to calculate its age and how long it's been dead so they can adjust the weight for drying. Where you bought your license.

State record? he said. I had no idea. What's the biggest pike ever caught in West Virginia?

That's a muskie. A muskellunge.

Aw, no, he said. I thought it was a pike. Like he'd set out to catch a fish and caught a polecat instead. In his eyes the naturalborn liar's thirst for an audience armwrestled with the idea of being made a spectacle of in public. With paying fines for not having a license. I dont want to jump through all them hoops, he said when his common sense eventually won the match. Cant you just weigh it and take a picture?

You'll be foregoing a lot of attention.

What I'm worried about is the reservoir, he said. Everybody and his halfbrother'll be out there soon's the word gets out.

You're a better man than I am, Lester. When my fifteen minutes of fame come by I'm going to roll in it. Like an old dog rolls in a dead groundhog.

Well, you aint me.

No. You got me on that one.

Lane wrestled the fish up and hooked its jaw on the scales and they stood back and looked at the scales, neither one trusting what it said. Thirty-two pounds four and a half ounces. Lane stretched a tape alongside the stiff body and marked a spot with his thumb just past fifty inches.

Since I aint going to turn it in, you think you might take a picture of it there? One that shows how much it weighed and with me holding the tape?

Lane found his old Minolta and deliberately unfocused the lens till he couldnt recognize Lester as human or the fish as any kind of a creature at all and took two pictures. Just to make sure, he said. Knowing that the minute Lester was out of sight he was going to strip the film out into the sunlight and then throw it in the trash. They didnt turn out. That's what he'd say and there wasnt a thing Lester could do about it.

It should have been Toby in the picture. Lane felt again the weight on the other end of the braided line where he bit it off and some small portion of the keenness Lane had felt crouched in the cane returned hard and caustic and he knew he wasnt finished with what had happened. I'll do my best to keep this quiet, he said. But if the DNR catches wind of it they'll make a record of it whether you want to or not. They're not as allergic to attention as you are.

I cant even show this thing off?

Do what you want to with it. I'm just saying. Knowing Lester couldnt resist. Knowing the word would get back to Toby. Half sickened and half intoxicated by the knowledge that he cared more about the fish, about the boy's feelings, than he really did about Billy Bean.

Long after Lester was gone, after Lane had scrubbed the counter with Lysol and propped open the doors to allow air to wash through, the shop still stunk of decay. When he went outside, he discovered that the whole world did. He smelled his armpit and though he detected nothing there he made a face. Knowing he'd found the source.

.15

IT WAS SUNDAY AND LANE WAS ALONE AND AWARE
of it and the baitshop filled with a silence as dank and dismal as the
bottom along Crupp's Creek. When the third carload of necktied
men and bright-bloused women passed on their way to the half-pint
Baptist church two miles out the road, Lane spoke aloud to himself
and realized he was really speaking to God. Belief, he said, speaking
to a God he didn't believe in. That's as far as I'll go. To believe in
belief. Maybe in purpose.

If you didnt, life got so uninspiring and insipid it was a chore to
keep it going. But once you determined there might be a purpose you
had to accept the concept of a purpose-er. Whatever He or She or It
might encompass. Not that Lane reckoned that nebulous force would
be encountered where the cars were headed.

The shop was so clammy and the day so warm in comparison
that Lane shed his sweater and dragged the old springback metal
chair outside on the walk where he bobbed and listened to a pair of
orioles working in the old lightning-busted whiteoak. A behemoth
that had survived not through exceptional health but because it was
so worthless and windshaken and had so many sign nails and fence

staples driven into it that no logger would touch it. As bright and lively as the birds were, Lane couldnt spot them.

What he did see was a slow movement through the forest, caught in his peripheral vision. A patch of manmade brown that eased close to the ground through a ragged splotch of sunlight that found its way through the canopy. It didnt move like an animal, unless it was a snake, and the brown was marked with a maroon stripe. The colors of the Union County Sheriff's Department uniforms.

Martin, Lane yelled when he realized there was going to be nothing more to see. What you doing skulking in the woods?

Nothing.

He walked down to the road's edge and looked both ways but there was no cruiser and after a bit he suspected his brain was still staggering under Friday night's load. A little jag of alcohol that once wouldnt have given him a buzz.

When Martin drove past fifteen minutes later, Lane wasnt so sure. The department not likely to waste time out Lane's way. Lane considered what he had to hide and felt shamed in some small perverted way. Like the man Mark Twain wrote about, without a single redeeming vice.

Five minutes passed before Martin returned. Like a dog to vomit. Long enough for Lane to vector whatever powers had crossed lines at that one instant where he'd bit the braided line in two. For sixteen years the muskie swam loose. Toby, his twelve years accumulating toward that moment. Lane waiting for it all his life. Three factors that compressed the odds of the event infinitely toward zero. Then it happened anyway, along with an entire new set of variables overlaid like a transparency. Twenty years of Billy Bean. Plus the factors the outsiders brought to the equation.

Which brought Lane back to the idea of a plan. A purpose. But if one by a loving and benevolent God, Lane had missed something along the way.

The prostate didnt have to go around the urinary tract so it would cause misery in old age. Slugs could have craved dandelions, not green beans. Kentucky bluegrass could have been vested with the authority to choke crabgrass by the neck until dead. Cockroaches might have thrived in rotten stumps instead of in the kitchen. Life made sense, but only if considered from an antagonistic, perverted perspective. With malice aforethought.

Unless humanity was to serve as comedy for the folks in heaven. Since in that eternal resting place there was no pain or sorrow, no suffering, no embarrassment or loss of face. The things we could laugh at. The thought cheered Lane, and he tried without success to think of anything that was funny that didnt come at someone's or something's expense.

While he was still wrestling with that, Martin pulled into the lot.

Mr. Hollar. Martin stepped from the cruiser, hitching at the heavy belt that dragged his pants low like a plumber's. Dandy day. A smile on his face but hard feral eyes locked tight on Lane's. Like rifle bolts chambered on a pair of steel-jacketed rounds.

Lane stood and slid his chair back out of the way. What can I do for you, Boob?

There's people can call me that. But you aint one of them.

Deputy Boob. That better? Pleased with his pry point.

All right. If that's the way you want to play it. Just remember. What comes around goes around.

Just say what you got in your craw and go around, then.

When I'm ready I will.

I might be in bed by that time. Lane stood and made to enter the shop. Planning to lock the door behind him.

Last evening. You were taking the canoe back?

Lane paused in the doorway. I was doing what the sheriff told me to do. The right and lawful and duly elected sheriff.

But when I saw you, over to Billy Bean's house. That's when you took it back?

Your tone of voice isnt one I care for. If you're accusing me of something, do it outright.

I'm just attempting to get a timeline straight.

A timeline.

Placing what I know in chronological order. Arranged the way it happened.

You ought to take up writing law enforcement textbooks. But when you do, put in a chapter for when things dont happen in order. Like you want them to. Lane felt himself radiating hostility, like a campfire too big to cook on.

Things dont happen out of order. Ever. It's just our perceptions that are flawed.

And you're out to bring the twain together.

Yessir. I am.

Lane knew that hassling a law enforcement officer was stupid but couldnt imagine how it could make him more ignorant than the man before him. Things happen out of order all the time. Folks get jobs long before they're qualified to perform them. Sometimes they never will be. Sissies are born without tallywhackers.

Martin worked his tongue in his lip and a tiny black speck appeared on the end of it and Lane caught the heavy smell of tobacco though there was no visible lump. Realized that Martin was closer than he had been. Than Lane wanted him to be.

You took the canoe back earlier. When I saw you out there, it was your second trip. That's the timeline. What I want to know is why.

That's your opinion. Not that it makes any difference

I drove past yesterday and the canoe wasnt in your truck. My memory's good.

I'm sure that's an asset to the county. Lane wondered if the memory applied to multiplication tables. Why are you driving past here every fifteen minutes all of a sudden? Tramping through the woods? Spying on me?

There's an investigation underway here, sir. One you requested.

You investigate somewhere else. Off of my property.

Wherever the facts lead me. That's where I go. That's my business.

Lane stepped into the baitshop and Martin followed as far as the door. Silhouetted, a squat splitting wedge. Splitting into Lane's business. Time to call your boss, I think.

Go ahead. Who do you think sent me? While you got him on the line ask him who he thinks will be sheriff in a few months.

Not a thought Lane wanted to dwell on. It's an elected office. You're not a lay-down for it. I might run myself. If it means denying it to you.

What is it you have against me, sir?

Lane leaned back on the minnow tank and felt its bubbling through the thin seat of his jeans. Just this general abhorrence of power in the wrong hands. Words rolling like rocks ahead of a plowpoint, impossible to put back, destructive and damaging.

Martin remained in the doorway like a dog who smelled territory not his own and respected the marker. Maybe I dont use all the big words you'd like me to, Mr. Hollar, and I cant help it that I'm not a big old fuzzy backslapper like Dick is. I know my job, though, and right now you fall dead square in the middle of it.

The quick uneasy thought that he'd misjudged Martin, followed by gut-deep animosity that Lane trusted. The law is something I respect and obey, and I dont care to hear it insinuated otherwise.

Why were you under Billy Bean's pickup?

A day earlier, when Lane had tried to share what he'd known, he'd been beating on a locked door. The temptation to step through this wide-open one was strong but his instincts stronger. NoBob hadnt denied tampering with Billy Bean's brakes, but he hadnt admitted to it, either. Martin had been there, too. I see why they call you Boob, he said when he could think of nothing else.

We're on the same side here. Unless you're not.

Lane figured he could outstare anybody but after a while his eyes dropped away. Feeling like he was on the wrong side of the law when he hadnt done anything to deserve it.

If there's something going on in my county, I need to know it.

If I ever visit your county, I'll keep that in mind.

Whether you like it or not, you're in my county.

Lane felt a fight he couldnt win ratcheting out of control and he moved behind the sales counter and stood there waiting until Martin walked away. Before Lane could breathe clean air again he reappeared on the other side of the screen door. The sticker's about to run out on your truck.

Lane didnt dignify the observation with a response.

Does Greasy do your inspections?

Lane turned to a shelf and straightened the dusty items there.

He's getting a hard look from downstate. Since that woman wrecked up on I-68. Stickers he issues might not be any good one of these days. I'm just saying. To save you trouble.

While he watched the deputy leave, Lane pondered just what manner of man he might be and when he'd processed what he knew with what he suspected he knew less than before.

• • •

The boy stood in the baitshop door that Martin had vacated minutes before and rapped lightly with brown knuckles against the jamb.

Come on, Lane said. You dont have to knock on a store's door.

I wasnt sure you were open. The boy came in with his tin can and Lane dumped it into a Styrofoam cup and stuck it into the refrigerator without counting the worms. How many is it?

Five.

Lane fumbled a quarter from the moneybox and passed it over and the boy looked at both sides of the coin and slid it into a threadbare pocket. Thank you, he said.

It'll likely rain soon, Lane said. The farmers got a lot of hay down right now. The weather gods wont let that pass unmolested. Chico, you live in that old farmhouse sets back in just beyond the substation, dont you?

The boy looked puzzled.

The thing with the wires and transformers. That buzzes.

Yes. Past that.

How many live with you?

I'm not sure. I never counted.

Six? Eight?

More than that. But they're not all there at the same time.

No kidding. How many brothers and sisters you have?

Just one sister. The other kids have different parents.

They live there too?

Yes sir.

Lane pondered that for a while. You know who your landlord is? When the boy got that look again he added, The man you pay money to for staying there.

No sir. He drives a truck. Like yours but with a different back part.

With a flat bed? Made out of wood?

Yes. Like that.

That's NoBob Thrasher then. He's got some rental properties. What's your daddy do?

He helps a man milk cows.

That's an honorable thing, Lane said. The boy turned to leave and Lane felt like he shouldnt allow that to happen. That there was something needed doing first. You didnt see a cop car sitting out along the road awhile ago did you?

No sir.

How old are you, Juan? Trying his best to say it right.

Eight.

I was probably eight once, but I dont remember it. How about a soda? I'm going to have one.

The boy's hand worked in his pocket where the quarter had gone. No sir. I'm not thirsty.

It wont cost you anything.

The boy's eyes dropped. I have to go.

The boy dodged out the door and left Lane feeling like he'd somehow offered insult through his kindness. Till he got to the door the boy had disappeared.

Just before noon he picked at a tin of sardines with a plastic fork and they lay restless in his gut. After lunch a slow but steady inflow of bait buyers kept him occupied but toward evening they dwindled away and left him alone like he wanted and dreaded.

At dark he locked the shop and put the moneybox in the refrigerator and stood and watched as the constellation of fireflies emerged. Mixing their God-given chemicals to attract and deceive. To mate and kill and die and perpetuate the process for another generation. As they were made to do.

And Lane was adrift and lost, designed for nothing.

Lane drove to his house and to Mary's soft bed, where he slept restless and cramped. Like his thoughts. Sometime during the night, though, when he least expected it, they rowed up and he knew what he had to do.

.16

HE AROSE WELL BEFORE DAYLIGHT AND DROVE past the farm where the buffalo were and through the tree farm to the edge of town and dodged into the short lane that led to Darlene's little ranch house. He entered without knocking the way he did when he knew she wasnt asleep. She and the boy were eating breakfast at the kitchen table and she turned down the radio and took her plate to the stove and got more bacon from the refrigerator and set it to hissing in one skillet and bathed two pieces of bread in French toast batter and slipped them into the other.

Here, Pap. Take the dregs and I'll get another pot going. She emptied the carafe into the heavy cup she reserved for Lane.

Dont go to any trouble, he said. I've been needing to trim up a little bit anyhow.

You look like the running gears out of a katydid. I'm the one that needs to cut back. But after I serve sausage gravy and biscuits and New York strips all day bran flakes just dont satisfy.

Lane sat at the table beside the boy and savored the dark rich coffee and evaluated his daughter-in-law. You just keep doing what you're doing, he said. That would be my advice.

He studied the top of the boy's head. Mornin Toby. Wondering how many other boys that age were up at this hour.

Hey.

Monday's a fishing day but I wont be able to today.

Why not, the boy asked without raising his face.

You are watching him today, arent you? Darlene said.

Well. After you held him back from me all weekend I kind of got to liking it.

Does that mean no? Darlene threw up her hands. Thanks for all the advance notice.

Until the middle of the night I didnt know what I had to do today. Got to run up to Cumberland. Cant you get Phyllis to watch him? Just till I get back?

Phyllis is working too because Judy's off.

Can I go with you? Toby said. Please, Pap?

Not this time, Toby.

Water welled in the boy's eyes and he placed his fork on his almost empty plate and fled toward his bedroom. The fork might as well have been prong-deep in Lane's heart.

I'm sorry, DeeDee. There's some things . . .

Dont worry about it, she said. The little bawlbaby. He's been doing that a lot lately.

He's just sensitive.

Yeah, I know. I tell his teacher that. That if he does wrong to just slap the boy beside him and he'll learn his lesson from that. Darlene sat the plate in front of Lane and pushed the butter and syrup closer. You want some milk or juice too?

Not milk for sure, Lane said, louder than usual, hoping the boy could hear. He lightly buttered the golden brown slabs and inquired of them with his knife and added more. I read somewhere that milk makes you effeminate. That they feed the cows estrogen to make them give more milk. And then the milk's got it in too, and when guys drink it they got female hormones in them.

Darlene laughed throaty and deep, her anger already diffused. I dont believe you're in danger yet.

That's what makes boys cry nowadays they say. It's not their fault. It's that daggoned milk.

You're full of something that comes out of a cow. That's for sure, she said. But she laughed. Big softie. Darlene poured fresh coffee and sat with him at the table.

The boy needs a dad.

The boy's got a dad, last I heard.

One he can see. Not one that runs off and leaves him to grow up on his own. Lane drank his cup of coffee down and savored the burn against his anger and rose and refilled it and topped off Darlene's cup though she hadnt even tasted hers. You heard from the shitass?

We talk all the time. And he sends money regular. If Frank's who you're talking about.

You best not be talking to him. Give me a smoke. I bought some but I smoked them all up. Dont worry, I wont turn into a serial bummer. He lit the cigarette she pushed his way and again cringed at the taste of menthol.

Dont be so hard on Frank. What happened is as much my fault as his.

Or yours, he suspected she wanted to say. Dont stand up for him, he said.

Lighten up on him. That's what I'm saying. Do you think incessant airing of what you think of his father is good for Toby? Frank is your *son*.

He was.

Is. You cant change that and he cant either.

Lane stubbed out the half-smoked cigarette with more energy

than the task required. Maybe I'll be able to watch Toby later today and maybe not. Some things have come up.

Get your butt back down off your shoulders, old man. Dont throw down your opinion on the kitchen floor like it's a deer you shot and then get your dander up when I give you mine.

I really do have things to do. If it throws too much of a sprag in the cogs I'll try to find somebody to watch him.

Better men than you have tried and failed to sprag up my cogs. I'll either take him along to work or leave him here. He's old enough.

Lane considered the idea with more unease than he'd have felt two days earlier. He ought not be left unattended.

She shrugged. We do what we got to do.

Maybe I better talk to him. Just so he knows I havent abandoned him.

You know where he is, Darlene said and started clearing the table.

The boy was in the small cluttered bedroom bent over the fly vise, his face puckered in concentration. Lane looked down along the top of his nose at the fly. As though he were wearing bifocals. You got that hackle mastered. And that purple really sets off that red.

It's not perfect. Not as even all around as I want it to be.

Good enough to fool me. And if you can fool me you can fool a fish. Easy. You got a name for that one?

Not yet.

Lane rested his hand on the back of the boy's neck and glanced at the closed door and lowered his voice. Toby, I'm sorry I cant take you with me.

I never get to go anywhere.

Yes you do. Trying to remember when.

The boy took his scissors and cut the entire fly from the hook and blew away the feathers and hair.

Now what did you do that for?

I didnt like it. It wasnt right. He laid on a knot and secured it with a drop of cement and started winding thread again.

Anyhow, Lane said. I'll come get you when I can. Dont think I've forgot about you.

The boy cut the thread off again and removed the hook from the vise and stared into the tacklebox of fly-tying materials.

I need to ask you something, Toby.

The boy closed the box.

Out at the reservoy. You called those men a name.

A shrug.

You called them niggers. The word foul on his tongue. Did you see them?

No. He flopped onto his bed and pulled the pillow over his head.

Then why did you call them that?

Because that's what they are. I hate them. And I hate you.

Lane patted him on the back. Feeling old and awkward and dumb and not knowing whether to be relieved that the boy hadnt seen the men or concerned that he had seen them and had reason to lie about it. Now in the light of day, that thought seemed both more preposterous and believable. Well I dont hate you, Toby. I love you with all my heart.

Now I have to spend all day at the diner. And you called my dad a shitass.

Sometimes it was better just to walk away. A shitass is what he is, Lane finally said. But not until he was a mile down the road.

•   •   •

Before the sun was up the baitshop was open and after an early flurry of anglers in quest of worms and minnows which Lane supplied and gossip about Billy Bean which he wouldnt, Lane strained the dead minnows out of the tank and sniffed each of the cups of nightcrawlers and dug down in the stinky ones and disposed of the dead worms and consolidated the remainder. He swept and straightened the baitshop and tried to perceive it with the eyes of a newcomer and hoped it was different than that.

The Colt .22 Woodsman pistol wasnt on the shelf below the cash register where it belonged. He shook the rag he kept it wrapped in as though he'd overlooked it. By the time he'd found it in a cardboard box of expired fishing license booklets he was getting worried.

You rotten little punk, he said and tried to figure out when Toby could have had it out. Lots of times, he realized. He suddenly wondered how much the boy knew about girls.

Lane removed and emptied the clip and cleaned and oiled the gun and refilled the clip with long rifle hollow points and slid it back up into the butt. He squinted at the thermometer and got a sweater from the closet and locked the shop and went to his truck and opened the door and stood looking in for a while. He felt down inside a long tear in the upholstery in the driver's side of the bench seat and then worked the pistol down where his hand had been. When he got in he could feel it there under his left cheek and liked the sensation.

• • •

Lane cut through Hardly and stopped at the Get-n-Go and purchased an entire carton of Marlboros and blanched at the price but didnt remark on it. Marveled at the cost of suicide as he lit the first out of the pack. He'd always considered smoking an emblem of either financial or intellectual poverty and relished violating his own mores.

He drove slowly with the window down out Sugarcamp Road to the end and turned the pickup around and said, Dadblame it, NoBob. You said you were working out here. He idled back out the road and stopped and reversed when he saw the edge of a sandpile spilled out from behind a little cedar-and-stone house. Lane parked with two wheels on the pavement and walked down to lean on the fender of NoBob's truck and nod at the two Hispanic laborers. They smiled and dropped their eyes. Hard little men, all rawhide and lean muscles, wearing open sandals and worn-out polyester slacks and dingy dress shirts with rolled-up sleeves. Handkerchiefs stuffed under their ballcaps to protect their necks from the sun. Both of them exuding a quietude to rival the rocks scattered on the ground.

NoBob was piling drystack stones on a retaining wall that already extended far above ground level. He picked up the rocks without looking and each fit as though designed for its place and the trowel never gathered too much mud off the board or too little. Occasionally he'd strike a stone with the trowel's edge and a chunk would peel away as though it was already cracked just there. He talked to himself all the while, too softly to be understood. The helpers demonstrated little need for instruction, replenishing the supply of stones, keeping fresh cement on the mudboard.

When he straightened to stretch his back, Lane said, Hows come you need two helpers? Looks like a girl could keep up with you.

NoBob didnt flinch or look Lane's way. As though he'd known Lane stood watching. I considered puttin on a girl or two. For break time.

You do this all this morning already?

No. The boys started it on Saturday. They dont care to take weekends off.

What they need you for then? I dont see any difference in what they laid and what you did.

NoBob grinned. They need somebody to pay em. And to make sure they're working at the right place. Not putting up a wall where there aint supposed to be one.

You reckon they got any kids that would mow grass? Someone you could trust?

They got kids would mow grass with their teeth if they got the chance. The ones old enough to have teeth.

From what Lane had seen of their quick white smiles, their teeth were better than his own. He remembered Chico—Juan—and wondered why he'd never considered asking him to mow the lawn at his house. I'll keep that in mind.

You come out to help, or you got a bee in your bonnet?

Now that he was here, Lane wasnt so confident about what he'd decided. How's come the wall's so high? You're way up above the ground.

NoBob arched his spine and pushed in on his lower back with his fist and said, They're puttin in a swimmin pool. He lowered his voice and glanced toward the house. The woman's uglier than a week-old crap and the more clothes she takes off the homelier she gets. Both helpers giggled like schoolboys.

You sound like you got inside knowledge.

I wasnt never that horny. Not even when I was a teenager. You know them two-bag women? You put two bags over their heads in case one busts? This is a steel-reinforced solid-rock privacy-fence woman. For the wellbeing of the general public.

This is a climate I never could figure a swimming pool for.

They'll freeze their dingleberries a time or two and then put the cover on and not take it off again. Look, NoBob said. In your business you can stand around and jaw and people will pick up stuff to buy while you're doing it. But in mine you have to put rocks on the wall.

I've been thinking.

Did it hurt?

I need to run up Cumberland way and talk to Larson Henry. See if I feel the same way about him you do.

NoBob threw his trowel at the mudboard and for a moment Lane thought he was going to jump off the scaffold onto Lane. You aint going to let it be, are you.

I'm not getting any cops involved. But my mind needs put to rest.

You got that part right. Permanent would be best. Please dont dig into stuff you dont know one stinking thing about.

I'm letting you know before I do anything. Like you asked. So dont treat me like something you found on your finger after you picked your nose.

NoBob picked up his trowel and returned to his work as if Lane wasnt there.

Could you tell me where to find him? Since you worked for him.

After a while Lane nodded at the helpers and left.

.17

LANE DROVE WEST ON UNION HIGHWAY TO 219
and turned north. Taking the long way to Cumberland. Time to
think. Dank hollows filled with nettles flavored the air till freshcut
hay took over just beyond the Maryland line. A daytime moon hung
over corn leaves rolled into spikes against the sun and the dry. Past
Deep Creek Lake it smelled of nothing—the farms long gone but the
knots of houses and buildings not yet clabbered into a city with its
smells of exhaust and waste. One day soon the spaces between the
buildings would disappear and Lane would not come this way.

The red- and- blue-roofed castles that claimed the ridgeline gave
him a claustrophobic feeling. Like he was being watched. He passed
a couple on bicycles and remembered when kids rode them. He took
the back way through the Savage River State Forest and was sad-
dened to see all of Meadow Mountain laid waste by timber crews.
He'd hunted ginseng there a time or two and decided right then that
he'd be the first one back in when the briars thinned.

At Hilltop he hit the interstate and endeavored to maintain the
speed limit but his mind would wander till a blast of horns would
prompt him to accelerate. Interfering with their constitutional right to

break the law. Everyone that passed stared at his pickup and he knew it was the color that pulled their eyes: robin-egg blue with a touch of ugly stirred in. Not the rusted fenders. Or the old hillbilly behind the wheel.

The air changed again when he topped Big Savage Mountain and the heat from the valley below rose to meet him. A few crooked steel I-beams had finally been erected where the weathered sign had long proclaimed that Noah's ark was being rebuilt. It was a start. But it wasnt ready for the rain to fall just yet.

The grass there was burned brown, the water wrung from the clouds by the mountains behind him. But they didnt get as much snow. That would almost make living there worth it.

Lane daydreamed without a specific topic and when he was again aware of his surroundings, Cumberland lay below him. Church spires spiking from the trees like a picture he'd seen of New England. He coasted down the hill and double-clutched into second gear and dropped off the overpass at the downtown exit. The only exit he knew. The one to the Veterans Administration clinic. Where they ran a finger up your tailpipe and told you to watch what you ate. Like a better diet would improve the smell of their finger.

He idled at the stop sign and looked both ways and allowed two opportunities to pass in indecision and then lurched out in front of a battered compact car running too fast and ignored the horn and upraised finger when the kid shot around on his right. A pair of diesel locomotives were building a string, blocking the tracks and his way to the VA, so he edged into the downtown mall and parked at the McDonald's and rolled down the passenger side window and wiped his face on the same blue paisley handkerchief he tied around his head when it got this hot at home. The locomotives hammering at the air turned it so harsh Lane could taste it. I'd as leave take up residence in hell, he said. Knowing that as towns went this one was as good as they come. He went inside and ordered a sausage biscuit and a coffee and counted the exact change from his green plastic change purse and sat under an airconditioning vent and watched people pass by. As happy as if they had their right minds.

The train was gathering steam and pulling away so Lane went to the bathroom and then rattled across the tracks and turned the wrong way up the street to the VA clinic. Just for a short piece. Like he did. Not because he didnt know better, but because it was ignorant to drive clear around the block when the entrance was right there.

He sat in his truck and watched old men shuffling in walkers and old men pushed in wheelchairs by daughters and sons and old men in one shoe and one bedroom slipper and old men towing oxygen bottles on little wheeled carts. Somebody needs to start coming out pretty soon, he said to himself after a long string of entries with no exits. What are they doing to them in there? After a while a desiccated bony old man with tattoos on both arms arrived on foot. Someone that lived within walking distance. Lane followed him into the clinic and read a brochure while the man checked in and then Lane sat with one empty seat between them.

Going to be a hot one, he said when the man glanced his way. The man smelled as if he were formed of tobacco.

Hot enough, the skinny man said. A voice like a rock crusher.

You like this place or the old one over by Memorial better? I kind of like it here.

I hate this. Now you got to go clear across town to get tests done at the hospital.

I'm lucky that I havent had any tests done. Just the ones they do here. You live close hereabouts?

Two blocks. The man pointed but the chopped-up waiting area had turned Lane around, and inside with no windows he couldnt get a fix off the mountains or tell which way the river ran.

Maybe you can tell me where to get hold of Larson Henry.

By the nuts. With a pair of waterpump pliers. The only way to hold that slippery sonofabitch. A laugh faded into a fit of coughing.

I meant do you know where I might find him.

Well I knowed that. A touch of outrage in his voice. He might be at his warehouse or maybe not. He's got fingers in things he aint got fingers enough for.

Where's his warehouse?

The man offered meaningless directions until he mentioned the Dingle and Lane vaguely knew where that was and collected his bearings from there but before he could recite his understanding a nurse appeared and said Mr. Shank?

Here's the ragged end of what's left of him, the man said.

The nurse looked at her clipboard and at Lane. Have you signed in, sir?

I will directly. Soon as I catch my breath.

When the door closed behind them Lane walked to his truck feeling old and decrepit by association and set off to find Larson Henry.

•　•　•

The warehouse was a faded tan steel building in a dirt lot filled with what might have been the assemblage of a giant packrat. Or the deposit of a wide-ranging tornado. A motor home with a cracked windshield and one wheelless axle propped on a split railroad tie. Half of a doublewide mobile home with blue numbers painted on the dingy white plastic that covered the open side. Wheels sunk in the mud but no tracks leading to it. Like they'd misplaced the other piece. Or the customer just decided he needed only half of one. A pile of secondgrade cutstone that overlapped a snarl of scrap steel. That crowded a D-6 bulldozer so uniformly rusted it might have been sculpted from a single chunk of iron ore. An old yellow Mercedes with a blue tarp duct-taped over the rear end. Four ricks of weathered sawmill lumber stickered but uncovered and rotting. The faded doorless box from a semitrailer set flat on the ground and overflowing with spent tire casings. A brownish Plymouth Reliant with one white fender and an old Chevy pickup with no fender at all on the driver's front side. Rear glass gone.

Lane parked behind the pickup and knocked at the walk-in door and after a while tried the knob and opened it and from back in the gloom a stocky man was coming his way and he stopped and said, Dont park there. I got to get out. His voice vaguely familiar. Maybe like the tobacco man's at the VA.

Lane looked back at the fenderless pickup and said, I didnt realize it was being run. He relocated his pickup beside the lumber piles and caught the sour smell of red oak.

When he returned to the building the man had disappeared. Lane yelled a hello into a darkness ten degrees warmer than the outside air. Far back a dim bulb shone like a pinhole in the siding. Lane shut the door behind him and allowed his eyes to adjust to an interior version of the lot. Appliances of various shapes and hues. A mountain of carpet remnants. An ancient forklift with an LP gas cylinder mounted behind the driver's seat. Stacks and stacks of store shelving. Buckets and cans and barrels of every imaginable size, few with labels.

Just beyond the single bulb was a walled-in room and another door. Lane picked his way there and heard voices and smelled coffee over the chemical smells and knocked on the door and the voices stopped. He opened the door and looked into an office that was yet another version of the past two spaces. Papers and mismatched furniture. Office machines that had gone out of style when the abacus was becoming popular.

The stocky man was stirring coffee above a dirty sink. One side of his face a purpling bruise and swollen to where you couldnt discern where one feature stopped and another took over. Like the nose and eye had become one multipurpose organ. A ponytail greasy and ragged. The armholes on his tank top so big that the top wrinkle of his love handles showed. Shorts and workboots. He was muscled and tanned despite his general condition. Behind a cluttered desk sat a small thin man with thin hair and liverspots on his bare arms. A black telephone and a cellphone like brackets on history. Hello, he said. With a question mark at the end.

Hope I'm not interrupting anything, Lane said.

How can I help you? the man at the desk said. A shirt like Mexican cooking and a blue tie snugged tight around his skinny neck.

I'm Lane Hollar. I was hoping to find Larson Henry.

Hang on, the man said. Harold, you go get the place redded out and I'll be along after a while.

Lane edged aside to allow Harold passage and said after he'd gone, Looks like he got the short end of whatever he took hold of.

What can I do for you?

Are you Mr. Henry?

I am. His eyes were not on Lane's but above his head and Lane glanced up and realized the premises were monitored. From high up where the cameras were mounted the place looked even worse. Like a topographic map of hell. In the black-and-white screen Harold stood staring at Lane's pickup before he climbed into the one with no fender.

Lane sat on a plastic chair with spindly chrome legs and said, I'm from down Hardly way. Run a baitshop outside of town.

Henry's eyes dropped to Lane's but he didnt say anything.

Folks tell me you're the man to see if you'd be wanting to relocate here. The winters on the mountain have about got the best of me.

A baitshop wouldnt work here or I'd have one. They fish the Potomac some but not that much. Bucket fishermen.

It would be just me that would relocate. Not the business.

Are you wanting to buy a business? Impatient.

Lane wished he'd thought his approach through a little better. Maybe. I have to do something.

I buy businesses, not sell them.

What all businesses are you into?

Where is your baitshop? I know that area some.

Outside of Hardly. Close to the reservoy. Not the big lake. Out on Ford Road.

Crooked little shack still has Insulbrick siding.

That's it. Irritated at the description though it was exact.

I've been looking at property out that way. Close by the school.

If there was a snake behind Henry's eyes Lane couldnt see it. But you never could. Whose property, if I might ask?

Fitzel, I think the family is. The parents have passed and the kids are looking to sell.

Lane knew the property, knew that to be true.

How much you take for your baitshop?

I wasnt wanting to sell. Summertime's nice up there. I'd keep it for that.

The business must do all right if you can afford a winter place.

Hardly pays the light bill. But I dont need much. They examined each other with a touch of belligerence. What kind of business are you starting out by the school? Lane said.

Nothing in mind. But the town is growing thataway.

Close to a school doesnt seem a good place for any business I know of.

What would you take for your property if I'd put in the deed that you could live on it and run your baitshop till you died?

A watersnake had kept at Lane this same way once. Following him and jabbing at him till Lane grabbed it by the tail and threw it into the bushes. But the snake had been shedding. Had an excuse. It's not for sale. I have family that will get it when I'm gone. Lane sat up straighter on his chair and rested his palms on his knees. I'm not very good at this kind of a thing. I didnt come to sell property. Or to buy any.

Nosir. I'd just about figured that out.

I heard a tale the other day that I felt obliged to check on.

Henry stared up at the monitor but nothing moved on the flickering screen.

A tale that Larson Henry was running drugs into the school and managed to run into the wrong fellow in the process.

A professional actor couldnt have faked the surprise in Henry's face. Drugs?

The word is somebody got caught redhanded and got his butt whipped for it. You were named, but it's right clear it wasnt you. Your man's plainly taken a thumping, though. And you just said you were looking at property up by the school. Where it happened.

Lane's eyes shied off from the color of the pants when Henry rose and turned off the coffeepot without offering Lane any or pouring any for himself. Like he was fixing to leave. Or maybe he just didnt like to waste electricity. He stood on the other side of the desk, taller than Lane had given him credit for but still not very tall.

My grandson goes to that school, Mr. Henry.

If you think I'm involved in drugs you're just flat out confused. Go back to whoever started this nonsense and find out the truth.

He's hard to talk to.

Mr. Hollar is it?

Yessir.

I have irons in a lot of fires, but I can assure you none of them is drugs. Wherever that came from is beyond my imagination.

What kind of businesses *are* you into then? There's no secretary here. And those phones arent ringing off the hook.

Henry sat on a corner of the desk and tore off a page from a daily calendar. Not that this is any of your business. But there's two ways to make a lot of money. At least two.

I'd say so.

One way is to take a single business and make it outstanding and make it the biggest and the best. Sam Walton did right well at that.

Lane looked around at the dust and clutter and already knew what the other way was.

The other way is to own a passel of little businesses making a little bit of money. That's where I shine. My little ventures run cheap, on cash, with unskilled labor. They're not so complicated that ordinary folks cant handle them. Not overburdened with paperwork. But they run honest and as legal as a small business can be. I sell groceries and gas and carpet and factory-second housewares and reclaimed furniture and used vehicles and scrap steel and roadside produce and manufacturers' closeouts and pawned guns and cleaning rags. That's just what comes to mind right off. I dont sell drugs or even liquor or beer. I hate anything that makes people more muddled than they already are.

The way he said it made a believer out of Lane and he ran his fingers through his hair and said, What about that fellow that works for you? Could he be into something bad?

Harold? He's a hard drinker and I suspect he smokes a little marijuana but I cant picture him being a dealer. Not enough smarts to get away with it.

He didnt, judging from how he looks.

I mean with the law. With the people he'd come into contact with. No. Not Harold.

Henry had been so stunned at the suggestion of drugs that Lane felt foolish introducing the idea of murder yet to boot. What's he do for you?

You appear to be someone that wont give me peace till you get it straight in your head.

I been known to be persistent.

Harold hauls vehicles for my used car lot. That's a lot of what he does.

Wont they run? Knowing as he said it what Larson meant.

I buy cars in Virginia. North Carolina. Where they havent been run in the salt. Harold takes the rollback to pick them up. He can haul two and I dont have to license them.

Salt's hard on stuff.

When he's not doing that it's just whatever I got to do. Run errands. Haul trash. Pick up the mail. Clean up. The rest of the time he's figuring how to steal off me or get paid for loafing.

It might pay to hire on a better class of workers.

Since the tire plant pulled out there's not much to pick from. Folks live here because they're rich enough they dont have to work or because they dont have ambition enough to go somewhere else. He's what I got.

Hows come you have closed-circuit television here?

The man looked at Lane long and hard enough to make him uncomfortable. You wont quit till you're done, will you?

No sir.

Just because I can. Because I want to. Because I feel like it. Now get the rest of it out of your system. So tomorrow you dont think of some other thing and have to come back. Get it done.

All right. Sensing an opportunity that might not return. What was Harold doing up at Hardly?

I told you already. I'm looking at a piece of property up there. Harold got sent up to check if the lines were run like Mountain High Surveying said it was before I cut the check. I've dealt with that company before.

It all rang too true to be made up. Well, Lane said and stood. I thank you for being honest with me.

If there's drugs getting into your school they're not coming through me.

I believe you. Thank you.

I'll stop in someday and talk about your property.

It flat just isnt for sale. Lane opened the door and shut it again without leaving. Just to put my mind clear at ease would you object to my talking to Harold myself?

Henry had opened a drawer in a dented gray file cabinet and was thumbing through greasy-looking folders. I had a dog like you. Chased cars till he caught one.

Sometimes I feel like I already have.

Not the way he did, you havent. Not by the front bumper. But you're likely to if you keep on. Larson Henry withdrew a file and put it on the desk and sat beside it. You know, he said, talking to Harold is probably the thing to do. If you still think he's capable of dealing drugs you have a better imagination than I do. Larson Henry dug the calendar page from the trash and on the back drew a map to where Harold was working.

What's his last name, anyhow?

Harold Bright. One of life's little ironies. Be careful. He's grumpy when you wake him up.

Lane thanked Larson Henry again and picked his way back to the daylight and climbed in the truck and said Whoowee and leaned forward so his back wouldnt touch the seat. He waved at the camera in the gable end and set off to find Harold Bright.

• • •

The old gas station Harold was cleaning lay south of town limits past the brown brick buildings that had been boarded up when Kelly-Springfield lost patience with the unions and moved to Ohio. The faded Sunoco sign said 1.29^9 for regular unleaded.

The left garage bay door was open and from the shadows protruded the rear of the fenderless pickup he'd parked behind earlier. Lane got out and looked around the neighborhood and decided he didnt trust anyone who lived there. Just as a starting point.

Inside was the odd combined odor of grease and mildew. Hey, he said into the gloom.

By the workbenches was movement and Lane shaded his eyes and saw Harold watching with the look of an animal with its forepaw caught in a steel trap. Get the hell on out of here, he said.

Harold Bright? Larson Henry sent me out.

Harold squatted for a three-foot section of crooked rebar and swung it to test how it cut the air. Well, from the sound of it. I aint talkin to you.

Lane took a step back and watched Harold's eyes go to Lane's pickup.

Lane turned and looked at it himself. It is a right unusual color. Maybe one you saw before. Up at the reservoy.

Harold's feet scuffed on the concrete and Lane ducked and his arm came up to protect his face but the rebar clattered against the floor and Harold charged by him in a blast of sour sweat and dodged past Lane's pickup and around the corner. Lane after him before he'd decided to.

Lane's feet skittered on loose coal shale behind the gas station and he went to one knee and clambered up to see Harold duck between two buildings not four feet apart. Lane was limping when he got there but he forged ahead down the narrow alley and squeezed between a brick wall and a rusty fuel-oil tank and when he was almost past it Harold rose up like a battered haunt from its shadow and hit Lane over the head with a length of two-by-four.

•   •   •

Lane opened one eye and contemplated a jagged fissure in weathered concrete. A dandelion had taken root in it and at that point another crack ventured forth perpendicular to the first. He felt his head and discovered blood on his hand said Ow and sat up beneath a long slice of sky between brick buildings and recalled where he was.

At the end of the alley a scruffy white kid in baggy shorts and a man's T-shirt sat on a balloon-tired girl's bike. When Lane looked his way the kid stood on the pedals and disappeared in a rattle of loose and rusting parts. Lane leaned against the oil tank and fought down his nausea and when he thought he had it whipped he bent over and threw up and dragged himself to his feet and staggered from the alley to the open air where he couldnt smell what he'd done.

The sun beat at him like a hammer and he slid down the bricks and the skin sloughed off one elbow and he sat with his head in his hands. He spit between his legs and a string of slaver fell across his belly and he wiped it away and got up and went back to look behind the oil tank. Like Harold might still be hiding there. He wasnt but the two-by-four was, a patch of Lane's hair wedged under a splinter. Lane used it for a cane back into the sunlight where he looked up and down and recognized nothing. Like he'd just arrived on the planet. After a while he collected his bearings and returned to his truck the way he'd come and tossed the two-by-four into the back and opened the door and felt in the seat for the gun. Thank goodness for that much, he said.

Harold's pickup was gone and the garage door was shut and locked and the panes of glass so greasy Lane could see only his own shadow.

In the truck he examined himself in the rearview mirror and with his handkerchief cleaned his face and felt along the edge of where his contusion had burst and wondered why he couldnt see the skullbone. I never knew stupid to leave such a mark, he said and started the engine and drove back toward Larson Henry's warehouse.

The Plymouth Reliant was gone and the door was fastened with a fist-sized padlock. Lane stood back and looked up at the camera and said, Is anybody in there? and felt foolish. Like he was hollering at God. He clanged a piece of gravel into the pile of scrap iron and got back in his pickup and headed for home.

Instead of driving back through Cumberland to the interstate he lit a cigarette and took Old 40 up through LaVale and on impulse or

maybe because his throat was afire and his head clanging like someone beating on a barrel with a frypan he swung into Bob's Discount
Liquors. Bleeding from his cut had nearly stopped so he cleaned his
face again and tied the handkerchief around his head in a do-rag and
tossed his smoke in the gutter and went inside and felt his way to the
back where the beer coolers were. The clerk watching him like Larson
Henry's TV had.

At the sight of the beer his stomach roiled sour and mean so he
walked down an aisle of bottles till he saw one he recognized by name
and color if not by what it might contain and he took it by the neck
and nearly dropped it so he clutched it like a baby and delivered it to
the counter. The clerk stood far back and said, How many you had
already, pops?

Not a one, Lane said. I hit my head. Hearing how that sounded.
Not from drinking.

I could lose my license. Selling to somebody already in the can.

I havent even had a taste.

The clerk stepped to the register and said $18.70 before he'd even
pushed any keys.

Lane felt for his wallet and found only dryer lint in that pocket.
Hells bells. Where'd my wallet go? It must be in the truck he said and
started that way.

Uh uh uh. Leave that bottle here.

Aw, I wouldnt . . . Lane set the bottle down and returned to his
truck. The wallet was nowhere inside it nor was it in his other pockets.
The change from the cigarettes he'd bought—a five-dollar bill and a
few coins—was in his front pocket so he went back inside and said, I
must of clean lost it.

Nice try, dude. The clerk set the bottle on a shelf behind the bar.

I wasnt trying to pull anything, Lane said. I found a five here. I'll
just have to buy something else. The first thing he found in that price

range was a pint of blackberry brandy for $3.95 and he took it to the counter and told the clerk to keep the change.

The clerk examined the bill longer than Lane deemed necessary so he started to leave. Here, I got to put it in a bag. You cant just carry it out like that.

Lane left the store feeling as though he'd just taken part of some transaction too foul for human consideration. Like he'd just purchased a child for personal use.

The pickup was boiling inside but as soon as he hit the interstate he was chilled. The rumblestrip startled him when he veered off the road trying to roll up the passenger-side window and a horn blew when he overreacted back into the fast lane. To heck with the highway, he said, and exited to pick up 36 at Frostburg. As soon as he was back to a road like a road ought to be, one lane each way, he relaxed and held the flat bottle between his legs and twisted off the cap and checked the mirror and took a long pull that eased his headache but sent his stomach into instant revolt. He gagged and spit out the window and screwed the top back onto the bottle and jammed it in the crack between seat and backrest. Saw himself pouring the rest of it down the sink so as not to kill the grass.

The papermill stink lay dank and oppressive till he was past Keyser, and as he wound back up into his mountains his spirits lifted.

Just past the Union County line, though, a sheriff's deputy Lane didnt know was waiting to pull out where Lane turned off of 220 onto Union Highway. The deputy glanced at Lane as he passed and did a doubletake and made a U-turn and followed him. Lane was trying to finagle the open bottle behind the seat and dropped one wheel onto the berm and the lightbar lit up and the siren gave a single *whoop*.

Lane kept going till he found a place where he could get completely off the highway and pulled off and opened the door to get out.

Get back in the vehicle, sir, the deputy yelled. Get back in the vehicle and shut the door.

Lane shrugged and got back in and watched the deputy sidle up to where he could look inside the cab without exposing himself to any danger. It's all right, Lane said. I'm not going to hurt you. I'm just an old man with a headache.

Let's see your license and registration and your proof of insurance. A stumpy little toad with little glasses in a fat face and a double chin where his hatstrap dug into it. Deputy Ferguson.

Lane rummaged in the glovebox and found a dozen or more registration cards and at least that many insurance cards. He leafed through them till he found a couple that seemed current. Aware of the lump of the pistol under his cheek.

As he passed the cards out the deputy crowded his head in the window, smelling for alcohol. Lane tried to hold his breath and suspected he was just going to make it ranker when he let it out.

The deputy withdrew his head and looked at the insurance card and registration and said Your operator's license too, sir.

Well. That one I'm going to come up short on.

The deputy checked for traffic but only one car had passed since they'd stopped. He stepped away a step or so and said, You dont have a driver's license, sir? Standing like he was going to whip a quickdraw on him and shoot him dead.

I have one but it's not on me. First time in fifty-eight years but I lost my billfold just a little bit ago.

What did you do to your head, sir?

That happened at the same time I lost my billfold. No way could he not look at it in the mirror while he said it. Blood had seeped through his handkerchief and was starting to gather for a run down his forehead. He removed the handkerchief and wiped at the wound and when he smelled the blood his stomach turned upside down and bile surged into his throat. He unlatched the door and pushed his way out and the deputy yelled something Lane didnt decipher and stumbled back into the path of a car that had to lock up all four wheels and dodge into the other lane to keep from hitting him.

Lane held onto the bedrail and blew out the brandy and what little else was left in him and while he was doing that the deputy kicked his legs apart and grabbed one arm and attempted to twist it up behind Lane's back. Before he could think not to he pivoted into the smaller man and his elbow came around and clubbed the side of the deputy's head and knocked his hat loose and his glasses askew.

When the deputy caught his feet his service revolver was pointed at Lane's head. He pushed his glasses back up his nose and said, Get on the ground. Do it now.

Lane got himself spread out in the gravel and while the deputy was cuffing his hands behind his back Lane said, You could screw up a cheese sandwich.

The deputy hauled him up to his feet and said, You'd best just watch your mouth, sir.

It wasnt you I was referring to, Lane said.

The deputy pushed Lane's head down as he put him into the backseat of the cruiser. I'd like to search your vehicle, sir, he said. May I have your permission? I can get a warrant if you dont.

Go ahead, Lane said. What you're looking for is under the seat on the driver's side. Hoping he'd stop there. Well you've screwed the pooch now, Lane said, and lay over sideways onto the seat and tried to still the throbbing in his head and the churning that had begun in his guts again.

• • •

I'm sorry you had to do this DeeDee, Lane said when they'd gotten outside the jail. I'd have called somebody else but I didnt know who. The bandage they'd put on his head protruded into his vision and felt like a new appendage but she'd only glanced at it and not questioned.

Her hair was a mess and her eyes were bleary and her pink pull-over didnt go with her green sweatpants. You're lucky I was home. Not working.

At least she was talking. He got in her Taurus and adjusted the passenger seat back as far as it would go and waited for her to start the car so he could roll down the window. Then he hawked and spat and felt better for it. Like he'd gotten the taste of jail out of his mouth.

Darlene drove like she did everything else: with efficiency and with little apparent thought for the job. She turned off the radio and said, I suppose you'll tell me what this is all about when you're ready to.

Well. I might. But I might not either.

When I threw Frank out I thought maybe I was done with this. What is it with men?

It's just the way we are, I reckon.

You got that right. You're all alike.

No, we arent. Thinking of Frank. Just that we share the same instincts.

She made a sound that was neither word nor curse and he looked and saw that she was crying and he'd never seen her do that before. Didnt know she had it in her. He looked out the window to hide the wetness that had sprung up in his own eyes without warning or accompanying emotion. I reckon the tree doesnt grow far from where the apple falls. If you want to turn it around that away.

Is it going to be Toby next? How long till I have to get out of bed to go get *him* from jail?

No. Toby's a good boy. You dont have to worry about him.

That's what I thought about you. She snatched the paper he'd signed off the console and read without her driving showing any signs of inattention: Assault on a police officer. Resisting arrest. Open alcoholic beverage container. Operating an unsafe motor vehicle. Operating a motor vehicle without a valid driver's license.

He wanted to tell her it could have been worse. If they'd found the gun. But he wasnt clear nuts yet. Just 99 percent. It's just bullshit.

Yes. That's exactly what it is. The paper was crumpled when she tossed it onto his lap. This is my son's role model.

Could I bother you to run me out to get my truck? he said when she slowed to turn toward his house. It's out past Crupp's Creek. Alongside the road.

No, I wont. You can walk out if you need it that bad. Ten miles would do you good. Give you time to think.

Please, DeeDee. I never got a chance to lock it up.

If you think anybody would steal that rusted piece of iron you're even crazier than I thought.

It's not the truck I'm worried about. Lane looked away so he wouldnt have to share her reaction. My pistol's in there, and it's loaded.

She loosed a visceral sound barely audible and whipped the wheel hard onto Lane's road and said nothing else on the way to his house. Then she spun gravel against his shins when she pulled away.

Well. Hell. Lane let himself into a house that felt not much different than the place he'd just left.

•   •   •

Do you know who it was that came by while Deputy Ferguson was cuffing you? Phil McKevey said. He didnt look like a lawyer with his ragged-necked sweaty T-shirt and shorts. Called away from a softball game. His big Dodge Durango throbbed with power as it almost imperceptibly slid up through the gears.

It was that old couple used to have the gas station where the Citgo is now.

The Yosts?

Might be.

They're stand-up folks. They'll say how it was. In my opinion you dont have much to worry about. The assault charge is bogus, and the rest of it is just window dressing. A man cant walk home just because he lost his wallet.

I wasnt worried about it.

Cutting off my own business isnt something I make a habit of doing, but by morning you probably wont even need a lawyer. If Dick Trappel doesnt throw this one in the round file I'll be mighty surprised.

I'll pay you anyhow. For taking me out to get my truck, if nothing else.

You watch getting home. Ferguson would love to stop you again. And dont drive again till you get your driver's license replaced. That advice wont cost you a thing.

That might be hard advice to follow. How do I get down to the Department of Motor Vehicles without wheels?

Surely you have someone who can take you. Your son? Or your daughter-in-law? Dont you have any friends?

Lane looked out the side window. Wondered how his life had deteriorated to the point where he had to call a lawyer for a ride to get a truck.

Oh, come on, Lane.

DeeDee's not too happy with me right now. And Frank and I havent spoken in years.

McKevey said nothing.

Lane probably wouldnt have either, had it been the other way around. It's not as bad as it sounds. Just a temporary situation. Just till one or the other of them died, he thought.

All right. How about the mall? You want to pursue anything there?

No.

Are you sure? Most people who trip and fall and hit their head on a curbstop cant wait to get the lawsuit underway.

No. We wont do that.

Good. It's my job to ask. But I'm glad you're not the type.

That dont have a thing to do with it. I never went to the mall. Not even close.

McKevey raised his eyebrows and looked hard at Lane.

What I told the deputy never happened. The part about falling down didnt.

Uh oh, McKevey said and slowed without braking.

Lane figured it a response to his revelation that he'd lied until he looked ahead and saw a sheriff's department cruiser backed into a side road not a half-mile from his pickup. Keep going, he said. Dont stop. When they passed he couldnt tell whether Deputy Martin noticed his presence or not.

You cant drive your pickup home. They're waiting for you to do just that.

There's something in my truck I got to get anyway.

This other stuff you're telling me, I'd just as soon not hear. Not unless I need to at some point. When they were around the turn, out of sight of the cruiser, McKevey braked and pulled the Dodge nose-to-nose with Lane's pickup. Like a sleek dark moose nosing a roadkilled and mutilated calf.

Lane got out and checked for traffic and extracted his pistol from the slit in the seat and without unloading it stuffed it in the back of his pants. Thinking McKevey hadnt seen.

Huh uh, Phil said when he opened the door. That thing's got to be in a case.

I dont have one for it.

The lawyer rummaged in the backseat and brought forth a sports jacket. Wrap it in this. At least it will be covered. And there damn well better not be ammunition in it.

Lane popped the clip out and put it in his pocket and worked the slide to show there was nothing in the chamber.

Shuck them out of there. Every one of them. If it's going in my vehicle.

Lane slid the shells out one-by-one from the clip with the edge of his fingernail till the follower showed in the end and he showed it to the lawyer and put it back in the butt of the pistol. McKevey took it and wrapped it in the jacket and placed it in front of the console in plain sight. That's where it's got to be, he said. It's the law.

Whatever. I didnt say anything.

I ought to be bored for the simples to have any part of this. Whatever it is.

Wait a minute, Lane said. He jogged back to his own pickup and took the two-by-four from the bed and carried it back to McKevey's Dodge and slid it into the backseat.

McKevey turned in the seat and looked the board up and down and reached back and touched the tuft of Lane's hair caught under a splinter.

You think we might could go, Lane said. I'd just as soon not be sitting here if Martin should decide to mosey this way.

McKevey started the engine and made a U-turn and accelerated back the way they'd come. That—he nodded at the two-by-four—is the curbstop you mentioned in your arrest report? The one you fell and hit your head on?

Dont it kind of look like one to you?

Jesus, McKevey said.

As they passed Martin again, Lane kept his head turned toward the lawyer, as though they were talking.

You want to tell me what you're into here, Lane? I'm not a defense attorney. If you're fixing to need one of those, I can hook you up with one.

No. There's nothing I've done going to make me need a lawyer.

Then tell me what it is. What you *are* into.

Lane thought for a while. Phil, I dont know. But I can assure you that I've not done one thing wrong. That's the God's honest truth.

Then why are you filing a false report to the police? And for the record, I wish you wouldnt have told me you did. Unless you're going to tell me everything?

Lane thought back to the way Martin had looked at him when Deputy Ferguson had brought him cuffed into the station. How Ferguson had mashed him down over the desk to unlock the handcuffs. Like he was fixing to cornhole him. How the blood roared back into his fingers when the cuffs came off. It just seemed like a good idea at the time, he said.

After a while McKevey smiled, and then he laughed out loud.

You going to let me in on it? Lane said.

Lane, you're how old?

It's not as old as it looks from where you're at. When you get here, you'll think you're a young man yet. Though he didnt himself.

Anyway, here you are after all these years out playing Rambo. You either got to laugh or cry, one.

It's the way we're made, Lane said. Fearsome and wondrous and demented to the marrow. There were probably folks laughed at Auschwitz. At Calvary.

.18

he unlocked the door of the baitshop. The smell. Nightcrawlers at
the wrong temperature. He'd only been gone for eight hours or so,
but it didnt take long for that smell to emerge. Something piney
accompanying it.

His first thought was that he'd left the refrigerator door open but
the door was closed and the residual cold inside would last a long
while.

The sound. Or lack thereof. The aerator in the minnow tank was
silent.

Lane stopped at the end of the counter and attempted to comprehend the mess on the floor. Currency and coins and earthworms
tramped indiscriminately among black peat and pieces of Styrofoam
cups. Like hogs had rooted it up from some subterranean level Lane
hadnt known about. The stink of urine. Tracks of it wandered out
from under the counter. Black rivulets like dirty searching fingers.
The extremities of earthworms writhed still attached to their flattened
portions.

Lane stepped back to the door but Phil McKevey was already

accelerating down the road. Lane slipped a round into the .22's chamber and stood very still and listened. For breathing not his own. For the small sounds of another presence. When he'd gathered a modicum of certainty that he was alone he loaded the magazine and slipped it into the pistol's butt and stepped across the mess to the minnow tank.

When he lifted the stainless steel lid the smell of industrial cleaner assaulted him. The gallon bottle that usually sat in the bathroom floated on an oily slick with hundreds of dead shiners. Lane closed the lid softly, as though not to wake them.

He leaned back against the tank and contemplated a new world with tired old eyes. Or perhaps a tired old world with new eyes. If there was a way to differentiate, he couldnt grasp the concept. After a while he opened the lid again.

Lane reached over the counter and retrieved the phone so he wouldnt have to wade through the mess but he saw where he'd already tracked through the streamers of peat and urine. As careful as he'd been. He dialed two digits of the three and put the receiver back in the cradle and said, Let's think about this first. Not go off half-cocked. As though there were another way to accommodate life. As though life might adjust its methods and procession to accommodate him. He recalled the look on Martin's face when Lane had called him Boob.

He leaned over the counter and looked again at the mess on the floor and saw that papers from the cardboard box where he'd kept the pistol hidden were scattered there too. The empty box tossed to the side. When he stood his vision slipped a cog and he held the counter hard till the dizziness passed. His stomach churning again.

There's enough mess here, he said. Dont be adding to it. When he could feel the floor under his feet again he slipped the pistol under his belt in the small of his back and fetched a dustpan and a broom and a mop and swept the whole—money and worms and dirt and urine—into the cardboard box he first lined with pages torn from a Cabela's sale flyer.

As he was backing out the door to take the box to the burn barrel, NoBob Thrasher slowed and started to pass by and when he saw Lane in the doorway braked hard and pulled into the lot.

Lane turned to hide the pistol and waited. Wishing he didnt have his hands full.

NoBob stopped a few feet short and looked him over, head to toe, then back to his head. What happened?

I fell, Lane said. Hit my head. Not a lie. Just not chronological.

Where's your truck?

I got a ride home.

The hell. His eyes dropped to the box that occupied Lane's arms and his hand went out to one of the now-ragged and soggy bills that protruded from the dirt.

Dont, Lane said and pulled it away. It's been pissed in.

NoBob withdrew his hand but leaned closer to where the coins reflected in his eyes. You're gonna have to do one of two things. Either hide your money somewhere besides your mattress or outgrow pissing the bed. One or the other.

Whatever, Lane said. Not in the mood for it.

What's going on here, anyhow?

I got vandalized.

Kids? Or what?

No. I dont know. Lane backed toward the burn barrel behind the shop but NoBob hung right with him.

There's money in there. You aint going to throw it away are you?

I dont dig in other folks' offal.

Give it here, then. I'll hose it off and let it dry and it will be good as new. It wont be the first time I laundered money. His laughter was like a rusty spring shackle shifting under a load.

There's not but forty dollars or so in here.

Half a day's wages. Wont take me but five minutes to clean it. He took the box from Lane's hands and as though he'd taken away the ability to speak as well. Lane watched mute as NoBob set it on the bed of his pickup and reconsidered and put it inside the cab on the seat.

Dont be shopping here anymore. Not unless you pay with a check or with new money.

If you knew where all money had been you wouldnt touch it with the end of a twelve-foot flyrod. The bills in your pockets have laid on bartops and been puked on and in the pockets of them drunk enough to shit their pants and dropped in the urinal and slobbered on by AIDS-infested faggots and . . .

That's enough. Lane turned and went inside and NoBob watched from outside the screen. When did you start packin a pistol?

Lane turned to face the dark squat stump of a man. What is it you want?

I come to find out what all you stirred up in Cumberland that might fall on me when it comes back to earth. From the looks of things, it's even more than I figured.

Where were you all day?

NoBob's hair flared under his hat when he turned his head and spat. Dont be saying what I think you're saying.

Lane said nothing.

Dont stand there and look at me like you found me on the bottom of your shoe.

The hot churn in Lane's gut had given way to a very cold boiling. This traveling salesman spent the night at a farm, back during the Depression, he said. There was a two-hole outhouse and the next morning he was out there alongside the hired hand and when the hired hand stood up some change fell out of his pocket and went down the hole. The hired hand looked down in there for a while and then he got out his wallet and threw a twenty-dollar bill down the hole. The salesman said, What do you think you're doing? You know how long it takes even *me* to make that much money? And the hired hand said, I just didnt want you to think I was the kind of person would go down in there for thirty-nine cents.

Why dont you just say it right out.

Only one kind of person goes down a shithouse hole for money. All's left to argue is the price.

NoBob's eyes glittered like lumps of coal and he stepped inside the door. It must be easy to look down, sitting here in your easy-chair waiting for people to come give you money. He extended a palm rough and chapped and more an implement than an extremity. Try earning a living once. Pick up another brick and another and another till gloves wear out faster than your skin does and you dont need them anymore. Tomorrow just like yesterday. Or last year. Or thirty years ago. Earn your money a brick at a time, a penny a clip. Then you wont stick up your highfalutin snoot just because a boxful of money had a germ or two on it.

Like I said.

You stuck up prick. Some day you'll wake up and wonder why you're all alone in a world of umpteen billion people. But there wont be anybody will talk to you and explain it. That will be a hard day, Lane Hollar.

Where were you today, NoBob? While I was gone.

You saw where I was.

No. I saw where you were when I left. You were pissed. And now I've been pissed on.

You think I'm the only person pissed at you? What about your grandson? Or that deputy you give such a hard time to? Hell, what about your *son*? There's a hunderd'd like to do it. I aint got the time to wait in line.

Strange it never happened before, then.

NoBob shook his head as though frustrated at making sense to an idiot. Why dont you tell me what I can expect after today. And then I'll help you clean up. We'll go have a beer.

Nothing's going to happen. I'm done with it.

Sure you are.

All I've tried to do is the right thing. It's got me knocked in the head and arrested and vandalized and treated like dirt. Somebody else can do right from now on.

Thought you fell.

I did. But I had a little help.

Arrested. So you're done with it but the cops aint.

I got stopped with an open bottle in the car. No driver's license. Not one thing to do with what happened in Cumberland. I told them I fell.

So who busted your head?

Lane looked out the window and felt the fire go out of him. A fellow named Harold Bright. Works for Larson Henry.

What did you do to him?

I showed up in a pickup that he saw here at the reservoy. While he was drowning Billy Bean.

NoBob clasped his hand to his eyes and shook his head. And you're going to let that ride? Is this the Lane Hollar we all know and love?

There's not one other person seems to give a rat's kazoodie what happened. You know what I want?

I'd hesitate to guess.

For life to be like it was. Not twenty years ago. Like it was last Thursday morning. Before all this. He waved his hand at the mess that still remained. That's all I want.

I got no argument with that. What about that mule's ass you were all worked up about?

It's the most beautiful thing I can bring to mind at the moment.

NoBob looked Lane over as though for ticks. Friends aint plentiful enough that I can discard them just because they call me names. Treat me like dirt.

Lane couldnt detect ticks on NoBob either. What I said was out of line.

NoBob nodded. Let's see if we can get you hitched up to that mule again. He took up the broom and began digging in the corners Lane had missed with his first cleaning.

Did you do this, NoBob?

You think I'd trash your place and then help clean it up?

You didnt answer.

You didnt have to ask either.

After a while Lane removed the pistol from his belt and placed it on the sales counter and filled a scrub bucket in the bathroom sink. You take me to get my truck after bit?

It's what friends are for, aint it.

.19

of used vehicles like a fly looking for a place to light. He compared
a window sticker to the pickup to which it was attached and wondered if there'd been a mistake. Driving through the Charleston traffic had left him sweaty and with a headache. It didnt matter that
Charleston wasnt Los Angeles. The cars were just as thick. Just as
fast. And Harold didnt anymore know where he was going in West
Virginia than he would in California. Close to the river, away from
the interstate, he could still taste exhaust fumes, feel the crowdings
of the automobiles.

The salesman didnt come bounding out like a doberman from a
dog box but hung in the doorway of the trailer where he likely thought
Harold couldnt see him and watched with his dark wetback eyes.
Like Harold was the one wasnt supposed to be here. Hair trimmed
and all dressed up nice in khakis and a shirt and tie but underneath a
fruitpicker to the bone.

When it became clear that Harold was going to have to initiate
the conversation he picked his soggy T-shirt loose from his skin and
threaded his way through the vehicles and stopped where they could

talk but where Harold couldnt smell the shorter man if he stunk. Like some of them did.

You got some decent enough looking automobiles here.

Yessir. Did you find anything you liked? I like to allow customers time to look around.

It's a shame your prices aint as good as your vehicles are.

The salesman offered a shrug that seemed a natural gesture of every Hispanic Harold had ever been around. *No, Señor. We no cross el rio. We swimming, Señor. Por fun.* Prices are established by the market. And we generally stay under that.

Established, Harold thought. Like he'd been studying the English language. Where's Nickel at? He's the only one around here I ever been able to deal with.

The man's eyebrows humped like tomcats squaring off to fight. I beg your pardon?

Harold pointed at the sign over the car lot. Nickel. The man owns this lot. This establishment. Take that, he thought, if you want to throw big words around like Nerf balls.

Mr. Ballew? He doesnt *work* here. Never has.

Why not? It's his place.

Are you wanting to trade the Ford? I can help you with that.

Harold looked at his sister's car—a four-year-old Crown Vic that rode like a wet dream, that made Harold feel like a prince behind the wheel—with the same expression he'd give to maggots in his lunch-box. No. That junker aint mine. I just borried it.

The man's eyes lingered on Harold's bruised face. You wreck yours?

Harold nodded.

You looking for something similar? Along the same line?

That there's a old man's car. I'm a pickup man myself.

I'll show you what we have in stock.

Where you reckon I could find Nickel at? Mr. Ballew.

You are . . . ?

Harold looked around at the vehicles like maybe there was a clue there he'd missed.

Your name?

Aw. Bright. Harold Bright. Nickel knows me good.

He doesnt get involved in the actual sales.

It wasnt just that the man was a beaneater. It was the whole nose-in-the-air package that stirred Harold's mush. Well, the fact is I aint looking for an actual sale. I'm looking for Nickel Ballew, and he's going to be one high-brassed compadre if I dont find him. Comprende vous? Spika de English?

The dark eyes didnt change that Harold could tell but the light they reflected did. Like the day had gone cloudy, but the sun still beat down like a copper blanket. I dont know where Mr. Ballew is.

Hell you dont. Give me his cellphone number then. I'll find out where he's at.

I'm sorry, sir. That shrug again. We dont give that out.

You think he might be out at the golf course maybe? There'd been a set of clubs in the jumpseat seat of Ballew's pickup. I'm tellin you, man, you're gonna think your member is caught in a weedeater when El Jefe finds out I couldnt find him to tell him what I got to. And that you're the reason I didnt.

I dont know where he is. Do *you* understand English?

I seen a course just out the road. Is that where he plays?

What Mr. Ballew does in his leisure time is none of my business.

How many courses is there around here?

I'm not a golfer. I couldnt say.

Rage sat heavy in Harold's belly. Like he'd eaten hot bread right out of the oven. Tell you right now, Chico, one of these days you're going to wake up in the land of your birth and wonder how you could of been so damn immigrant. You'll remember this day, right here.

Indianapolis is not so bad a place, he said. The teeth were so white and shiny Harold could see the colors of the vehicles in them. Better than Dogpatch.

•   •   •

Harold made a wrong turn and found himself in a ritzy development, all the houses the same but different colors, and he followed a jogger with a nice butt for a block until she started glancing over her shoulder. He took a side street and found his way back to where he could see the golf course and from there made lefts until he spotted the entrance between two pressure treated posts. He parked at the far end of the gravel lot and entered the clubhouse and stood with his hands clasped in front while a skinny man in a calfpuke green pullover scheduled a lesson for a spindle-legged old man. Ten thirty, he said. Late enough for the cobwebs to be gone but before the heat kicks in.

The pro tracked the old man out the door and then turned to Harold. What you need?

I'm supposed to play golf with Nickel Ballew today, but I never wrote down which course. Or if I did, I lost it. Along with his phone number. He shook his head. It was one of them nights.

Everybody in the whole world had took up shrugging. What do you want me to do about it?

Does he have a time wrote down? When he could play? Harold knew the right word but couldnt flag it down.

The pro looked Harold over head to toe and then back at his battered head and walked over and stared out the window. You'd have to check with the starter.

Where would I find him at? Or her, he said when the pro's head turned around like an owl's to stare at him.

The same place you always do.

Well, hell. Harold combed his fingers through his hair till they hit the rubber band that bunched it into a ponytail. Nickel might still be at home. You probly got his number here. How about giving it to me and I'll just give him a ring.

What did you say your name was again?

Aw, the heck with it. I dont want to tie up your phone. I'll just run out to his place. He lifted his hand in a little wave and started to leave and stopped and laughed and shook his head. You know, I dont even remember how to get there now.

Somewhere inside the pro was another fruitpicker. Same eyes except blue.

You reckon there's anybody might could tell me? I'd dearly hate to miss my appointment with ol Nickel.

Like security cameras, the eyes set far back in a deeply tanned face. There's lots of things I hate, the pro said. He flushed Harold away and turned his attention to a young woman with bad acne who was entering the shop.

Dont be surprised if he cancels his membership, Harold said. He aint going to be a happy girlscout. Back outside in the heat he watched a bowlegged woman on the putting green and then turned his attention to a pair of teenaged boys at the driving range. Hooting and hollering at each other's slices and duckhooks. When Harold crossed the pavement they stopped and watched and one said something and the other laughed.

Close up the green grass was leprous with dry spots and frecklings of weeds. Like a cheap new carpet after a party. A little black man in dark pants and a striped shirt and a mashed-down-in-the-front hat lounged in the shade of a tree beside the first tee and Harold intuited that this was the starter. An old-fashioned cellphone, big and boxy, hung on his belt and endowed him with an official air that made Harold more polite than he was inclined to be. As Harold walked his way the little squinted eyes picked at him like crochet hooks. Hey, stud, what time is Mr. Ballew playing? Nickel Ballew.

The man slapped a clipboard against his leg and said, If his name aint on my list I dont have no idee. A faded little voice that matched his wardrobe.

Well look on there and see if it is.

It aint.

Harold hawked and spat over toward the proshop and followed its track and left without looking back.

He drove all around the area, and out of town a ways he found another course but one look at the vehicles there and he shied off. He could make an ass of himself on his own if he got that desperate for the experience.

Closer in he passed a bar and a craving hove up and he braked hard and turned into the lot and stepped inside and when his eyes adjusted, Harold realized he was in a black bar and though Ballew had some nigger in him it wasnt *that* kind of nigger or near so much and so Harold backpedaled out the door and spun away in a cloud of dust.

The search was corrupted now with thirst and he located another bar with clientele that looked more promising—high dollar shirts and expensive cowboy boots and fat black cigars—but he studied his own reflection in the mirror behind the bar and lost his nerve and his sense of place and stood looking around like he was a blind man who'd suddenly gained his sight and was finding the visual world one hell of a disappointment. He left without ordering.

He needed to get shed of town and his growing dread of what Ballew was going to do when he found out they hadnt gotten away with knocking the redneck in the head—*Ballew's* knocking him in the head—and he found again the interstate but the moment the city pizzled away in the mirror he was dry again and he glimpsed ahead at the next exit a lowslung long building in a gravel lot across from the tall Citgo sign and he turned onto the exit though he was going way too fast. The Crown Vic nearly brushed the guardrails but the antilock brakes snubbed it down like a bumblebee hauled down by a spiderweb.

From the worktrucks and multi-colored outside Harold could already see the interior in perfect detail: the ratty felt on the pool table, the jars of pickled eggs and beef jerky on the pitted bar top, the dim little naugahyde booths that smelled of spilled beer and ashtrays, french fries fresh and ancient stuck in the cracks, wifebeater shirts and workboots and ballcaps and tattoos. Ballew wasnt going to be there but the cold lump in Harold's gut was starting to fester and it was hot and he needed a beer to still the quivering that had started when the old man in the babyblue pickup had come looking for him.

He went in like he was in his own home without pausing at the door and found a place at the bar and told the girl, Whatever you got on tap.

She snubbed her cigarette in the kind of aluminum ashtray that tipped if you werent careful and she wasnt and she scooped the ashes off the bar and into her hand. We got Coors Light and Bud and Yuengling. Her body was young and tight but she had a hominy face and her eyes were tired and her hair had that fossilized quality barsmoke imparts. Pretty nonetheless.

Bud, he said and got out his bill clip with the whitetail buck on the side and slipped loose a ten and two ones and put the pair of twenties back in. The girl took the ten and brought back nine dollars. Making sure he'd have change for a tip.

The man two stools down was pugnosed but not from birth with eyebrows like busted milkweed pods though he was Harold's age and he wore a white undershirt crusted around the neck and armpits with dried sweat and his hands were coarse and white-cracked. The earthy smell of concrete stronger than the sweat. I can see by your outfit that you are not a cowboy, Harold said.

The cement man glanced at Harold and then again for a longer appraisal and said, Holy damn dude. What happened? Someone say shut up and you thought they said stand up? A voice like a can being crushed.

Harold's beer was tooth-cracking cold and yeasty and before it even hit his stomach eroded the fear that worked in his belly like potato salad too long in the sun. He grinned and said, That's about the size of it. When he gets out of the hospital we'll likely take the issue up again. If he still wants to argue. Harold lit a cigarette and blew smoke toward the ceiling. Somebody tell me where I can find Nickel Ballew, he said. The feller that's got the used car lot the other side of town.

What you wanting him for? the bartender said.

He come in here?

You a pool shooter? the cement man said.

I been knowed to sink a few.

You want to go a game? Already reaching for quarters.

No, no. Not just yet. Got to settle the trail dust first. He drank more of his beer and felt it nose toward his extremities. I got to get ahold of Nickel. Some lumpy stuff's comin down.

What kind of stuff? the bartender said. Her face and voice familiar with various types and particular brands.

That there's for me to know and for you to find out. Just give me his number and I'll tell him myself, sweetiepants.

Right, she said and started to move off down the bar and Harold didnt want her to go. Give me five of them Captain Jacks. I feel lucky.

She rammed her hand into the ten-gallon aquarium half-filled with the little bundles of tickets instead of water and brought out about fifty and counted out five and took his five-dollar bill and stood waiting for Harold to peel them open so she could count out more.

Harold tilted his head to keep smoke from his eyes and with a forefinger pushed the bundles into a line. The little clown faces pointed the same way. With his fingers outstretched over the bundles he went *Hommmmm* and trembled with psychic energy.

The girl looked disgusted and threw the extras back into the aquarium.

Naw, I was just fooling with you. I'm going to open them.

She ignored him and worked her way down the bar discarding empty cans and bottles.

With a single practiced motion Harold licked his thumb and grasped the center bundle and popped the seal and spread the three tickets inside just enough to reveal a flash of yellow in one. Yeah buddy, he said and replaced the opened bundle back in line with the others.

How much you win? said the pugnosed cement man.

I aint opened it all the way yet. But it feels good. Feels big.

Harold drained his mug and rattled it against the bartop and the girl returned in a rush and said, You do that again you'll find yourself on that list right over there. Push your mug out where I can see it's empty and I'll get it when I can. Dont be banging it on the bar. She pointed at a dry-erase board behind the bar with a long list of those barred from the premises. A permanent marker rested in the lip and Harold could smell it when he saw it there.

Get me another one and yourself and my buddy here, Harold said.

The cement man drained his mug and said, Thank you dude.

When she returned with the drinks Harold nodded at the list. Gosnells are either a rowdy bunch or there's a surplus of em in these parts.

They're not that many but ever last one's a ass-pinchin turdhead. She had either a mixed drink or a Coke and this time she took four dollars. Thank you, she said and started to move away again.

Me and Nickel Ballew has been around the horn. The things we done together. Breathy with awe.

Like what? she said.

If I told you I'd have to kill you.

She didnt smile. What's your name?

Harold Bright. Maybe Nickel's mentioned me.

Bright? she said.

Pick the lint out of your ears, sweetheart.

She worked down the bar again and ducked behind a curtain into another room.

This'n aint nothing, Harold said to the cement man and spread the leftmost bundle to reveal three tickets with black numbers and no clown face. I could feel it.

The man laughed. I can feel losers on about nine hundred and ninety-nine percent of em. Feelin the winner, that's something else.

Harold touched three fingers to the three unopened bundles and felt a winner inside though he couldnt tell which one it was. I can do it. I got the gift. Knew that he really did, and marveled.

You got a gift for somethin.

Harold looked hard but there was no malice in his face or voice. Just the scab-picking brand of boozy humor that Harold fancied he himself possessed. You aint had a good butt kickin lately, have you. Careful with his tone. A touch of grin.

You could teach a class in how to take one. Your diploma's all over your face.

Harold offered his mug for a toast and they touched and drank. Folks are the same everwhere, he said. I knew before I come in that this was a dandy place. People that aint got a corncob crostways in their tailpipe.

The girl returned. You still aint opened those Jacks?

I will. Harold straightened the line. When I get ready.

I havent seen that much foreplay in bed before.

Imagine that, the cement man said. Doin it in a bed. But I bet it could be done. Lots of times I used a pickup bed but not a regular one.

You know why women dont blink during foreplay? the girl said.

They dont? the cement man said. Mine's all had bags over their heads. Cept the one real pretty one that didnt have eyelids.

They're scared they'll miss it. That's why they dont blink. But the cement man had stolen the thunder from her joke, even if it hadnt been a tired one.

They's at least two winners in here, Harold said. I'm savorin the feelin.

She pointed to the single fully opened bundle. They got to have a picture. Not just numbers. Under the picture it says how much you won.

I peeled a million of em. I know what they go to be. Harold lit another smoke and then fanned the edge of the middle bundle and exposed the yellow glimmer inside. There's one. And I feel another one right over here. He squinted at the payout schedule taped to the side of the aquarium. This one feels like a twenty, but there's a hunderd in here. Maybe a double hunderd. I can *feel* it.

She reached high to a shelf above the mirror and Harold admired the bare skin where her top pulled up. She tossed a foil packet of Mylanta to Harold. On the house, she said.

What's that for?

To get rid of those feelings before they make a mess in your shorts. She laughed and the cement man laughed and he said, Dude, you done put me off enough. Let's shoot that game of pool.

Harold collected his beer and unopened tickets and change and carried them to a booth near the pool table. They flipped for the break and Harold won and his beer goggles were working, steadying his nerves and sharpening his vision. After a solid and a stripe on the break he ran two more before he miscued and squibbed the cue into the jumble he'd left at the end of the table.

Harold laughed inside at how the cement man made a bridge, a fist with a thumb sticking out the side like a beginner might do, and unsteady on his feet. We playing for anything?

Just a beer. The cement man closed one eye and stroked a long shot down the rail, easy and sure, and Harold's confidence disappeared down the hole with the ball. The man was slow and careful, parking the cue perfect for the next shot.

The door opened and closed behind them but Harold was intent on losing and didnt notice. The cement man glanced up and hurried his shot and the cue squirted off the rail funny and nudged the eight-ball from a group of three and into the side pocket. I got to go anyhow, he said, and threw two dollars on top of Harold's change.

One more, Harold said, but the man was gathered and gone and another, tall and dark, was squatted at the coin slots. Can just anybody play? he said, and a shot of ether, cold and startling, replaced the warm glow in Harold's veins. The bar suddenly so quiet Harold could hear the icemaker in the back room. Nickel, what you doing here?

The man peered across the table, squinting beneath the hanging light. Harold? Harold Bright? I'll be derned. He dropped the balls and gathered them into the rack before he stepped across to shake hands. What you doing down this way, son?

Let's slip outside, Harold whispered. I got something to tell you.

Let's shoot a game first.

This here's important.

A gold filling flashed far back in Ballew's mouth when he smiled. Nothing's more important than pool. Break em up, pardner.

Harold looked toward the bar but it had mostly emptied and the few that remained were ignoring the poolshooters with diligence. When he set up for the break Harold's hands were shaking and the shot skimmed the rack and barely loosened the balls.

That's the way I like em, Ballew said. Anybody can win on a busted-wide table. With each shot he pocketed one ball and picked another lose from the jumble and when the eight fell Harold loosed a breath he hadnt known he held. Relieved he didnt have to shoot.

Let's go see what's festering in your gut, Harold, Ballew said as he slid his cue into the rack.

Harold reached for his mug but missed the handle and it upset in a wash of beer that swept his tickets onto the floor. Aw no, he said and crawled over the seat after them.

Dont embarrass me, son. Ballew's fingers were like meathooks dragging him back to his feet. The bartender was there with a rag, sopping the table. I cant take him nowhere, Ballew said.

It happens all the time. Dont worry about it.

Ballew slid a folded bill into the hip pocket of her jeans. Thanks for the call.

Thank *you*, she said without checking to see what he'd inserted there.

Wait, Harold said as Ballew pushed him toward the door. Them tickets got winners.

Gambling's a filthy habit. Destroys the mind and cheapens the soul.

Harold was looking back when they passed through the door and cracked his elbow on the jamb and said, I'll be go to hell. Not about his elbow.

Come. Ballew didnt look back to be certain Harold trotted behind like a puppydog. He hopped up into his pickup and Harold hustled to start the Crown Vic and waited for Ballew to back out. The big pickup sat and idled and after a while the horn blew and Harold switched off the ignition and walked to Ballew's passenger window. The window came down and Ballew shook his head and said, Unbelievable.

What is?

Jump up here.

Harold climbed inside the pickup but left his heart in the parking lot. What?

The door locks popped down and Ballew backed out and before Harold could find the lock button they were rolling, accelerating down a narrow road that wound away from the interstate. Why'd you lock the doors? he said. The keys are still in the car and it's my sister's. She'll kill me if something happens to it.

The locks go down on their own when it's humid, Ballew said. Detroit junk. He pushed the button and the locks popped up but by then it was like an unlocked door on a submarine. Not a whole lot of use.

Harold stared backwards through the black glass as though he could see through the mountain, to the crew he knew were already stripping his sister's car.

Nobody will steal your car, Harold. These are good folks.

Hell they wouldnt. Harold was no psychologist but he knew one thing for certain about his fellow man.

What's burning a hole in the pocket of your heart?

Huh?

What's so important that you disturb my business and insult my employees? Scatter my name like tissues thrown out the window?

Harold watched his reflection in the side mirror and with some revulsion watched words spill from his mouth. We're in trouble. You are. Someone saw you kill that redneck. That old blue pickup parked at the water dam came clear up to Cumberland where I was workin. There aint another truck that color that I ever seen and it had that same dent atop the tailgate. I told you it was totally insane to kill him and I never wanted to. All I wanted to was to teach him a lesson but no, you had to knock him in the head and drownd him.

Ballew laughed like Harold had told a joke too raw for the company and not especially funny. This pickup that's looking for you. Did it have a driver or did it arrive on its own recognizance?

Smart-aleck, like Harold didnt know what recognizance was. I said it did. He came to Mr. Henry's warehouse and I lit out but dreckly here he come to where I was workin.

Did you ask his name? Smiling like it was a big joke.

I whacked him with a board. Someone comes looking for who killed the redneck I dont ask how the chickens is doing.

Whacked him with a board.

With a two-by-four. Not a board board. Wanting to get it exact. There wasnt no doubt what he wanted cause when I ran he took after me.

Ballew downshifted and turned up a gravel road that wound up a hollow, the rocky creek on Harold's side falling away as the road steepened. The truck lurched and bucked and the tires chugged in loose stones. What did he do when you whacked him with a board?

What you think people do when you apply a board to their heads?

Did he fall in a way that would indicate that he might rise again someday? Like the Christ? Or did his descent have a more permanent quality?

I didnt kill him. I aint stupid.

Harold, you're so contentious you even contest my thoughts.

I aint contentious either. I dont have clue one what you're thinkin.

That I can believe. Ballew commenced whistling as though Harold were talking to someone else and he was trying not to overhear. I wish you'd gotten the name, he said.

I never said I didnt. Harold opened the wallet he'd taken from the old fart's pocket. Lane Hollar.

Ballew steered with one hand, his arm jerking as the pickup bucked at twenty miles an hour on a five-mile-an-hour road, and took the wallet with the other and examined the picture on the driver's license and glanced into the money pocket. Where's the credit cards?

There wasnt none. I aint dumb enough to use no credit card.

Ballew flipped through the pictures—most of the man and a boy—then shifted in his seat and withdrew a small key from his pocket and unlocked the center console and tossed the wallet inside and shut it again.

Not before Harold caught a flash of something dark and metallic and the residue of his breakfast turned to water. I got to be gettin back or my sister'll have the law out looking for her car and she knows where I went. Ballew's plan as plain as a pubic hair in the butterdish.

Do you know the parable of the ten lepers, Harold?

Harold looked at him with dread. Jesus Christ.

Yes. Exactly.

Please let me out, Nickel. I wont tell nobody what you done.

Tell me about the lepers, Harold. He spoke like a preacher, loud and insistent, and that scared Harold more than the words.

I dont know nothing about no leopards, Nickel. Please let me out. I'll walk back.

They are not found that returned to give glory to God, save this stranger.

Harold was blindsided by the idea that there was someone else in the jumpseat and he started and whirled but there was nobody else there.

Ten were healed, but nine went their selfish little ways. Consumed by their mean-spirited little lives. *Where are the nine?*

Harold had kept tears from his eyes but not from his voice. Leopards dont even live in these parts.

In the midst of your suffering I was *there* for you, Harold. In your *pain* and *soulsickness* I was there to guide you. When you managed to get yourself caught with my little gift to you, before you did the job you agreed to do, *I was there.* To restore your station. His voice went low and still. Now you want to cast your pitiful sins at my feet. Not in supplication for forgiveness but to make them *mine.*

A lump of dread blossomed in Harold's lungs and seized them in place and expanded into his head and with no more thought than he'd given to breathing up till now he snatched at the seatbelt buckle and heaved the door outward and shoved off into space and watched the world rotate below him.

. 20

ON TUESDAY MORNING LANE CALLED DARLENE
instead of going over for breakfast and to get the boy. When she
didnt answer he said, If that's the way you're going to be. Picturing
her ignoring the phone. Talking to the boy over its ringing. Telling
him what a certified butthole his grandfather had turned out to be.

He drove to the baitshop and scoured and rinsed the minnow
tank and started to refill it and as he watched the water gurgle from
the end of the hose it seemed as though he were pumping time into his
life, not in a manner that would turn back the clock but would merely
make the days interminable without extending his existence. Like life
tended to do anyway.

After he'd turned away the second customer looking for minnows and worms he hand-printed a sign NO BAIT and stuck it in the
door glass.

Watching the water imperceptibly and inexorably rise in the stainless tank was more riveting than his life and when the door opened
and closed behind him he didnt look up but said, Cant you read? I'm
out of bait.

Yes sir. The voice small and dark and firm like its owner.

Lane turned and examined the boy and his tin can with its sharp, chewed edge where it had been opened with a pocketknife. Juan, am I ever glad to see you. How many you got for me today? Trying his best to say the name the way it should be said, soft and stretchy and fluid.

Nineteen.

You had a good night, dry as it is. How long did it take you to find that many?

The boy shrugged.

An hour?

Maybe six. Or seven.

Six hours? He did the math and tried to fathom finding an earthworm every twenty minutes. Fifteen cents an hour. You came at the right time, Lane said. I'm clear out of worms. Minnows too.

What happened to them?

They expired, near as I can tell. You know that word? Expired? Yes sir. It means they died. Why did they do that? All at once? They had a little help.

Why would someone kill a worm? Or a minnow?

Just because they can, I reckon. That's the usual reason the weak and the helpless get done in. It's the way of the world. Knowing he was preaching because he was alone and frustrated and had nobody to vent on. Or just because he could. Let me get your money, he said before he remembered that he'd dumped all the urine-soaked money into a Pepsi flat that had disappeared into NoBob's truck. That he'd spent what money he had left on a bottle of brandy that had deposited him at the jailhouse. Behind the paper towel roller in the bathroom was an envelope with five twenty-dollar bills—just in case someone tried to catch him unable to make change for a hundred—but he recalled the look of disdain the boy had given him when he'd attempted to overpay earlier. He looked at his watch. I'm going to have to run to the bank for change, he said. Could you ride along with me?

The big brown eyes examined Lane in a manner that made him distinctly uncomfortable. I'll drop you off at your place on the way back. Save you the walk, so you'd get home about the same time. Could you do that for me?

If you're not going to be gone long. There's garden work to do.

Do you need to call anybody? Lane pushed the telephone in the boy's direction.

No sir.

You do have a phone, dont you? At your house.

No sir.

Lane felt bad that he'd asked. He locked the baitshop door behind them and the boy vaulted onto the pickup's seat in a way Lane could but vaguely recall.

As they pulled onto the hardtop Juan said, Did Mr. Thrasher kill your worms?

NoBob? Lane laughed. Why would you think he would?

The boy shrugged and Lane remembered that NoBob was likely the boy's landlord. Satan personified. The boy sat still and Lane felt compelled to make small talk around the silence. You said your daddy milks cows. What's the other men at your place do for a living?

One works for a man that sells cars.

They were at the bank and Lane pulled into the drive-through and wrote out a check and sent it through the capsule and told the girl what he wanted and she sent the check back and said, You'll have to come inside, Mr. Hollar. We cant send coin through the container.

I forgot that, he said. I just forgot. He pulled ahead and parked as close to the door as possible. You want to come inside? Wondering if the boy had ever had occasion to enter a bank. If he ever would.

I'll wait.

Dont fool with anything. As though the old bare-bones pickup had much to fool with. Lane nodded at a man in a gray suit and disheveled hair smoking out his death sentence outside where he wouldnt take others with him. As he pushed through the double doors of the airlock he met Deputy Martin coming out and Lane recoiled as though he'd encountered a skunk.

Martin laughed. Mr. Hollar, he said and slapped a vinyl money-bag against his free hand.

Lane stood aside and found himself shut off in the cubicle with the man he'd least enjoy being shut in with. Smelled his cologne and breath, pine woods and coffee.

Martin paused and considered Lane's pickup. Who's that with you?

Lane felt under no obligation to speak.

You're hard up for friends. Unless you're hauling him to jail. Getting a head start on the system.

I'm not hard up enough to be cooped up with the likes of you. Lane tried to push past Martin but the shorter man didnt move and Lane found him to be like brushing past a whiteoak stump.

If you're still wanting to play detective, start in that nest of wet-backs. Find out what *they* were doing when your buddy got drowned. Except that would be like accounting for all the ants in a hill.

He wasnt my buddy. Just a human being. There's a distinction.

Between animals like you got in your truck and human beings, too. You'd do good to keep that in mind. Martin crowded Lane out of the way simply by moving in his direction and continued out the door.

Lane's voice trembled when he instructed a different girl on how to break down the check and she misunderstood his quaking.

Dont you just *hate* airconditioning? she said.

He didnt answer and when she'd counted the bills and coins she gave him a look that made mechanical refrigeration compara-tively warm.

•   •   •

At the substation that marked the unpaved drive to Juan's house Lane downshifted and slowed and asked the question that had been working on him. You said one of the men at your house works for a man that sells cars and your daddy works on a farm. Are there more than two men in the one house?

There were, the boy said. One is in prison.

Lane turned up the drive and the boy's face turned panic-struck and he grappled for the door handle. Let me out here. The road's not good.

Lane ignored him and eased up the potholed drive, one used so little that grass grew in the center. You mean jail, right?

Please. Let me walk. My mother wont like that you brought me home.

Lane hadnt considered that he'd get the boy into trouble. He stopped and held the boy by the shoulder for a moment. Tell me about the man in jail before you go.

Marcos was driving a car that had drugs in it and now he's in prison at Clarksburg.

Running drugs? Somebody from your house? Rearranging his images to accommodate the new information.

He didnt know they were in there.

That's a common enough defense, I reckon, Lane said. But the boy had opened the truck door and slid out and walked away without looking back.

Lane sat for a long time thinking before backing out the drive and returning to the baitshop but before he killed the engine he realized he still hadnt paid the boy for the nightcrawlers and he pondered whether he'd cause trouble if he went back now and decided not.

•　　•　　•

The farmhouse rotted in a grove of lightning-scarred maples that once were majestic but had gone as tired and fatalistic as the dwelling. The ridgeline sagged, the paintless siding was weathered and cracked, and the brick chimney had pulled loose from the house to threaten the garden.

The garden was large and dense and lush. Pole beans waved above eight-foot-tall sapling tripods and bright turquoise and pink strips of cloth tied five long rows of tomatoes to tall stakes. The corn was squat but already in tassel, and pumpkin vines crawled among the stalks. Squash plants the size of washtubs, a blue-green expanse of cabbage and another of purple-blossomed potatoes. Two women and an improbable number of children worked among the rows when Lane first came in sight, but by the time he'd parked at the end of the drive, still thirty yards short of the sloping porch, they had disappeared. Like bean beetles hiding on the underside of leaves.

The junk Lane recalled from being here years before—expired stoves and ruptured water tanks and a cracked bathtub and uncountable bottles and cans—had been collected into a pile far back in the trees. An application of weed killer would have turned the yard into a barren desert but all was neatly trimmed and a coffee can of flowers sat at each corner of the rotting porch steps. From inside the house came music, strange and lively, that died suddenly like an echo of the truck's exhaust.

Lane stepped out and a small man all sinew and skin like worn dark-tanned leather appeared in the open doorway. *¿Señor?* he said.

The boy, Lane said. I forgot to pay him for the worms. Talking loud and slow so he'd be understood. Juan.

The man turned and spoke and the boy appeared in the doorway.

The money, Lane said and fumbled in his wallet for a dollar bill. It's a nickel over but we'll call it interest for late payment.

The boy came down the stairs, skipping the second one down, and took the bill and gave Lane a nickel from his pocket. My papa, he said and when he did the man came forth and took Lane's hand in one made of rough-worked granite. Teeth white and straight and the faint odor of manure that never quite left those who worked with cattle. Not a smell of waste but of the earth.

Señor, he said again.

Does he have any English? Lane asked the boy.

Yes, I speak it, the man said.

The boy is a good worker, Lane said. The worms he brings are top-notch. Took good care of.

The man shrugged as though Lane had pointed out that the boy had arms.

You work on a farm? Wondering why the man was idle this time of day.

Yes. I milk the cattle. At 3 AM and 3 PM. He looked at the sun and Lane wondered if there was a watch or clock anywhere in the house. For Mr. Eberley.

Henny? Or Clark? Either farm at least five miles if you took a straight shot at it.

Yes.

Lane looked around the empty driveway. You walk that? Every day?

The man held up two fingers and grinned. Twice times.

Twenty miles to pull tits, he thought. Why dont you just stay over between milkings? That's a far piece.

Work is here too.

He was eating breakfast, Juan said. Sounding apologetic.

In the garden the women and children had reappeared without Lane's notice. One small girl smiled shyly at Lane and a woman said something low but sharp and the girl bent to her row again.

Lane felt corpulent and moneyed and debased. I best be going, he said. There'll be people wanting bait.

Thank you, Juan said. For bringing the money.

Thank *you*, Lane said. He shook hands again and tried not to look in the mirror as he drove away.

•   •   •

Not until he returned to the baitshop and saw the sign did Lane recall that he had no bait to sell and he wondered if he was losing his mind. All at once instead of the daily pilfering of old age. He sat in the truck and compared his own sagging building to the one he'd just left and was not gratified by his conclusion. The place was without warning too dank and rank and depressing to enter and he thought to go to Darlene's but he suspected he'd dirtied his nest there and was not up to making an issue of it. He looked at his watch but Rooster's was not yet open.

Lane rested his head on the back of the seat with his eyes closed and after a while he straightened and examined himself in the mirror and combed his hair with his fingers and started the truck and drove to his home. Feeling as he entered the house as though he were letting himself in the back door to hell.

. 21

WHEN LANE WOKE ON WEDNESDAY HIS HEAD
felt fresh-wounded and raw and not till the phone rang again did he
realize that his wake-up call hadnt been issued via a two-by-four. He
collected his bearings and what was left of his head and stumbled
out into the hall and looked at his watch and wondered who would
be calling him this early. Or at home any time.

Without the accompanying body, Larson Henry's voice was that
of a younger man's. Resonant with vitality.

Lane picked the phone off the table and walked till he was out of
cord, where he could look out the bedroom window at the sun breaking over the ridgeline. It's all right, he said. I had to get up to answer
the phone anyhow. Seeing no need to explain that it had been years
since he'd slept this late.

Lane listened and nodded and pictured the truth as a banjo string.
Once you put a kink in it, it never straightened again. There's where it
would break. Lane shook his head. Nosir. I havent seen Harold since.
I never even got to talk to him, Mr. Henry. After one look he lit out
like a bear with a bumblebee up his behind.

Lane wandered back to the little table and tore two pages off the calendar there to get it caught up. Nosir. That puzzles me too. Far as I know I never set eyes on him in my life. When I met him in your office was the first time and he didnt show any reaction then.

Because the monitor was black-and-white. And Harold didnt see the color of my truck till he went outside. But Lane didnt say those things. I came back to tell you what had happened but you were gone, he said instead.

If you say Harold has a sister I'll go along with it. But I dont know her. Sisters are notable for throwing fits, from what I've seen. But she doesnt have call to throw one my way.

He frowned and shut his eyes for a second and leaned against the wall. Yessir. William Bean was who drowned. And he was the one that gave Harold Bright a good thrashing. That's my opinion.

He listened some more and said, Yessir. Any intelligent person would call that an unbelievable coincidence.

Nosir. The cops are privy to some of my life but not to that particular event.

That's just the way I am.

Lane listened a long time before he spoke again. Do what you have to. I reckon the cops will be tickled to hear what you have to say.

He hung up the phone and considered driving down to the station to talk to Dick Trappel but realized the opportunity had passed. Once you had a polecat in the trap it was best to give it a chance to get loose on its own before you climbed in to help. Determine which individual lies needed fixing rather than light into the wrong ones.

The truth would realign without his assistance. Larson Henry would see to that. Missing people were difficult to ignore. More so than when they were around.

Lane looked up at the ceiling and sensed that there was someone there to curse but nobody to hear it if he did. In the bedroom he looked again at the clock but saw the disgruntled fishermen waiting at the baitshop. Lane not there. No bait when he did get there. Darlene already gone to the diner, again with nobody to watch Toby.

You're looking for reliable, he said to the empty house, buy yourself a Maytag.

Lane stood in the shower till the hot water ran out, and when he emerged felt no cleaner or dirtier than when he'd entered. Just twenty minutes older.

• • •

When Lane figured the breakfast rush was over, he drove to the diner. He stood in the doorway till he spotted Toby sitting alone in a corner booth. He nodded at Darlene and she turned away and slammed through the swinging doors into the kitchen.

Phyllis or Judy—he could never keep them straight—said, Sit anywhere at all, and he picked his way through the tables and chairs and sat across from the boy. Morning, he said.

Looking up from a *Vacation Guide*, the boy considered Lane's scabbed head. Does it hurt?

Lane touched the place and wondered if he shouldnt have bandaged it. Even if a bandage did make him look like a hypochondriac. Only if I breathe, he said.

Phyllis or Judy showed up at the booth and said, Coffee, hon?

You just as well tell Darlene to come out. I'm not going away.

I'll tell her. Sounding dubious.

Lane touched the boy's arm and he didnt pull it away. You'd just as soon I did that, I reckon. Quit breathing.

I didnt say that.

I'm done with the things I have to do. You can go with me now if your mom says you can.

I'll stay here. Toby turned a page in the magazine.

Lane withdrew his own arm and leaned back in the booth and

watched the boy till Darlene arrived with eggs and bacon and toast and a cup of coffee.

Is that what I ordered? he said.

It's what you eat. And you damn well better eat it.

Well. Lane picked up his fork. I thought you were mad at me.

I feed possums. Coyotes. Cant stand to see the most pitiful creature go hungry.

How you know I didnt already fix for myself?

Get real. She started to wheel away but Lane caught the edge of her skirt and held tight. I need a favor. Need you to run me to get my license.

Not now. I'm working. You drove yourself here. Drive yourself there.

Lane looked around the nearly empty diner. I could probably spring for what tips you'd miss while you're gone. Driving yourself to the DMV to get a driver's license isnt the smartest thing to do. They do have windows in the place.

Darlene looked at her watch. No way can we get to Clarksburg and back before lunch. When I *have* to be here.

They come to Parsons on Wednesdays. Down at the courthouse. We could be back in an hour and a half.

Darlene looked at her watch again and said a word Lane thought he might have misheard. Since he couldnt imagine a woman knowing it. That food better be gone when I come out of the kitchen, she said. Lane had already started on it when she'd looked at her watch.

•   •   •

Making up with Darlene involved about what Lane expected. While she drove and spouted blasphemy toward the entire Hollar line, all Lane had to do was grovel in the dirt and eat roadkilled crow feathers and all without salt and cut off his own gonads with a dull butcher knife and put them in her lockbox for safekeeping. Nothing serious.

The woman didnt have it within her not to forgive. If Frank would show up on her doorstep she'd forgive him.

Toby wasnt going to be so easy. He stayed in the car while Darlene accompanied Lane into the courthouse. She stood at his shoulder and didnt allow the bureaucrats that got their jollies making old folks' hands tremble get away with it. When they mumbled she repeated what they'd said and explained that Lane didnt *have* a photo ID because that's what he'd *lost*, was that so *hard* to understand?

The lady state trooper that took his picture said, Are you sure you want to be looking like that on your license?

Lane touched his head. People look the way they look, I reckon. His eyes dropped of their own accord to the innertube of fat that stretched the shirt creases above her waist. Sometimes you cant do anything about it. His license still had frost on the edges when he slid it in into his pocket, but it was legal.

•   •   •

Back at the diner Darlene kissed him on the cheek and her boob poked him in the belly and made him think thoughts he didnt care to think. Thoughts he hadnt fooled with for years. Till lately.

I was going to take Toby but he said he didnt want to come, Lane said.

He'll get over it. Another day here in the diner wont hurt him.

Three in a row, though. He must be madder than I thought.

Just two. Monday he threw such a fit about not going to Cumberland with you, I left the little bullhead at home. Then I worried about him all day. About what he'd get into.

You did? Lane always made a point of never showing surprise, but that one caught him with his guard down. You didnt get into anything, did you Toby.

Toby wheeled off without answering. Like kids do when their stupid old grandpap acts like a dork.

Nobody called, at least. So if he did anything he got away with it.

Lane tried to catch the boy's eye but it wasnt going to happen. Tomorrow I'll get you. You can watch the shop some.

No he wont, either.

Not by himself. I'll be around. All right, Toby?

The boy shrugged but Lane figured the bait was about right.

•　•　•

Lane drove the short distance to his home and looked at his watch and calculated when Dick Trappel would arrive. Despite Larson Henry's fears, Lane wasnt worried too much about Harold Bright. The way he'd been scratching gravel to get shed of the place the last time Lane had seen him, he was likely breaststroking across the Gulf of Mexico. Waving at the Cubans headed the other direction.

Lane misfigured Dick's arrival by a half hour but only because Dick stopped at the baitshop first. Customers were more than Lane was in the mood to put up with even if he had bait to sell. The porch swing was a good place to wait. How long it had been since he'd sat at his own house and relaxed, he couldnt recall, but suddenly it was the most pleasant undertaking he could remember. After a bit it felt as though he'd swung back through the years and if he went inside Mary would be fixing supper. Fried mush and brown beans and whole milk from a half-gallon jar.

Then the cruiser rumbled into the driveway and Lane blinked and understood with agony as sharp as the first that Mary was no more. That happiness runs in one direction only, like time, but pain operates under no such limitation. The shards would never ascend to the table and reassemble themselves, but the same plate could break again and again and again.

The sheriff parked beside Lane's pickup and stepped forth and straightened his shirt. His uniform was starched and pressed but he'd spilled coffee on his pantsleg and undone his appearance. Like one little housefly caught in the cheese on a twenty-inch pizza would. Howdy Dick, Lane said.

Mr. Hollar. He glanced around like the house had just jumped up out of the dirt and said, How much property you own here?

Four acres in this lot and a couple more in one that butts up sideways to this one. Enough to make my taxes high but not enough to do anything with. Lane spat over the porch rail. What can I do you for?

You can answer some questions. Down at the office.

Right here's the best place in the world to answer questions. Come in and I'll get you something to drink. Lane's arm had a notion to rub the knot on his head but he browbeat it into submission.

I want you in town. You best call your lawyer.

What's going on?

Just come.

The hard old edge Lane sometimes thought was gone rippled the surface. If you're trying to say I'm under arrest you got it surrounded but you havent hit it yet. You'll have to move in on it a little.

Dick slapped the handcuffs that hung on the back of his belt. Either come peaceably or I can hook you up.

When Lane came down the stairs the sheriff took a step back and tensed up like a dog with whitethorns in his stool but Lane was loose and easy and he saw the sheriff relax. Instead of stopping, Lane walked past, heading for his pickup.

Mr. Hollar. You stop right there.

Lane opened the door to his pickup and placed one foot in the cab and paused and said, Go ahead and shoot me if that'll make you happy. I've been cuffed and given a free ride in your cruiser already and I wasnt crazy enough about the experience to want another round right off. I'll see you down at the station.

Holding what he had, what little it was.

. 22

DICK TRAPPEL RODE HIS TAIL ALL THE WAY INTO
town and when Lane switched off the engine he was at the door.
Driver's license. Let's see it.

Lane passed it over and the sheriff glanced at the picture and
handed it back. Havent you been a busy little boy, he said. Come
inside.

The police department was old, corners rounded with layers of
paint, but it was airconditioned and clean with no smoking signs
everywhere Lane looked. Each one bumped his craving up another
notch. The sheriff directed Lane into his office and then disappeared
down a hallway. Till he returned the grit under Lane's saddle had
grown into a fullblown burr.

The sheriff was crisp and official again in unstained pants and
Lane wondered what kind of a person kept a change of clothing at the
office. He considered the clothing he kept at the baitshop and decided
it wasnt the same thing. You want to get Phil McKevey down here,
Mr. Hollar?

I havent done anything to bother a lawyer with.

All right, sir. Sounding skeptical. If you change your mind we'll stop and you can call him. The sheriff pushed one button on the phone and said, Martin, get in here. The deputy pranced in hardfaced and unsmiling and Lane loathed him at a gut level. Set there and listen, the sheriff said. When Martin had taken a chair along the wall the sheriff opened a folder and removed a photograph and pushed it across the desk to Lane. Can you identify this person?

Lane slid it back to the sheriff without picking it up. Harold Bright. A gofer for Larson Henry, up Cumberland way. He caught the little end of a fracas with Billy Bean a few days back and that's everything I know about him.

How did you come by that knowledge?

Billy Bean told folks and I heard it from them. And it's not classified information that Bright works for Larson Henry.

But how and when did *you* learn of it?

From Jodie Preston's girl. Sandy.

Where? When?

Lane thought. Seems like a week, but it was on Thursday. At Rooster's.

I was under the impression you'd given up drinking.

Lane shrugged. Impressions are personal and liquid things.

The sheriff leaned back in his chair and held a pencil by both ends like an ear of corn but his eyes never left Lane's. You went to visit Mr. Henry. Why?

Sounds like you know more about it than I likely do.

Deputy Martin leaned forward in his seat like a heavy dog testing the little chain that tethered him to the doghouse.

How often have you spoken to Mr. Henry?

I never saw the man till I went there. Lane scratched at the tuft of hair in his ear and shook his head and said, I'll tell it like it was. Regardless of how it sounds. I went looking for Harold Bright but I didnt even know what his name was. Billy Bean said he fought with someone that was running drugs into the school. Someone that worked for Henry. Since you didnt show much interest in what happened at the reservoy I went to see for myself.

The sheriff's eyebrows slid up onto his forehead. The autopsy showed what I thought. Billy Bean hit his head and then drowned.

I dont doubt that those two events took place. Just that they were self-inflicted.

They were, Martin said.

His blood alcohol content was point one two. Before breakfast.

For him that was sober. Lane bit down on his words and thought, If you dump your words out like a sack of groceries nobody's going to help pick them up.

After a while the sheriff said, On Monday the 11th you went to visit Larson Henry.

If Monday was the 11th I did.

The sheriff opened another folder. The same day you were arrested. With a busted head. Is that correct, Martin?

Yessir.

The sheriff closed the folder. The same day Harold Bright turned up missing.

I've known people to go to the post office and not get back for a week. Maybe he got the hankering for a drink. Some do.

There's reason to think otherwise. And that you might be involved in it. Seeing what all went on with you on Monday.

Lane shrugged. On Monday babies starved and wars were fought and incest occurred in the best of well-bred families. If you're going to insinuate I was somehow responsible for everything that happened on Monday, be comprehensive. He looked at Martin. That means throw it all in.

Those that laugh last . . . think slowest, Lane finished for him.

That's enough, Trappel said. Let's hear the details of your encounter with Harold Bright.

Lane crossed to the window and admired the parking lot. There's not much to tell. I saw him at Henry's warehouse and again at an old filling station he was redding out. We never spoke at the warehouse and when I got to where he was working he said he wasnt talking to me and lit out. That's the sum total of it.

What did you say to him?

Lane turned and leaned against the windowsill with his arms crossed. I never got a chance to say anything. He just took off running.

Why do you suppose he did that?

Maybe he's just the type to. Or has a guilty conscience. Maybe he thought I was Billy Bean's buddy.

Then you went to the mall and hit your head on a curbstop.

If Martin hadnt been perched like a buzzard on a fencepost Lane might have told it right, but he was so he didnt. What's the report say?

What did you buy at the mall?

I busted my head before I got inside and lost my wallet too. The last time I was in one of those places money was still a requirement. How it is now I dont know. I reckon it's still not appropriate to go in public places leaking brain matter from the head. Unless that's changed too.

The sheriff opened the first folder again. When did you last see Harold Bright?

Monday. Before that I never laid eyes on him, and I havent since.

The sheriff lifted the papers in the folder and from the back took another photograph and pushed it toward where Lane had been sitting. Who is this?

Lane sat and studied it for a long while. Memorizing the heavy-lidded eyes set incongruously in the chiseled features. Small ears nearly hidden in the dark hair long enough to keep the curl under control. The blunt slope of the nose in profile. Dont have any idea. Who is he?

The sheriff leaned forward. Eyes boring at Lane. You've never seen this man.

Nosir.

Does the name Nicholas Ballew mean anything to you?

Never heard it.

How about Nickel Ballew?

Nosir. I take it he's implicated somehow in Harold's turning up gone?

The name's come up. Harold told his sister that's where he was going. Took her car. The car's why she's throwing such a fit. He shook his head as though embarrassed about answering a question instead of asking one. When were you last in the Charleston area?

Charleston West Virginia or Charleston South Carolina?

West Virginia.

I dont know that I ever have been to either one. In fact, I'm right certain I havent.

I'd just as well question a stump, the sheriff said and rocked back into his chair and laid his head back and stared at the ceiling.

Martin, he said. Go apply yourself to that stack of paper on your desk. It doesnt appear that Mr. Hollar is going to be a wellspring of information this morning.

Deputy Martin got up and grinned at Lane and left without a word. Like a trained dog being sent back under the house. The sheriff sat without talking for a long while and that suited Lane. I remember when that little MG went under that coaltruck over on Cheat Mountain, Dick finally said. Tore that bald head off.

Yeah. Lane acknowledged it happened, not that he recalled the event or cared to.

You still hunt ginseng?

Not much. The boy dont care for it. He'd rather fish. Not Frank. Toby.

You ever take Frank out?

Frank and I never did much of anything together.

You and Frank are too much alike.

If I need somebody to tell me what a piece of crap I turned out to be I'll go take up with a woman. Or join a church. Lane leaned forward with his hands on his knees. If we're reduced to reminiscing I got things to do.

Humor me a minute. He waited until Lane sat back in his chair. I still get out sanging once or twice a year. Next year, after I retire, I intend to get out a lot. You'll see me out at the baitshop, too. My fish pole dont have all the limber wore out of it yet.

I intended a lot of things that never came to be.

The day that old drunk tore his head off, you stopped to dig a sang while you were carrying it out. Of all the things that's happened to me on this job, that's the one I remember best.

It was heavy. I had to set it down to rest anyhow. And I never cared much how things looked.

I wasnt being critical. I was envious of you. Thought you had your priorities right.

Your envy was misplaced. That head changed my whole life. People got to thinking of me just one way and sometimes I did things just so they wouldnt be disappointed. Sometimes I consider myself self-confident, but I'm likely not. Or I'd be what I was. Not what I was expected to be.

The sheriff sat up straight and zeroed the dark little gunbarrels of his eyes on Lane's. Just me and you. Off the record. Tell me something I dont know. Something that's the truth.

Lane glanced at the door where Martin had gone and licked his lips. Some records are more off than others. I told you what I know.

Everything?

Am I free to go or are you going to charge me with something?

The sheriff wooled at that for a while and his eyes softened a bit.

I seen that porch swing was in bad need of rocking when I got to your place. Needed the rust worked off the chains. He stood and took his hat from atop a filing cabinet and put it on and straightened the hair displaced by the brim and said, I'll walk you out to your truck.

Even in town the air smelled of cut grass and wildflowers. As they crossed the pavement Lane breathed it in and said, You like it here, Dick?

Best place I've ever been. The sheriff opened Lane's door and said, You ought to lock your truck. At least take the keys out. I could write you a ticket for that.

Lane got in and pulled the door shut and started the engine and lit a cigarette and blew smoke out the open window.

The sheriff leaned against the mirror. I make half as much money here as I could anywhere else.

There's not a soul here couldnt do better elsewhere. But then they'd have to lock their trucks. Unlocked trucks dont come cheap.

This Harold Bright incident happened in Allegany County. Maryland. Not my county and not my state. We dont have drugs and killing and organized crime and rape and prostitution here. I'd like to keep it that way for one more year. Then someone else can daddy it.

Lane switched off the engine. There's two ways to believe we dont have those things. One's to make it the truth and the other one is to stick your head up your butt like I have. Till now.

Dick rubbed his eyelids with the tips of his fingers. I dont like what you're saying.

You havent liked anything I've said since Thursday morning. Since something happened in your bailiwick you dont want to consider.

Now dern it, Lane. A proper autopsy was done on Billy Bean. NoBob and your grandson both told a different story than you did. The things you heard, they didnt. I personally looked over the area and there isnt a sign of foul play. Martin's been assigned to it fulltime and he's come up with flat nothing.

Martin's dirty.

No. You think what you want. But this is my department and I know what goes on in it. We're not some big-city elite organization, but we're clean.

Somewhere there's a god or a god's helper or a devil maybe whose only job is to shovel manure into a big fan, Lane said. We dont have any more control of where it lands than when. Sometimes we get splashed up in the middle of our backs where we cant reach to scrub it off. Where we cant even see it's there.

If you're saying my department is corrupt you better say it clear and to my face. And you better have some evidence to back it up. Not just some imagination that got twisted over in a rice paddy somewhere.

Take your hat off, Dick.

The sheriff stared cold eyed. Like Lane had requested he drop his drawers.

Just take it off a minute.

The sheriff removed his hat and ran his fingers through his hair and looked around like he was doing something he didnt want to get caught at.

That makes you out of uniform, I'd say, Lane said. Not that it makes a lick of difference. But it makes me feel better. Now I'm telling you something man-to-man and I'll deny every word if you decide to make an issue of it. Let me give you an alternative scenario to what you got inside on paper. Not that I'm saying it happened thataway. Just that it could have.

The sheriff nodded. You got the floor.

Let's say I went to look for Harold Bright and he ran off exactly like I said. Lane started to flick ashes out the window but dribbled them onto the floor instead. Just before he ran away, though, he lammed me in the head with a two-by-four. Instead of me falling down at the mall. Let's say the story was just that much different.

Dammit, the sheriff said. Sounding tired.

You know what that means?

It means you're coming back inside. And this time you'll call your lawyer whether you want to or not.

Elected officials are expected to talk stupid but that particular statement is beyond the call of duty. What it means is that Harold Bright was scared enough to assault me. The only reason for that is if I knew something could put him in a world of hurt. Like that I saw him murder Billy Bean.

What it means is that you've just become the number one suspect in Harold Bright's disappearance. People dont utilize a board on someone's head without good reason. And a person that gets struck with a two-by-four doesnt normally say he fell down and hit his head unless he's got something to hide.

How about when Lisa Gnegy shows up at the diner with another black eye? I know Gnarly smacked her and you know Gnarly smacked her but if you haul him in she'll swear she fell down the steps. She's got her reasons. But that doesnt make her a criminal by any measure that I'm privy to.

The sheriff put his hat back on and stood back away from the truck. If Gnarly turned up missing the same day Lisa showed up with a shiner it might.

Lane drew the last fire from his smoke and tossed it out at the sheriff's feet and said, Dick, I'll tell you square I never had one thing to do with Harold Bright disappearing. I dont know a thing about it, either. I cant say we've ever been friends but you know me good enough to know my stated word's as good as any sworn affidavit. And that's my stated word.

You said you never saw the people at the reservoir, and that they never saw you. So why would Harold Bright go into such a tizzy when you show up?

Because of this truck right here, Lane said and patted the outside of the door. It was parked at the reservoy that morning. You ever seen another one that color?

The sheriff pursed his lips and looked back toward the station.

NoBob lied. Maybe he's got reason to, maybe not. He's said what he's going to say. Toby was just confused. And mad at me for biting off the line when he had the biggest fish he'll likely ever have hold of in his entire life. He's but a boy. Lane held up one hand to still the sheriff's protest, then raised his index finger. Someone messed with Billy Bean's emergency brake; if you crawl underneath, you can see where the drums have been beat on to make them release. A second finger: The truck was out of gear when I first looked inside, but when we came back it was in. A third: There was no paddle in Billy Bean's canoe; it was still hanging on the wall when I took the canoe back to his place. His little finger: The tacklebox was his live bait box, all sinkers and swivels and whatnots, but the rod in the boat was a fly-rod. He closed his fingers into a fist. And Martin knew the last two. He was lurking in the woods watching me figure it out. And who was there at the truck while you and I were gone? You want more?

Is there more?

Yeah. My baitshop got vandalized. All my minnows and worms killed.

Why didnt you report it?

Because you would've sent the man I think might have done it to investigate.

Breaking and entering.

No. But everybody around knows there's a key under the rock. And one more thing. Where I told you I got shot at? I went to look for a shell casing. What I found instead was the butt off the kind of cigarette NoBob smokes. Not even wet yet.

That dont mean anything.

How many Sonoma butts you see around?

There's enough. This other stuff. You sure of it?

I am, but that doesnt help you much. You dont have but my word about anything but the brakes, and those dings on the drums could have come from anywhere. But they didnt. And since Billy Bean's up in smoke, you wont get anything there.

Will you swear to this in court? If we could get it there?

I told you going into this conversation, I'll swear I never said one word of what I just told you. It's over. Done with. Dick, you dont have any crime. Let the Allegany County sheriff look for Harold Bright. Maybe some good will come that way.

What are *you* going to do? In the meantime?

Not one dadblamed thing. I already stuck my dipstick where it didnt belong and it came back with something other than oil on the end of it. Got my head busted with a board for obeying my civic duty, and now you're contemplating arresting me for that. I'm out. Before this thing spills over onto my family. He started the engine and eased the shifter into reverse. Every now and again you screw up so bad you just draw a line through the whole thing and try your best to forget it. That's what I'm going to do. In the meantime, I'd recommend you take a good look at what Martin does with his time. And what might be going on in the schools you dont have the first clue about.

What goes on I know about.

Our parents figured the same thing about us.

I'll not create trouble where there isnt any.

Right off, I dont know just where that idyllic place might be. Lane backed out and pulled away. When he looked back the sheriff was stooping to pick up the cigarette butt Lane had discarded. Like that would keep the county clean. Dick straightened like an old man, rubbing his back.

Nicholas Ballew, Lane said. As soon as he was out of sight of the station he pulled over to the curb and found a pencil in the glove box and tore a corner off an expired registration card and wrote it down. Just in case.

.23

HAROLD LEAPED FROM BALLEW'S TRUCK, SAILING
out over the hollow like a bird of prey. He twisted his face away as
the ground approached and struck on his side and felt his shoulder
give and he was airborne again, legs and arms spun outward like a
ragdoll and he caromed off a tree and his face plowed into the rocky
ground and his mouth scooped dirt and vegetation but he was up
and scrabbling downward through nettles and Christmas fern and
rusted cans and broken bottles, over a worn-out tire and into the
creek. A great cork driven tight in his throat.

Behind him the engine roared as Ballew powered back in his
direction. Tires sliding in the gravel, the slam of a door.

Harold's shoes skittered on the creek's flat wet stones and he went
to one knee but pushed forward and up the far bank into a laurel hell,
pulling himself through the twisted black trunks, sliding on his belly
where he couldnt clamber over.

His breath came back in a rush and with it the pain he'd not yet
felt and he cried out and pushed forward and there was a deer path,
narrow and low, and he crawled along it like one of Ballew's leopards for half a football field, spitting out spiderwebs and blood from

a cracked lip. When he could go no further he collapsed and covered his head with his arms and waited for Ballew to come shoot between his fingers into his thoughts.

But when his breathing slowed to where he could hear again, the big engine still rumbled where it had been, and he could hear Ballew's voice low and coaxing, but couldnt make out the words. The note of the rumble changed and came closer and Harold realized he'd fled downhill like a wounded animal, like Ballew had known he would. Tires softly rearranged the gravel and he realized he was no more than fifty feet from the road. That Ballew would be looking straight down into his nest. *Valet, bring my brown pants*, Harold thought. *Not the red jacket that would hide the bloodstains.* Knowing he'd lost his mind.

The tire sounds stopped above him and the door opened and closed. Harold lay tight and still, barely breathing.

Harold, my man, fear not. No harm shall befall those who believe in me. But you have to trust me. Blessed are those who not seeing, yet believe.

Harold put his fingers in his ears to the first knuckle. When he removed them, a long time later, the forest was silent but for the chatter of a red squirrel and the tinkle of the stream.

•   •   •

When the hollow began to dim in late afternoon Harold sat up and inquired of his shoulder and felt where the collarbone was likely broken and spat away the sour syrup that gushed in his mouth. His cigarettes were smashed and broken and he threw them away and then found them again and took the longest piece and straightened it and lit it and smoked it in long trembling gasps. Wished it was a doob.

He drank from the stream and washed the worst of the mud from his shirt and jeans and then pissed where he'd drunk and followed the stream uphill, no damned animal he, half a mile to its head at a concrete-encased spring, cradling one arm in the other and limping as though it were his leg that had been damaged. Across an overgrown hayfield dotted with chest-high cedars stood a gray plywood-sided shanty surrounded by an aureole of bright junk. A battered Toyota pickup seeming merely a larger chunk. Smoke drifting from a crooked stovepipe though it was easily eighty degrees. Harold watched until dark, pinned to the earth with dread and indecision, till a dim light appeared in a dirty glass. As though his circuits had been energized by the same switch, he crept forward and looked inside the Toyota and the keys were there but he calculated the distance between where he crouched and where the driveway dropped over the hill's brink and the relative speeds of rifle bullets and Toyota pickups and his nerve drained away.

Among the junk he recalled a bicycle and on hands and knees he found it—a girl's bike with one flat tire—and when he'd nursed it to the top of the hill he pedaled down into the night, wobbling one-armed, grunting when the wheel found a pothole or an emerging boulder, finding the rhythm he hadnt used for twenty-five years or more.

When he hit the hard road he turned opposite the way they'd come, following the road more by feel than by sight. Occasional headlights sent him into the ditch with his hand over the bike's reflector.

Finally, three or four miles later, neon beer signs marked the windows of a roadside bar. He checked quickly for ignition keys and finding none chose the most decrepit vehicle in the lot—a Dodge Reliant with rusted fenders and a downslung front corner. One likely lacking proper registration and insurance. One not likely to be reported stolen, at least for a while. With a dime he unscrewed the rear license plate and cursed and tried the next car up in the parade of decrepitude, a salt-perforated Subaru wagon with plastic duct taped over the missing passenger-side rear window, and that one *did* have a spare key under the plate where every redneck kept one. He took the car out of gear and drifted it to the bottom of the hill before he started it in a rattle of valves and a cloud of oilsmoke.

Near Jane Lew he stopped for cigarettes and five dollars' worth of gas, and after he picked up Route 50 at Clarksburg ran with his lights on bright so he could see deer in time to miss them. The Subaru not likely to survive the impact. Just outside of Red House he traded tags with a Chevy pickup with two flat tires parked in a barnlot.

Harold parked the Subaru on the dark end of the WalMart lot in LaVale in a covey of similar vehicles and grunted as he worked the bicycle out of the back with one hand.

From LaVale it was all downhill to home.

. 24

ON THURSDAY MORNING LANE WOKE RESTED AND refreshed and flabbergasted that only a single week had passed since he'd crouched in the reeds. The commercial bait truck was waiting at the shop when he arrived with Toby, and they restocked the refrigerator with worms and dippered eighty dozen shiner minnows into the tank.

While the boy stood behind the counter and looked excessively proud and important, Lane burned trash in the barrel behind the shop. Walking around and around it to escape the smoke that anticipated his every movement. If he incinerated more often, the trash wouldnt be so soggy and hard to burn, but it was a job he dearly hated and he put it off as long as possible. Some day he'd die first and wouldnt have to fool with it. So far he hadnt been that lucky.

He could always haul it to the landfill, but he hadnt yet deteriorated sufficiently in morals or hardheadedness to pay to get shed of garbage. Nor would he dump it along the highway like white trash did.

He stepped back to listen to a loud exhaust from someone pulling into the baitshop's lot and fought down his urge to go take care of it. Let the boy do his job. As hard as the fence had been to mend, he didnt want to tear a hole in it right off.

Later that afternoon he planned on taking the boy fishing. He'd said nothing about Lester Kelso bringing in the muskie, but it was apparent the boy had heard from somewhere. If Lester was worth the price of a .22 shell, Lane thought he might put him out of his misery. What's the use? Toby said when Lane mentioned fishing. To be truthful, Lane agreed with the boy. Fishing wouldnt be the same, knowing the fish of a lifetime was no longer there. Another like it existed nowhere in the state. Or another of any size in the reservoir. Like Lane. The last of his kind.

Lane closed his eyes and recalled the weight he'd sensed for one brief moment on the line, his teeth on one end and the monster fish's on the other, the line an umbilical that made them one. He smelled again the mud and rotting vegetation, heard the ripples of the water in the reeds as he shivered. The flat bark of the pistol. The loud pipes fading away when Billy Bean's killers left.

His eyes snapped open and he looked toward the baitshop and dropped his stick and hurried around the corner and pulled up short at the sight of a tall black Ford pickup with a rollbar. An acorn caught in his throat as he peeked in the corner of the window.

Toby was behind the counter, laughing and talking to a tall gangly man in black jeans and pimpled ostrich-skin boots, a faded but clean and pressed chambray shirt. Standing loose and easy, jingling loose change in his pocket. The man in Dick Trappel's picture. Nicholas Ballew. Looking more of a black man than in the picture.

Lane inventoried his surroundings for a weapon and finding none pushed in the door. You all right, Toby? Getting himself close, in between the boy and the man.

Sure, the boy said.

He's doing a fine job, the man said. His voice slow and southern and with a touch of the evangelical. One Lane had heard before, if only briefly. Toby was telling me you got some monstrous big old fish in that reservoir. That you and he are fishing buddies. One doesnt go without the other.

Lane probed the face and eyes for evil and found nothing but warm pleasant amiability. We dont go out that much.

Ballew looked at the corkboard covered with pictures of people holding fish, most of Toby and Lane, and grinned. You must do daggone good when you do go, then.

We catch one now and again. What do you want here?

I was just driving past and saw the baitshop and it reminded me of when I was a boy. Probably been thirty years since I wet a line, but I recall it being restful for the soul.

Some say it is.

I read someone drowned out there a few days ago. I hope his soul is at rest.

I wouldnt know a thing about that.

Some of the warmth leaked out of Ballew's eyes. It's hard to even think about. Drowning drunk. Meeting the Lord with liquor on your breath might be an awkward moment.

We all got our own beliefs.

You know what I believe? He laughed at the look on Lane's face. No, no. I'll not give you a sermon. I believe I'll take up fishing. What all would I need?

Lane felt he was away off somewhere else, unable to affect or ameliorate what was happening though he was part and parcel of it. Like in a dream. It takes a raft of stuff to get started, he said. More stuff than I likely have on hand.

Ballew looked around the shop, inventorying the shelves' contents.

Lane considered the pistol under the counter and wondered if Toby had moved it again. Or if he'd even put it back where it belonged. You'd need a good rod. The ones I sell here are just cheap ones. For tourists and whatnots. My reels are the same way. Just junk.

You sound like you dont want me going fishing.

This reservoy is hard to fish unless you know it. With the weeds and all.

I like a challenge. Maybe the boy could go along. Show me how to do it right.

No. His mother wouldnt allow that. I wouldnt either.

I'd pay him well. The workman is worth his hire, the Good Book says.

Come on, Pap, Toby said. Let me go.

No, Lane said. His voice like the bark of a pistol. If there's nothing you want . . .

I'd like to buy a fishing license.

Lane looked out the window and tried to think of a reason not to sell him one and couldnt. He just wanted the man gone. West Virginia resident?

Absolutely. Almost heaven will do till time for the genuine article. Ballew looked at the form. I havent seen an application like this for a coon's age. Most everything's done by computer nowadays.

When Ballew was through Lane completed the vendor's section and tore off the license and handed it to Ballew. What kind of work you do in Charleston? If it's any of my concern?

Ballew's fat lips spread wide to reveal a glimmer of a gold filling somewhere in the back of his mouth. Used cars. He nodded toward Lane's pickup. You ever get ready to trade that old F-150 in, I'll give you a good deal. It's a right peculiar color, but I bet I could sell it anyhow. But it does stand out. Once you see it, you dont forget it again.

It's not ready to be traded yet. Lane's skin felt too tight on the back of his neck. You should fish somewhere else more friendly to one who dont know the place. Vepco Lake, maybe, up at Mount Storm. Or Randolph Jennings on the North Branch. Those lakes are better suited to someone that dont understand what's going on.

I'm not as much an outsider as you think. Got a business at Clarksburg, too.

Then Tygart Lake's where you should go. At Grafton. Close to where you are. You wouldnt have to come in here at all.

My newest lot's right here at Almont. Just opened it up.

Almont? The word jumped out of Lane's throat like a frog.

I'll be around quite a bit, so I best learn the place. Like you say.

I wouldnt have thought there's enough people in Almont to make an ice-cream shop go.

That's why you're not in the car business. Just like me. I hardly see how you can hang on here selling worms. But you do, I reckon, or you wouldnt be telling me how to run the car business. Just shows it's best to stay out of business you dont know anything about.

That advice goes both ways.

That is a certified fact. Ballew put the license in his pocket. I'll just take the license today. If I'm not mistaken I saw some tackle up at the garage.

I'll need paid for that.

Ballew picked up the wallet that had been left lying on the counter and when Lane's eyes focused on it he realized it was his own and his hand started out for it before he caught himself. That looks a lot like a wallet I just lost.

Ballew straightened and placed the wallet between them. Looks can be deceiving. The warmth gone from his voice. Oft times the crooked path seems straight.

Or crooked like it is. Crookeder. Bile in his throat at being bearded in his own den. In front of his grandson. Lane considered the contents when it had left his possession: a few dollars with no distinguishing characteristics; a driver's license he'd already replaced; a few pictures for which he still had the negatives.

Would you like to examine the wallet, sir? Before your unprovoked hostility exceeds my natural grace? His voice ratcheting up like a preacher's.

Lane calculated whether he could kill the man with fists and feet and teeth and whatever he might bring to hand and decided probably not but that he was ready to make a run at it, not sure he had a choice in the matter anyway, and he shifted his feet into a better position to get over or around the counter. What I want is eighteen dollars for the license. Then I want you out of here.

Do you fear God?

The unexpected question derailed Lane's move, and he suddenly understood that he wasnt afraid of anything, not for himself, that he was not brave but warped, lacking some essential element of humanity he couldnt recall or fathom. Right now I'd like to get my hands on Him, he said. Maybe I'd change my mind then. But you're not God. Get out of my baitshop.

Ballew looked at him for a long time, long enough for a car to pass with a toot of the horn, before the shine went out of his eyes and the tension from his face. You're a hard man. His voice normal again.

Life's a hard thing. A man's got to stand up and meet it.

Ballew peeled a twenty from the wallet and placed it on the counter and on top of it a piece of folded paper. Mr. Hollar, I wish you the best in your business. Hope other folks keep their nose out of it. Like folks should.

Out.

Toby, Ballew said. I get back up here maybe I'll swing out to Foxhollow Road and pick you up and you can teach me how to catch the big ones. I bet fish are just like folks. Just not so grumpy. They get old, they're smart enough to keep their mouths shut. Keep em out of a heap of trouble. Keep the faith, he said.

Lane started around the counter, but Ballew was leaving.

Bye Nickel, the boy said as the door closed behind him.

When he had gone Lane looked at the paper on the bill: a religious tract, made on a copier with misaligned text. Hell is an eternal price to pay for a moment's indiscretion, it said.

. 25

THE BOY WAS CRYING AGAIN BUT LANE DIDNT
care. Dont *ever* give your name to a stranger. Or where you live.
Lane slammed the pickup into second gear and slowed just enough
to make the turn into Darlene's driveway.

I didnt, Toby said. His face hidden in the crack between door
and seat.

Then how did he know it? Dont you lie to me boy.

He acted like he knows *you*.

Lane slid to a stop in front of the house and for a moment rested
his forehead on the steering wheel. You didnt tell him? Hopeful and
afraid the boy was being truthful. Did you ever see him before?

Maybe. The voice small and scared.

Where?

I'm not sure.

How'd you know his name?

When he came in he called me Toby and said his name was
Nickel.

Come on, Lane said, and by the shoulder led the boy to the house.
Not releasing his grip when the child squirmed. Darlene, he yelled

when he opened the door and she was there, her eyes big but her mouth set in a hard line. Prepared to be scared or mad as required.

What are you doing back already?

I'll be back soon. Right now I got to go to the sheriff's office. If anybody comes that you dont know, keep the door locked and call 911.

What's happening? she yelled at his back.

I'll tell you later, he said.

•   •   •

Lane threw the vendor's copy of Ballew's fishing license onto Dick Trappel's desk. This man just threatened me and my grandson. He's right here in the county. Driving a big black Ford pickup with a rollbar and loud pipes. There's the license number. His finger trembled where he'd scratched it down with a ballpoint pen.

Nicolas Ballew? Threatened you how? The sheriff looked old and tired and sick.

He was too smart to say anything straight out, but his meaning was clear. That if I didnt keep my mouth shut about what happened out at the reservoy he was going to hurt Toby.

Anybody else hear it?

Just Toby. Lane suddenly wondered what the boy had heard, whether he'd heard any threat at all. Arent you looking for him?

The sheriff shook his head. Not anymore.

What about Harold Bright?

Harold's home. The Allegany sheriff called and said it was all a false alarm.

He had my wallet, then. The one that was stolen.

I dont recall a wallet being stolen. Unless there was something you failed to mention. Other than what really happened on Monday.

Lane had more air in him than he could get out in one sigh but it contained little oxygen. Ballew's bad business. Pick him up before he gets away.

He's not going anywhere. Has a business up at Almont.

A used car lot. Almont couldnt support a donut shop. That's enough to know he's into something illegal.

Maybe I should investigate all the businesses that dont appear to do enough trade to keep at it. What time would be good for me to have a look at your baitshop?

That's different. I saved money all the time I worked at the lumber company. And I dont live high on the hog.

The sheriff pulled opened a lower drawer and cocked one foot on it and leaned back in his chair with his fingers interlocked across his belly. Close that door.

While he did, Lane glanced into a small office and at the back of Martin's head and fought the urge to plant his fist there. Dont trust your help? he said when he'd taken a chair across from the sheriff.

Martin's easily distracted. And he's got a raft of paperwork. Dick leaned close and lowered his voice. This is none of your business. I'm only telling you so you'll know we're watching Ballew.

Go ahead.

The Maryland boys are antsy. Ballew's set up right on their line, and they want to know what's going on with that car lot.

Drugs. That's what got Billy Bean in trouble. How about that name, Nickel? There's a drug dealer name if I ever heard one.

Word is he got that from jingling change in his pocket. The problem with the car lot is that he's selling a ton of cars. He brings cars from down south that havent been run in the salt.

Lots of dealers do that.

But Ballew's are cheap, and they're the right ones. Deep Creek Lake is all tourists and high dollar second homes, but there's still a passel of local folks live there. They dont drive Beemers and Escalades. More and more are in a Ballew Beauty. That's what he calls them.

Then hows come the Maryland cops are taking such an interest?

The lake area's had drugs for a while, but till lately it was what the tourists brought with them. For their own use. Now it's everywhere. In the construction workforce and the golf course workers and the down-home folks. Into the schools.

There you go.

Ballew has all his permits and licenses. Doesnt have a record. Had some juvenile trouble and later an assault and battery that he didnt start but it was with the wrong person so he did a spell in a county lockup. That's it.

Where's he from?

Kentucky, to start with. I got a buddy on the force down that way. He's a mixed-race reject that grew up in a foster home. The old man there beat him and quoted scripture while he did it. Hell and brimstone and pass the razor strop. One of those kinds of places.

What kind of a system they got, that would let that go on?

A lazy one, like bureaucracies everywhere, I reckon. The problem rectified itself. The old man got overcome with silo fumes. Somehow a pitchfork got jammed in the latch and he couldnt get out.

One of those.

One of those. Nothing was ever proved. Not that anybody tried too hard.

There's got to be something on him. If the cops are watching him.

Everywhere he expands his business—Charleston and Sutton and Clarksburg—drugs show up in a big way. Anybody else in the drug business either moves out or disappears. A few of his employees have been busted, but they take the ride. Dont rat him out.

He's not selling cars. He's peddling drugs. The cars are just to haul them in.

Maybe so, but some of the used car lots run into trouble when he moves in. I'd say he's serious about the cars too, along with the drugs. But until he screws up somehow, there's nothing I can do.

They sat and examined their feet for a while, then Lane stood and stretched his legs. Maybe you cant do anything but I can. If he comes around my grandson I'll kill him. You can know that ahead of time.

If you do, I'll put you in jail while the State's Attorney arranges for a longer stay. This isnt the Wild West.

No. There the lawmen had balls and some sense. Lane paused at Martin's door. You want this open?

Dick Trappel combed his hair back with his fingers. I'd as soon it stayed closed but it wont. So you'd just as well open it.

. 26

Bright raised his head from a plate of baked beans and half of his
just-eaten breakfast reassembled into a choking lump in his throat
and the balance turned to water and went directly to his bowels.
Those loud pipes were unmistakable.

He scrambled to the trailer's window and from behind a smoke-
and-grease-stained curtain watched the black Ford pickup ease down
his trash-strewn driveway, followed by his sister's Crown Vic.

The pickup pulled forward toward a horizontal doorless refrigerator and then backed around, headed out, and the Crown Vic
stopped where it had been. A short dark man stepped out of the car
and removed a swath of butcher's paper he'd been sitting on and wadded it and threw it into the refrigerator and then he climbed up into
the passenger seat of the pickup.

When the pickup swung around Harold saw that another
Hispanic was driving, not Ballew, and without further thought
he threw open the door and yelled at the departing vehicle: Hey,
you damn greasers, what you doing with my car? Then his brain
caught up with his mouth and he dodged back inside and clutched

his damaged arm with the other and tried to wrap sense around the returned car.

The phone rang. He stared at the dirty beige implement for fifteen rings or more and when he accepted that it wasnt going to stop he lifted the receiver and let it fall back into the hook and jumped when it immediately began again. He brought the receiver to his ear and heard not Ballew's voice but his sister's, tearing at his ear like fence wire dragged through a rusted staple. He listened for a long time, opening his mouth to speak every now and then and closing it again. Give me a break you old battle axe, he said at the first smidgen of an opportunity, I just walked in the damn door and I need any shit out of you I'll knock the top off your head and dip it out—not sacrificing momentum for breath—dont you know I got a broke shoulder, dont that mean nothing to you you self-centered whore, I'll bring it back when I can. The receiver chattered in the hooks and his jaw quivered with outrage and half-vented adrenaline.

The ringing commenced again and he jerked it up and yelled, Fuck you, you hear me, fuck you, and the third curse got cut off halfway and his voice was very different when he said, Sorry, Nickel, I thought it was someone else.

While he listened he stared at the wall, his thoughts like a wheelbarrow full of frogs.

My shoulder hurts bad, he said. It might be broke. Harold shrugged and clasped it with his free hand. No, I dont have insurance.

Because you was acting *crazy*, man. Talking about leopards and stuff. What would *you* of done? Riding despair like it was a freewheeling tractor going too fast to touch either brake. I dont know that much about the Bible, he said.

I dont want to do it anymore, he said after a while.

I know I did. But I'll give your weed back to you. Wondering where he'd get it.

Not when you got a broke shoulder, a deal aint a deal.

He shook his head. I dont care if there is more in the car. It aint the price I'm haggling over. I dont want to do whatever it is you want done. When he realized he was talking to a closed circuit he looked into the receiver and hung it up and went directly to the bathroom and retrieved from the top of the medicine cabinet the little that was left of the bag of marijuana Ballew had given him and rolled a joint, spilling grains into the sink from the quivering paper. He stood in the trailer's doorway and stared at the Crown Vic until the joint was gone and he'd swallowed the roach and only then did he venture out to the car.

The envelope was on the seat as Ballew had promised. Harold counted it and wished it were less, so he could return it, but more because he knew he wouldnt.

The interior of the car had been detailed and shone with Armor All and upholstery cleaner and the gastank was full and a new oil-change reminder was stuck in the upper corner of the windshield. On his soul.

Harold peeled off two of the bills and put them in his wallet and put the rest of the stack in his sock where it felt like a sweet potato. When he started the engine the radio blared a Bible message from an AM station and every button he pushed merely changed the voice, not the subject. He switched it off and turned and headed out the driveway, sensing that he was driving straight for the gates of hell but finding no sideroads or places to turn around.

. 27

away in Lane's mirror the churning in his stomach had given way
to hunger and to dread of facing Darlene again so he stopped at the
China Wok and shuffled along the buffet behind a fat woman with
glossy black hair and ankles too slim and shapely to support her
while he filled a Styrofoam takeout box. Embarrassed to be seen eating foreign food in public. Guilty for eating with so much going on.
At the register he started to pay and on impulse said, Hold on, and
went back to fill another. Then he drove to Jodie's with his stomach
growling.

A light was on back in the depths of the house, indistinct as a
candle in a cave, but this time the door was locked. Though he rattled
the door glass and went around to the side windows and peered in,
nobody stirred. It's me, he said. Lane. Wondering if that was why the
door was locked.

He considered assuming something was wrong and decided it
likely was but was nothing that would require an ambulance so he
left one of the containers on the doorsill and yelled, There's food here
for you, young lady.

As he backed out of the driveway he thought he saw a figure in the door glass but when he stopped it was gone. He pulled under a whiteoak that overshadowed the road a quarter-mile down and ate in silence but for the ticking of the cooling engine. When he bit into the egg roll, grease dripped from his chin and it hit his stomach the way the whiskey had but settled quicker. He tore open a packet of whatever was in the bag with the nameless items he'd dished from the buffet and stirred it in and tasted it and wished he hadnt but he shoveled away at what seemed like five pounds of rice. Wishing he'd have gotten more shrimp and less filler but he always felt like a thief when he loaded up on high-dollar dishes at a buffet. After a while the food got traction and he slowed and belched and rolled down the side window and when the rustling of paper bags and creak of tired seat springs had stilled, another soft, steady throb remained. One in Lane's good hearing range.

The sound of an engine idling.

Lane stepped out and cupped his hands to his ears and caught the flash of sun off glass through the trees behind him and a second later the uneven acceleration of someone backing up. Lane jumped into his pickup but by the time he'd started the engine and turned around only a cloud of dust remained where the other vehicle had been.

He drove faster than he was comfortable with to Darlene's and stopped short and backed into a side road and waited for five minutes but nobody came by. Lane felt both relief and dread when she opened the door.

She peered through a tiny gap between door and jamb. I've had enough.

Lane dug at his ear and said I understand how you feel.

Then go home.

Home's where your family is. You and Toby.

Go find Frank. Take your trouble to him.

Lane sat on the porch railing and hawked and spat. I came to explain what happened. Then I'll go.

I'm not sure I want to know, she said, but she opened the door.

Where's Toby? He needs to hear this too.

He needs to keep out of this. Whatever it is.

DeeDee, he's already in it. I've been trying to get him out. Or keep him safe till it comes to a head.

Sit, she said, and Lane took his usual chair at the kitchen table. She drew water into the carafe and dumped it into the commercial coffeemaker she'd brought home broken and Lane had fixed. I'll get him, she said.

The way Toby held back when she dragged him forth stuck Lane in the chest. Hey, Toby.

The boy stared at his feet.

That man in the baitshop means us harm. He talked from both sides of his mouth, but he was threatening us.

Toby slid into a chair and looked at Darlene.

That means he said one thing but meant another, she said.

All he wanted to do was go fishing.

You're not ready to accept it yet, but Billy Bean didnt drown on his own. This Ballew fellow and another one helped him along. Now he's found out we were there. It's my fault. Talking to the boy but apologizing to Darlene. The words hard to chunk out, unsuited for his throat.

Can I have some coffee, Mom?

See how you influence him? she said to Lane. She poured a half cup and finished it off with milk. If it stunts your growth dont come bawling to me. When she'd filled two more cups she sat across from Lane. Speak or forever hold your peace. Or maybe even if you do.

Lane studied the wrinkles around her eyes that he hadnt noticed before and then the rest of her pretty face and said, Frank is a corkbrained idiot to leave a woman like you.

Dont beat around the bush. Get on with it.

Lane sipped from his cup and found himself stalling. He swallowed the coffee and spit out the words. I'm certain Billy Bean had help drowning. We happened to be close by when it happened.

Darlene put her head in her hands and ground the heels into her eyes. Toby says different.

His mind was on a fish.

Today it wasnt. He told me what the man in the baitshop said. Nothing to get all worked up about like you did.

Like I said. He was saying one thing, but meaning something else entirely. Lane saw his reflection in the coffee and drank so it would go away. If I had it to do over I'd do different. If these people would leave me alone I'd look wherever I have to not to notice them. Just so they'd stay out of our lives.

The more we want something out the more in it comes. The other way too.

Lane swirled coffee in the bottom of his cup. I dont know what else to say.

Since the day I met my first Hollar my life's been screwed up.

Everything was perfect before that then, I take it.

Since Frank left I've been hanging on, making the best of it. Trying to keep the rug clean without anybody tracking more dogcrap on it.

What I tracked in, I'll clean up.

For that I ought to be grateful. Instead of caring about the rug to start with.

Rip Van Winkle said a woman's tongue is the only edge tool that gets sharper with constant use. You've brought blood, so ease up a bit.

Ask Deputy Martin, Toby interjected. He said the old fart's got one oar out of the water.

When did you talk to Martin? Lane's voice sharper than he intended.

Toby shrugged.

Darlene looked at the clock and took their empty cups and rinsed them at the sink. I have to go to work.

Let me watch Toby.

Are you nuts? With this going on? I'll take him with me.

Please, Mom?

The pleading in Toby's voice surprised Lane until he fathomed in the boy's eyes the endless hours at the diner, sitting on a kitchen chair or in a corner booth after the supper crowd departed. He'll be safer with me than with you half watching him at the diner. I'll keep him overnight. So you can get a good night's sleep. Or you could come over too. Not that I think you're in any danger without Toby being around.

Your track record on safety wont win no ribbons at the fair.

Well what do you intend to do if Ballew does show up? Give him a thrashing with a flyswatter?

Are you staying at the baitshop? Or are you going home?

We'll go to the house. There's work I need to catch up on, and he can play outside.

All right. But you better do a better job of keeping him out of trouble than you've been.

She kissed him on the lips, Lane conscious of her body contours. Of his own. Of his need and of his depravity.

• • •

The moment they headed home, Toby turned tight-lipped and cold, his enthusiasm for the idea of a night with his grandfather quenched by the reality of it. Lane tried to make small talk. How's it feel to be grown up enough that your mom lets you stay home alone all day.

Okay.

How'd you like to learn to pick the banjo? Lane said as they turned onto the hard road. Working the evening through his mind. Looking for common ground.

I'd as soon eat dead possum.

You dont like the banjo? Surprised.

I hate it.

What dont you like about it?

Everything. People make fun of you if you play one.

Who does?

At school. On the TV.

For playing the *banjo*?

Toby rolled his eyes.

What do they say?

Nothing.

Come on now. A big grin, from a good buddy. You have to tell me what it was they said.

That banjo players are homosexuals.

The hard small place inside Lane expanded to make him hard and small all over. You heard that on the *TV*? No doubt about it, the damned thing was going to the dump.

The boy nodded. On that movie.

Lane saw Burt Reynolds shooting the rapids in his canoe, the inbred albino hillbilly boy strumming the opening chords of "Dueling Banjos," the stupidest song ever composed. Those things dont really happen, he said.

The boy gave him a look that said he barely had enough intelligence to sustain life.

And Lane had been worried how much the boy knew about *girls*. Around here, I mean.

Again the look. They tell jokes, too.

About me? Or five-string pickers in general? Getting the distinction clear. Cutting right to the shaft.

Both.

Tell me one. Unable to quit. Not believing that kids talked about him, not disbelieving either. Since there werent any other banjo pickers around that he was aware of.

What do you do when the banjo picker falls out of the boat?

I give up.

Throw him his banjo.

He relaxed and felt the hardness diminish and his self regain its place. Nothing perverted. Nothing disgusting. He laughed with more feeling than he had. That's a good one.

How do you tell a banjo picker in disguise?

How?

He plays with his worm.

Here now, Lane said. Stung and perversely flattered that a joke had been expressly written for him and his baitshop. Knowing he had to have a talk with the boy and fearful he'd know less than his student. The buffalo were out when they passed the farm and Lane slowed to savor their hairy black bulk. Buffalo were almost extinct once, he said. After being so many you couldnt see the end of them.

The boy shrugged. Can I sleep in the tent tonight?

Lane weighed the boy's safety against his wants and found the result acceptable. I thought being out there by yourself gave you the creeps.

Not anymore.

Not since he was ticked off at Lane.

You going to set it up? Or do I have to do it?

I can do it. I'm not a kid anymore.

Lane ruffled his hair and cherished the way the boy shied away and straightened his bangs behind Lane's hand. When a fellow becomes a man he gets what he wants, I reckon.

Does that mean yes?

It dont mean no. But you have to stay close by the house. Where I can keep an eye on you.

Will Mom care?

What she dont know wont hurt her.

Toby grinned, the first Lane had witnessed for a while.

Evening was approaching and they rolled up their windows, spurred by some sensor common to their core.

.28

THAT NIGHT WAS THE FIRST SINCE BILLY BEAN
died that Lane slept well. While Toby set up the tent Lane opened
the bedroom window so he could hear the boy and the boy could
hear him and then he played the banjo for a while. Wondered how
the instrument had become such an emblem of inbred redneck ignorance. Why not the fiddle or mandolin or the hammered dulcimer?
What could you expect from an instrument you played with a hammer? The dulcimer, though, had acquired genteel respectability
while the banjo was as labeling as a wifebeater T-shirt or a chain-
drive wallet.

Bothered by the senselessness but more by the fact that he cared
what others thought. That caring, more than the banjo, likely what
made him ignorant and redneck. Not that he had any more frame of
reference than did a hog eating bacon.

In consideration of his audience he played Clementi's "Opus 36
in C-major" and "Somewhere Over the Rainbow" and what remnants of Pink Floyd's "Wish You Were Here" that he could bring to
mind. Instead of "Shuckin the Corn" and "Pig in a Pen" like an ignorant inbred redneck might. Suspecting as he played that these tunes

he considered modern and cosmopolitan would be viewed by Toby as emerging in the Paleolithic Period. Composed with a rock on a hollow log.

Like Lane had when his old man sang "Moonlight Bay" and "Red River Valley," nostalgic whiskey tears in his eyes as though before he'd become a drunk he'd done nothing but sit on the porch and sing Stephen Foster tunes. The memory drained the music from Lane or curdled it till he didnt recognize it as such so he put the banjo away and walked out to check on Toby's progress. Walking manly so the boy could see a banjo picker as one really was.

The tent squatted back in the woods in a swale where a good rain would wash it away but it was pegged square and tight as the mildewed canvas would ever be. Gamy and musty as a rubber boot containing a dead fish, its smell opened windows in Lane's memory he was careful to keep curtains over.

The boy sat inside like a hippie, eyes closed and hands palm-up on his thighs. If he'd heard Lane picking or seen him walking he was hiding it well.

When Lane said Yo the boy started and looked as if he'd been caught at something. What are you doing out here?

Thought I'd see how to set up a camp right.

Nowadays kids learned about homosexuals before they had hair on their balls but not to say thank you when it was called for.

No fires, Lane said. It's too dry.

He nodded and Lane reached in and ruffled his hair again and the boy didnt pull away.

When he'd zipped the mosquito flaps and re-stuck the duct tape across the tear Lane returned to the house and took a long hot bath and put on the pajamas he never wore and stretched out in the bed that had been Mary's. The bed her father had made for their wedding, from cherry that had grown on *his* father's property.

Sometime during the night Mary came to visit. Just like the song:

"Come Back to Me in My Dreams." Lane and Mary didnt talk, nor did they need to, but sat on the bed's edge holding hands, her head on his shoulder where he could smell her skin and feel the wrinkles in her hands. She knowing the words he needed to say.

Words he should have told her anyway, if only for the telling and the listening. When she'd been there he'd slid off to sit at the bar or to go fishing. When he could have talked to her. Then when she died he'd stayed home. When it was too late.

The phone was ringing and Lane could hear it but couldnt drag himself back enough to answer, or wouldnt, even when it ceased and began anew. Then it quit and he sat up wide-awake and stared at the phone, afraid it might have been DeeDee but lacking nerve to find out.

There was a number to dial that returned to the person who'd called but Lane had never had occasion to use it and couldnt bring it to mind. The longer he sat staring the less certain he was that the phone had even rung.

Now that he was awake, but with the past fresh on his mind, his boy Frank found a way around his defenses and gnawed at his thoughts like a rat inside the wall. A good boy all those years and then a good man and husband for more till one day he quit his job and walked away and took to drinking and whoring and gambling and likely stealing and cheating to support his habits though Lane didnt know any of that for certain. Only that he was gone.

Lane had been tough on his son. What doesnt kill you makes you stronger. But effects from that should have either manifested early or worn off when he got away.

Sitting in the middle of the night staring at a phone that wouldnt ring it occurred to Lane that perhaps Frank had grown tired of looking at the mule's hind end too. Frank, though, never failed to enjoy whatever he undertook to do. Another failing, Lane thought, an ambition killer if ever there was one. And if Frank and DeeDee werent as much in love as any couple after ten years of marriage, Lane hadnt noticed.

If Frank could break stupid without warning, why not Lane?

Maybe he already had.

Lane recalled the grandson outside and rose and shuffled through the familiar dark to the living room picture window and peered into the blackness and was reassured to see nothing. Then heat lightning flickered far off and Lane glimpsed his reflection superimposed over it, a microshot of himself sufficient to understand that it didnt match the one he was carrying of a tough old geezer who'd maybe lost a step and couldnt see to distinguish the color of a man's skin from two hundred yards and close up wouldnt care to note the difference. A good man running over with moral fortitude and tolerance and virtue and common sense. A man you could count on when the defecation hit the fan. A good ol boy who could get er done without making a fuss.

That glimpse instead revealed a lazy old loser in sissy pajamas who'd given up and didnt have the character to admit it. A man who'd allowed his mind and his body and instincts to go soft and wormy. A man who'd dug a foxhole just large enough to accommodate him and his grandkid and his daughter-in-law, then pulled down the lid and said to hell with the rest.

A man ought not to look at his reflection in the middle of the night just after he dreams his wife has returned to visit.

Lane felt Ballew's fat lips and dark skin eroding his unprejudiced nature, tasted it. A flavor he'd spit away in his youth that now returned with such intensity that he could smell it as well. And some part of him savored it.

Out beyond his reflection, amid the heat lightning but lower, down among the trees that surrounded the lawn, another small fire flickered and a fist slammed into his side as the glass exploded in his face.

.29

LANE LAY IN THE SHARDS OF BROKEN GLASS
and inquired of his side and groped for the sense of a world gone
horizontal and numb but not numb enough. His breath was sliv-
ered like the glass and as brittle and cut at his throat. His nightshirt
wet and sticky and the flesh beneath his fingers ragged and misshapen and not his own and the carpet against his nose all mildew
and decay.

His first thoughts were that Toby had somehow shot him, but
very close someone not Toby coughed and Lane rolled to his hands
and knees and crawled from the window, broken glass slicing palms
and knees. Air an endangered commodity. The porch step creaked
and glass crunched beneath a shoe and as he found the entrance to the
hallway the house shuddered and drywall dust sprinkled the back of
his neck and he knew not if he'd been shot again or merely flattened
by the sound.

Stay still, Toby. Stay where you are. Be quiet. Please be quiet.
Wanting to yell it, hoping Toby had sense enough to do it on his own.

Lane pulled himself up on a doorknob that he thought was
the basement stairs but was a hall closet that prohibited forward

movement and he regathered himself and discovered the proper door and dragged it open and the floor fell away and he slithered down the stairs and stars flickered behind his eyes as his head rattled against the worn yellowpine treads and hit the cinderblock wall at the bottom and he rolled sideways and found his feet.

Above him a gun sounded twice and glass shattered in the closet where he kept his liniments and rubbing alcohol and cough medicine and a door slammed and the one at the head of the stairs opened and the basement lights came on and his hands were not just sticky but red. They slipped on the knob but he wrenched the exterior door open and stepped out onto the moss-covered stairs and heaved upward against the rusted steel panels that covered them. They opened with a reluctant groan and he slipped through the crack and allowed them to fall shut again.

He was running, staggering on the uneven ground and his bare feet turned back toward the house without his permission and in the dark his hands groped for the great rough sausage of concrete he'd levered from the ground when the clothesline post rusted off, a useless foundation he'd torn from the earth but had never hauled away. It floated into his arms as though it weighted no more than a sack of potatoes and he fell with it in one mighty crash onto the doors just as light flickered between the steel panels. The panels buckled downward into the hole and someone below cursed and the gun bellowed again and light bloomed in a jagged circle beside Lane's arm and he was up and running away.

His head beginning to work. Knowing where he was. Knowing someone had come to kill him. Knowing where he was going, taking them away from Toby.

When he sensed the barbedwire fence ahead he slowed and waved his arms vertically to the fore till his pajama sleeve caught on a barb and he tore it free and felt his way to a post and using it for support vaulted the fence. He glanced back as a shadow detached from the front porch and he stumbled ahead in the cleared place beside the fence, stripping off his white pajama top as he ran and falling as he hobbled out of the pants and then running free with one arm in front of his face to ward off overhanging branches. Seeing more as his eyes accustomed to the black. Feeling naked and vulnerable in nothing but his boxers and glad they were dark-colored. Blood black on too-white skin. He eased onward through the night, seeing and hearing nothing behind. When the neighbor's dusk-to-dawn light showed through the trees, Lane stopped and felt amid the grass till he found a rock and he threw it toward the light and felt something tear further in his side. The rock rattled through branches close to the neighbor's house and the big redbone hound opened up like Lane knew he would and the chain rattled from the doghouse and now that Lane had created evidence of which way he was headed he turned and went back the way he'd come, ran back toward his pursuer until he dared go no further and slipped off to the side and lay facedown in the meadow with his thigh in a thistle but he didnt move. Believed he could hear blood gurgling from his wound above the bucksaw rasp of his breath though he knew it wasnt so. Almost immediately he heard cloth tear against a fence barb and Lane held his breath until feet swished through the grass and past toward the baying dog and when all sounds of passage faded he was up and moving back toward his own house. Stopping to listen behind. Hearing nothing but the dog.

He vaulted the fence again and tore his leg on a barb and slipped along the perimeter of the yard until the blacker shadow of the tent hove up amid the trees. A guy rope caught his ankles and he fell into the flaps and found it open and hissed *Toby* but the tent felt empty and it was. As he raced across the yard toward the house, his heart stuck in his throat, he heard a soft metallic thump—the closing of a door or an elbow against a fender—from the direction of his pickup and he veered toward the sound till the truck slouched up from the black, pale and formless. He jerked open the door and the domelight blinded him but not before he could verify its vacancy and he said again *Toby*, as loudly as he could without being heard and the only answer was the pounding of feet down the driveway. Lane was up and running, fighting with the knowledge that they had to get away, and his sanity forced him back to the truck.

Lane shuttered his eyes against the domelight and found the keys he'd left in the ignition and he pumped the throttle once and hit the starter and the engine caught and the truck bucked forward as he almost stalled it. Conscious of the wisdom of always backing into his parking place.

He hit the lights and far ahead was a pinwheel of fireflies, reflective patches on the boy's sneakers, and he gunned the truck after them, yelling out the window for Toby to stop. To wait. To come to safety.

As he drew close Toby dodged off into the roadside weeds and Lane slid to a stop where he'd disappeared and went after him, gravel like spikes being driven into his tender feet, goldenrod slashing at his face wet and cold as icicles and the boy cried out as Lane fell over him and gathered him like spilled groceries and hustled him back to the truck and rammed him up over the seat past the steering wheel and they were underway again. Lane looked in the mirror and saw nothing, no lights, no vehicles, and what could have been the roar of an engine starting could have been the thunder of his own heart.

The boy was down on the floorboards, whimpering, hands over his head and when Lane leaned to help him up he recoiled and cried out.

It's okay, Toby. It's all right. We got away.

In the instrument lights the boy's eyes shone like coals in a campfire. I'm sorry, he screamed. Just leave me alone.

• • •

Lane missed Frank's street the first time. If you could call mud and gravel roads through faded roundshouldered trailers streets. Lane had been there only once and then he'd driven past without stopping and now his mind looped and darted like a bat eating millers. Every trailer unique and homogeneous, every wornout vehicle, every overgrown yard.

Since he'd been past, Frank had built an enclosed porch against the front door that looked like an outhouse backed up to the trailer. Beside it a stack of garbagebags. A waterheater on its side in foothigh grass. A white Neon with a blue door and a dented red front fender. Bald tires. The smell of leaking propane. The trailer dark and abandoned-looking. From two trailers down came the shrill voices of those together too long to rectify their association.

Is this it? he said.

Toby peeked over the dash. I think so.

Lane steered the boy by the shoulder as he limped tenderfooted across the gravel and slipped onto the porch and leaned against the roughsawn board wall for a moment to stop his head from spinning and then beat with the heel of his hand against a corrosion-frosted screenless aluminum door.

From far back in the trailer's dark warren some small sound and movement and Lane waited and then banged the door again. After a while the porch light flared and revealed him bloody and nearly naked and disheveled. Open the damn door, Frank.

The door creaked open and Frank's unshaven face loomed in the crack and he looked at the boy and blinked and his eyes wandered across Lane and off to the side like he couldnt get them to catch hold. What do you want? He wore a pair of jeans and nothing else. Shorter than Lane and chest hair going gray but the stomach flat and washboarded as ever and shoulders as broad as the door. Like Lane once was.

I came over for a cup of coffee. Cant you tell? Lane pushed the reluctant boy ahead of him and past Frank and was startled at the trailer's interior neatness. A rack of books and a stack of CDs and a good sound system. Photographs of a steam-driven sawmill and of men building a bridge matted and framed on the wall.

The boy had eyes only for his father. Liquid and brown and piercing and Lane was grateful they were not focused on him.

You cant just come busting in whenever you feel like it.

Lane steadied himself with one hand on a worn recliner and said, Let's start over. Try something like, Hi, how you doing? Like anyone else would if you showed up at their door in their skivvies and gutshot and blooded and damn near killed.

Frank stared at the place on Lane's side where the blood had stopped running. Dont sit on that chair.

Mark off a place where it's safe to pass out and I'll wait till you go fetch a tarp to put down so I dont foul anything up. I'd hate that.

Frank slid a vinyl-covered chair from beneath the kitchen table and Lane sat on it and felt the adrenaline drain away as though he'd sprung another great leak. Like he'd been shot again, lower down. He bobbed his head toward the bedroom. You got anybody with you?

You had to bring your trouble here. To your favorite son. Get your grandson in it, too.

Lane examined for the first time the wound in his side and found it both better and worse than he'd thought. More ragged. Not as deep. Like he'd been winged by a brushhog.

You're bleeding on the floor, Frank said.

Give me a minute and I'll die and quit disturbing your evening. His voice found resonance with a pane of glass, and it whispered in its frame.

Frank looked at the boy as though for guidance and then he grasped Lane's elbow and raised his arm with the kind of roughness Lane associated with mule handling and peered closely at the wound and then at the cuts on his hands and at his bloody footprints and said, You always did think you were Jesus Christ. He disappeared back the hallway and returned with a bottle of rubbing alcohol and rolls of gauze and tape. He wet a washcloth with the alcohol and said, This is going to burn.

The vapors from the rag struck at Lane's nose and made his eyes water. I dont recall Christ getting shot.

No. You had to do Him one up.

Lane flinched at the fire that touched his side. I didnt come just for you to patch me up. The mess I'm in's not my doings but I can take care of my part by myself. But Toby's in it too and maybe Darlene.

Frank threw the cloth on the table. What does it have to do with me?

Toby and I witnessed a murder and now someone's tried to kill me. They'll be after him too and that will drag DeeDee in.

What does that . . .

Where do you think is the *last* place anyone would expect me to go?

Frank wasnt *exactly* like Lane. He said nothing.

Take the boy and Darlene away somewhere. Get them out of Dodge.

You got the nerve.

Lane reached over and picked up the cloth and poured more alcohol onto it and jammed it into his torn flesh and bit off his gasp. To ask you to keep your wife and son from getting shot? Maybe I should ask the welfare agency.

Frank looked at the boy and the boy back at him and whatever worked between them Lane had no label for.

Does Darlene know she has to leave?

Seeing how I dont have clothes I most likely didnt take the time to phone either.

Jesus wept, Frank said and went back the hallway and shut the door.

A dresser drawer slammed and shortly thereafter doors opened and closed and water ran in the bathroom sink and a commode flushed.

Lane worked what dirt he could out of his side and slopped

alcohol directly into the wound and cried out and slopped once more. A thin pink mudpuddle forming on the vinyl floor beneath him.

Are you going to die? Toby said.

Yeah, but not from this. The wound was bleeding again when he jammed it full of gauze and bit off long pieces of adhesive tape and fastened it in place. He turned his attention to his feet and his hands and found the wounds there deeper than he thought but superficial in comparison and wiped them with the bloodied rag and called out, You have any clothes I can put on? Something it wont hurt to bleed in a little.

Frank returned in a chambray shirt and ballcap and sat in his recliner and laced hightopped workboots and from a nail by the door took a worn leather jacket. Frank turned as he went out and said, Lock the door when you leave. Make sure. Everyone here's a thief. The door closed and opened again. Everyone. The door closed and the single step thumped under his boots.

Lane limped to the door and opened it and said, What about the boy?

A dog inside the next trailer barked twice and yelped and was still.

Frank stood with one foot inside the car and slammed his fist down onto the top among other dents. He got in and slammed the door and started his car.

The car door came open again and Lane gave Toby a shove and the boy was gone like a shadow running ahead of the porch light. Lane saw him reach for the shoulder harness before the dome light went off.

Take Darlene too, Lane yelled. She's in danger. The dread of what he'd just done—placed his grandson's life in the hands of the man he trusted least in the world—clotting in his throat.

Frank pulled forward enough to clear Lane's pickup and backed into the grass and swung around and accelerated out of sight.

Lane went inside and looked around like he'd waked from a dream of heaven to find himself afoot in Baltimore. Thirst struck at him unexpected and he took a jug of orange juice from the refrigerator and opened cabinet doors until he found a glass and filled and emptied it three times and felt sick to his stomach.

Outside the bedroom door he said Hello though he was sure he was alone. He located the light switch and studied the single cot along the wall and a desk covered with stapled texts and heavy books and a gooseneck lamp and a laptop computer. On the back corner a framed photograph of Frank and Darlene in a happier time and on the wall was a laminated picture clipped from a newspaper of Toby holding a largemouth bass. You parasitic asshole, Lane said and slid back the plastic curtain closet door and rummaged through its contents until he found a T-shirt that wasnt too baggy and a pair of sweatpants with enough elastic to take up the slack. With his pale skin covered by clothing Lane felt stronger. Or at least less vulnerable.

The clothes were clean and pressed and a dresser drawer was filled with socks and underwear neatly folded. Lane examined a pair of briefs and decided to stick with his boxers but took a pair of dark socks. He sat on the bed and pulled them on and felt the fibers grab at the cuts on his feet. Without white socks he felt vaguely ungrounded. As though he wore women's clothing under his own.

Fatigue hard and heavy struck at him and he lay back on the bed and closed his eyes for a moment and when he sat again he was confused and laden with the sensation of a vast amount of time squandered and lost. He struggled up onto his elbows and looked at the bedside clock and cursed it and himself and stumbled to the living room and picked through the shoes lined against the wall on a folded newspaper and found them too small so he took a pair of moccasin-like bedroom slippers and eased his feet into them and took one last look around a trailer he couldnt comprehend and went out into a night dark and liquid but already fading.

•   •   •

Lane idled along through the back roads and then onto a log road that deadended in a grove of white pines a half-mile from his house and followed an old fence that intersected the one he'd vaulted during the night. The sky was lightening in the east as he gathered his dew-soaked pajamas from the grass.

He squatted for a long time behind a chestnut stump and heard nothing but a cardinal singing as though it were full light and a pulp-wood truck pulling the grade on Peck's Hill and a cow desperately wanting milking and the rumble of his own stomach.

He slipped to the rear of his house and put his ear against the wall and listened again and could hear only the refrigerator. The compressor nearly shot.

The cellar stair cover caved in. A jagged tulip of metal where the bullet had exited.

He stood looking for a long time at the tent and cold seemed to radiate from the earth into his core. The canvas slashed into ribbons. The pillow gutted and its foam scattered like some horrendous perversion involving poultry had taken place here.

When he crossed the front porch he felt no further need for caution other than to watch for the broken glass. Just a sense that he'd been violated. The inside damp and foul and his feet and hands were afire and his side crusted and brittle and raw. Blood had leaked through the dressing onto Frank's shirt. Lane removed it and went to the bathroom and doubled a towel and with tape from the medicine cabinet fastened it over the gauze and poured Tylenol directly from the bottle into his open mouth and chased it with two glasses of water.

In the bedroom he discarded the pants and socks and as he was buttoning a longsleeved flannel shirt over his chest his fingers stopped and he stared at a whiter spot on the yellowed drywall amid the mosaic of photographs. Where the picture of he and Toby and a stringer of gold and purple bluegills stretched across the tailgate of his babyblue pickup had been.

He stepped around the bed to find the picture on the floor, not so much broken as ground into the carpet. Anger rose from it like smoke.

Gypsum dust from the bullethole in the hall wall freckled the little table where the phone sat. Lane listened for a dial tone and dialed Darlene's number and let it ring fifteen times and as he put the receiver down thought someone picked up.

Who is it? he said but he'd broken the connection and he heard the fear in his voice and dialed again and let it ring for five minutes without an answer. He threw the phone and watched it come to the end of the cord and keep going, the colored ends of the insulation snapping back at him like Christmas trees and bumblebees.

Frank, he said as he went out the door, you had for once better have done what you were supposed to or I swear I'll slit your bag and run your leg through it and make you run.

•   •   •

Martin rubbed heavy-lidded eyes and attempted to return from his nap. The station smelled of scorched, stale coffee and shoepolish and industrial pine cleaner. All right, he said. You've been shot. And your daughter-in-law and grandson are missing. I got that much.

Something's happened at her house. The place is busted up and there's no trace of them. Get the sheriff in here. I'm not talking to an idiot.

You ever been told you have a smart mouth?

Not by anyone your age or intelligence.

Martin stared at him for what seemed a long time before he picked up the phone.

. 30

FRANK SWUNG AROUND A WORN-OUT PLYMOUTH
Valiant parked along the road and with a clatter of cv joints and
squeal of padless brakes herded the Neon into Darlene's drive. Stay
here, he told Toby, and left the motor running and the lights on and
stood up onto the porch without using the steps and rapped on the
door and looked back to where his keys hung in the ignition. He
tried the knob and found it unlocked and opened it and said, Hello,
and amid the smells of home—of cooking and laundry and tobacco
smoke—he might never have been gone. He stepped inside onto the
rag rug and said, Darlene?

She stood at the mouth of the hallway in the dark, bisected by
headlight and shadow, wearing the same ragged-out robe she'd always
worn. Frank, she said. A volume. A voice galled and troubled and the
parts more than the whole. What are you doing here? Why have you
been nosing around?

I just got here. Get dressed.

It's five in the morning. I thought I heard you earlier.

Get dressed. Please. You're in danger.

Her one visible eye was a singlebottom plow cutting deep. Danger from what?

From whatever mess my old man's made.

Feet scuffled on the porch and he turned to see Toby silhouetted in his headlights. Headlight.

Darlene's shriek was visceral in the small space. Toby! Not yet making the connection between the boy and his father and when it came her eyes shot wide and she said, How did you end up with Frank? Words like bursts from a machine gun.

He got shot, Toby said, and buried his face in his mother's chest.

Shot? Shot? Dragging the boy toward the bedroom. What do you mean, shot? What's he talking about? Darlene said. What is he talking about? Everything coming in pairs.

Darlene, Frank said. We need to go.

The boy's face was buried in his mother's nightdress and showed no signs of emerging soon. I'm calling the cops, Darlene said and tore free from Toby but Frank caught her by the arm. We need to go. Right now, Darlene. We cant stay here.

Her fingers toyed with the ties of her robe as though she couldnt decide whether to release them or throw in an extra knot. She spun away and Frank followed her to the bedroom door and watched while she fastened a bra and spun it backwards and slid her arms through the straps. She hauled a sweater over her head and grabbed a pair of jeans from a closet shelf. How long will we be gone?

I dont know. But you dont have time to pack.

How bad is the old fart shot?

Not bad enough, he wanted to say. He'll be all right.

Where is he?

He was at my trailer but I dont suppose he'll stay there.

Is that where you're taking us?

This—Darlene's—the only place there'd ever been to go, an ideal always within grasp when the days got too lonely or the nights too long. Now that refuge gone. Or expended. No. Not there. We'll just drive away somewhere.

The dream of my life, she said.

He found the boy crouched in the corner of the hallway, his gaze fastened on the far end and for a moment Frank thought someone was there but it was just unfocused fear of what *might* show up there. Come on, he said and lifted the boy up and after a moment's resistance the smaller body clung to Frank's and the boy said Daddy and without knowing he'd moved, Frank's nose was buried in Toby's hair and some ancient undiscovered or newformed hymen ruptured inside him and all that he was gushed forth and was gone and he knew not himself nor this boy in his arms. Hardmuscled and tall and smelling of manhood while they trembled inside, still children.

Darlene was behind him and they crept to the front door and she gripped the closet knob and said, Do we need coats?

This close to escape he felt disaster looming like overhanging rocks already in motion. We need to get out, right now. She didnt recoil when he grasped her arm again, the blood and bones and skin pulsing with life.

He killed the lights and peered out and said Go and they swept together to the Neon and the boy got in but Darlene looked inside and said Good Lord and as though the car were insulted the engine hesitated and died and the lights went dim and Frank knew it wouldnt start for twenty minutes. Like it did.

I'll be back, she said. Get in my car.

Darlene, where are you going? Come on.

The keys. She reappeared in the headlight's dim yellow glare, headed back to the house. Dont go back, he yelled. Come on. The lights made him feel exposed and vulnerable and he switched them off.

Shut up and get in the other car, she said from the darkness, and the front door closed behind her.

. 31

BY THE TIME LANE AND DICK TRAPPEL ARRIVED
at Darlene's the haze was wasting away in the foreplay of a hot day.
Frank's car slumped and battered as a runover can. The keys in the
ignition.

Darlene's car gone.

The front door unlocked.

The inhabitants gone. All as when Lane had been here earlier.

Lane listened at the door but only the clunk of cubes in the icemaker testified to habitation. There's nobody here, he said, but the
sheriff unbuckled his revolver and drew it at the ready as Lane eased
open the door and stepped inside. DeeDee? Toby?

Lane pointed at the jagged hole in the drywall, at the entry closet's contents spilled across the floor. See? What do *you* make of it? he
said. I think something happened here. That someone was here that
shouldnt have been.

I dont know, the sheriff said. It dont look good.

They walked through the house not knowing what should be
gone and what should be left behind and found nothing to be right.

Lane imagined he smelled flesh and sweat and hate and lust and understood he sensed nothing but his own fear.

Frank, he said. Not knowing why he said it or what he meant.

.32

INSIDE DARLENE'S ENTRY CLOSET THE MAN shifted and pulled the warm robust fabric of a coat against his face, the way he'd done when he'd been locked in the closet as a child, and breathed of the delicate perfume lodged in its fibers that never matched the ugly women that made them. Then he smelled of a low-heeled shoe and recalled feelings though he had none now. No arousal, no contempt, no remorse, no love, no hatred. Tears streamed down his cheeks or felt like they did without cause or effect. Water from a rock in the desert.

Two feet away on the other side of a thin hollowcore door life lurched onward and beings grappled for twining amid sorrow and failure and waste and here nothing.

He felt for and found his pistol and smelled of the bore and put it in his mouth and tasted of the hard round hole and felt the rifling with his tongue and as he did the twisted weal rose anew within and he eased up hunched under the clothespole and grasped the knob and listened to the small sounds of life just beyond. A soft cough. Footsteps returning from the bedrooms. *Do we need coats?*

The presence of a hand on the other side of the knob and the bloodrage surged and with it life and the pressure against the knob was gone and he stepped forth and over the sights of the pistol watched them hurry down the walk to the wreckbattered junk that clung to motion with some desperate mechanical tenacity the man understood more than himself.

Or not. The engine faltered and died and the single headlight dimmed and after a moment went dark and the world with it. The rattle of a loose board on the steps and the door opened and the woman passed not a foot away in the dark and the gentle scraping of her hand against the familiar wall and the rattle of keys in the bedroom and when she returned he reached out for her but she was not where she sounded like she was, just the thistledown of her hair against the back of his fingers and she was gone like she'd never been. Like everything he'd ever wanted. Like everything he'd ever gotten only to find it fleeting and unsatisfying.

Headlights flared and the car backed away and the night returned harsh and crowded with the jangle of a phone like an alarm clock in hell that tolled eternal. He turned and buried his face in the coats and tried to find again the emotions he'd not quite grasped and found them gone as well. He stripped them hangers and all from the clothespole and flung them to the floor and kicked a hole in the wall and fled. Knowing what he fled rode with him. In him. Comfort small and knotted in the idea that he couldnt escape.

What would the hard old vet do now? A frisson of unease speared him as he recalled those eyes.

.33

the sheriff said, Not in here you dont, so he put it back but it stuck partway in and rather than fiddle with it he mashed it into the hole with his thumb. Ruining a couple others as well. You havent answered my question, Lane said.

Because he's my deputy. Because investigating crime scenes is part of what he does. The sheriff looking pale and old. Like sheriffs that didnt want problems but had them anyway looked.

The coon dont investigate problems in the henhouse. Not if you got any sense, he dont. Not if you nurse some affinity for the chickens.

Martin was on night duty. Right here.

Says who? Did anybody see him?

You did. Other than that, there's just not a regular parade of folks out that time of the morning.

When I saw him here it was a long time after the fact.

The sheriff shrugged. Lay off Martin.

You picked up Ballew?

We havent found him.

Are you looking? Like you're paid to do?

At the moment I'm sitting here catching grief from somebody that doesnt pay enough taxes to own a private sheriff to boss and insult. We swung by Ballew's lot in Almont, and I have calls in to Clarksburg and Charleston. But I'll tell you right now, we dont have any probable cause to pick him up. Not unless Martin finds something I couldnt see.

Martin couldnt find his bellybutton if the directions were tattooed on the head of his pecker.

Dont underestimate Martin. He knows what he's doing, and he's got more training than I do. The sheriff swished his coffee cup and a bit slopped over the rim onto his pants and he dabbed at it with his handkerchief. I've been trying to get the county to switch to coffee-colored uniforms.

Dont slop it around like that.

We all slop at something. Mine just as well be coffee. The phone rang and the sheriff picked it up and leaned back in his chair and listened for a while. I thank you for getting back so quick, Jimmy, he said. How's the girls doing?

You got to be kidding, he said. Last I remember they didnt come up to my beltbuckle.

I'll do that, he said. And you too. He hung up the phone and said, Ballew's in Charleston.

Lane looked at his watch. He's had time to get there. Five hours that seemed like five weeks.

He's got witnesses say he was there all night.

What kind of witnesses?

What kind of witnesses are there?

There's witnesses that saw what they say and others that say what they saw.

I dont know which these are. But they're what we have to work with.

I dont believe them. How about Harold Bright?

Harold is in North Carolina picking up vehicles for Larson Henry's lot. That will be easy enough to check out.

Larson Henry was at a birthday party in his honor, I reckon. Or giving a speech at the Rotary club.

Mr. Henry's not a suspect.

Lane leaned forward with his head in his hands and attempted to glue the world back together in some semblance of order. It's Ballew or Harold Bright. If not Martin. There's not another soul in the world would shoot at me.

There's been times I'd done it myself if I thought I'd get away with it.

Martin packs a pistol.

Dont even go there.

I want the bullets in my house checked against his pistol.

Martin's not stupid, and he's an officer of the law. Knows how evidence works. You just gave me a perfect reason why he didnt do it.

Somebody would have seen him if he was here when he said.

If it wasnt the weekend *nobody* would have been here. We dont have a *staff*. Two deputies and a dispatcher. She works eight to four, and when the Homeland Security money dries up she'll be back checking groceries. She's better qualified for that anyhow.

Martin's the only common denominator here.

What about me?

That's different.

Or the boy? Maybe Toby laid a couple of rounds at you. You said you been on his list lately.

Toby doesnt even . . . Lane bit off what he was going to say. If you dont investigate your own deputy, I'll get someone else in here to do it for you.

The sheriff picked a mic off a stand beside his telephone. Martin, he said, his lips touching the black grid like a lover's kiss.

The rattle of static. Yes sir?

Where you at?

Passing the Get-n-Go.

Get in here.

Two minutes.

The sheriff put the mic back in the clip. You can make your accusations to his face.

That a service you offer to every ordinary two-bit criminal you haul in here?

If there's an ordinary criminal I've never met him. Every one has his own little perverted twist. And Martin's not two-bit. He's a first class deputy. We're lucky to have him.

Folks will be tickled to hear they got a sheriff prefers to focus on semantics than crime. Parse a sentence while the electorate gets shot.

They wont have long to get worked up about it. This time next year Martin'll be sheriff.

Not if I have anything to say about it.

You'll have one say. Like everybody else.

Lane stood and walked to the window and watched through the slats of the Venetian blind as Martin pulled into the lot and got out and glanced at Lane's pickup and adjusted his belt and hat like he was headed into a gunfight. He's a cocky little turd, Lane said.

Anyone that age wasnt cocky wouldnt be much force.

Martin disappeared from Lane's view and almost immediately appeared in the doorway of the office. Yes sir?

Mr. Hollar here has a question to ask you.

It's not a question.

It will be now.

Where were you when I was getting shot? When my daughter-in-law's house was getting busted up?

Martin's expression went cold and blank with more contrast between his face and neck. Exactly what time was that again?

I dont know for sure. Two-thirty. Maybe three.

Right here. On duty.

Anybody see you here?

Martin looked to the sheriff. Do I have to put up with this?

For a little bit.

Are there any witnesses to your being here at that time?

Not to my knowledge. There's not much happens here at night.

You sleeping again? Dick asked.

Martin shrugged. Like I said.

Anything else you want to ask, Lane?

Did you do something to my family? Did you shoot me?

Martin looked at the sheriff. This is about enough.

If you did those things, just say so so he can sleep better.

Martin looked at Lane and his lower lip trembled and he spun on his heel and disappeared into his cubbyhole and slammed the door behind him.

There you go, Lane said. He wont deny it.

He'll shoot you but wont tell a lie. That the way you got it figured, Hollar?

I'm putting in a call to the state boys, Lane said. Someone that takes this serious.

They're already here. The technicians are out at your place and at Darlene's right now. Dusting everything down. Ferguson's out there too. Not that the state boys know any more about it than we do.

Lane's anger and frustration had gelled into hard cold rage and started to swing back the other way. He began to speak and felt the tremor in his voice so he swallowed his words.

You got anything else, Lane?

Not that's going to get answered here.

Hollar, the sheriff said as Lane started out the door. In my experience, folks sometimes have a tendency to help the law out a little bit.

The law around here could use help. From what I've seen since I've come in contact with it.

Helping the law is seldom a good thing. People tend to break it while they're trying to help. Then you'll find out just how efficient I am at prosecuting lawbreakers.

If you are you've done a good job concealing it.

Remember what I said, sir.

Some things are hard to forget, but anything that's run out of your mouth lately doesnt fall in that category. As he walked to his pickup he felt eyes tracking him like crosshairs in a scope. He started his pickup to drive away but as he passed by the office, Martin stepped out a side door and raised his hand and Lane's foot stepped on the brake even as his mind told him to run the deputy over.

What? he said out the open window.

Martin tossed a plastic bag onto his lap and Lane stared at it mute and frozen. Like it was a scorpion on his tallywhacker. Not a bag of dried leaves that Lane didnt have to smell to know what it was. That was in the boy's tent, Martin said. Thought you might want to take care of it yourself. Instead of us. Not put him off to a bad start like some have had.

.34

DOING NOTHING WAS KILLING LANE BUT HIS
only hope was that Darlene would call the baitshop if she was okay.
When customers came he shook his head and waved them away from
the door and let their insults bounce off and added some of his own.
The minutes dragged past and his thoughts were like a carpenter ant's
nest he'd dug out of the wall one time, black and churning and exuding the collective stench of a million tiny stinks. The phone dragged
him from wherever he'd gone and when he levered himself up from
leaning into the minnow tank his side was sore and burning. He lifted
the receiver and listened until Darlene said, Hello? Pap? Hello?

DeeDee, he said. Where are you?

It does matter, too, he said. Are you all right? He crossed around
behind the counter and sat in his chair and there he could still smell
urine and worms though he'd scrubbed it with bleach and he returned
to the front of the counter and pulled up his shirt and examined his
bandaging.

That's the stupidest thing I ever heard of. You dont have to pick
between me and anybody. And I can take care of yous again. Now.
He sat in the chair again.

Because I dont *know* what to say.

After a while he said, Well I'm glad you're all right, anyhow. But he said it too late, to a dead phone.

Lane put his head down against his knees and breathed the stink the same way one would pick at a scab earned in a barfight. For punishment.

Though he didnt hear the door he felt a presence and when he looked up Ballew was there.

.35

THIS AINT EVEN MY TRUCK, HAROLD SAID, BUT the Virginia state trooper mashed him against the rollback's bed and yanked his wrists to the small of his back and ratcheted a nylon cable tie around them. All I'm doing is driving it back up to my boss's lot. I aint never even had the spare tire off of this thing. He imagined he could feel pulsating heat from the flashing lights that pinned him against the car at a reststop on I-81 just north of Roanoke.

The words Harold had heard before—*can and will be used against you*—but this time they didnt apply to him because for once he hadnt done anything wrong.

What is it? one trooper asked the one who'd found the package hidden behind the tire.

Meth, I think.

I'm just a driver. Picking up a car for my boss. Larson Henry. You can call him and ask him if you dont believe me.

Yessir. We intend to talk to him as well.

Then Harold knew exactly what had happened. I been set up. Back at the reststop. Some greaser went running away from the truck when I come out. I thought he was trying to steal something. It aint no wonder I was supposed to stop there. Knowing now what the job was Ballew had paid him to do.

The trooper who'd cuffed him was big and black and pushed Harold ahead of him toward a cruiser. Harold recoiled from the pinkly hands. I wont hit my head, he said, but the big greasy palm set down on Harold's skull like a road-killed possum and crammed him down and in.

You should shut your flapper, the trooper said. So I dont have to remember in court what all you said.

This is a frame job, Harold said, but the trooper had shut the door and joined his buddies from the other two cars. They talked as though this was just any other day and one jabbed at the other and danced on his toes like they were boxing and they all laughed.

I want a lawyer, Harold said when his trooper returned.

Yessir.

I know who done this. It aint me they're after. It's my boss. I'm just a errand boy. Got nothing to do with the business. All I do is haul cars home. This here's the last time I do. You can bet your last bottom dollar on that.

The trooper laughed. How many bottom dollars does a person normally carry?

Huh?

Never mind. Just lean back there and relax.

The interstate spur into town was nearly deserted at this time of night and as they humped across the overpass and dropped into the downtown exits Harold felt like he was riding a boxcar into Auschwitz. Like once the cruiser made the exit there'd be no return. Not in this life. He looked for the door handles and found none and groaned and lay over in the corner and tried to think back to where he'd gone wrong and couldnt ever remember even *having* a choice. Much less taking the wrong one. It aint fair, he said.

Nosir, the trooper said. There's times it's not. There definitely is.

. 36

BALLEW STOOD STILL JUST INSIDE THE DOOR.
We need to talk, he said.

Lane glanced at the box containing rags and papers and pistol and tried to remember which way the butt pointed when he'd felt for it earlier. Pictured himself hauling it forth upside down with the barrel on the bottom. Or pointed back at him. We might be beyond that point, he said.

You need to disengage.

Disengage.

While you can.

Lane picked up the phone and dialed 911 and when Ballew had no reaction he put the receiver back into the cradle before anyone answered. I thought you were in Charleston.

A man is wherever enough people say he is.

Lane dropped his eyes to the box below the counter and grabbed the gun and when his eyes came up over the sights he was looking down the bore of Ballew's pistol. A much bigger pistol than Lane's.

The wages of sin . . .

Lane considered how many times he could shoot the man before the bigger slug stopped him and decided not enough and then who would look out for the boy and he put the pistol back into the box and when he looked up again Ballew's pistol had disappeared. You're being watched right careful, Lane said.

Yes. Disposing of you would be inconvenient at this point.

I'm just an old man in a baitshop. Disposal wasnt something I felt I was requiring.

You're a zealot. You wont be able to let getting shot pass unanswered.

A zealot. Nobody's ever accused me of that before.

One ruled by his beliefs.

And who said I got shot, anyway?

At some point you'll decide that I'm the one who shot you. Then I *will* have to.

And that would be inconvenient. While you're being watched so close.

Ballew shrugged. I didnt do it, or you wouldnt be here.

Who did shoot me, then?

Another shrug. I dont know.

So I disengage and after a while it gets a little more convenient and first thing I know we're reengaged only I dont know it till I look down and see an extra hole in me.

I dont know that you have a choice.

I have a lot of choices.

Not good ones.

Let's see. I know you killed Billy Bean. And you're going to say I cant prove it, and you're right. I can hound after it until I convince someone what happened, or I can seek out some justice on my own. There was a day I'd have had to do that, when I wouldnt have been able to let it be. When I was a zealot. But I think I'm past that. I'm not going to ruin my life trying to fix things I cant affect. I'm making that choice. On my own.

I stand corrected.

Dont think that if I ever get the chance to help put you where you belong, I wont do it.

Another shrug. Take no thought for tomorrow for the evil today is sufficient thereof.

You got that right. I could dwell on your wrecking my shop, too. Let it eat at me. Eat me up.

Ballew looked around the shop. What is wrecked?

You're the only one could have done it that wouldnt have taken the money.

A shop? Whatever.

Whatever is that it's my living. My property. But I'm going to let it pass. Not because I'm afraid of you. Dont ever think that. But because I just recently found out that I got a life to live. That's another choice I'm making.

Not a bad one.

You're small time and dont know it. That's my take. Back in Charleston you've hid out with the rest of the small time punks where the cops are paid off, but now you're stepping out here where real folks and honest cops are, and you're going to stand out some. My money says it wont be long till you're either laid out on a slab or looking through bars.

The steps of man are ordered by the Lord.

Your steps had better be going out that door right there. Before I change my mind. Before I do something stupid and you have to kill me whether it's convenient or not.

A soft answer turneth away wrath. Ballew paused at the door and looked at Lane not with hate or fear or malice in his eyes but with curiosity. Like a cardinal seeing himself in a windowglass. Say hello to the family, he said, and nodded and was gone.

Not until Lane carried trash to the burn barrel did he find the tract stuck in the door's crack. He burned it without reading it. Having endured all the Godly wisdom he could tolerate for the moment.

.37

time and relished the way his side felt when he did. Like he'd earned
the privilege. Despite the way Frank looked at him. Sitting at the
kitchen table where Lane always sat. Drinking out of Lane's coffee
cup. A new piece of drywall already nailed fast where the hole was
kicked in the wall, gray joint dope turning white along the edges
of the patch. Toby wiggled out of Lane's grip and sat across from
Frank and looked at him with the same kind of adoration he might
have given Jesus Christ if He'd have lighted there. Lane tried to
imagine the boy with a marijuana cigarette between his lips and
knew it never had happened, and never would. That Martin along
with everything else was a liar. He put it from his mind.

Darlene pulled back and examined his eyes and said, Let me see
where you're shot.

It's nothing to fret over. A couple of days it'll knit.

She pulled his shirttail loose and peeled back the adhesive tape
and touched off to the side where the skin was red and angry.

Lane didnt look. He already knew too well what it looked like
and it felt better when he didnt.

This needs stitching. And it's inflamed.

It's nothing to be bothering a doctor over.

You didnt let your insurance drop, did you? Aw, Pap, Darlene said when she saw the confirmation on his face. You need insurance.

I got the VA. If I need a doctor bad enough.

He knows what he's worth, Frank said.

Dont start, she said.

I'm worth two of you. More than two. What was I thinking?

Stop it. Darlene's voice had venom in it Lane hadnt heard for a while. She flattened the tape back against Lane's side. You'd better go.

You mean I'm not even welcome here?

Just for a while, she said. Till things settle down.

I came here to make sure you were all right.

How long's that take? Frank said.

Frank's here now.

Lane stared at his son and wanted to see a man that could protect his family. That could be depended on. Wanted to love him but could find no love for nor confidence in the man.

Pap, Darlene said. Meaning it was time to get out.

Lane speared Frank on his gaze. If you let anything happen to them, I'll have your family jewels for breakfast. If you have any. Whoever shot me was right here in this house. Right there in that hall closet. You cant count on the sheriff's department. They might even have done it.

Pap, Darlene said again and opened the front door.

He stood a few minutes on the front porch trying to fix in his mind the smells and sounds of DeeDee and Toby and their home but they were gone before he got to his pickup.

●　　●　　●

You wont be happy with this, the hardware clerk said as he scored and broke the sheet of Plexiglas. Not quite straight and not quite square but close enough, Lane figured.

You dont have glass big enough, and I cant wait for an insulated pane to get made. I got a hole in my house.

It'll scratch, and it's not clear like glass. I'm just saying.

Lane had never encountered a salesclerk as eager to talk him out of buying. There's nothing to see anyhow. Nothing I care to look at.

You wont be able to bring it back for a refund.

If I do I'll get some other clerk. So you wont have to fool with it.

He puttied the Plexiglas into the windowframe and spackled the holes in his house and rewired the telephone and swept and vacuumed the floor and sprayed Liquid Wrench and oil onto the nuts that held the cellar entrance to the foundation and when they surrendered to the socket he turned the steel canopy topside-down in the grass and with a knapping hammer beat the bullethole closed and the panels into some semblance of straight. Enough that it would close again. When he'd finished his side was leaking pale fluid but when he rebandaged it some of the red was gone from the edges and the sting wasnt as sharp.

When he'd finished he felt restored and sat on the bed and reached under it for the banjo. When he drew it forth the clunk of loose parts where there'd been none. He opened the case. The head a collapsed lopsided star, the neck broken and ruined in a tangle of strings and maple splinters. Belt buckle scratches now a jagged hole where a heel had smashed through the resonator.

His guts cold and plastic. Reshaping and hardening to accommodate a world that could accommodate this. He touched the tension hooks gone loose. A sliver of mother-of-pearl that jutted from the fretboard like a broken tooth. Then he closed the case and slid it back under the bed and when he stood again his eyes were damp. He again opened the banjo case and touched the ruined top, caressed the jagged splinters that had once been a neck. The banjo made a sound though he'd done nothing to prompt it. A death rattle. Or a promise. A threat. A haunting that made a hole in Lane he knew only one way to fill.

.38

and allowed his eyes to embrace the dim depths and when they had
he walked to sit where he always had at the bar. Larry placed a draft
beer in front of Lane and he took a long pull and dug for his wallet.
The beer a cold billet that warmed as it went.

I can spare a drink for a man's been shot, Larry said and pushed
Lane's twenty back to him.

How this stuff gets around is beyond me, Lane said.

From further down the bar a man that Lane didnt recognize called
his name and lifted his mug in a toast and Lane raised his own and felt
cheap for it. Like he'd won a carrion-eating contest. He'd no sooner gotten comfortable on the stool till NoBob popped up on the next one.

Hey, Lane, he said. I seen your truck. I got his next beer, Larry. A
five-dollar bill crept reluctantly from a worn, dark-sweated wallet.

Lane downed his beer and the second went as quickly as the first
but wasnt half as good. This stuff is lumpy today, he said. What you
got back there for whiskey?

Larry removed the mug and returned with a short fat glass dark
and tinkling with ice.

Did I say what I wanted? The liquor hard and clean and hot.

You dont have no idea what you want. Wouldnt be drinkin if you did.

Lane turned up the glass and let the whiskey run till it was gone and still held the glass there and cherished the sensation of cubes against his lip. Make it a double this time.

That was a double, Larry said.

Make it twice whatever that was. You do the math.

While Larry refilled his glass Lane went to the jukebox and fed in a five-dollar bill and turned it the right way and fed it again and when his credits came up he looked for the bluegrass album and was surprised to find a new IIIrd Tyme Out and a Rhonda Vincent and the Rage and the new group he'd heard about but never heard, The Grascals. The liquor working at the sides of his head, making the hair feel ruffled. He punched numbers till the credits went away and went back to the bar and drank from his glass.

Thank you, Larry said. Loud to be heard over the music.

For what?

For playing some bluegrass. It's good to hear it again without putting in the quarters myself.

Quarters? How about five-dollar bills.

I wish you boys would pick again. Come do one more night. One last get-together. Like Peter, Paul, and Mary do every three-four months.

Turn it down a tad. I cant hear what you're saying. Bluegrass shouldnt require earplugs. Seeing in Larry's eyes that he'd hurt him and not caring enough to listen to it that loud. Lane took his drink to a booth and slid in and NoBob followed and his mug had transformed into a glass too. Dont you have to be someplace? Lane said. Home or somewhere?

Naw. The old woman'll just think I'm working late.

Maybe I need to be alone.

What you need is to get drunk. Fall down off your high horse.

Ah. It's been a bad day. Thanks for the drink.

Least I can do. We likely aint set down together in a bar since we played together.

Probably not. Lane recalled how it was to have a band, the banjo warm and lively, picking vibes from the crowd, how playing it tapped him into some primal current and in so doing made him more human. How it would be to have a whole crowd of people clapping and talking to him between sets, telling how their daddy and their brothers used to pick and how warm and fuzzy it made them to hear that good old-time music. I'm done with it, he said.

You're just put out about your banjo. I can understand that. But dont be clear done with it. We ought to do like Larry says. One last fling for old-time's sake. You can get another one, or borry one. And I aint forgot the bass.

If you did, you could learn it again in five minutes. Bass aint exactly rocket science.

I guess banjo playing is.

Lane took a long drink to ameliorate the memory of the smashed head and the caved-in resonator. No, I'm done with it. I just need to put it behind me.

Like I said, what you need is a good drunk.

What I'm even doing here is beyond me. I should be at the bait-shop getting the place in order so I can open again.

A good drunk will do you good. Get the cobwebs from between your ears. I aint been on a whiskey drunk for a coon's age. My head's hair near cobbed shut.

I dont recall much good in a whiskey drunk.

Maybe you aint never been on one. You aint really been drunk till you've shit your pants and lost your hat.

Lane thought about it. I never did lose my hat.

There you go.

Lane lit another smoke and liked the way he could feel it again, teaming with the whiskey to put a ringing in his ears.

There's something I been wanting to ask you, NoBob said. These here suspension cables they hold up bridges with. All wove out of little wires.

What about them?

Would one of those wires support itself? Without the others? If you just tried to string one little wire across the whole span.

What are you asking me for? I'm not a bridge builder.

I figured you was most likely to know. Being smart. And maybe the general principle involved being apropos to our relationship.

Apropos.

I get the *Reader's Digest*, NoBob said.

To our relationship.

Such as it is.

Yeah. It would. It would have to. If one wasnt strong enough to carry across, ten thousand wouldnt be either.

I dont think so. You could make a rope out of hairs that would reach across the Chesapeake Bay but there's no way one hair could. The least little wind would break it.

It's a wonderful country we live in. Every single person's got the right to be wrong. Is that what you think about while you're stacking bricks? It's no wonder you put them up so crooked.

NoBob snagged their empty glasses and made another trip to the bar. Lane evaluated the jukebox banjo and wondered what kind it was to have such a good bottom end and figured the sound was done electronically. Probably a hundred-dollar string-rattling banjo with a thousand-dollar microphone. His senses sharpened by the liquor when he prefered them dulled.

A tall hard man that could have been in his twenties or his forties—it was impossible to determine whether years or miles had tracked him up so—staggered over with a glass hidden in his hand

and raised the other flat-palmed and froze like an Indian saying howdy until Lane realized the man was looking for a high five. He nodded without slapping the callused hand.

The man scratched a nose riddled with broken capillaries that would someday turn it plumlike and said, Man, I hate to hear that you got winged right there in your own house, man. But I'm glad it was someone tough like you instead of some woman with a bunch of kids. You done good, man.

Thank you, Lane said and wished he wouldnt have.

You ever need any help you just give me a call.

I'll do that. The whiskey had quit ruffling the hair on the side of his head and was blowing in his ears directly on the exposed brain. He was about to offer to buy a drink to get rid of him but when the man turned his head to watch NoBob's return Lane saw he had a greasy ponytail and changed his mind. The man watching NoBob, primal instincts working hard in his eyes, deciding whether to attack or flee, to excuse himself or bust his glass in NoBob's face.

Scuse me, NoBob said with a lot of sarcasm and crowded past the man and bumped his arm and his drink slopped onto his hand.

The man looked at his hand and drained his glass and Lane saw the drink hit bottom in his eyes. I was just tellin Mr. Hollar this county was lucky whatever crazy fudgepacker is loose with a gun run up against a real man. Someone would stand up on their hind legs.

Lane recalled lying in his undershorts in a thistle. Wondering if his pursuer could hear his heart pounding.

You told him. Now get along. NoBob picked at and enlarged a scar in the tabletop.

Aw man. What's your problem, anyhow?

Let it go, NoBob, Lane said. He addressed the ponytail man again and with his fist bumped him lightly on a bicep as hard as the tabletop and said, I thank you, sir, for your kind words.

I was braggin on you, man.

Appreciate it. Thank you.

Take your bragging somewhere else, NoBob said.

Thank you, friend, Lane said again. Giving him a way out if he wanted it.

The man looked at NoBob and at Lane and Lane saw himself within and pitied himself but not the man.

You're a righteous dude, the man said and turned and walked away with his legs splayed for balance. A T-shirt with Cheat River Triathlon on the back Lane knew he'd bought at the ragshop. Runover work boots that had been on the job.

Dont talk to them faggots, NoBob said.

You were about to have to tell your mama a faggot whipped your scrawny little butt. NoBob snorted and his spittle freckled Lane's arm and a soft facet within rolled over to present another surface. There's probably a number of things that fellow is but faggoty dont strike me as one of them, Lane said. He's hard as a locust post.

Then why dont he cut his damn hair?

Maybe he's got better things to do with his time than cut hair. Or maybe he's man enough to look how he wants to. Instead of how his granddad did.

NoBob tilted his eyes up to Lane's and at that angle something reptilian could be seen in their depths and the same thing in Lane recognized it and wanted to either mate with it or kill it. He drank about half of his whiskey and swished the rest in the cubes for a moment and swallowed it down.

Dont let your alligator mouth overload your hummingbird ass, NoBob said.

It wont, Lane said, knowing he was drunk by the way he felt so extraordinarily reasonable and coherent and unapologetic.

NoBob spat in a napkin and wadded it and tossed it back with the ketchup and shakers. I dont hardly know how to take a friend that'd as soon take up for one of them dirtbag Sitzels as for me.

Lane cut his eyes toward the ponytailed man. He's a Sitzel?

Yep.

All right. I got that much. Now which one's the friend? He laughed at the expression on NoBob's face and slid off to the bathroom and found another drink in his hand from somewhere he was in the booth again and the conversation had boiled down into the resurrection of slights unintended and forgotten until the alcohol raked them back up into the smoke and racket of the barroom. After a while Lane felt that he was afar off watching strangers bicker about subjects he wasnt privy to.

He slid out of the booth and said, I got to see a man about a dog. The pool table shifted as he passed and caught his thigh and he knew it hurt him but he didnt feel it. Somewhere in his memory was already being to the bathroom once—twice?—but he didnt know how that could be since he'd just gotten here. He stood a long time at the urinal without results but felt no fullness or frustration because maybe he hadnt had to go after all. He lathered his hands and tossed the towel toward an empty wastebasket and watched in puzzlement as it came up short.

Lane pushed against the door and when it didnt open his momentum squashed his nose against the faded rough paint and he rattled the knob and found it locked. With no discernible way to unlock it. All right, he said. You had your little joke. Now open the door. When there was no response he whacked it a couple of times with his fist and then stood back and gave it a kick but found himself off balance and did it little damage. You can open it or I can tear it off the hinges, he said.

Off to his right another door opened and a man he didnt remember knowing said, What's all the hollering about? You cant get in the closet, man. It's locked up.

When he'd reoriented himself in the bathroom he said, I know that, and the man withdrew from the doorway. Lane washed his hands again and went out and stood at the end of the hallway looking over the bar like he'd just arrived on the planet. NoBob's back was to him and from that angle Lane knew him better than he wanted to.

The backside of the bar was deserted so Lane flipped up the drunk-stop and as he passed behind the bar he snatched the biggest fullest darkest bottle he could find and ducked under a curtain that smelled of smoke into kitchen air heavy and thick. Hot grease roared as Larry dumped chicken wings into the deep fryer and when he turned he jumped and ashes fell from his cigarette and he said, You aint sup-posed to be back here, Lane. His eyes caught on the bottle and again on Lane's face. If I let you everybody will be doin it. There aint nobody supposed to be back here but Gilpin and she didnt show tonight.

With fingers as thick as the air Lane located a twenty in his wallet and said, Is that enough?

If you're plannin on drinkin yourself to death do it on something better than that. But when Lane stuffed the twenty into Larry's shirt-pocket he didnt resist.

Lane examined the bottle and found it to his liking or at least nothing to dislike. After he'd located the back door and outsmarted the lock, he let himself out into the parking lot and discovered that despite all previous evidence to the contrary it had gotten dark. He turned to ask what had gone crooked with the time and the drinks he'd forgotten about rose up roaring in his ears like the chicken wings had bellowed in the grease.

I sure hope you aint driving, Larry said from the open doorway.

I'm too drunk to walk, Lane reasoned. His fingers found the bot-tlecap but couldnt hold onto it and he watched it skitter to a stop in the gravel and stood spraddlelegged and turned up the bottle and gagged on the hot treacly mix and forced it down and drank more.

I got to get back out front or they'll steal me blind, Larry said. The lock mechanism snickered shut and Lane felt his way along the vehicles till his hands and eyes agreed that one was familiar and parked front-end-out like he always did and after a try or two he managed the seat. When he'd rested and drank awhile the starting procedure returned and when the truck began to move he jammed the bottle between his thighs and gripped the wheel with both hands and watched with fascination as the graveled lot got smaller and the road approached and dwindled and became a cutbank and when the front wheels dropped into the ditch and the pickup lurched to a stop and the engine stalled he steered on for what seemed a prudent interval before he drank again. Too many wrecks happened from folks quitting steering too soon. So simple he couldnt fathom why he'd never figured it out before.

With the seat out of level his leg cramped against the door and he located the handle or something similar that moved and the door fell away and he grabbed at the steering wheel but his arm went between the spokes and his shoulder mashed the hornring and the noise startled him till he figured what it was and how to make it stop. When he turned the bottle up again a loose hard weight in his head like the klunk in the gastank of his chainsaw shifted and in slow motion the pickup rolled over onto its side and the ground tilted up and hit him hard in the ear and when his environment settled down the pickup and the world were upright where they were supposed to be but he was on the ground with his feet still in the truck.

The smell of liquor rank and sweet and hot and he found the bottle and held it to the hard raking light that had appeared like the sun coming up under the truck and shook it and drank what little remained.

After a spell of time he couldnt rightly gauge gravel scuffed beside his head and soft hands caressed his cheeks. Pap. What are you doing to yourself?

DeeDee? You come to dance? Like you used to?

Come on. Let's get you out of here before the cops wander past.

You better stay back. That truck just bucked me off and I dont think it's all out of its system yet. It's one strongwilled sonofabitch. At the thought his stomach rebelled and he extracted his feet from the door-hole and tried to sit up and there were stronger hands than DeeDee's under his arms and a voice said, Come on, dude, help just a tad here, man. But the arms under his didnt seem to need any help. Lane felt himself levitate off the ground till only his feet dragged in the gravel.

Wait, Lane said. I lost my hat somewhere.

Grab his hat there if you see it lady. The man held him with one hand while he opened the door to Darlene's car and with a tenderness alien to Lane's remembered experience tucked him into the seat and buckled the shoulder harness around him.

I'll move his truck back over there where it belongs.

Thank you so much, she said. Tell Larry thanks for calling.

It aint no problem, maam. He's one righteous dude. I told him I'd help him anytime he needed it.

I lost my hat, Lane said and felt his head to make sure and still wasnt positive.

You better get gone, maam. If I find his hat I'll pitch it in his truck.

Darlene started the car and U-turned and headed back the way she'd come.

I got to get my hat. Suddenly that seemed more important than life itself.

You dont wear a hat, Pap. You never did.

Maybe that's what the problem is. Lane felt again of his head and then under the seat of his pants. I aint drunk, he said.

No, she said after a while. Why would anyone think you were drunk.

He leaned back into the headrest and a great warm peace came over him like he was being immersed in the stuff he'd just drunk. I think I'm gonna grow me a ponytail, he said.

You do that, she said long after he'd forgotten she was there. He could tell from her voice that she was crying again and the knowledge was a comfort in the midst of hard peace.

.39

LANE WOKE ON THE KITCHEN FLOOR, HIS HEAD deep under the table among the chairlegs, and though he wasnt exactly sure about anything else, he knew he'd been shot and who had shot him and who had destroyed his banjo. Why, he had no idea. Nor what he was going to do about it.

When he'd extricated himself he ciphered the day and decided it was morning, not confident of how he'd arrived at the conclusion. Where he'd lain, blood had dried on the linoleum and when he twisted his head enough he determined that his bandage was gone and the wound had opened and bled and crusted with a scab that felt like a cast-iron stovelid grafted directly to the nerves.

He made his way to the refrigerator to search for orange juice he knew wasnt there and found instead his bandage, bloody and muddy and half-wrapped in shrinkwrap like a sandwich he'd intended to eat later. He abandoned the kitchen for the bathroom and discovered he'd been there as well and what he'd done turned his stomach again and he found the porch a much more pleasant platform for a morning piss that smelled of alcohol and ammonia. Then he sat on the stairs with his head propped in his hands and revisited the night passed and the years and the decades and encountered the memory of carrying the bald man's head, how after the thin cartilage webs had surrendered, the fingers went right in, and he wished it had been his head. The bald man carrying it. But the bald man was dead and Lane had to carry his own.

●　●　●

When Lane had showered and found clothing that didnt smell like a bar rag he walked the three miles to Rooster's without raising thumb or eyes to passing vehicles, and by then the leftover alcohol had oozed out of his pores as thick as industrial sludge but not nearly as sweet smelling.

The truck sat alone in the back of the lot, sitting at an angle that made it look not just old but confused. The driver's side door was caved in, the rough knobby tread of a workboot visible in the paint. The windshield wiper fractured and hanging askew like broken eyeglasses. The side window down and a half-empty Coors Light can on the seat beside a dark stinking stain. The keys in the ignition. Not worth stealing.

Lane tried to comprehend why anyone would do such things and failed and was surprised when the engine started and again when the truck pulled ahead as though it were just another day. His hangover had turned his vision punky, the peripherals all gone or jumpy and the straight-ahead washed-out and pale. Lane drove like a student driver, rabbity and overcorrecting, until the feel of driving came back. Or enough of it to tell that he'd done it once or twice before.

Praise God from whom all blessings flow, he said and headed out toward Sugarcamp Road where he knew NoBob would be working. Hangover and Saturday or not. Not one to let a dollar unturned.

●　●　●

NoBob was nearly done with the privacy wall around the pool. The sandpile nothing but a white smudge in the gravel. The mortar bags empty and flapping under a stone to keep them from blowing away. One brown man knapping dried mortar from the mixer while the other gathered scraps of stone rubble into a pile. Lane stood for a while watching the capstones fall into place as though they'd been designed for each spot. As before, NoBob talked to himself as though nobody were around. Especially Lane.

Lane sized his questions against the man who'd provoked them and knew with some visceral intelligence that confrontation was the easy way out. That he didnt want this to be over, not this easily. That he was going to suffer for a while, that the banjo would stay broken and his side would always hurt, and he didnt want to do it alone. He finished a cigarette and flipped it toward the scaffold and turned to leave.

Was there something you was wanting? NoBob said. Some insult you forgot last night, maybe?

Lane turned again and watched NoBob dig at the sole of his workboot with the point of his trowel and with clarity as good as his vision had ever been he also knew who had kicked in the door of his truck. What's the matter? You got paint in the tread?

NoBob looked at him sharply. What's that supposed to mean?

I could come take that boot off you and hold it up to the side of my truck and see if it matched or not. But I dont need to.

Before you decide to go taking my boots off, you'd best consider what you're fixing to do. The laborers stopped their work and drew close together and watched. If not understanding the words, knowing the tone.

Maybe I could take you, maybe not. But I'll lay money you'll be barefooted when I'm done. Whatever it takes.

NoBob tossed the trowel onto the mudboard and scratched his ear and shook his head. You aint the only one was drunk last night.

But you're the only drunk I know of went around kicking truck doors in.

No, but you was the only one dragging up every piece of past shit in the world and dumping it on my head. A man can take so much.

And a truck dont fight back.

I dont fight with people too drunk to stand up. Get it fixed and send me the bill.

You'll get the bill all right. And it wont be one you can pay with a check, either. How you think you're going to replace a banjo that's not made anymore? How you going to replace blood that's been spilled? Shooting from the dark. Not even enough nerve to look me in the eye while you do it.

I dont know nothing about them things. I swear to God I dont. I admit I kicked in the door of your truck. Dont even care who seen it and told. I shouldnt of done it, and I'm almost glad I got caught. But not the others.

You took away something precious to me that I can't replace, and you took my blood. That's the way you're going to pay it back. With blood. And with something precious. And it will be when you least expect it. Like you took mine.

Lane, I didnt do those others. I swear it on my grandma's Bible.

It didnt sink in on me when you said it. But it worked on me overnight.

Said what?

How did you know about my banjo? When I never told a soul. Not a one. Lane turned and didnt look back.

Lane . . . hold on a minute.

You sleep good, my friend? Your life insurance up to snuff? Lane said. But when he accelerated out Sugarcamp Road he felt as at peace as any time he could recall. Like the accounts had been squared, the bills paid in full. They probably were, he realized when he felt for his anger and found nothing there. He laughed, the last thing he'd expected to do. NoBob, he said aloud. You poor pathetic pitiful worthless piece of dog crap.

.40

WHEN LANE RETURNED TO THE BAITSHOP TWO brown forms in worn white shirts and dark pants and sandals sat leaning against the building. Juan and his father.

You got worms? he said when he'd dismounted from the pickup.

Not today, Juan said. You remember my papa? Emilio?

Señor, the man said and Lane was again impressed with the consistency of the man's hand. Like a brick by some miracle made flexible.

You going fishing? Lane found the key in his pocket instead of using the one from under the rock like he usually did. But not while they were watching. Wondered if he'd have shown the same caution if they were white instead of Hispanic.

No sir, Juan said. My papa needs to talk to you.

Come in, Lane said. Inside he could still smell rotted worms or thought he could and his nervous stomach rolled and he allowed the door to stand open behind them. He cleared a box of cleaning rags from the other chair for Emilio and sat in his rocker and motioned for Juan to sit on the counter but the boy stood beside it.

A house, Emilio said after what felt to Lane an interminable wait. The auction? To sell for the most money?

You want to sell your house? You have to own one first.

Yes. To own.

He wants to buy a house, Juan said.

Houses cost a lot of money.

How many? Emilio said.

How much? It depends on what you buy. He thought of Jodie's slowly subsiding dump. You might find something for twenty-five or so, but it wouldnt be fit to live in. Thousand, he added. Then again some of the vacation places go for a million or more.

No vacation, Emilio said.

No, there dont seem to be. I could keep my eyes open, I reckon, but if anything affordable comes up someone will snatch it up quick.

How much for Mr. Bean's house? Juan said.

That one will be tied up forever in probate. Even if you could buy it, you'd probably be looking at seventy-five or better. You know how big a pile of money seventy-five thousand dollars is?

The boy looked at his father and the man nodded and the boy said, You dont have to pay it all at once. The mortgage.

Lane studied his shoe tops for inspiration and found no more than he'd expected. You'd need a bunch down. Money up front. Probably fifteen thousand dollars or so.

Yes, the man said. *Mil.*

But it takes a lot of time. Paperwork. And that place wont be for sale for a long time.

Two *semanas*, the man added.

In two weeks, Juan said. It says so in the paper.

I dont read it. When the editor dies I might start.

Two weeks, Juan insisted.

Whatever. Sick and nervous and tired of the whole conversation. Even so. The banks would have to check your credit history and stuff. It takes a long time.

We work hard, Emilio said. Pay every week.

We work. We save, Juan said. All of us.

Go check with the bank then. Maybe they'll go for it.

He has no papers, Juan said. Just the kids.

Then you have a problem for sure. Even if you could get the loan.

In your name we could pay for it. When my sister is old enough you could change it over to her.

Lane felt these people attaching themselves to him like pubic lice and he pictured dozens of them, hundreds of them, *mils* of them moving freely in and out of his life and belongings. I'm not the kind of man you think I am, he said. Not if you think I'd do something like that. You'd be way better off to hang onto your money till you raise up a legal one to own it. Instead of all this rigamarole. It's cheaper to rent anyhow.

No rent, Emilio said. Own.

What's so all-fired important about owning property? It just ties you down.

Is why we come. To own.

We dont want to move anymore, Juan said. There is enough property that we can build more houses. When we save more money.

You dont have a handle on how much money it takes.

We work hard. And Marcos gets money for going to prison.

One of you in prison, that'll cut through the paperwork for sure. Look . . .

He didnt know about the drugs in the car he was driving but he did not argue it, Juan said.

If he's that ignorant he likely needs to be in jail. Locked up somewhere.

Dos pay, Emilio said, and again held up two fingers. Like he was just learning to count and two was the number he was giving special attention to.

For going to jail he gets twice as much as working. Juan nodded his head, making it the truth. And no expenses.

Wait till he gets out. Then ask him how easy money it was.

Is not hard, Emilio said. Milking the cows is hard.

I dont have all day for this. Where you got the idea I'd do something like you're suggesting is beyond me.

You treat me fair. Nobody else does.

No. I'm a crooked old man that lives in a crooked old house. I'm likely the crookedest one around. You dont know anything about me. The events of the week swirled around him, and he said, *I* dont even know anything about me. Now you get along. There's stuff I need to get done.

Juan touched his father's sleeve and after a moment's hesitation Emilio followed him to the door. The older man stood in the open door a moment longer until Juan tugged at him and then he eased the door closed.

Lane watched them go. Again the older man stopped and looked back, his mouth working like a possum's in the cat dish, but the boy shook his head and kept walking till the man had to run to catch up with him. When they'd gone Lane felt like they'd stolen something, but he knew nothing was missing. Nothing he could take back.

Lane looked around the baitshop and deemed it a tomb but not as nice as one and he locked the door and drove to his home.

• • •

The old cruiser sat in his driveway, Martin inside eating a sandwich. Lane pulled in beside him and walked to the deputy's open window. Now what? he said without preamble. Martin chewed awhile and swallowed before he answered. I stopped in to tell you what all we were doing to find out who shot you.

Put this in your file: I already know who did it. And he dont have the guts to do it again.

The deputy paused with the sandwich halfway in his mouth and withdrew it and changed his mind and took a bite. Eyes boring at Lane. Really, he said after a while. Who might that be?

Lane had thought about it just as long as Martin had, and he just couldnt see anything wrong with them chasing after NoBob. Making him sweat. Do you all good to figure that out on your own. Good practice. Like the Search & Rescue boys had on Billy Bean.

You're making serious allegations.

It's no allegation. Just a fact.

Then you're obliged to tell me who it is. People that shoot others cant be walking around loose.

The only thing I'm obliged to you for is what you did for Toby, if it was like you say. But it wasnt. He's no doper. I know the boy.

Martin's chiseled jaw took on an extra facet. You got a funny way of saying thanks.

I got a funny way of asking folks to leave me alone, too. You want to hear it?

Martin shook his head and started the engine. That's twice I've tried to do something nice for you.

You still wont get my vote.

I'm not sure I'd want it, Mr. Hollar. In fact, I'm right certain I wouldnt.

.41

sat on the edge of the bed and examined his wound and found it sore and puckered and ugly but less inflamed and pulled on a shirt without fooling with it further. As he drank his coffee and thought about the fishermen waiting at the baitshop to complain about the quality of the last minnows they'd bought he realized how tired of it all he was. That worms were no different than two-by-fours, just as homogeneous. As nameless and uninspiring as the customers. That whatever life he had left wouldnt be found in a minnow tank. If it was, he'd just as soon pass on it.

Without making a formal, definite decision not to go to work he found himself sitting on the porch swing drinking the last of the coffee when Darlene's car crunched up the driveway, Frank at the wheel. Alone. He parked and stared blankfaced out the windshield. After a while he got out and came up the walkway and stopped at the bottom of the stairs. Darlene's got Toby with her. They're not alone.

It's all right. Whatever danger there was is likely past. I should have let you know.

Can I come up?

This is your home. You dont need an invitation. Like some places I know. Wanting to be surly but not finding the raw ingredients. They went into the kitchen and Frank sat in his old place and Lane put on another pot of coffee and sat across from him feeling slippery in time. Like Mary should be there at his right. Like Frank shouldnt have gray whiskers. But she wasnt and he did.

They catch who shot you? Who was it?

No. But I know who it was, and it wont leak off onto anybody else. It was personal. Wont happen again, and dont worry, I'm not going off on a vigilante run.

So all this was for nothing.

I reckon.

You'll tell me when you're ready, I suppose.

I might. Might not. What's up?

I caught Toby smoking grass, Frank said when the coffee started to gurgle down. Thought you ought to hear it from me. When he wasnt around.

Lane's perspective of Martin did a somersault and it took Lane a moment to rearrange the world to fit it. You sure? he said. For no applicable reason recalling the cornsilk he'd smoked as a boy.

Smelled it on him, Frank said. And then when I confronted him he owned up to it.

You ought to know what it smells like.

Same old dad.

Lane sat across from his son. Where'd he get it?

He wont say.

Yes he will, too. I'll find out.

No you wont. That's why I came. I know how you are.

You dont care to stop whoever's bringing it in here?

I care about the boy. That he doesnt get browbeat and shamed and driven away like I was.

Lane swept the salt and pepper shakers and the napkin holder off the table and felt foolish for doing so and hit the table with his fist and felt more foolish yet. He retrieved the shakers and stuffed the napkins back in the holder before Frank could do it. Gone all these years, he said. Leave your wife and kid when they needed you the most, then lay it off onto me.

They didnt need me at all. They had you, you blind arrogant asshole.

That's reason to leave them?

I left you. Not them. Frank looked up from the saltshaker he'd been inspecting for chips and Lane saw himself in those dark eyes. Not the reflection. I couldnt compete with you, old man.

If we were racing it somehow slipped past me.

When Mom died you took Darlene. And Toby.

Lane shook his head. As befuddled as if Frank had hit him with a bumper jack.

Frank shook some salt into his palm and touched his tongue to it. Anything I could do you could do better. I put a new starter on Darlene's car and the next week you put a clutch in your truck.

It needed a clutch. What was I supposed to do? Pedal it? Wait for you to grow up?

The evening after I killed a copperhead in the flowerbed you told Darlene about night patrols in Nam.

Lane sensed that the more he kept his mouth shut the quicker this would be over. But restraining words was like wrapping a bobcat in toiletpaper.

All day long you could influence Toby, show him what a wonderful grandfather you were, while I had a half hour in the evening. If he wasnt with you.

Life works out thataway.

When you helped us move you grabbed the heavy end of

everything. I sold the .30-30 and bought an ought-six and right off you show up with a 7 mm Mag.

It wasnt intentional.

That's the problem.

All right then. I meant to do it.

Alpha male comes natural to you. When I had a science project, you werent satisfied till it was good enough for the national fair. Till it was your project. What other twelve-year-old ever built a steam engine?

Lane threw another wasted wrap around the bobcat.

When I ran cross-country you ran with us at practice. Or ahead of us. *Run through your pain boys. If you're not hurting you're not running.*

The coffeemaker burbled the way it did when it was finished and Lane filled two cups and poured milk in one till it approached flesh-color and sat it in front of Frank. Lane leaned back against the counter and cradled the heat in both hands. The team went to States that year, he said.

We didnt care about States. Fun was what we were after.

I never figured last place was an enjoyable position.

Frank rose and poured his pale coffee down the sink drain and refreshed his cup and sipped it without additives. When I took guitar lessons and learned "Red River Valley" you took first place in the Mid-Atlantic Regional Banjo Championship.

Lane shrugged.

The only time you ever entered.

If I could say something to make you feel better about life in general and you in particular I'd do it.

The best job I ever had was when I signed on as a draftsman for Borman.

Could have fooled me. You worked a week and quit and left home.

I dont suppose you remember what you said about the job?

The coffee was too hot to drink but Lane drank some anyway. Probably something about shortsighted career choices.

How was it? If brains were shit you couldnt raise a bad smell, boy.

There's not a draftsman left on the planet has a job. Everything's done now on computers. Like I predicted.

The inference being that I'd be too intellectually challenged to change with the job. To learn AutoCAD.

Lane combed his face with his fingers and felt it go back the way it was. Disapproving and stern and aloof. I'm sorry, he said and wondered if he was. If he wanted to be.

That's like a lion apologizing for eating meat.

Then I'm sorry you feel that way.

There's the Lane Hollar we know and love. Be sorry for someone else.

They sat for a while both looking into their cups. When someone outdoes you, do them one better, Lane said. That's the way the world works. Dont quit when you get one-upped.

When God beats you, you do. You dont say, *Wine?* I'll turn the water into Jack Daniels. You dont try to feed *twenty* thousand. You dont make the blind man *fly*.

Somehow I missed when religion sneaked in.

You were a god to me. There was nothing you couldnt do. Even when I hated your doing it, when it made me look weak and useless, I was in awe of what you did. Of what you could do. Of how you kept above the rest of the world.

If I made you feel . . .

Then Mom died and I saw what you really were. That Mom was the god.

She was special.

You were just a stingy old man who took from your wife and when you felt the need for more you got it from a bottle. You should have kept on drinking. Instead of moving in on us.

The bobcat had blown out of the toiletpaper and departed without Lane's noticing but had taken words with him. Frank was wrong or Lane hoped he was wrong but if there was evidence that he was, Lane couldnt locate it.

You didnt keep your feelings under control. You didnt have any.

You're wrong.

When did you laugh? Your jokes turn into sermons. I watched you smash your finger with a hammer one time and you didnt even blink. You bit off the nail and spit it out like it was a sliver of dead skin and went on like nothing happened.

Dead skin's what a nail is. Uncertain if he'd said it aloud.

At Mom's funeral you sat there like a wooden Indian. Did you ever cry? Even once?

Yeah.

When?

Lane thought back and didnt have to go far. Monday. When DeeDee brought me home from the police station.

Frank looked at him like he'd confessed to wearing women's underthings. Why?

I dont know. She was crying and it made me cry too. Lane considered sharing how he'd felt when Mary died, when he'd held her hand and felt something he couldnt name or fathom pass from her to him but he had no words for it. It would be like trying to explain gravity to a piece of dandelion fluff.

Did you feel anything? Do you ever *feel* anything?

I dont know. The man across the table looked like his son and sounded like his son but he was someone Lane didnt know and he didnt even know himself anymore. Two strangers discussing his most intimate traits. I felt something. But I dont know what. It wasnt anything to cry about.

Before that? Is there another time you cried?

Lane considered that and saw no gain in answering. If you

realized what a worthless unfeeling parasitic corpse I was, why didnt you throw me out? Instead of running off to let your family suffer?

Frank picked up Lane's cigarettes and then put them back down.

Go ahead, Lane said.

No. I quit. And I wont take it up again.

Lane lit one for himself and smoked it halfway down before he spoke again. I never felt like a god. Maybe just the opposite.

Like a devil?

That's not the opposite of a god. Being helpless. That's the opposite.

After a while Frank said, Mom always took me to church.

I never held that against her. Just so it didnt get to be her whole life. Or yours. Folks get tangled up in it and forget they got this life to get through first before they go to heaven.

In Sunday School they taught the earth is six thousand years old. That dinosaurs never existed. That some scientist found a little piece of bone and from that shard they extrapolated an entire T-Rex. That science was a conspiracy against religion.

Lane nodded. I wasnt worried. You had enough sense to see past ignorance. To learn that blind obedience is a screwed-up offering to the creator of the human mind. If that's what you believe.

That might be the first time you've ever complimented me.

That's ridiculous.

Tell me when.

I always bragged about you. At work. At the ballgames.

To *me*. When did you say anything complimentary *to* me? Or even *around* me.

It's not because I didnt feel that way. The words sour paste. I didnt want you to be like those people that always want to get up and sing with the band but they cant carry a tune in a dump truck. But nobody's ever told them.

Your favorite maxim. There's too many inferior people walking around without a complex.

It's the truth.

Anyway. In the ninth grade our class went to the Smithsonian, Frank said.

I remember. Past midnight when you got back.

In the very first building a brontosaurus skeleton was on display.

I've seen pictures of it.

Around it were photographs of scientists digging it out of the ground. It wasnt just a little piece of backbone. It was there all of a piece, like it was when it died. It felt like someone kicked me in the belly. Because I knew what they'd taught me in church was a lie. I must have stood there for ten minutes with my mouth open. Sick.

That's why I didnt worry about you going to church. You have enough sense to get away with it.

You dont understand.

You still believe the earth is six thousand years old?

No. I believe in something. In God. In creation. In a hereafter.

Lane examined Frank as though he were newformed.

But I dont know what it is I believe. Or why. You know how horrible it is to not be able to get shed of a belief you have no evidence for? No evidence that man hasnt tampered with for his own benefit. Or through stupidity.

Just saying forget about it dont work, I take it?

Mom had no doubt. I envied that. She didnt *care* what God was or when He created the universe or why. She just trusted in Him as though He was what they said He was.

She was an exceptional person.

The same thing happened with you. When I saw what you really were, it was too late. You'd always be a god. It didnt matter if you were a drunken god with no feelings, a god that fed off his followers and used them and discarded them as he wished.

I thought that's what gods did, Lane thought but didnt say. I'm sorry, I really am, he did say, and parts ground inside Lane that did not normally come into contact when he said it. Some small piece shifted into a new location, a mechanical shifting without any trace of softness or warmth. Like a bolt cross-threaded in a hole, one that wouldnt go any farther or come loose without breaking but an improvement over no fastening at all. You're saying you left because of me? Still trying to get ahold of the thought.

Frank shrugged. Who knows. It's what I've told myself all this time, anyhow. It's my story, and I'm sticking to it. I'm as screwed up as you are. Maybe I'm just like you.

If you thought I was a god, you were even worse off than I thought.

I shouldnt have come. But I could see it all starting over again. With Toby. Frank put his head in his hands. The pot smoking isnt all of it either. He vandalized your baitshop, too. The day Darlene left him home alone. Rode over on his bike.

The concept was too much for Lane to get his thoughts around. How do you know that?

He told me. Had to get it off his chest.

But why?

Frank shrugged. It's one of the things kids do at sometime or another. He was mad enough at you.

That I know.

And he's afraid of you.

Afraid?

You just wont accept that you intimidate people, will you? He's scared to death of what you'll do when you find out.

After Lane had sat silent for a while, Frank said, I need to be getting back. I dont feel up to it, though.

You are, Lane said, and felt tears in his eyes and brushed them away with the back of his hand and looked at the wet smear in amazement. I didnt feel anything, he said. Just the water.

Did you ever consider that's what there is to feel? What do you expect? For your heart to split? For your lungs to seize? For your brain to go into convulsion?

Why carry on so about such a thing as water in your eye? Truly puzzled.

Because it's so precious. Because that little detail lifts us above the apes. Frank glanced at his watch and drained his cup and rinsed it in the sink and set it on the drainboard.

What are you going to do about Toby?

I'm going to try to love him. If I know how. What he's done isnt the end of the world. But it might be the start of a bad one if somebody doesnt do something.

It's still hard to imagine that he'd smoke pot. That he trashed my baitshop. He's such a good boy.

Yes. He is. I can see that. Frank looked at his watch. I've got to go. I'm glad you came.

Are you?

Yes. I think so, anyhow. Wanting to get it right while he had a chance.

Frank paused at the kitchen door. Two weeks from Friday I graduate. I'd like you to come.

Graduate from what?

From college.

College?

WVU.

When did you go to college?

I've been going nights and taking days off when I have to. Seems like forever. But I'm about to get my degree.

In what?

Mechanical engineering.

No kidding. Lane examined Frank head to toe and couldnt see

the difference though he knew there was a big one. Nobody in our family's ever been to college.

I know.

I figured you for whoring and drugging.

Women I never did take up. Maybe I never acted like it, but I *felt* married all along. The bottle caught my attention for a month or so but I got to the bottom of one and saw there was nothing on the other side of the glass so I quit. My money went for tuition. Driving back and forth. It's not cheap.

Did Darlene know?

Frank took a deep breath and looked at his watch. I'd just as well tell you. We've been sleeping together once in a while.

The hell.

We have needs, Pap. And it's scary out there. You can pick up stuff that a shot or a pill wont get rid of.

Does Toby know?

We've been careful to keep it from him. Dont want to mess him up any more than we have already. But he suspects, I think. He's a sharp kid.

It dont seem right.

We are still married.

I mean about Toby.

Just so you know, we've been thinking about moving back together. What's just happened will likely push us to decide.

Lane considered that for a while. The boy could use a daddy.

Frank looked at his watch again. I have to go. Arent you going to belittle my major before I leave? Ask what good an engineering degree will be here in Dogpatch? Suggest I fix wringer washers?

No, Lane said and left it at that.

Thank you. I have to go. Just give us a little space, okay? Give us some time to work it out.

Butt out for a spell. Leave the three of you alone. That's what you're saying.

Just for a while.

I'll try. Thank you. Frank spun away and out the door and down the stairs but not before Lane saw the welling in his eyes.

Lane wanted to chase him and hug him but knew better than to hug another man. Frank, he yelled from the doorway.

Frank stopped but didnt look back. What?

Lane had intended to ask Frank when *he'd* last cried but those words had to pass through the hole with the cross-threaded bolt so he said instead, You're not like me. And I'm glad. I'm proud of you, son.

.42

LANE SPENT A LONG LONELY NIGHT AFTER THE catharsis of his talk with Frank wore off and the reality of the problems that remained sunk in. Just after daylight on Monday morning he rinsed the coffeepot and when he'd made a new pot and drank it he knew that he had to do something even if it was futile and senseless, at least till DeeDee and Toby were talking to him again, so he drove to the baitshop and found it as lonely and as smelly and as depressing as a groundhog's hole. He compared his watch to the calendar and tried without success to fathom how it could still be less than two weeks since he'd taken Toby after the muskie.

He settled in behind the mule and replenished his supply of worms and minnows from the wholesaler and attempted to be pleasant to the customers, not that there were that many. The hours passed like Februarys, the days exponentially slower. By Thursday he was out of smokes and as lonely as a seventeen-year locust in an off year. Tired of worrying over his grandson. Tired of trying to figure out why NoBob had gone so crazy on him. Knowing that he hadnt even been able to figure out his own son or even himself. Twice Lane called NoBob's number and got the answering machine and hung up without leaving a message, not knowing what he'd have said if the man had answered. His anger rekindling all the while.

He wooled at Emilio's request to help them get a home and though he knew he'd given the right answer worried that he could have done it in a nicer manner. Perhaps helped them along some other way. Maybe if he hadnt been hungover. The auction was coming up, if they'd had their facts in the right bucket. He thought about who might be bidding on Billy Bean's house. Who would have the money to. Phil McKevey or some of the other lawyers and doctors from town, but he couldnt imagine why they'd want it. Larson Henry, if he knew about it. NoBob would. And Lane could, if he wanted it. But he didnt. Then there were the folks who'd love to have it but didnt have the means. No use to try and count them.

After a long spell with no customers he locked the shop and drove to the Get-n-Go and purchased a six-day-old copy of *The Weekly Herald* and a carton of cigarettes and tried without much success to forget the price while he sat in the pickup and smoked one and leafed through the newspaper looking for the auction notice. He tried not to see the editorial, but the title—"County-wide Zoning Past Due"—jumped out at him and the paper tore when he folded it back to the want ads.

There it was: a picture of the house and garage. 8.4 acres with improvements. Like Juan had said. But the owner's name was wrong: Sybil Tasker, not William Bean. After he'd read and pondered the listing he drove to the sheriff's department and found nobody there but Martin.

The deputy slid his chair back and got to his feet when Lane came in. Lane remembered when he could get to his feet like that but it had been a while. Dick's not here, he said.

That's all right. You're the one I'm wanting to see. To thank you for giving the boy a break. I'm ready to accept that now.

I shouldnt have done it. Are you going to get me in trouble now for it?

No. And I dont think you'll have cause to do it again. Not with that particular kid anyhow.

I've seen it happen before. A kid gets in trouble and then he cant get shed of it.

Well. You're probably right. I'm sorry at how harsh I was to you the other day.

You ready to say who you think shot you?

No. But I'd just as soon you dropped the whole thing. It's over.

The investigation's going on full-bore. Fingerprints and bullets are off to the lab. I didnt say anything to Dick.

Why not?

Martin shrugged, and for the first time seemed remotely likeable. Who knows why we do what we do. Or dont.

Well, let it go on then. It wont hurt anything. Doubtful they'd figure it out.

I'd figured that Harold Bright for it. But he's in jail down in Virginia, was when the incident happened.

That dont surprise. What for?

Got caught with a load of drugs. You want to give me a hint who you think it was?

No. You all need something to do. Earn your pay.

Lane left and walked down the street and climbed the long cracked concrete stairs to the courthouse and examined the waterstains on the ornate rotunda ceiling while he waited ouside the REGISTER OF WILLS office until the telephone conversation ended. He stepped inside and said to the man who'd been a fixture there as long as Lane could remember, Jack, how you doing?

The short and slightly heavy but athletic-looking man said, Lane. What brings you out? I hope you havent died and I'm the first to find it out.

Lane barely knew the man but talk was always loose and comfortable between them like it would be with old friends. I been feeling poorly lately and I thought I'd stop in to see if *you* might know any-thing about my passing on that I hadnt heard.

They laughed and shook hands and Jack motioned to an oak chair on rollers and when Lane had deposited himself there said, How can I help you today?

The William Bean place, Lane said, not knowing whether Jack knew Billy or not. How can that be up for sale so quick? There's no way the estate can be settled yet. Is there?

There's no estate to settle, Jack said. I ought not be telling you this but it's no state secret, I dont imagine.

No estate? How can that be?

Billy Bean has a sister. Her name was on everything he owned but for his old truck—somehow that must have slipped by—and it was appraised at two hundred dollars and that's not considered an estate. It all passes to her. Since she's owned everything right along with Billy Bean.

Sybil? Is that her name?

Jack nodded. Married Thurman Tasker used to live past the bowl-ing alley before it burned. Moved from here ten-twelve years ago.

Lane conjured a featureless couple that walked and talked but not much more. I kind of recollect them. She was Billy Bean's sister? Cricket's girl?

Yes indeedy. It wasnt something she flaunted, and now she wants to be rid of it as quick as the ink can dry. Not that there's much to be rid of other than the property.

I'll be daggoned, Lane said. Who set it up that way? With both their names on everything?

Cricket. I suppose he thought Billy Bean wasnt up to it on his own.

I wouldnt have figured Cricket to care one way or the other.

When you start figuring parents and children, you're likely to fig-ure wrong.

There's that.

How's Frank doing?

Real good. Did you know he's an engineer now?

Get out. You dont mean the train driving kind, either.

Nope. The kind that has brains. Like his pap.

Here I always thought you were the father.

You keep tending your wills and stuff. Leave the thinking to those that's qualified. They laughed.

•   •   •

Lane drove back to the baitshop and sat and waited for customers that didnt come. Once folks came a time or two and found you closed when they expected different they found another place to go. He tried to care and couldnt bring it to a head. When he'd picked at his side long enough to learn that it had healed to where it wasnt satisfying to torment it anymore he dialed Darlene's number but pushed down the button before it rang, keeping his promise but doing something, at least, and then he called NoBob and again hung up without leaving a message.

After he sat and smoked and rocked and thought for a while he realized it was evening and if he'd accomplished anything that day he'd hidden it well. He pulled the pickup next to the baitshop door where he could hear the phone and removed the window crank and door handle and inner panel from the kicked-in door and examined the damage from the inside. With the window down, the glass was in the way, and up, the mechanism blocked any hopes of kicking the panel back into the same zipcode it once occupied. The discovery sapped any ambition that might have coagulated and instead of replacing the panel he tossed it into the pickup's bed.

Lane knew he should go home but the house was full of Mary, a Mary who wasnt there anymore, and even the thought put an ache in him that he didnt care to tolerate if he didnt have to. He went back inside and smoked a cigarette and located the paper and read again the description of Billy Bean's property and then it was dark and he was again asleep in the chair for the fourth time that week.

. 43

THE AUDITORIUM WAS HUSHED BUT HUMMING
with too many people in too little space breathing and farting and
perspiring. The stage was bright and the auditorium was dark and
the floor was steep and disorienting and Lane felt as though he were
on Mars or perhaps in heaven or hell looking anew on a world he'd
not yet seen. The amplified voice mated with the applause and cheers
till he couldnt differentiate one from the other and once he thought
he saw Frank reach for a diploma and he cheered and DeeDee said,
Not yet, Pap.

When Frank did cross the stage Lane couldnt discern him within
the long black robe and flat hat and despite the announcement he
held his applause until he was certain and ended up rendering it to
the next in line.

His boy an engineer. As unreal as his surroundings.

Darlene stood on her tiptoes and kissed Frank on the mouth and
when it lasted longer than appropriate in that kind of a surrounding
Lane had to look away. Embarrassed. Already he worried how to find
their way out of Morgantown. Even though he wasnt driving, he felt
responsible for delivering his family forth from the city's maw.

In the car Toby sat between Frank and Lane, and didnt push Lane away when he pulled the boy tight to his side. You been behaving yourself?

The boy nodded and after a while said, Yes sir.

That's good. You going to keep it up?

Yes sir. Sounding like a boy that age ought to sound. Innocent as he could be and contrite where he wasnt.

Lane looked in the backseat at Darlene, pretty as a picture, and at Frank. Whatever might happen, he said, I want you to know that I love you. Every one of you.

You got something planned to happen? Frank said.

No. But you never know what the morrow holds, Lane said. I just wanted to say it. While I could.

Frank nodded and Darlene touched his arm and the boy seemed to snuggle a little tighter. Making Lane just about as happy and as unnecessary as he could ever remember being.

. 44

LANE UNLOCKED THE DOOR AND FLIPPED THE
sign to OPEN. Somewhere the sun was shining and birds were singing
and people were fishing and buying bait but it wasnt there. It should
have been more depressing than it was but after last evening with
the family it was going to take more than the same old depressors
to get it done. Lane examined the minnows in the bulk tank and
scooped out another half-dozen dead ones. He'd scrubbed away all
the pine oil he could but the traces remaining endowed his minnows
with a propensity to swim upside down without moving their tails.
The lucky ones that wouldnt get turned into fish droppings.

Then he sat in his chair and read again the auction notice and
watched the Trilene clock snicking splinters off the time and started
to get up and sat down again. He studied his watch like the smaller
timepiece might consume life with improved regularity and finally he
jumped up and put the cashbox in the produce drawer and turned off
the lights and headed for the auction.

Lane parked along the hard road at the tail end of a half dozen
or so cars and pickups that spilled from Billy Bean's driveway and
evaluated each one and wondered if he'd been wrong about who

might want the place. Half excited that there werent a lot of bidders and half trepidatious that everyone else knew something he didnt. He walked up to join the paltry crowd that milled through the garage and driveway where what few possessions Billy Bean owned were spread and boxed on a row of folding tables. The day was overcast and smelled of rain, and a pile of blue plastic tarps lay to the side at the ready. The tarps the only minor things that Lane would be interested in owning but not for sale. Lane wandered inside the open door, feeling that he should have knocked, and found the inside as clean and organized as the garage had been. Everything with a little age on it, a little quality you couldnt find anymore in this day of flakeboard and plastic.

Outside, he examined the people and if there was one with the means or ambition to buy the property they hid it well. You here to bid on the place? he asked a squat, hairy man in bib overalls big enough for a pair of him.

Huh? he said and edged closer to a cardboard box half-filled with cheap hand tools. The kind you bought from the back of a truck behind the armory. Aw, no. The real estate dont go off till noon.

That different buyers might come at different times hadnt occurred to Lane. He looked at his watch and decided that two hours of squabbling over the junk on the tables was more than he could tolerate and maybe that was the final nudge that made up his mind.

•   •   •

Yes maam, Lane said to the bank teller. I understand that there is a substantial interest penalty for taking it out early. Instead of paying me the princely sum of 3.4 percent interest on my CDs you're going to charge me some for taking good care of my money all this time. But if you keep fooling around the daggone things will mature first and how much interest you *would* have paid me will be hypothetical. Your point will be moot.

The teller got a little bit rosier under her cosmetized cheeks as though the frost had leaked out of her voice to chap them. Ever since he'd removed the two green plastic sleeves from the safety deposit box she'd treated him like a thief. She looked away and back again and when he was still there she proceeded with a bewildered determination. I'm required to make sure you understand the terms and conditions.

I know that. What a commendable job you did. If you need me to sign off on a paper that says I'm the same Lane Hollar that owns the safety deposit box and the selfsame one put the money in the bank, lay it out here and give me a pen. Just dont put anything on it that says I havent lost my mind. I'm old enough I can go insane without your permission. Give me a cashier's check for twenty-five and the rest goes in the checking.

Lane fiddled while she typed the check but not as much as she did, by his reckoning. The money in the checking wont be available until Monday at noon, she said.

Where does money go in that interim? he said. Between when you quit paying me to use it and when I get to utilize it again? He laughed at her expression. You're supposed to tell me it offsets the time between when I pay my bill with a check and when the money comes out of my account. That it keeps the float afloat.

Well. It does.

There you go, he said. So we'll just have to call it square. He examined the check and found it suitable and folded it and put it in his shirt pocket. We friends? he said.

Her smile showed pointy little teeth she'd like to bury up to the gumline in his neck. Of course, Mr. Hollar.

When he left the bank it was 9:35. To settle his fidgets, or maybe just to tick off the teller again, he stood on the sidewalk and smoked a cigarette. For a nickel he'd go back inside and apologize for being crazy and put the money back into CDs and reclaim his right mind but nobody came by with a nickel or a desire for Lane to be sane and nobody had ever yet possessed enough sense to apologize for insanity so he tossed the butt into the street and headed out to Billy Bean's.

•   •   •

Most of the mangier cars and pickups were gone when he returned and the earlier rows of vehicles were gap-toothed. Lane paused when he saw NoBob's pickup but thought Oh well and walked on past an elderly but clean Lincoln Continental and a new Lexus and a half-dozen shiny SUVs all alike but for the names. Looks like the price of poker just went up.

The tables all but one were folded away in the garage with a couple of boxes of junk they couldnt give away and the auctioneer was reading over his handbill in preparation to start the real estate auction. Lane waved at the little brown boy who stood back alone and nodded at the bidders who looked his way and examined the others who wouldnt. He nodded at NoBob but the dark eyes jerked away and took the man a step or two with them. Lane had expected a shot of anger or maybe pity but what hove up was the humor of the situation. He stood at the remaining table and ran his finger down the list of registered buyers: Larson Henry; Robert Paul Thrasher. Paul. All those years he'd never known NoBob's middle name. Jason Martin. Lane's finger paused there and looked around again and spotted the deputy leaning at the corner of the garage. Sandra Foster. Jodie's girl Sandy. Looking older than she should, but maybe just the too-tight clothes making her look that way.

They're about to start, sir, said the woman behind the table. If you're wanting to register.

With some small difficulty Lane remembered his contact information and signed the form and stuffed the file card with his number into the shirtpocket with the check and before he joined the bidders he stopped and said, Juan, and shook hands with the worm boy for the first time. Found his hand as hard as his father's.

Are you buying? the boy said. Hope in his eyes.

I dont know. Not how you think, anyhow.

The boy's expression said that Lane had taken something from him. By force.

Lane again evaluated the crowd. A few realtors overdressed for the disposition of a dead man's possessions. Each one talking on a cellphone or punching at some handheld device Lane didnt know the name or purpose of. Like one thing wasnt an acceptable accommodation of time, even if that one thing was snarfing up the sum of a man's life. Sandy looking as nervous and eager as one waiting to hear the eighth number on the Powerball ticket. Tapping her front teeth with her file card.

Martin had stepped forth into the daylight and stood at parade rest like a rural lawn ornament. One carved out of a stump with a chainsaw. Lane felt a touch of envy at one with muscles like that who could stand still and relaxed.

Larson Henry nodded and Lane tipped a finger to his forehead to show that there were no hard feelings about the call to the sheriff. NoBob fidgeted and shook his head and came close enough to talk but far enough away to get a running start. That's the deputy over there, he said. In case you didnt know it. His eyes were red and tired.

How you doing, NoBob. You can relax.

You crazy mudsucker. Locked away somewhere is what you need. I'm warning you, stay away from me.

All right. I'll stand right here. Does that suit?

NoBob shot a stream of tobacco juice toward the woods and followed it and stood where he could see both Lane and the auctioneer who had stepped up onto the front porch and adjusted his ballcap and said, Gather round here, people. There's not that many of us so I'm not setting up a PA system. They all shuffled forward and tightened a bit but not much. NoBob removed a dry-looking tobacco cud from his jaw and hurled it into a pine tree at the yard's edge.

There's a floor price on this particular property, folks, the auctioneer said, but it's the owner's intent to sell. We'll need from the winning bidder fifteen thousand dollars in the form of cash or a certified check with the balance at closing within sixty days. His voice didnt sound hurried but if he'd taken a breath, Lane had missed it.

Lane felt for the cashier's check and unfolded it to assure himself that it still had the right numbers on it and felt NoBob's glare but didnt respond to it until he sensed the shorter man close beside him.

You're not living in the house you got now.

Well, that's kind of why I'm here.

You bastard, NoBob snarled.

We need to talk. Not here.

Sandy, just in front of them, turned and said shhhh.

Is there anybody who dont have a number? the auctioneer brayed. All right, then, who'll give me a hundred thousand for it. One hundred, who has a hundred, who'll give me a hundred thousand for it here. His finger dancing across the buyers, trying to single one out to bid.

Twenty-five, said NoBob, and right behind that Sandy said twenty-six but the auctioneer ignored her and said, Twenty-five who'll give me fifty, who'll give me fifty for it. Fifty now seventy-five, he said. Lane had seen or heard no bid but the auctioneer's finger pointed in the general direction of several realtors each time he said fifty.

Sandy said, Fifty-one, and the auctioneer again ignored her and she looked down at her number like what she was doing wrong should be printed there and Lane felt embarrassed for her and moved over to stand beside her. You have to bring it up in fives for now, he said. Unless nobody does, then you can bid just a thousand. She looked at him like he was talking Kentuckian or some other unknown exotic tongue.

In a quick flurry that Lane didnt keep up with the bid went to eighty and two of the realtors left, the cellphones already in their ears, and from the corner of his eye he saw Sandy slump and shake her head and he wished he could somehow slip some money into her pocket without her knowing where it came from.

We have eighty thousand here, the auctioneer said. Lady, do I hear eighty-one?

She shook her head and Lane called out, Who has the bid, anyhow?

This gentleman right here, number thirteen, has the bid at eighty thousand dollars. He pointed at Larson Henry.

Eighty-one, NoBob said.

Eighty-one now eighty-five. Larson Henry shook his head and took a step backwards. Eighty-one now eighty-two. Eighty-two. The voice loud but somehow hushed, like a preacher's at a tent-revival altar call. Eighty-two. All done at eighty-one? Eighty-two? Going once.

Eighty-two, Lane said.

Eighty-two now eighty-five. Back into high gear.

Eighty-three, NoBob said.

Eighty-three now eighty-five.

Eighty-four, Lane said.

Eighty-four. Eighty-four eighty-five.

Eighty-five, NoBob said.

Now eighty-six.

Sandy had moved close beside Lane and he caught a whiff of her perfume and it was the one or one close to what Mary had worn and then Mary was there with them too and Lane looked around like he'd just awakened from sleepwalking and shook his head.

Eighty-six sir? The auctioneer pointing to him.

No. What the hell am I doing. The bid's not mine is it? Fearful that he'd lost track, that he'd just purchased another place for Mary to haunt.

Eighty-six and it will be. Eighty-six, a bargain, sir.

I'm done. Lane stuck his number in his shirt pocket where even he couldnt see it and turned and left the gathering. Behind him he heard what sounded like Martin's voice take up the bid, and then another's, going by hundreds now.

Sandy walked beside him, bumping him when their strides mismatched. I was wishing you'd get it after it got too steep for me, she said. I hate it when these outside people come in here and run up all the prices. The people that live here cant afford a place anymore.

There'll be something come along. Just be patient. He watched her go, wanted to go with her.

Larson Henry caught Lane as he was climbing up into the truck. Mr. Henry, Lane said. I kind of figured you'd pick this place up.

Not at that price. If I didnt own the property next door I wouldnt even have bothered to come.

You bought that one, did you?

Yessir, I did. Out here close to the school, it's a good investment. That's what I think, anyway. But I wanted to tell you I'm sorry if I caused you any trouble a while back.

No. It was good for you to look after your buddy, even if he's not much account.

I'm what he had. Everybody has to have someone.

How is ol' Harold. Last I heard he was in a jail in Virginia.

Yeah. Seems he's been hauling drugs home in my cars. Looks like you knew him better than I did.

You normally get cars from down South?

When I can. They're not so eaten up with rust.

How long's Harold in for?

There's not been a trial yet. I've declined to bail him out. For a spell I was thinking I'd be in the pokey with him. Being my rollback and my cars. Used up all my egg money getting them loose.

You ever wonder if you were set up? That maybe it was aimed at you instead of Harold, maybe to shut down your business?

He shrugged. If it was, it missed. I'd never even seen the cars. Bought them through a broker I use once in a while.

Well, good. I'm glad you're out of it.

You ready to sell that baitshop yet?

Lane started to say no from habit but he paused and said, I dont know. Tell you the truth, I've lost interest in it lately. Till I dont hardly care one way or another.

I'd like to look at it.

Go right ahead. I'm going to the bank before they close and then I'm going to visit my family. He described the rock that hid the key. Just make yourself to home.

If Henry was surprised, he didnt show it. I'll put the key back under the rock. What's a good time to call you?

Whenever I'm there.

When will that be?

That's a good question, Lane said.

•   •   •

It never even slowed down, Lane said to the same teller who'd given him a lecture about pulling money from his CDs before they matured.

Excuse me? she said.

The spaceship. It was supposed to pick me up at the buffalo farm. But the brake lights never even came on. Went right over.

She turned and gazed through the tinted glass at the drivethrough like she wished she were just driving through. What would you like to do with this, sir? She unfolded the cashier's check she'd created a few hours earlier and flattened it on the countertop.

Buy some CDs. I got some money in checking I'd like to move over, too.

If it's the money we just put in this morning, it wont be available until Monday.

Yes maam.

For what period of time would you like to invest? She pointed to the rate chart propped on a big easel by the door.

Lane considered the chart. Six months, I reckon. The ship will be back a year from today and I fully intend to get it flagged down this go around. A year from Monday will be too late.

I'm required to tell you that there is a substantial penalty for early withdrawal.

Would you like to go along? When it comes back?

Excuse me?

Thought I'd ask, he said. You seem the daring type. The kind likes to live on the edge.

If there were any more rules regarding what had to be told a customer buying CDs, she broke them.

.45

asked if he could come in said, Of course. They sat at the table and drank coffee and talked about nothing. Darlene not as tired-looking as usual and Toby buried in an oversized book about engines. When did you get to be a bookworm? Lane asked.

Did you know the Wankel engine only has one moving part? the boy said.

I didnt even know it had the one. When it's broke down, I bet it's broke down good. Lane imagined he could feel Frank's smile on his skin. I'm thinking on selling the baitshop, he said. That's why I stopped over.

Aw, Pap, Darlene said. You need *something* to do.

It's got to be more like something that keeps me from doing anything. An excuse not to *have* to do anything.

How you going to spend your time if you sell it?

Fish. Hunt sang. Maybe buy a camper and go to bluegrass festivals. Plant a garden. Anything I feel like doing. Get a life of my own so I dont have to suck off yours, he thought but didnt say. I got enough money to get by. My stabling costs arent that high.

Are you looking for our blessing? Frank said. Do what you want to.

Before I let it go I need to make sure you dont want it.

Even if we did, right now money's tight.

If you want it, I'll *give* it to you.

Toby looked up with possibilities dancing in his eyes. Then they were dismissed and the boy went back to his reading.

We might be moving, Darlene said. It depends where Frank gets a job.

I suspected that, Lane said. And offering you the baitshop isnt to try and keep you here.

We dont want it, Frank said. But thank you for the offer.

You going to keep this place? If you move.

Try to. It'd be nice to have a place here in the mountains. To come to when we could. If wherever we were got too unbearable.

You all right with moving, Toby?

Sure, the boy said without looking up. It'd be cool. He looked at Frank as though for approval.

He could visit, Frank said. Maybe spend whole parts of the summer. If you wanted him.

Any time, Lane said. I'd be tickled.

Would you like that, Toby? Darlene said.

The boy's pale eyes examined Lane and he imagined he saw humor flickering behind them. Like it used to. I dont know. You going to bite the line off when I have a big fish on?

I been thinking about having my teeth pulled. So there'd be no chance of that happening. He laughed at the boy's expression. Or maybe I'll just promise not to gnaw line anymore.

Okay, Toby said. Did you like Dad's graduation?

Wouldnt have missed it for the world, Lane said. Pain and pride tearing at his eyeholes like tomcats hung over a clothesline.

. 46

MARTIN ENDED UP WITH IT, DICK TRAPPEL SAID.
He slid open a lower desk drawer for a foot prop. Paid too much,
if you ask me. But I'd like to go back and buy up all the property I
thought went too high at the time.

Wouldnt we all, Lane said.

They sipped coffee for a while till Lane said, Where's Martin get
the kind of money to buy property? Doesnt he already have a place
over on the far side of town?

The place he lives in now is lucky to be standing. One of those
ranch houses the Koster boys put up back in the sixties. Corn fod-
der and molasses and skimpy on the molasses. But he didnt buy Billy
Bean's place for himself.

He's got money enough to buy property he dont even need?

Martin took a thirty-year mortgage. I co-signed it.

Lane shook his head.

He bought it for his mother. She's never had a thing in her life.
The old man was a sot, and now that he's gone she lives in a rental.
The boy drives a Plymouth Valiant for his personal car, for god's sake.
Like riding a dinosaur. Packs a lunch to save money. Buys his clothes

at Goodwill. Works all the overtime I'll give him. Above and beyond that he's putting in extra time on a drug interdiction task force the state's set up. Plus takes classes at the community college. Still finds time to keep in shape. Runs marathons. I wish we had fifty Martins in this county. A hundred. Boys with ambition and the willpower to back it up. That would take care of their family before they lit off to stack up a bank account for themselves.

I'll admit that I figured that one wrong.

He's the young man you wanted to be. Me too. But we never got it done.

Lane let that lay on him and smart for a while. To see if he could take it. Like the time he'd watched a hornet sting without swatting it. Just to see if he could.

The sheriff rose and went to the door and looked up and down the hallway to make sure nobody had slipped into the building while they were talking. He closed the door. What I'm going to tell you stays right here.

All right.

You were right about how Ballew gets his drugs in and out. Martin's pieced together the rest of the operation, and he's set up a sting to bring him down.

How's the rest of it work?

Like you thought, Ballew's using Mexicans to do the dirty stuff. He buys cars at auctions down south. Never even gets near them. Takes Mexicans to drive them home. If one of those cars happens to have a spare tire full of coke, what does he know? His buyers take car and all. Ballew's never even gotten close to drugs.

Except for one time that might have backfired on him? Because that's what I think the Billy Bean thing was all about.

That's a possibility.

And the Mexicans dont rat him out because he takes care of the family if they go to jail.

That and the fact that they dont know anything *to* rat. They get to court everybody can see they dont have the money or connections to be druggies. Worst case they get shipped back to Mexico and have to work their way back but he pays for that too. If they go to jail, that's the big time. Good wages and a lot easier than what they have on the outside. It gives them a stake to get started on. Ballew wont use them twice. They move on.

How they going to sting him? If Ballew never touches the product.

He's got to touch the money. That's where we'll get him. I'm not free to share the details.

He's slippery. Maybe smarter than you. Maybe even smarter than Martin.

We'll get him. I'd bet my badge on it.

That's not much of a wager. You're going to give up sheriffing in a couple of months anyway.

I'll give it up, though. Not lose it in a bet.

Ballew got away with Billy Bean. But he'll get brought down.

We dont really have a case to pursue with Billy Bean. Not unless Harold Bright decides to confess to it. But the other thing, your getting shot, I havent given up on that. We have the slugs from your place, but they dont match up with any guns we've found. They're 9 mm. We havent even found anyone that owns one of that caliber.

Well. I'm not going to loose sleep over it. It was all tied together, I think. Did you know that Frank came home?

You think there's anything in this county I dont know about?

Couple, maybe. Thought that might be one of them.

I'm glad for you. But worried too. Just a little bit. How good a liar are you, Lane?

Speak English.

You go from a man that carries heads by the noseholes and stops to dig a sang in the process to one that doesnt worry that someone blew a hole in him. I'm not buying it.

I never was that man.

Tell somebody that wasnt there.

Lane extracted a smoke and when the sheriff said nothing lit it and drew it deep and held it while he rowed up his words. I been doing a lot of thinking. All I did in Nam was survive. Try to stay alive. I didnt do one thing a rabbit wouldnt have done or a boxturtle or a cockroach. Just because I wasnt as good at it as some and got myself in more of a mess that took longer to get out of, folks thought I was a hero. Then when I didnt talk about it folks took it for a sign that I was even tougher than they imagined, and when folks treat you one way after a while you start to believe it yourself.

Dont sell yourself short.

Not sure I could. But then you drink a lot and that erodes what you really are and after a spell you're left with what you think you are, which isnt necessarily so. Me carrying that head wasnt really me. It was the man people around me had made me into. Then I had that head to live up to. Am I making any sense at all?

No. Keep trying.

Maybe because I wasnt drinking when this last thing happened. Maybe that's why I saw it different for a change. But even then I jumped right back into the bottle, trying to live up to what I was sup-posed to be. Instead of what I am.

You know what I think? I think you're the exact Lane Hollar you've always been. Every day that you dont carry a head in here and lay it on my desk, I'm more surprised than if you do. There's some that become what others expect them to be, but you're not one of them.

I been wrong about everything else lately. So I wont argue with you. But I feel different. Like I've finally figured it all out.

You're more likely just bored with being a hardass. Feeling sappy because you and Frank made up. But I'm by necessity a student of human nature, and I have yet to see a person change from what they are and stay there. The hand you're dealt is the one you have.

Lane stood and killed his smoke against his thumbnail and put the butt in his pocket. I'll play this one till it runs out. At least till then.

Dont ever light up in here again. I let that one slide.

All right. I wont. I got to go. Thanks for letting me wear out your ear.

Here's your hat. What's your hurry?

Yeah, I'm going. I got some bridges to fix and then I might travel some. See the world. At least the parts my old truck can get to.

When you carry that head in here, bring a newspaper to lay it on. Dont mess up my whole office.

Lane laughed. That much I could do, I reckon.

What about your baitshop?

I dont reckon it will care one way or the other what I do. Since I never cared what it did.

•   •   •

Lane called Larson Henry and listened to his offer for the baitshop. If I was to sell it, were you planning on keeping it open? Or do you want it just for the land?

I know somebody might run it for you, he said. A man and his boy. If you got nothing against Mexicans. With someone that cared about it, you could likely make some money.

The boy can. Like a native. And the man's a hard worker.

He listened to the silence and admired Larson Henry for allowing it to run on. Is that your best offer? he said. Knowing he was no more suited to dicker over price than a hog would be to negotiate feeding times. When do you want me out? he said. Not that it'll take me more than ten minutes.

Yessir. That will be fine.

No. You can pay it all when we transfer the deed. Closing, they call it. I never thought about it before, but that's a strange word for it.

Yessir. For me too. That's why I said it's a strange word.

.47

flatbed truck was there the door was locked and nobody responded to his knock. The lawn needed mowing and the garden was producing more weeds than vegetables. He considered leaving a note but wasnt sure what to put on it.

The baitshop was closed and he liked it that way and the old pickup seemed to want to go for a drive so he gave it its head. On the backroads he'd not been on for years houses had sprouted everywhere. Farms chopped into building lots, fields grown up with cedars. At a crossroads he saw he was only seven miles from Almont, and he wandered that way.

Just beyond the half-dozen houses and the single gas station that made the town, just short of the North Branch of the Potomac and Maryland, he eased by the long row of used cars under the blue and red and yellow banners. None of the vehicles new or even close to it, but each one sparkling and sharp. The lot newly graveled, a new already-underpinned construction trailer serving as a sales office. The whole thing as out of place as a stalk of ginseng in the middle of a WalMart lot.

The black pickup with the rollbar was parked beside the trailer and on the small porch Ballew leaned against the rail talking to another dark-skinned man and as Lane drove past they waved and with only a slight hesitation Lane returned it. He drove away without slowing or accelerating, feeling he'd closed a door on a dirty room that he'd never have to clean.

Back at his home Lane mowed the lawn and trimmed around the foundation and the fence and then he sat in the kitchen and drank coffee and enjoyed the fireflies in the gathering dusk. Just after full dark he went inside for a sweater and dialed NoBob's number and hung up before the answering machine came on.

The porch swing had nearly rocked him to sleep when headlights flickered through the trees and NoBob's pickup eased down the drive like a cat into a doghouse. He parked beside Lane's truck and the engine died and the lights went out.

Lane opened the front door and switched on the porch light and sat again in the swing and said, Come up.

NoBob's shirt was visible before the rest of him. It paused at the edge of the light. I'm carrying a gun, he said. I want you to know that. Before you do something crazy.

Come on. I'm not fixing to hurt you.

When NoBob moved to where he was visible, he carried an old rusty singlebarrel shotgun. A 16gauge, it looked like, though Lane hadnt seen one in years. Whatever it is that you got in your head, NoBob said, it's a crock.

Come up and sit down.

No. I aint. I dont trust you one bit. NoBob was close enough that Lane could see the bags under his eyes. The red tinge in the whites. What is it you want from me?

Nothing. Maybe you can tell me why you shot me. That much I'd like to know.

I busted your banjo, and I'll buy you a new one. Or pay for

getting that one fixed. But I swear I dont know anything about you getting shot.

You swore you didnt know who broke the banjo till I caught you in that lie.

I shouldnt of done that either. But how you got a hole in your love handle I dont have no idea.

Come up here and sit and pretend like you did. Just for the fun of it. Tell me why you *would* have done it. Even though you didnt.

If you dont quit stalking me I'm taking it to the sheriff. My woman's had to go to her sister's and I aint slept for a week. I never shot you before, but if you come around one more time I will. No more calling either. I'm warning you, Lane Hollar.

Stalking you?

You might think you're crazy and mean but I aint taking any more of it. I wont shoot you in the gut, either. Right between the eyes. And it will be self-defense. You leave me alone.

You just happened to stop by the house when somebody else just happened to be shooting me and you just happened to stomp my banjo.

I dont even own a gun other than this old thing and I aint even sure it will shoot. But I aint afraid to find out, he added.

All right. Let's hear your story. It ought to be interesting, anyhow.

No. I'm going straight down to the sheriff and file papers on you. I cant live like this.

Well let's say I'm out to kill you, like you say.

No. Like *you* said. In front of witnesses.

Whatever. Tell me how it happened. Put up a good defense before I kill you.

I dont know how it happened. Like I said, I didnt do it.

Just tell your part then.

I was at home. And my woman can attest to that.

And you stomped my banjo from there. This ought to be good.

We heard it go out on the scanner and I high-tailed it over here and I reckon everybody else went to the boy's house. The window was busted out and I just stepped in and looked around to see what all had happened. And I seen your banjo sticking out from under the bed and I done it. I wasnt even done stomping till I was sorry, but there aint no way to put it back together.

But why? Why would you bust my banjo?

NoBob shuffled his feet and leaned against the post. You know how I am. I get pissed that—he showed a space between his fingers— quick. And I do stuff I shouldnt.

So what was it that pissed you off? That I wasnt killed? Just had another bellybutton?

No. Not a-tall. Just that here you went again, getting all the attention, and that now I'd look like a fool and a liar about what happened out at the reservoir. I seen that picture smashed all over the floor and I thought, hell, I'll bust his damn banjo and let somebody else get shafted for it. Instead, I screwed up and drunk too much liquor and let the cat out of the bag and ended up gettin blamed for the whole deal. But I swear on my mama's open bedsores that I didnt have nothing to do with any of the other.

But why would you want to bust my banjo? Or kick in my truck door?

You just dont get it, do you?

Lane swung and brooded for a moment and knew that he had no clue. Not a one. The boy's tent. You slash it up like that?

It aint the boy I got issues with.

The shotgun barrel waved around when NoBob got animated, and Lane found himself looking down the hole more often than not. Unload that thing, he said.

I dont even have no shells for it, NoBob said. He leaned it against the porch post.

As the new facts rearranged themselves, Lane felt the soft peace of the last days being crowded out. He went inside and called Darlene's number and got no answer and tried it again to make sure he'd dialed the right number and when he returned to the porch NoBob was nowhere to be seen.

NoBob, Lane hollered, and saw the man lurking behind the pickup. What are you doing now?

I thought maybe you went after a gun.

If you didnt shoot me, then who did? Knowing it had to have been Ballew. Knowing he'd let down his guard, believing a killer not to be a liar too.

I told you, I dont have no idea.

Lane ran to his truck and it was rolling downhill before the motor caught and the passenger door flapped open and NoBob vaulted up onto the seat, the rusted shotgun trailing behind and preventing the door from closing. Dont you go runnin off till we get this settled. Like I said, I cant live like this.

Lane grabbed the gun by the barrel and threw it out the window and roared away toward Darlene's. As much as the old blue pickup could roar.

• • •

The house was dark, no porch lights or nightlights showing anywhere, and the car was gone. The door locked. Lane beat on the aluminum storm door and yelled, DeeDee. Frank. Toby. Sensing that the house was empty. Like Lane's gut.

What's going on? NoBob said for about the fiftieth time.

I might kill you anyhow. For making me let down my guard.

They're probably out to a movie or something.

And they might not be, too. I havent even talked to them in two days. Lane looked at his watch and ran back toward his pickup.

• • •

To Lane's surprise, Dick Trappel's cruiser sat in the lot instead of Martin's. Dick looked up at the wall clock when Lane and NoBob entered. Try that Tylenol PM, he said. It'll knock you out like turning off a light. That's what I do when I cant sleep.

Darlene and Toby are missing, Lane said. I'm afraid something's happened to them.

Dick looked at NoBob and he shrugged. They aint there. That's all I can say.

I just saw them around noon. And Frank. They were fine then.

The sheriff shook his head. They're all right. They're out to dinner or something.

Ballew's back in town, too.

That much I am aware of. It's not for my health I'm working after dark.

It's not like Darlene to be out late. She has to get up early.

If they're still gone in the morning we'll look around a little bit. But they wont be.

I should have known better than to come here, Lane said and headed for the door.

No you dont, the sheriff said. You take a seat over there and rest your motor. Both of you.

I dont have time for it, Lane said without slowing.

Hollar. You stop right there or I'll arrest you.

For what?

For whatever it takes to keep you from screwing up what we've got going down. I mean it. Park your butt right there.

Daggone you, Dick . . .

We're in the process as we speak of busting Nickel Ballew. If you go chasing off crazy like you've been known to do, he'll get wind of it. We might not get a better shot at him.

What about my family?

If he had anything to do with them, we'd know it. Especially now.

What's got you all fired up again, anyhow? Last time I saw you, it was all dont worry about it.

Let's just say I was wrong. Lane looked at the sheriff's badge and what it stood for and he said a word he hadnt learned in Sunday school and sat and NoBob shrugged and took a chair beside him.

The phone rang and the sheriff picked it up and listened for a while and said, Just stay right there. Keep watching. And stay off the radio till it's time.

Lane had started to light a cigarette and the sheriff said, Not in here.

You said I couldnt go out, and I'm going to have a smoke whether you want me to or not.

If you take off I'll put you in jail and charge you with obstruction of justice. And I'll make it stick.

Lane shrugged and went out the door and NoBob went with him. Lane sat on a bench near the front door and when he'd gotten his cigarette going he said, That banjo was a pre-war Gibson. With an original neck. Not a tenor banjo with a five-string neck scabbed on later. Having no clue why the banjo was important again in the midst of this other. Just that it was.

Your mind does light around here and there, dont it.

You know what that banjo was worth to me?

Yeah. I'm afraid I do.

Not in dollars. To *me*. It cant be replaced.

There's people could fix it up. Some guy up at Deep Creek builds instruments. Fixes them good as new.

But not good as old. The way it was before you put your boot through it.

If I could take my boot back out of it I would.

NoBob took from his shirtpocket a can of Skoal and filled his lip and put the can back and the stiff blunt fingers refastened the button through the flap. He worked at the snuff for a long time before he spit. You know what it's like to play the bass? Boom boom boom boom, one five one five. Like laying damn bricks. One after another. One five one five. Like a retard learning to choke his chicken.

Whatever complex you got, I dont have a name for it.

When I was a kid I had an inferiority one. The old woman licked me for it till I give it up. But listen. There you always were, doing all that melodic crap up and down the neck. Eddie on the mandolin and Paul on the flattop, all of you talking about minor sevenths and augmented ninths and hammer ons and pull offs and then you turn to me and say, D chord, NoBob. Dog. You know how that makes you feel?

I hope you're making this up as you go along. That you havent festered and rotted over a D chord. Play something else if the bass makes you feel stupid.

I cant. I *am* stupid.

Did you ever consider quitting? Not doing something that made you feel stupid? That ever cross your mind?

Then what would you have done for a bass player? According to you, we could have called down to the slow school for a retard. Or maybe just hit somebody in the head with a brick. Or run a coathanger up their nose and stirred their brains into a proper semblance for bass playing. Or after a couple of lessons we could teach the bass to play itself.

NoBob looked at his hand and smelled it and wiped it on his pants. I loved it, though. Loved being part of the band.

Lane tried to keep his anger fired but it was going out despite his best efforts. I'll tell you what I loved. You remember the songs we did where we'd kick off with just a singer and the banjo or the mandolin? The vocal lead and a single instrument. Like "Some Things I Want to Sing About." Or "C&O Canal Line." Then we'd bring in the other lead and then the guitar. Last of all we'd bring in the bass. And *that's* when the music started. When that big old doghouse spoke up. Every time it did, no matter how many hundreds of times we'd done it, it

made the hair stand up on my arms. Maybe it is like laying bricks.
But the bricks better be straight and solid and spaced exactly right.
Because that's the foundation for the whole band. Lane felt like a tent
evangelist frothing up the crowd for plate-passing time and he said,
Shit, and spit in the grass and scrubbed it in with his foot. You didnt
bust my banjo over playing bass. If you were that crazy you'd have
come unraveled before that.

No. That was just part of it. So I wouldnt ever again have to listen to one of those fancy riffs up and down the neck. Or twisting the
damn tuners. Showing off. It aint no wonder there's all those banjo
jokes. Like how do you play redneck ring toss?

If you're asking me, I give up.

I aint privy to all the rules but it involves a banjo and an
outhouse.

I reckon you heard about Fancy and Hoab Dillard. Used to live
over past Leadmine?

Heard of them.

Hoab rigged a meat grinder up to a gasoline motor. It worked
good but he had the pulleys wrong. It ground meat so fast it would
stick it against the wall if you didnt head it off with a dishpan. But
it didnt have any power, running that fast. Anyway, Hoab poached
a deer and they were grinding it into hamburger and he was feeding the grinder with his fingers instead of a plunger so he could feel
of the power and not stall it and after a spell the auger nipped him
and pulled him in almost to the second knuckle. Clipped his index
finger off clean but then it stalled the motor before it ground it up.
Hoab was dancing around bleeding everywhere and trying to wrap
his stub up in a dishrag and hollering, Take me to the emergency
room, Fancy. Just as calm as a cowpie she said, Now you just sim-
mer, Hoab, and let me get this finger out of here first. She got the
wrench and tore down the grinder and felt around in the meat and
said, Aha. Out with his finger she came and looked at it and went

out on the back porch and hurled it out into the bottom and she said, There's *one* finger that wont be sticking in my face anymore. Come on, Hoab, she said. Let's get you in town and get you patched up so you can work tomorrow.

You're thinking *I'm* the one shy one egg of an omelet?

Fancy said that was the best tasting burger they ever had.

NoBob made a face and shot a stream of snuff juice out into the night.

There's a parallel there. Fancy throwing away Hoab's finger and your busting up my banjo.

You just showed what the problem is. Right there while we were talking about it.

Lane thought for a while. All right. I give up again.

Anything I ever did, you had to top it. Just now I told some sorry little worthless joke and without even laughing you come back with one that's twice as funny and has meaning to it and fits the situation like it was wrote for it.

Lane started to ridicule the statement and without warning he saw Frank there, if not saying the same thing something close enough to bring blood.

I found an old bass stowed away with the high school's band stuff and bought it for two hundred dollars, and it aint but a month till you run into an old woman with a pre-war Gibson banjo you pick up for half what it's worth.

What it's worth now. Or was before you busted it. I paid the going price then.

Whatever. Every time I came into the lumberyard after cement or wall ties, head-to-toe crusted over with mud and sunburn and my ass dragging along behind me like tin cans tied to my tail, there you were perched on your stool in front of the airconditioner.

You think that's not work?

W equals fd, he said. Work equals force times *distance*. That's what they taught me in school. And I didnt see nothing moving where you were.

I'd forgotten you went to school.

There you go again. Always had a little plastic thing in your shirt pocket so you wouldnt get ink on your good shirt.

I did that for Mary. People made fun of it but I didnt care.

Mary. Pretty Mary. Sweet Mary. Loving Mary. Sexy Mary. Mary, go to hell.

Here, now.

You got Mary and I got Cindy the bitch from the wrong side of the tracks in hell. No we cant go on vacation. No you cant go fishing. No you cant go drinking with the boys. No, Bob. No, Bob. NoBob.

Lane lit another cigarette from the butt of the first. Not any more. Mary's gone.

Yeah, but Cindy aint.

Well. You married her.

For better or worse. The one thing I never counted on was that she'd stay the same. You see what I mean?

I can see that I wont win this argument. Because it will never be over.

You retire and buy you a baitshop where you sit with your feet up and tell fish stories. So I think I'll finally get one up on you so I go into rental houses and do good at it for a while till the damn banks start writing one-hundred-and-fifty-year mortgages to anybody can make an X with a little assistance and all of a sudden the only people dont own their own house is the ones cant make the X or dont dare to for some nefarious reason. You like that word? Nefarious? First thing you know the only way I can make a go of it is fill the houses up with wetbacks. Then the roofs start needing replaced and the furnace goes out and the kids get hungry and eat up the wiring and they put Kotex down the toilet and glom up the septic works and I jack up the rent and they move ten more in to cover it.

Get out of it. I did.

Would I could. The law wont let you put em out. Nobody's going to buy a house has four families of greasers squeezed into it.

Then why are you buying more? Out at Billy Bean's?

I really hadnt decided to or not. Not till you showed up. If you got into renting you'd right off make money at it and find nice married couples to rent with no kids or dogs and that liked to dust and paint. Ended up almost buying the place over keeping you from getting it. Martin baled me out at the last bid.

You do have some issues.

It could be looked at that way, I reckon. If you had a mind to do it.

Before Lane could respond Dick Trappel rapped on the window and Lane tossed his butt and they hurried inside just in time to hear the tail end of the radio transmission. *No big hurry. They're as dead as they're ever going to get.*

.48

HAROLD BRIGHT CROUCHED BEHIND A FIVE-YEAR-
old Suburban as Nickel Ballew's pipes shut down and the headlights
died and the pickup door closed and feet crisped across the gravel
toward the sales trailer at the Almont used-car dealership. Ballew
whistling "Amazing Grace." Harold waited until keys rattled in the
doorknob before he eased around where he could see without being
seen. Like the predator he'd become. Like a panther waiting to jump
on a deer.

Ballew let the keys dangle in the doorknob and turned and smelled
the air. Who's out there? he said.

Harold held against his cheek the chrome barrel of the .38 revolver
he'd bought from a man in Romney that Dandy had steered him to.
The barrel trembled not with fear but with adrenaline. With power.

You ought to see me now, Dandy. Not the terrified weasel they'd
brought in handcuffs into the Roanoke jail but hard and dangerous
and mean. He touched his tongue to his knuckle and tasted the scab
from where he'd smacked his sister. Stupid bitch. Let him stew in jail
for two weeks before she bailed him out.

Ballew smelled the air again. Is that my buddy Harold? Come

on in and we'll catch up the news. Ballew set his briefcase on the makeshift porch and scratched his back. Or pulled up his shirttail so he could get at his gun. With the porch light beside his head he was half black and half white the way he ought to be. Instead of mixed together.

You got every right to be upset with me, I reckon. Ballew stepped down off the porch in Harold's direction. Blessed are ye, my son, when men shall revile you and *persecute* you and shall say *all manner of evil* against you falsely. For *my* sake.

Harold raised the pistol and it clunked against metal and Ballew moved closer but to where he was hidden behind the Suburban.

You are *blessed*, my son. The voice directly opposite the vehicle. Your *trials* are but a test. To see if you're *worthy* to follow me.

Harold eased down to his rump and sat where he could turn either way, front or rear, and held the pistol in both hands in front of his face. The way he'd seen it done on the TV. At the ready. His heart like a lawnmower.

A soft clunk at the front of the vehicle and Harold wheeled and watched a gravel bounce from the hood and when he spun around Ballew was standing in the space behind him. The porch light reflected from the barrel of his gun.

Put it down, said a voice but Ballew's lips didnt move but instead he turned away from Harold and beyond a short man in uniform sidled into the edge of the light. A pump shotgun at his shoulder. Throw it out on the ground. You're under arrest. Step out in the open. Both of you.

Ballew looked back at Harold and grinned. It is hard for thee to kick against the pricks, he said. He turned his attention to the uniformed man. Boob, my man, what's the problem. You bucking for a raise?

Just lay it down, Nickel.

Ballew looked at Harold again and said, Why does somebody

always have to be in a mood? I'm just going to lay it down easy, he said to the uniformed man. So I dont tear up the blueing. It was my daddy's gun and it means a lot to me. My foster daddy's.

Ballew leaned forward and placed the gun on the gravel. Blessed are the *peacemakers*, he said. When he stood his hand palmed a hard shard of steel that Harold pictured sticking from the officer's heart. From his own. Harold aimed his pistol at Ballew's back and it roared and bucked louder and harder than Harold thought possible and then again and once more till Ballew fell beside the pistol and his hand unclasped the knife. The roaring proceeding after the pistol was still as though trapped inside his head.

The officer was there, close, where Harold could see he was a deputy. Crisp and compact and trim. Well, well, he said. What do we have here. He stood not six feet away, where Harold could smell the Hoppes solvent and gun oil on the shotgun. Where he could feel the black void of the barrel focused on the side of his head.

Dont shoot, Harold said. He was going to knife you. And I know stuff. We can work a deal. I'm going to lay down my gun.

The problem with deals is that when it's all said and done, another sleazeball is out on the street. Walking around loose. I got to admit, though, you been a big help.

Harold looked through the deputy's spread legs to where the only hope of things ever working out for Harold Bright lay dead and useless and silent in the gravel. The only one who knew the truth would never share it. Look, he said. There aint no use for anybody else to get hurt. He caressed the pistol's cylinder and felt a winner in there, at least one. Felt the truth as well. But I bet someone will, he said. He raised the pistol again.

• • •

Martin wiped his shoes on the backs of his pantslegs and stooped to pick up Ballew's gun. He walked around behind the office where he'd hidden his cruiser and exchanged the .45 auto for the pistol under the seat, a 9 mm he'd brought for the purpose. Back at the bodies he wiped it clean and worked it into Ballew's hand and took one look around and went to call it in. He stopped and looked at the briefcase still sitting on the porch, tried to imagine how much was inside. What it would feel like to own it. He shook his head and went on toward the cruiser. Money wasnt what he wanted. Never had been.

. 49

I AINT BELIEVING I LET YOU TALK ME INTO THIS,
NoBob said. His pants were muddied where he'd slipped on the
shaley rocks that underlay the thin soil on the near-vertical hillside.
Hat askew and far back on his head where a branch had knocked it.
His gray workshirt wet under both arms.

I have to do something since I sold the baitshop. And the fish dont
bite during dog days.

Sittin at Rooster's doing twelve-ounce curls works for me.

We've done what you wanted the last three weekends. It's my
turn to say. He who would have friends must show himself friendly.

Friends is something I'm not sure I want anymore. Since you got
to be one again.

There's another one, Lane said. Right behind you. Caught up in
that Christmas fern.

I dont see it, NoBob said, but he hauled back the fern to expose
a squat three-prong ginseng with two red berries yet clinging to the
stalk.

Lane ambled down and sat on a windfallen tree beside him

while the shorter man cursed and grubbed with a screwdriver at the stubborn root. Tell me that's not fun.

I aint had that kind of fun since last time I got the intestinal flu.

You know what an old-woman whiner you are, NoBob Thrasher?

I'm going to take a break. Go ahead if you want. I'm ragged out.

No. I'm wore out too. Lane dug inside his shirt for a cheese sandwich gone soft and fragrant and fished the flat glass syrup bottle from his pocket and drank the water warm and clean and sweet with the faint maple flavor that never left the bottle.

NoBob put the root in a breadsack and opened a beef jerky and threw the plastic wrapper where he'd just dug a sang. Lane looked at it but didnt say anything.

You got any water left?

Lane handed over the syrup bottle and NoBob wiped his mouth on his sleeve and turned it up and swallowed and shook the bottle and held it up to the light.

Finish it off, Lane said.

They chewed in silence but for the high-pitched drone of late-summer locusts until Lane pointed down the hill at a rough-barked vine the size of his bicep that hung straight down from where it disappeared in a poplar canopy. You know what that is? That vine?

A grapevine, I reckon.

Nope. That's a Virginia creeper.

Them little things that crawl around over the rocks.

Yep.

How'd it get so big?

When things are left alone sometimes they get bigger than they should naturally.

I reckon. Probly why I'm hung like a chickadee.

Right beyond it is where it laid.

Where? What?

That head. That time that baldheaded fool lost it.

It rolled clear down *here*?

Yep.

You could of waited till I was done eating to tell me that.

I wanted to come back to here today. Right here's where my life took a bad turn and I was hoping to get back onto the right fork.

I hope you aint going to bring up the banjo again.

You just did.

You aint done with it. I just know there's gonna be a price to pay yet, and I'd just as soon get done with it.

No. Not that you were justified in doing it. Dont go thinking that. My old man gave me a belting one time for something I didnt do. While he was drunk. When he sobered up I told him and he just shrugged and said, I never hit a lick amiss.

You're full of yourself today, aint you. And I'm full of something else. He came to his feet with a groan and walked down the hill and stood behind a tree for a while. I appreciate it, he said when he stepped out. Friends is one thing I aint overburdened with.

I know what you mean. Since I've not been able to remember but one, and I was fixing to kill him. Maybe I could be friends with Dick Trappel if he ever gets shed of his uniform, but probably not.

I wish Dick wouldnt retire.

It's time. Martin will do all right.

Maybe. He's sharp. I'll give you that. But I dont like him.

You'd just as well start, because he's going to be sheriff. For sure since the thing up at Almont. It might be better to have a sheriff nobody liked.

He'll be a world-class one then.

They sat for a while without speaking, even when a red fox flitted through the laurel on the opposite hillside. Finally NoBob said, You aint going to change your mind, are you? Come after me for your banjo.

Lane examined NoBob as he'd never done before. Looking at every gray hair on the side of his head. The shape of his ear. The way his jaw hinge worked as he tormented a grain of snuff between his teeth. The way the wrinkles beside his eyes crossed rather than forked. NoBob looking straight ahead. Allowing it. No, Lane said. A banjo is a special thing. But it's not worth a friend. Last week I was working around the house and I happened to unfold a six-foot rule and I saw the seventy-two on the end and it dawned on me that it was pretty symbolic of a man's lifespan. And then I put my finger where I was along the way. Makes you think what you're going to do with the time you got left.

What are you going to do? Putter around the house?

I've been thinking on that. First I'm going to go see that luthier guy up at Deep Creek. From what I hear he's a grouchy old fart that hates repair work. But I bet he'll work on a prewar Gibson. Then maybe round up some guys and do some pickin again. See if I can still. Dig some sang. Fish more. Start going to church with my boy and his family. Unfold that six-foot rule and look at it again and then go get right with the Lord. While I can. Do some volunteer work. Maybe down at the library. Gluing broken bindings and such. Take some kid that dont have a dad under my wing and teach him some things. Tell this fellow I know how he could sell his rental houses and help some good hardworking people in the process. Without having to throw anybody out on the street. If he had the time and imagination to get it done. And really wanted to. Lane extracted his cigarettes and lit one and sucked it deep and held it till it made his ears ring. Quit smoking. Go to a low-fat diet. Exercise. Learn to take the long view.

Bullshit. I cant see you doing that.

Some of it.

Maybe.

Thought about setting up a marital advice clinic, too. A free one. Where I could help people get out of bad relationships. People I liked.

Frog Friend tended me for a while before his back went out, NoBob said. One day at work he opened up his sandwich and set there and stared at it for a while and then he flung it down through the trees and said, If there's anything in the world I hate more than a egg sandwich, I dont know what it is. Well, why dont you say something to your wife? I said. Tell her to pack something else. And he looked at me like I'd took leave of my senses and said, Wife? I packed that damn lunch.

You ever consider me and you writing a Bible? The way we've taken to talking in parables it would come natural, I figure.

You know what I'm saying.

That you love your woman, I reckon. Or that you want to stay with her for some reason.

Not while I got her, I dont even like her. But if I was to cut her loose I can see that I would right quick.

Lane got to his feet and stretched his back and made a face when it cracked. He wasnt up the hill twenty yards till the shorter man had caught up with him. Long legs not such an asset on a vertical surface.

Where was you going to get a bass player at?

Have to look around. Wouldnt want to get any old one. It will have to be someone that can walk to town and home again and still be in time when he gets back. Like an atomic clock. One that dont show off and try to make it a lead instrument. That plays it the way it was intended to be played. That dont get bored with it and be picking his nose when you needed him.

If people would just say, That's a D minor there. Or a D fallopian major paragoric twenty-seventh. If that's what it was. Instead of *dawg*. It would make a difference.

It's all the same on a bass. D whatever is just a D.

No it aint, either. Maybe it looks the same and sounds the same but it *aint* the same.

It is to me.

That's why you're not a bass player. If people could just say things the way they was . . .

I dont know. You know they're using lawyers instead of mice for experiments nowadays, dont you?

Aw, shit. Go ahead.

They say there's way more lawyers than there are mice. And the scientists get attached to the mice. But the big reason is that there's some things mice just wont do.

They could.

But they probably wont.

They could try.

I guess they could. If they really wanted to.

NoBob stopped and jumped up and down and yelled and spun in a circle and Lane wondered for a moment if he'd been snakebit. Finally, NoBob yelled. Finally, by damn, you walked past a sang and I was the one to see it. He pointed to a four prong that had lost its berries and was already flat down on the ground, leaves wilted and yellowing.

I saw it, Lane said. Been walking past them all day trying to get you to see one on your own. So you'd like yourself better.

Well I thank you for that, my friend, NoBob said as he drew forth his screwdriver and commenced to dig. And I'm going to remember this spot and come back in a few years. As heavy as it's gettin fertilized, sang ought to be four feet tall.

You're welcome, Lane said. The urge to squeeze NoBob's shoulder strong but one he could still resist.

. 50

the reservoir and after he'd made certain nobody was around he waded through the cane and squatted till just his nose was clear of the water, his breath whistling from the cold. Tried to bring it back. The smell of human waste and water buffalo and the faraway chop of rotor blades. But all he could find was an old idiot man who, if he hadnt lost his mind, was driving close the edge. Vietnam might have been on some other planet, maybe even in another life, and hunkering down in the mud wasnt going to bring it back again. Some small hard sour thing inside grew harder and sourer at that bit of news but it got smaller too.

As he hauled out of the cane Lester Kelso came walking a dog that was a cross between a snapping turtle and a red squirrel. All jaws and tail. Lane, he said, what you doing down in the cane? I thought you was a muckrat. Hair near turned Myrtle loose on you.

He's out there, Lane said. Three times I've had him on now and this time I thought I had him. No way was he going to break this line and I had him hooked good.

Another muskie?

I reckon you could call it that. But it's some kind of a freak because muskies dont get that big. It made that one you caught look like a newborn.

What happened?

I was waded out to where I couldnt get ahold of anything and he pulled so hard he towed me out where it's deep. I'd got some line back but he hit it so hard it birdsnested on me and then he pulled me under. I held on long as I could but I had to let him go. Got one good look at him and it was scary. Probably have nightmares about those teeth. Lane shook his head and shuddered.

Gawd, Lester said. On one of them snakes, wasnt it.

No. He's too smart for that.

What then? What did you catch him on?

Lane looked up and down the bank and then at the dog.

She wont tell. What was it?

You'll tell. Or catch him yourself.

No way. If there's one thing ol Lester knows how to do it's keep his mouth shut.

Fudgesickles, Lane said.

Tell me you're lying, Lane Hollar.

I wouldnt tell you at all, but I know you dont have a license.

How you keep a fudgesickle on the hook. Dont they melt?

I've already told you more than I should have. You wouldnt get that much but I think it was hooked deep enough that it will die and float up somewhere. Probably way up in the far end where it's nothing but a swamp. Where nobody in his right mind would waller through the mud to look. The dog wagged its tail and Lane could swear it grinned. If a snapping turtle can grin.

•   •   •

Jodie looked out over Lane's shoulder and said, Tell me I'm not seeing what it looks like. Is this your midlife crisis?

Nah. That's just when you get to deteriorating faster than you can lower your expectations. I been in that state for twenty years. He turned to help admire the camper behind his pickup. How you like it?

How old is that thing?

Lane calculated. Twenty-two years.

Who painted it for you? And why? Maybe that's the better question. Why?

That's its natural coloration. Why I bought it. There could have only been one gallon of paint that color made before whoever mixed it got fired. Half of it went on my truck and the other half on that camper. If that doesnt make them made for each other, I dont know what would. Pure destiny.

Are you going to get it out of my driveway before someone sees it? People already laugh at me, I know, but . . .

I'll be going directly. Going out to Frank's for a cookout. Dont know why they cant eat in the house where it's comfortable but that's the way they are. Then I'm taking the boy for a day or two down to Spruce Knob. Where nobody will see us and embarrass him. But he's got to be back for a ballgame on Tuesday.

She looked dubiously at the round-shouldered monstrosity in the driveway again. Well, come in, she said.

No. I got to run. But I stopped in to ask you something.

What?

You ever been to the Grand Canyon?

Are you kidding?

Me either. I figured we'd go there and maybe Yellowstone if the weather doesnt get bad on us first. When we get back if we're still talking to each other you can give this house to Sandy after we fix it up a little and you can move in with me. If we decide to come back. If we dont, she can have mine.

Does anybody know you got loose?

Probably not. I put a cowpie in the bed and covered it up so it looks like me sleeping there.

I'm going to call the authorities. Before anyone gets hurt.

Lane opened the screen and leaned forward without touching but for the lips. She tasted of lime and of cigarettes and her breath smelled of milk and he could see yards deep into her eyes. Wednesday, he said. We'll eat a good breakfast and just drive till we get tired. There's two beds. One has a room that shuts off. You can have that.

A tear raced down her cheek and she shook her head. I havent even been out of the house for years. And you love Mary. You always will.

There's that, he said. I might never love you that much. Maybe not at all. I might not even like you after I know you better. But I'd like to find out.

Lighting out for the Grand Canyon's not the way to do it.

Lane looked at his watch. Probably not. But I dont have as much time as I used to. You either. Wednesday. Say eight o'clock.

He turned and walked to his truck on the balls of his feet because his heels had started hurting this morning for some reason he couldnt discern. Whistling. She might have said, I dont have a thing to wear. Or it could have been, Just get that damn thing out of here. His hearing wasnt what it once was. That should bother him more than it did.

. 51

MARTIN WATCHED THEM GO, EVEN WAVED AS THE
two old fools limped by in the color-matched-in-hell truck and
camper. He felt lighter when they were gone. The old man was on
Martin's side now, but Martin didnt trust him. Still sensed a hard
edge under the genial exterior. And he was sharp.

Martin shrugged it off. The old man had no reason to ponder it
further, and Martin certainly intended to give him no reason to start.
By the time the old man returned, Martin would be the sheriff.

That left the boy. Why couldnt the old man have taken him along
when he left? The kid knew something. Martin could feel it when
they talked. Spoiled little pampered shit. Didnt even know what an
ass-beating felt like. Or the inside of a closet. The kid would take
some watching. Maybe he needed something more than his tent cut
to pieces.

Time would tell. Just now Martin felt good. Happy. Powerful.
Healthy. The craziness that lit on him when he did too much thinking
about life's little inequalities gone for the moment

Soon he needed to get shed of Ballew's pistol. Not yet. He liked to
hold it in the dark, feel its black heavy power in his hand.

Acknowledgments

My heartfelt thanks to those who worked so hard on this book: Farley Chase, Richard Nash, Laura Mazer, Roxy Aliaga, and all the folks at Counterpoint. My sympathy and warmest affection to friends and family who make my otherwise small mean life large and gracious. My love to Connie, who makes it all seem worthwhile.